ANOTHER TALE OF
TWO CITIES

by

EZHUTH AANI

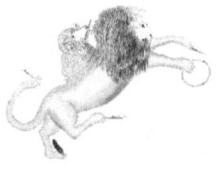

Myth Publications

Jamaica

New York

USA

Foreword

When a civilization faces annihilation, how far would they go to pre-empt the disaster and how much will they endeavour to preserve their way of life? How would they have felt when they realised that their efforts were failing? It is a sad reality that those civilizations that do not keep abreast of developments in the external world get swallowed up by others. This has happened in the past and is happening in some parts of the world as I write this. This will continue to happen as long as human race populates this planet.

What factors will decide which culture will prevail? What would be the feelings of the people who are trapped in these situations? How would their daily lives have been? Would there have been love and romance even in these times of crisis? Would there have been intrigue and politics even in the face of impending disaster? Thoughts such as these inspired me to write this story.

We have seen many examples where one people have been totally trounced and humiliated. The feelings of helplessness and powerlessness in such situations can be paralysing, or they can lead to greater human endeavour. This human story woven in the background of historical events still has an overpowering effect on me when I read some parts. So much so that I wonder "Did I write this?" at times. I have poured my heart on paper. I leave it to the readers' judgement whether it has the same effect on them.

The Khmer Empire lasted more than 600 years and encompassed a landmass of an area that is larger than most Empires that existed on the Indian sub-continent. The pinnacles of their achievement, the twin cities of Angkor Wat and Angkor Thom, still stand to bear testimony to their splendid architecture, engineering and culture. I have always been intrigued by these marvelous structures. The greater Angkor area had one million inhabitants at its zenith and was the largest metropolis of the pre industrial era.

The Khmer Empire occupied parts of Modern day Cambodia, Vietnam, and Siam.

In early 15th century Angkoreans faced their greatest challenge for survival yet. Many factors were at play. Enemies from neighbouring Ayutthaya and Champa Kingdoms, religious intrusions and, climate change conspired to create an existential threat that was faced never before by the Khmers. Did they succeed or perish? What did they do to preserve themselves? That is the story I have tried to narrate.

I am an early student of Buddhism and my interpretation of the concepts is as I understand them. I do not profess to be an authentic expert on this subject. I am happy to learn if there has been any misunderstanding.

Climate change is a hot topic and it may be politically incorrect to say that climate change is not brought about by humans. But it is a fact that the earth has gone through many cycles of profound changes in the weather. Little Ice Age (LIA) has been scientifically proven. Asia underwent prolonged droughts and intermittent deluges during LIA.

The international political situation too was undergoing a lot of changes in the fifteenth century. The great Mongolian Empire had run out of steam and had been supplanted in China by the Ming dynasty. After reaching glorious heights of international exploration the Ming had decided to pull back. The successors to the Mongolian Empire were still powerful in Central Asia in spite of the death of Timur (Tamerlane). The sleeping European giant was just waking up, undergoing early Renaissance. Gun powder had been taken from China to the rest of the world by the Mongols. An arms race was on.

Closer to home, India which was the cultural twin of the Khmers, was reeling under successive intrusions by Mohammedan invaders. A Hindu Empire, the Vijayanagara, had arisen and was serving as a bulwark in central and south India against the northern invaders. In Lanka, the last of the great kings, Parakramabahu VI was making preparations to invade Jaffna and unify the land.

All this would change within a century when the Europeans found sea routes to Asia. But the Khmers would have no way of knowing that.

This book was originally published in Tamil in 2015 and was acclaimed by scholars as ground breaking due to its international perspective. I am grateful to Prof Parvati Vasudev and Mr. Anandan Kasinathan, who helped with the English translation. I am also grateful to my own aunt Parvathi Nagasundaram, for inculcating English in me from early days and my wife Dr Mythily Ramanathan for enduring the long hard hours of research, writing and editing that went into this effort.

The English version was published in November 2016 and has done well and been acclaimed by critics. This is a revised edition which has incorporated the criticisms – the story has not changed. This edition is better than the first in my opinion.

Ezhuth Aani

(A. Ramanathan)

April 2022

PART-I

Ezhuth Aani

Chapter 1

The horse raced through the bush forest with the sound 'ladak, ladak'. Carrying Adithya, the horse called Vibhanji galloped thus for several hours, along the narrow track. Adithya travelled across the forest, avoiding the main roads and the hostels that lay along them. These had been constructed by the former Emperor Jayavarman VII.

It was a time when the movement of enemies had increased not only on the borders of the Angkor Empire, but sometimes even in the interior towns.

It was a period when the strength of the Angkor kings had begun to decline gradually. For the past 600 years, they had continuously kept under their control an Empire larger in area than that of most of the ancient Indian Empires.

Enemies like Ayutthaya and Champa were eating into the Empire's boundaries gradually, like termites. In China, the authority of the Ming dynasty was coming down from the dizzy heights attained during the reign of the Yongle Emperor, and the once powerful Chinese navy had run aground completely.

In India which had nurtured Angkor's religious and cultural traditions, Hindu Kingdoms were falling apart due to Muslim intrusions. Worse still, natural disasters such as severe drought and famine were wreaking havoc everywhere. Because of all these factors, the Angkor Kingdom was struggling to sustain itself. But, whether it was possible to succeed in that attempt was a moot question.

It was under these circumstances, that Adithya as the king's personal envoy was on his way to meet an important person.

As he rode, engrossed in various thoughts, Adithya was surprised to notice that both sides of the road that lay along the River Siam Reap were full of forest trees and shrubs, still green as ever, though the River itself had turned into a series of mud pools. Even the River Mekong, described as a perennial lifeline, had lost its former majesty, and was much less in width. Tonle Sap, the inland sea that had earlier been a vast Lake, had now shrunk in almost all the directions. Away from the waterways, in many places, small plants and bushes had withered away. Even big trees had lost their foliage and become mere stumps. Everywhere there was drought.

Despite such dryness, the forests on the Riverside had not lost their greenery. How long they would be able to withstand nature's fury, none could say. In several parts of the country, forest fires had reduced innumerable trees to ashes and burnt stumps.

Vibhanji's shod hoofs were making a rhythmic sound, as the horse trotted. The noise of the birds returning to their nests in the evening on one side, and that of the frogs and insects which announced their presence in the forest on the other was like music set to the rhythm of Vibhanji's footfalls.

As it was a mountain track, it was uneven and in some places very narrow. With the sun setting in the west, darkness began to envelop the area. In the hope that he could reach the hermitage of Vajragnani with a few miles' journey, Adithya proceeded on his way.

Suddenly, Vibhanji reared itself on its hind legs, neighing. At the same time, strong ropes tightened around Adithya's torso in front and at the back. Seconds earlier, he had already drawn his sword.

"Ha ha ha!" A woman's derisive laughter, louder than the sounds of wild animals, filled the air.

Ezhuth Aani

A beautiful maiden appeared before him saying, "Rider, you have no other alternative but to surrender." As the incident occurred on a hilly ascent, the lady who stood on a rock and Adithya who was on his horse, were nearly on the same level. She was on the left of the road.

Although she was dressed topless like the Cambodian ladies of that age, the garland of leaves and flowers which she wore served to cover parts of her breasts, but those that were exposed drew his attention like a magnet. The lady, who wore a dress below her waist, did not wear any jewels, but she wore ornaments made of leaves and flowers as bangles and a crown made of leaves. Adithya wondered if these were 'fruits hidden amidst leaves!' Was he a hermit or a monk not to wonder at her beauty, even in this hour of danger?

Dusky bodied, her eyes shone like stars, overcoming the mild darkness that prevailed then. She had knotted her hair into a bun, and wore a tiara of leaves around it. She looked like a beautiful goddess, but in her right hand was a huge sword. How could those soft hands bear such a heavy sword? And how does she wield it? Having lost a few seconds in such questions, Adithya managed to return to reality. He tried to cut the ropes that bound him.

With the metallic sound 'kling', his sword was stalled by hers. Taken aback by this unexpected move, Adithya tried to withdraw his sword and upset hers. This sword fight lasted a few minutes.

As she stood on his left, and as his legs had been restrained by the ropes, so that sitting on his restless horse he was unable to plant his feet on firm ground, he could not fight with his usual strength. The absence of footwork affected his fencing skills. Nevertheless, as far as possible, Adithya used his full force and jabbed her sword with his. Moving her legs skillfully in front and back, and the sides, the lady fought with him on equal terms. The woman being on high ground neutralised his height advantage of being on a horse. Finally, as he swerved left using all his strength and drew his sword, he experienced excruciating pain in his back and realised that he had sprained it. At the same time, as his grip slackened, Adithya's sword was flung far away. Simultaneously, the lady's sword also broke near its hilt joint, and fell just where his sword had fallen. Both were stunned.

It was the maiden, who stood with the sword grip, without the blade, who spoke first. "O' warrior! You have lost your sword to a lady" she taunted. He replied, "You have bound my lower part so tightly that I can't move. In such a condition, how can you call this your victory? Only if we can move our legs freely, can we fight as we wish; don't you know this?" He continued: "I have not seen even a man wielding a sword like you; perhaps you are a man in a woman's dress."

"How can I be a man? Having roved your eyes lustfully about me from head to foot, you should know whether I am a man or a woman" said the maiden. "If only you had focused your attention on my sword and not allowed it to feast on my chest, you could have won! But this is the first time my sword has been broken."

As what she said was true, Adithya fidgeted ashamedly, and said, "Lady, remove my fetters. I'll teach you how to fight."

"Both our swords have fallen. You are now inviting me for a wrestling bout? You'll regret your words" said the maiden. Only then did Adithya realise that she was not alone and that there were ten to fifteen soldiers standing behind her.

"Untie his knots" said the maiden.

"It shall be done, my lady" said the warriors, and removing his bonds, they lowered him from the horse.

Ezhuth Aani

Defenseless, Adithya realised that he could not escape from them, and hence obeyed their orders. They took him to an open ground, devoid of trees.

She then asked him, "Ready for wrestling?" As Adithya hesitated wondering 'How to wrestle with a lady?' she said, "I thought you had realised that I am not an ordinary lady. No man has overthrown me so far." She continued, "O' warrior! I shall give you another chance. If you fight with me and win, I shall release you. But if you lose, you'll have to fight with my pet lion tomorrow."

Understanding that he had no other alternative but to fight with her, he reluctantly accepted her condition. Her men stood around them like spectators. But he knew quite well that at her command they would surround him any time.

If he felt that he was fighting with a lady, the feeling vanished within a few seconds of the start. He had fought with innumerable men till then; but never before had he met a warrior who dealt blows all over so fast, like streaks of lightning. She folded the lower part of her dress, tucked it up and following the ancient Ayutthaya martial art known as muay boran, she fought with him. Her legs hardly touched the ground; but she attacked him from different directions in different ways. Her feet and arms descended on him ceaselessly. Wondering how such soft hands could be so strong, and how such soft feet could turn into such adamantine weapons, Adithya fought with her more defensively, avoiding the impact of her assault by moving sideways, and falling on the ground and rising dexterously.

It was at this time that the back pain which had started during his swordfight began to increase. Just then, one of her blows struck his back, and he felt excruciating pain. Before he could recover from this, another blow fell on his manhood. With that Adithya fell on the ground. His eyes began to close and he felt dizzy. Her voice seemed to come from somewhere far off. Laughing loudly as she readied herself to pounce on him, she said "You don't have the strength to fight with me; how will you fight with a lion? Come, fall at my feet and surrender. I'll then consider sparing your life."

She was hesitant to kill this youth, who had such a handsome face and robust body. So far she had defeated any number of men and fed them to her lion without any remorse. But now, deep down in her mind, she felt sorry for this man. That one second's hesitation was time enough for him to gather his wits.

The next time she tried to attack his body, Adithya who lay on the floor, rolled on his side, received her leg on his shoulder, and using her own momentum, flung her away. The Japanese way of fighting which he had been taught in his youth in the Vijayanagara Empire by the Jain hermit Madhura, now came to his aid. Before the lady who had been thrown down could rise again, he passed his hands under her armpits and entwining his fingers behind her neck, held her down tightly. For the first time in her life, the maiden struggled even to breathe, caught in the firm grip of a man and unable to move. The garlands which had covered her breasts had been dislodged, and in his iron grip her chest was nearly crushed.

Even though she felt humiliated that she had been defeated, she also felt a kind of joyous excitement in his strong grip. Was this a pleasurable pain? Perhaps. For the first time in her life she experienced such feelings. More than the thought that it was not a shame to submit to such a courageous man, she was overcome by a sort of bliss!

At that time, her men surrounded him with their swords drawn; but gesturing to them with her eyes to go away, she addressed Adithya: "O' warrior! I have never known what defeat is in my life; you have taught me a lesson today. Thank you. I am honored to have been defeated by you."

Ezhuth Aani

Loosening his hold, Adithya said, "Lady, I don't know who you are. But, I've never met a beautiful, courageous and skillful 'wonder-woman' like you till now."

On her orders, his sword and horse were handed over to him. However, she said, "I shall keep my word. But at this time of the night you shall not travel far in this dense forest where wild animals live. Moreover, if your back pain is not treated now, it will get aggravated when you ride a horse, and become a big problem in future. If you don't mind, you can stay for a couple of days with us, be treated by my father, and then continue your journey. But if you wish to go now you may do so too."

Adithya reflected. What she said seemed reasonable enough. Moreover, a part of his mind was eager to know more about her. Hence he agreed to go with them.

On asking her, "Who is your father?" she replied "You'll know when you meet him."

She tried to mount Vibhanji. Vibhanji, however, reared, leaped and attempted to throw her down. She too moved her body to match its movements, and lying forwards whispered something in its ear. Immediately, Vibhanji became calm.

"Lady! Vibhanji has never carried anyone except me so far. She will throw down anybody who tries to get on to it. How did you make her submit to you?" asked Adithya.

She replied, "There is no animal that has not obeyed my command. It was all taught to me by my father."

"You are, indeed, a wonder-woman" said Adithya, and followed them through the forest silently.

After several miles' distance through the dark forest, he saw
a   miracle   unfold   in   front   of   him.

Ezhuth Aani

Chapter 2

Yes. A small cluster of dwellings built in the middle of the forest appeared before him. Many thatched houses surrounded by landscaped gardens had been constructed, and in the centre was a Buddhist stupa. The buildings were all built with simple trees and thatch mounted on bamboo stilts. Adithya never knew that such a place existed in this forest.

A hut was allotted to him, and all his needs attended to. Saying, "O' warrior! Take rest; we shall meet tomorrow" she ordered her men to take care of Adithya and Vibhanji, and left.

Adithya could not sleep for a long time. He was surprised to think how, leaving aside his business, he had come here, and lost his heart to a lady. Where had his bravery and resolve gone? When he rose the next day from his sleep, the sun was at the zenith. He was ashamed that he had overslept due to exhaustion. Only a few moments after he opened his eyes did he remember where he was, and the incidents of the previous night. Usually, Adithya would get up before sunrise, and finish his prayers to the Sun, his yoga practice and his ablutions. But that day, his whole body, particularly his back continued to ache, and he felt tired. The lady he met the previous night, had hurt him very badly indeed. But when he thought of her, he only felt a sort of calm and respect for her.

It was strange and surprising to him to think what this beautiful, courageous and intelligent maiden was doing in this forest. Unable to shake off his memories of her, he went out of his hut; only then did he realise that although he was free to roam about, he was being watched all the time.

When he started walking, he became aware that his back pain had not left him. On the other hand, it seemed to have increased manifold since the previous night. Nevertheless, could physical aches deter a warrior like him? He began to carry out his usual duties, enduring the pain in his back.

"O' warrior! If your backache is not treated now it will increase in course of time" said a voice. Turning back, Adithya asked the maiden, "How do you know about my pain, lady?"

Laughing heartily, the maiden said, "I noticed it yesterday when you walked. Now too, you're walking leaning to a side. From this I could surmise your back pain." She appeared more beautiful in today's golden sunlight, than she did in previous night's growing darkness. Her long black hair, which had been knotted into a bun the previous night, was let down now, and covered her breasts on both sides, looking like a shawl. Her slender waist, large, curved hips and buttocks, and then the smooth banana stem-like thighs and legs, which though covered by a dress could be seen silhouetted in the sunlight, drove him crazy.

"Are you a doctor?" asked Adithya.

"Medicine is also one of the arts taught by my father. I know several other arts too" she said. "You are the only man who has not yielded to my sword and wrestling. I have decided to take you to my father. But before that, you should be treated for your ailment. You look as if you belong to a royal family. You must be having great responsibilities. If the sprain in your back is not treated immediately, it may turn out to be a big problem later, and affect your life in the future."

To his questions, 'Who is your father? Who are you?' she answered, "Everyone calls me The girl. My name is Mandagini. You will know who my father is, later. What is your name?" He replied, "My name is Adithya. But people call me Princeling, meaning Prince."

"Good day, Princeling. I have insulted you, not knowing your identity. Please forgive me."

"Mandagini, you've not insulted me. In fact, you have learned certain methods of warfare which even I do not know. It is my good fortune to have met a beauty like you" said Princeling.

Descended from Jayavarman's lineage, and recognized only as a member of the royal family, and not as the heir apparent, Adithya's name was known in every nook and corner of the Angkor Empire. Adithya had earned great respect not only from the king but also from the common people, by displaying his skill in various armed combat competitions and battles. Though there were many princes, it was Adithya who was affectionately called 'the Princeling'.

Adithya's mother was a relative of Harihara and Pukka, the founder kings of the Vijayanagara Empire of India. Having spent a few years of his childhood with his mother in the Vijayanagara Empire, Adithya had distinguished himself not only in warfare but also in Vedic learning. His mother, a Hindu, had married his father who was a Buddhist; hence, she had taught Adithya a lot about both religions. His guru Madhura, followed Jainism, but had explained to him the doctrines of all the religions.

In addition to being trained in wrestling, sword-fighting, archery, and riding horses and elephants, he had familiarized himself with the cannon that had just been introduced into India. On his return he had established his supremacy in the occasional skirmishes and battles with Ayutthaya, and become more popular with the people than even the veteran warriors.

Because of this, Mandagini had heard about him. When she knew that it was the Princeling who had defeated her, she felt that her defeat was in fact like a victory. She remembered her father saying that there was a proverb, 'If rapped, better to be rapped with fingers bejeweled with rings'.

The hills called Mahendra Parvatha were the birthplace of the Khmer Kingdom. It was there that Jayavarman II routed the encroachers from Java, and proclaimed his Empire. It was on the southern slopes of Mahendra Parvatha that many of the rivers which fostered the culture of Angkor originated. It was by using the waters of these rivers for several centuries, that the people of that country were able to cultivate the land and establish a powerful and wealthy Empire.

Although he had been informed that the person he had come in search of, lived in the middle of the dense forest north of Parvatha, even the royal spies did not know much about him. Strangers who had entered the forest without permission had never returned alive, according to legend. None knew whether they had been eaten by wild animals, or captured by this maiden and put to death, or magnetized by her charm had become her followers.

Even the rulers of Ayutthaya and Champa had ordered their soldiers not to disturb him. Thus, this forest area was treated by all the kings as a Peace Zone.

The man called Vajragnani was a Buddhist monk, but one who respected and encouraged men who professed other religions also. It was widely reported that he had learned and mastered not only the art of war, but also dance, medicine, and various other disciplines. Many of his disciples had served in the hospitals established by Jayavarman VII on the borders of the jungle. Several royal princes had come to him to learn and stayed for some time in his ashram. They would be examined by Vajragnani's men on the outskirts of the forest, and only then taken to him. They would also have to take an oath on their swords that they would never try to learn anything about his secret paths, either when they were his students or later, and that they would never at any time act against him. Thus, even those foreign princes who fought amongst themselves were united as students in his ashram. As long as they were there, the aristocrats behaved like siblings, eating and sleeping together, but once they returned to their respective lands, they fought with one another as enemies.

However, all the countries treated Vajragnani with a kind of loving respect. They offered bountifully all he needed, through the messengers he sent. Whenever they fell ill or had some problems, they would come to him seeking his advice. Rarely did he venture out of that forest. It was the others who went to him. There was an unwritten rule that those who went to meet him were not attacked incognito. But, permission had to be sought several weeks in advance, to meet him.

Adithya had been sent to meet him on a secret mission. Hence, no prior information had been given. Looking at her beautiful face and lost in all these thoughts, he was shaken awake by her question, "Why did Prince Adithya come to this forest?"

For a second, Adithya hesitated whether to tell her or not, but he felt an overwhelming trust and confidence in her. In life, sometimes when we meet some people, the mind does not wish to conceal anything from them but rather open up to them.

"I came in search of Vajragnani" said Princeling.

"Father is in meditation. He will not meet any body for the next two weeks. Hence, you may stay here, get treated for your back pain and then meet him" said Mandagini.

"I haven't heard that Vajragnani has a daughter" said Princeling.

"I'm his adopted daughter. Buddhist monks do not marry" she said. In Buddhism, there are two divisions: Mahayana and Theravada. Among these two, Theravada Buddhist monks observe rigorous celibacy. Hence, Vajragnani could not have had a daughter. He had become a monk in his youth. Most of the people in the land did not know about his adopted daughter. In fact, though the great man called Vajragnani was famous all over the country, nothing more about him was known except his name. Other details were mere guesses and rumours. Even these legends were mostly exaggerated accounts of his prowess; very little information was available about his personal life.

Adithya had no other alternative but to stay there. Apart from being treated for his back pain, the desire to learn the art of warfare from her was an additional motivation for his stay.

From the next day, medical treatment was given to him under her supervision, morning and evening. Though he wondered longingly whether she wouldn't massage his back herself, it was mostly men who carried out the treatment under her supervision. However, now and then she applied pressure on his neck and backbone at certain angles, to bring the spine back to the original alignment.

When he was not being treated medically, she taught him Thai wrestling. In addition, they exchanged their knowledge about different methods of wielding a sword and other strategies. In particular, she taught him Vajragnani's unique method of aiming two knives simultaneously at one or more targets, unerringly.

When men and women were learning to practice close encounters of this kind, physical closeness was necessary. Though it was under the garb of learning and teaching that they were engaged, it was unavoidable for their chests and arms to touch each other. Although she knew that he was excited by this, she feigned not to have noticed it at all.

In a few days, his back pain was completely cured. The two weeks passed quickly, and the day appointed for meeting Vajragnani dawned.

"Please remain in your room. When father rises from his meditation, I shall inform him and take you" said Mandagini. That day, Adithya rose with the sun. It was the first time that he was going to meet Vajragnani. While other princes had gone through Vajragnani's school at least once, Adithya alone had grown up with his mother in Vijayanagara, and had acquired his early education in India. His guru, Madhura, had taught him comprehensively about drawing, sculpture, and religions, apart from the various forms of warfare. However, since he had not travelled through Vajragnani's school, his thoughts and skills were different from those of the other princes.

Adithya's father had been killed due to internecine squabbles within the royal family, when the former was a child. Royal intrigue was commonplace in Angkor. His mother, unlike the other ladies, did not marry the victors and enter their harems. Instead, carrying the infant Adithya, she undertook a long voyage and reached Vijayanagara. There, she brought him up as a complete young man, and then brought him to Angkor in search of his father's inheritance. By the time he reached Angkor, there was a resurgence of internal conflicts, in which Adithya's uncle Indravarman had an upper hand. Because of this, the Princeling was not only accepted in the court, but various responsibilities were assigned to him. The more he displayed his skill and capacity, the higher his status rose. Though he was not the heir apparent, he stood tall, respected by everyone. He was also loved by his countrymen.

Ever since the Angkor Empire had been established by Jayavarman II, it had seen many wars. In most of them, it had routed its enemies and emerged victorious. For several centuries, it remained a militarily mighty and affluent empire. However, in recent times it had got entangled in various crises, and was struggling to sustain its integrity as a nation. Enemies were eating away the boundaries of the country like moth. Even within the ruling family, there was no unity, as several factions had emerged. In the meantime, the people had begun to embrace the newly introduced Theravada Buddhism in large numbers. Because of this, the tradition of worshipping the king as God's representative was gradually fading away. The practice of maintaining lakes and canals through free manual labor, as part of the service to the king, had begun to dwindle. Moreover, as the monsoons had failed for many years, most of the rivers had dried up. In addition, the mineral wealth of the soil that had made possible three to four seasonal crops annually had begun to decline. People, who had never known famine, now had to face it every day. During such hard times, social evils such as robbery, murder and prostitution began to spread in the country. Strong societal bonds had begun to snap. Under such circumstances, the danger of the Khmer culture itself disintegrating was quite clear to the elders of the land. The people were ready to unite and follow anybody who was capable of saving the land from such dangers. When a society faces annihilation, it will somehow strive to save itself.

It was in this context, that the king had sent his confidante Adithya to Vajragnani as a messenger. It would be more appropriate to say that he sent Adithya to obtain Vajragnani's wise counsel, rather than as a messenger. Though Vajragnani belonged to the Theravada religion, he spoke the Cambodian Khmer language. The King believed that the sage would desire to foster and preserve his culture and not let it perish. Moreover, the king's opinion was that Vajragnani, who was respected by all sections of people, would somehow restore peace to the land.

It was against this background that Adithya journeyed towards his forest empire in search of Vajragnani. Fortunately or otherwise, he had been captured by the sage's adopted daughter, and now after several days' delay, was finally going to meet him. As he had not seen him earlier, he did not know what to expect.

Chapter 3

He expected to see a saffron-clad tall man. He reckoned that the man, who held the key to the land's future, would be full of radiance and authority. When she took him to meet her father, Adithya went with great expectation and humility.

On the way, his attention was drawn to a man sitting under a huge banyan tree, in the lotus posture. Unlike saffron-clad hermits, this man wore a white dress, and was bare-chested. He had no ornaments either. Though he could not reckon his height as he was seated, Adithya was sure that the man was shorter than himself. He was slim. Neither his head nor his chest had any hair. As soon as he saw him from a distance, Adithya asked "Who is he?" "Ask the man himself" said Mandagini.

As for the man, for many minutes he was in meditation, with his eyes closed. Adithya was unsure as to what to do. Apprehensive of disturbing his meditation, he stopped talking to her, and kept looking at the man again and again.

Although he did not appear distinctive or majestic at first sight, he had some sort of a charisma and that induced Adithya to look at him repeatedly. He was slim and had a tanned skin. Apart from this he had no indications of his belonging to any particular religion or clan. Though his eyes were closed, there was some kind of magnetism in them. The closed eyelids had long eyelashes. These lashes radiated like the sun's rays in all directions. His eyebrows were arched like bows. A lady should consider herself blessed to have eyes like his. They were ever so attractive, despite their being closed. The eyelids alone could make women jealous. But his body was every inch masculine. Though there was not a single hair on his body, there was absolutely no trace of fat anywhere; his adamantine strength was obvious. But unlike a wrestling champion or a bodybuilder with protruding muscles, he looked like any other ordinary man.

His hands, with their veins bulging out, evidenced the fact that he had toiled hard. His palms, placed one on top of the other in his lap, and his feet in the Padmasana posture, faced the sky. These palms and inner feet were soft red in colour making one wonder as to whether they were lotuses doing penance to the sun. His appearance which was a combination of softness and solid strength, inspired respect and awe.

When the man who had such an aura even when his eyes were closed, opened them ... wow! How did such serenity and piercing sharpness inhabit those eyes simultaneously? The moment he opened his eyes, even the slightest doubt that Adithya had, left him. Undoubtedly, this was Vajragnani. She did not tell him this. The man too did not inform him. But he understood it clearly. When one approaches a great man, the latter needs no introduction. Circumstances and the man's personality make us understand who he is.

Opening his eyes, he looked at his daughter lovingly, and addressed Adithya: "Aggressive girl! Did she hurt you badly?" Even before he could reply, he continued: "I know that a man who will equal her will appear one day. You teach her your knowledge of warfare. Once she learns that also, there'll be none to equal her in this world."

When he said this, Adithya looked at her in confusion. Did the girl tell her father everything? When did she meet him? While he was lost in thought, Vajragnani observed him keenly. Unable to withstand the power of his gaze, Adithya looked the other way. "My son, I knew about the purpose of your visit, and the incidents that occurred on your way here, even as I was meditating. This is one of the strengths of yoga" said Vajragnani.

"In that case, do you know why I've come here?" asked Adithya.

"There is the danger of a centuries-old empire crumbling. Under such circumstances, the king is trying to get help and advice from all quarters. He has sent warriors in all directions. You have not been sent to talk to me. More than that, it is to seek advice on where to get help from and for guidance. Also, the king expects that I can bring about peace, using my goodwill with the rulers of Ayutthaya. He has sent an able messenger like you to persuade me to accept your request" said Gnani. "If you know the past, present and future, why don't you tell me what will happen to my country, please" said Adithya, pleadingly.

"Ha ha! Seems as if you'll corner even me" said Vajragnani, and continued: "Though I can predict the future to a certain extent, I can't say for sure that it will happen exactly as I said. It is crystal clear that a great danger is imminent. But it's my opinion, that with concerted human effort, it is possible to escape from any catastrophe. You should know the story of Markandeya of Hindu mythology. Destiny can be overcome by one's intelligence. Moreover, destiny is something that is shaped by us. You are the architect of your own future. Hence, don't lose hope. Carry on with your work."

"Whose side are you on, in this?" asked Adithya.

"Do you expect an answer to this from me, a hermit, who has renounced the world? In my view, both your king and the king of Ayutthaya are the same. To me, it matters not, who wins or loses. But..." Adithya asked Vajragnani who paused, "But what, O' hermit? What do you want to say?" Vajragnani observed him intently for many seconds.

Ezhuth Aani

"The matchless buildings and sculptures created continuously for several centuries from the time of Jayavarman should not be destroyed by your greed. They are not solely your possessions. They are wonderful artistic treasures that belong to the whole world. No one has the right to destroy them. They should last as long as the world lasts. They should be immortal. This is my first concern" said Gnani.

"In that case, won't you help us?" asked Adithya, with great expectation. "No, no. To whoever comes seeking my counsel, I shall speak nothing but the truth. After that, their success or failure depends on their effort and endeavours."

"You belong to Hinduism, is it not?" asked Vajragnani. "My mother is a Hindu, my father a Buddhist, and my guru a Jain. I myself do not know which religion I belong to" said Adithya.

"My son, it was Jayavarman II, a Hindu, who established the Cambodian Empire. For several centuries, the Angkor kings continued to be Hindus. The Brahmins who came from India held sway here. It was Suryavarman I, a descendant of the Sri Vijaya clan whose mother was Tamil, who was the first Angkor king to embrace Buddhism. Later, during the reign of the Emperor Jayavarman VII, Buddhism flourished here. However, the kings of that time followed Mahayana, a kind of Buddhism that had a lot of similarities to Hinduism." As he paused, Adithya interrupted him. "As far as I know there is only one kind of Buddhism. What is this new branch you are talking about? And what is the connection between these religions and the current problems faced by the country?" asked Adithya.

"Whether you like it or not, religions have entered politics. Have you not heard of the proverb, 'As the king leadeth, the people follow?' Through the use of religions, the aristocrats have been able to control the people. Similarly, it is possible for the religious leaders to acquire a high status in society by means of the king's influence."

"Are you also of the same kind?" asked Adithya. "No, my son. We are inhabitants of the forest. We do not involve ourselves in the politics of the land. But, in times of turmoil, we do not fail to give our advice. If there are no kings or religions, there'll be anarchy in the land. By preaching a disciplined and proper way of life, religions and politics help each other in maintaining a well-structured society. However, in their greed for power, when they try to use religion as a weapon to subjugate other countries, they deviate from the basic tenets of their religion" said Gnani.

"Please continue your explanation about the branches of Buddhist Dharma, which you began" said Adithya.

"Only after the Buddha attained Nirvana, the Buddhist monks collected the teachings of the Buddha, in accordance with the orders of King Ajaatha Sathru. The first book, the Vinaya Pitaka, consists of the rules for the Buddhist monks. Suddha Pitaka comprises Lord Buddha's preachments. They were uttered by the hermit, Ananda. Every stanza begins with the preamble, 'I heard thus'. That is, it is assumed that Ananda, who heard the Buddha's teachings, repeated that to others. Later, a section called Abhidamma Pitaka was appended. Together they form the Tripitaka. This was the first Buddhist Council. Buddha's preachments had been handed down orally from generation to generation, but not written for a long time. Hindu religious texts were also handed down from generation to generation only by oral tradition.

"Before the Buddha appeared, the Brahmins had been dominant for a long time in India. One's social status was determined by his birth alone. It was the Brahmins who established the social code called Varnashrama Dharma, or the caste system. They made the people believe that the Brahmins appeared from Creator Lord Brahma's tongue, and that the Sudras appeared from

His feet. Lord Buddha, who brought about a great spiritual revolution, was also responsible for a social revolution. In Agganna sutta, Lord Buddha debunks these Brahmanic creation myths. The Buddha has stated very clearly that one's status is not determined by his birth. On the contrary, one can become elevated only by his thoughts, deeds and motives. There are many other stanzas such as Vasala sutta that tell the same. In the presence of one who has renounced the world, even emperors will bow in obeisance. The Buddha did not totally reject Varnashrama Dharma. This was because, it was his contention that, if law and order were to be maintained in society, each individual had to carry out the duties allotted to him.

"Buddha, Dharma (righteousness), and Sanga (clergy), are considered to be three gems by the Buddhists. The concept was obtained from Ananda's Ratana Sutta. Through the prayer, 'Buddham Saranam Gachchami, Dharmam Saranam Gachchami and Sangam Saranam Gachchami', Buddhists bow their heads and surrender before the three gems. Of these, there is no confusion regarding Buddha and Dharma. But what does Sanga denote? Does it refer to all the Bodhisattvas who attained Nirvana earlier? Or does it denote the living Arahats who have renounced the world and have elevated themselves through their genuinely ascetic life? Or does it refer to all those who are saffron-clad? Surely, Ananda must have preached his sermons, having in mind the first two categories.

"But, both the kings and the monks have joined hands, and politicized the Sanga. The minds of the monks who had renounced the world, turned toward social status, power and wealth. At the same time, these neo-Brahmins, the only difference being that they were ordained rather than born into their privileged position, aided the kings in controlling the people. These monks are one with the kings in their lust for power.

"Do not even for a moment think that all Buddhist monks are political. Most of the monks live as faithful followers of Lord Buddha's teachings. I had to explain these facts just to make you understand why splits arose in Buddhism. Otherwise, how could conflicts occur in such a pacific religion?

"The third Buddhist Council was held during Emperor Ashoka's period in Pataliputra. It was organized with the aim of purifying Buddhism. Emperor Ashoka dispatched religious missionaries to all directions. Among these, his own son, Arahat Mahinda, was sent to Lanka. As soon as King Devanampiya Tissa embraced Buddhism, most of Lanka became Buddhist.

"A subsequent king Vaththagamini Abhaya built Abhayagiri Dagoba. The monks of Abhayagiri were influenced by Buddhist monks from South India. By that time Buddhism had evolved in most of the world to what we now know as Mahayana. But in Lanka, being an island, the religion had been preserved exactly the way Arahat Mahinda taught. We call this the pure form or Theravada. This difference in ideology brought the Abhayagiri monks into conflict with the powerful clerics of Mahavihara. This rivalry was not based on doctrinal differences alone. There was intense competition for political concessions and royal patronage.

"Finally, after several hundred years, Mahavihara won a decisive victory during the reign of Parakramabahu I. Abhayagiri monks were defrocked and became laymen.

"Paradoxically, Buddhism which once held sway over all of India had been completely wiped out from the subcontinent by the Hindu renaissance.

"Theravada Buddhism flourished in Lanka. However, the rulers of the island nation sent Theravada missionaries by sea to other countries. Due to this, there was a second wave of Buddhist revival. But the form of the religion that spread this time was

Theravada. Theravada spread to many countries along the coast of the great ocean. Cambodia (Kamboj) is one of them."

Interrupting, Adithya asked, "What is the connection between this history and our current problem?"

"A lot in fact. King Jayavarman was a Hindu. He was considered as an incarnation of God. The citizens worshipped the King as the Lord Himself. They felt that service to the King was the same as service to God. Thus, it was easy to construct and administer huge temples, tanks, reservoirs, dams and canals.

"Several tanks and reservoirs were built around Angkor, the capital of an empire consisting of millions of citizens. To fill these water bodies, dams were constructed across the Puok, Ruolos and Siem Reap rivers, so that they were either diverted, or their waters brought to these man-made lakes through canals. To maintain this huge irrigation network, mobilisation of the entire citizenry was necessary.

"Because of these irrigation schemes, it was not necessary to depend on Lake Tonle Sap, which obtained water from the Mekong River and monsoon rains. Tonle Sap swelled during monsoon rains but shrunk back during the rest of the year. The ingenious water management system made it possible to cultivate many seasonal crops every year to feed the ever growing population.

"The people worshipped the King as the Lord Himself. Kings were looked upon as incarnations of God. During this period, the kings and people followed Hinduism and Mahayana Buddhism. But for the past fifty years, it is Theravada, introduced back during King Sindiran's time that has dominated."

"What is the difference between Theravada and Mahayana?" asked Adithya.

"According to the Mahayana, there is an element of immortality in every living being. This is indestructible. We call this Buddha Dhatu. This Buddhist element is our real self. Everything else is an illusion. In the Mahaparinirvana Sutra in the Mahayana, Lord Buddha has said this very clearly. In this respect, there are similarities between Mahayana, and Advaitha (non-dualism) school of Hinduism preached by Adi Sankara. Our Buddha Dhatu is their Brahman. But in Theravada, the state of Nirvana is a vacuum; a void. But in my opinion void and fullness are two aspects of the same state.

"Moreover, according to the doctrines of Mahayana, the Bodhisattvas i.e., those who attained Nirvana before us, help us in many ways. Just as the Hindu gods shower their blessings on their devotees; these Bodhisattvas help us to cross the ocean of Life. It is in this respect, that Bodhisattvas like Manjusiri, Avalokateswara, and Vajrapani are worshipped. This is similar to the Hindus worshipping different Gods. The existence of Bodhisattvas is only possible if the entity continues to exist after enlightenment. Bodhisattvas are not compatible with pure Theravada beliefs. Every man is encouraged to elevate himself by meditation and reflection. When people follow Theravada, service to the king becomes meaningless. Due to this, the water management schemes face the danger of neglect and destruction.

"Monsoon failure is not the only reason for the famine prevailing now. The dams, canals and tanks, constructed to save and use the rain water, have been silted up. With the decline of fidelity to the king, and the rise of economic problems, the central control of the Angkor Empire has diminished. Every chieftain has begun to administer his province according to his will. Under the circumstances, the spies of Ayutthaya and Champa have been instigating rebellions and anarchy all over the country."

"It is my good fortune to have come here, seeking advice from one possessing such vast knowledge and sharpness of intellect like you" said Adithya.

"It is all due to the insight gained from my mentor, Tsongkhapa. The meditational practices and techniques which he taught me have been helping me" said Vajragnani.

"In that case, did you go to Tibet?" asked Adithya.

"Not only there; I was in China for many years and learnt many arts there" said Gnani.

"You have stated the problems very clearly. Will you give us their solutions also?" asked Adithya.

"The country's immediate need is water. Next, to fight against foreign intrusions you need military and financial aid. Moreover, you need modern arms for the army that you will recruit. We shall analyse these one by one. If you accept my advice, you will have to undertake long journeys. There is no immediate danger to the country. Hence, you have a few years' time. However, if you don't take preventive measures against the great disaster that will befall the land in a few years' time, you'll have to suffer" said Gnani.

"My son, you eat, rest and then come. At midnight, I shall show you a miracle. Then I shall tell you the solution to your country's problem" said Gnani, and closing his eyes, began meditating.

Princeling looked at Mandagini, as if to say, 'What next?'

Chapter 4

O warrior, eat and rest. If you come with me, I shall serve you myself" said Mandagini.

"It is my good fortune to be served by a beautiful lady" said Adithya.

"Warrior! Mind your words! Will you try to take advantage of even the hospitality shown to you?" However, the moment the words were out of her mouth she regretted, wondering if she had been a little harsh towards him and looked at him guiltily. She feared that she might be attracted to him if she were to interact with him flirtatiously; at the same time, she felt a sense of pride when he praised her! She realised that she would be disappointed if he stopped trying to interact with her intimately. But she also feared that if she revealed the fact that she liked his attention, he would lose his respect for her. Thus, both were in a state of distress, like those caught in the middle of a cross-fire not knowing which way to go – wishing to be close on one hand, and moving away on the other. It was a novel feeling for both.

Having been brought up in an ashram, Mandagini was accustomed to eating only fruits, vegetables and rice. Her adopted father too, ate only such food. But a warrior like Adithya preferred meat and non-vegetarian food. However, even if Mandagini had served him poison, Adithya would have consumed it as nectar. So the vegetarian food tasted good.

As soon as the meal was over, Mandagini sat in meditation. Forgetting her surroundings, she sat cross-legged for quite some time, with her eyes closed. Her breathing slowed down gradually until she breathed only once in several seconds. At the same time, with a beautiful lady like this in front, how could Adithya meditate?

He sat staring at her, without even batting his eyelids. So far, he had never observed her body closely, having spoken to her looking only at her face. This opportunity to see her body and relish it was golden.

As her 'magnetic' eyes were closed, he was able to see her face and body at leisure. Though her eyes were closed, they enhanced the beauty of her face, with their neem-leaf like shape. The arched eyebrows drew one's attention to the eyes and added to their beauty. The nose, sharp and small, formed the centre of her meditation, being in the middle of her face like an ornament. Though the lips were closed, they were constricted at the corners, so that she appeared to be smiling. Her high cheek bones bore witness to the fact that she was a resolute lady. Her long neck was like a stem that held her face like a flower.

As she did not wear an upper garment in accordance with the Cambodian tradition, the plumpness of her breasts could be seen clearly; however, the garland of leaves and flowers which she wore, served to cover her chest to a certain extent. The lower garment made of a very fine material covered the part below the waist; nevertheless, her slender waist and her rounded hips enhanced the beauty of the lady-goddess, sitting in the lotus posture. Her physical features indicated that she belonged to the category of Padmini, one of the four types of women, as described by Vatsyayana in his Kamasutra.

Adithya continued to take in her beauty. Opening her eyes suddenly, Mandagini said, "Have you seen enough, o' warrior?"

Startled, Adithya asked, "With your eyes closed, how did you know what I was doing?"

"My father has taught me the art of seeing my surroundings even with my eyes closed" said Mandagini. She continued, "Don't know why, I couldn't meditate peacefully. Your sharp eagle's eyes have been confusing me."

"No, no. They say you should not meditate on a full stomach. You tried to meditate soon after a meal; that is why this confusion" said Adithya, glossing over the situation.

"How is it that today alone I've not been able to focus on my meditation? I normally meditate at this time" said Mandagini.

Both knew that the other's presence affected them. They were not angry. Instead, an unknown feeling of happiness took hold of them.

"If you come with me I'll show you a wonder" said Mandagini.

"Ever since I met you I have been seeing only wonders" said Adithya.

They then mounted their horses and rode through the forest for quite some time. In the dense forest, along a rocky single track, Mandagini rode in front, while Adithya followed on Vibhanji. As it was a familiar track for her, Mandagini rode ahead fast, and then waited until he reached her. Thus, they travelled together.

After travelling for a few hours, that wonder suddenly unfolded itself before Adithya's eyes. Yes, it was a wonderful creation sculpted during the time of Suryavarman I. It was man's expression in art of Nature's beauty and grace. Although innumerable cave temples and stone sculptures had been created by man, how those sculptors could have imagined these creations, wondered Adithya as he took in the wonder that lay before him.

Though he had heard of this place called Kabal Spean, at first sight its mesmerizing beauty gave Adithya a never-before-experienced thrill. The place, under the River Kabali, could be seen very clearly as the water level had gone down considerably. The River Kabali, flowed first between two rocks and then on comparatively plain ground, before dropping as a cascade. Later, it joined the Siem Reap and Puok Rivers, which were the lifelines of Angkor city.

In that place, on the rocks at the bottom of the River, a thousand Siva Lingas had been carved out on the bedrock. The base of each lingam was in the form of the genital organ of a woman, the yoni. These artistic idols would be submerged when the water level in the River rose. Apart from this, there was a cluster of eight lingas arranged in a square with a linga in each of the eight directions. Inside the square were five more lingas, and the whole unit resembled the female genital organ. The square seemed to open out in the direction of the flow of the river.

In addition, various sculptures depicting Lord Vishnu in the reclining posture, with Brahma in the lotus rising from Lord Vishnu's navel, and Lord Siva with His consort Uma, had been very aesthetically carved on the rocks nearby. There were also carvings of animals such as bulls and crocodiles.

These sculptures, begun during the time of Suryavarman I, and completed during the time of Udayaadityavarman II, were the highest manifestations of the then Hindu culture. Also, one of these lingas was made of gold.

Gods such as Karthikeya and Ganesha, which Adithya had seen in India, were not found commonly there. Adithya wondered whether the worship of these gods spread later.

As the River Kabali, considered as one of the sources of water of Angkor city, flowed through such a sacred environment, it attained the status of a holy River. The water which flowed through this River was regarded as a sacred offering to the Lord. The rice grown using this water was considered as blessed, and therefore a holy produce.

When the kings were Hindus and Mahayana Buddhists, people believed firmly in such myths. But from the time Theravada Buddhism began to spread, these beliefs started declining.

"My father has said that this is the cradle of Angkor culture. I come here often and spend my time. I feel that there is a spiritual vibration here." As she said this, Mandagini slipped on a moss covered stone and fell, catching hold of Adithya suddenly; under the force of her weight, he too was drawn down and fell into the water. With the impetus of the fall, both of them rolled on the slippery rocks and approached the edge wherefrom the cascade dropped. Had he not, in the nick of time, seized hold of a creeper nearby, they would have fallen into the abyss. With their chests locked one on top of the other, and their clothes all wet, the man and woman were on the verge of yielding to their basal instincts, in spite of the disaster that lay ahead. Only then, realizing the reality of the impending danger, Princeling tried to get up, controlling himself. Understanding the possibility that if Mandagini, who was caught under him, were to get up suddenly, the rocks too would roll and fall down, he got up very slowly, balancing her also.

As he attempted to get up slowly, for many seconds their body contact continued, and once again their feelings held sway.

His comment, "Mandagini, it is not proper for us to be in this condition" drew only a deep sigh in response. Somehow they controlled themselves and got up, and sat on the rocks on the banks of the river. Their wet dresses, as they clung to their bodies, served to reveal their physical features clearly.

"You are wet. Are you feeling cold?" asked The girl.

Ezhuth Aani

"The heat of my body makes the water hot" said Adithya. She remained silent.

"We have rolled on a thousand lingams, which are manifestations of Siva and Shakthi, symbolizing the union of man and woman" said Adithya.

"To me it appears that placing our feet on this sacred ground and on these sacred symbols is an ominous sign" said The girl. "For so many years, this river has been considered as sacred, and our feet touching the origin of this river appears to me to bode some evil that is likely to befall Angkor city, which depends on this river for sustenance, and our friendship that has begun here."

"No superstitions please. I firmly believe that any danger can be faced and overcome by our intelligence and effort" said Adithya, as he embraced her.

She too leaned on him, as though accepting his embrace. Their lips met. After a few seconds, she said, "O' warrior! This is not proper. I shall marry only the man whom my father selects. It is not good for us to be intimate like this."

Reluctantly, Adithya moved away from her, "What you say is correct. I have the duty of protecting my country. For this I may have to travel to foreign lands. Allowing my objective and resolve to be diverted by problems of love and marriage, would be treason to my country. Moreover, I may lose my life during my exploits. I don't want to waste the life of a beautiful maiden like you" said Adithya, rising.

"Dear lady, thank you for having brought me to this wonderful place. It is time for both of us to return to the ashram. Vajragnani will be waiting for me tonight" said Adithya.

Both of them mounted their horses and began their journey in silence. The sun which had reddened the western sky, was gradually taking leave. Also, as they had to go through dense forests, it appeared in some places as though it was already midnight. As it was familiar with the path, The girl's horse proceeded without any hindrance. But, Vibhanji was very cautious and ambled slowly. Because of this, Mandagini had to wait for him several times. Adithya said, "How woeful that I have had to follow a lady's directions!" She replied, "Father often said I was equal to two men. Moreover, in our ancient myths, have goddesses not been portrayed as very powerful?"

"I have never met a lady like you. And I consider it an honour to follow you" said Adithya. She interrupted him saying, "Warrior, I had thought that there was no man equal to me on earth until I met you." They shared their mutual love and respect for each other and reached their homes.

"You take rest. I shall come and take you to my father myself" said The girl.

Chapter 5

She now took him to a mountainous area along tracks cut by Mother Nature, on the sides of vertical rocks. In some places, dents and handholds had been carved by men as footholds and handles. In total darkness, both of them went one behind the other, each carrying a lamp. The narrow path on the mountain face was on level ground, but gradually rose higher and higher. Here and there, some of the rocks jutted out; they served as seats for them to rest awhile, before proceeding further. Before placing her feet on the rocks, Mandagini checked to see whether they were firmly bound to the mountain side, and only then moved forward. Although she had travelled along this path many times, in the dense darkness she was very cautious. All of a sudden, there appeared a cave on the side of the mountain. A natural cave, it had been bored and expanded. As they went through the cave, it was clear to Adithya that apart from the cave seen from the outside, there were many others connected with one another. They appeared to be like a small palace. Adithya and Mandagini entered a cave, and through a narrow passage on the right, reached another cave. There were several lamps burning in this cave. There were stone seats also. In addition, palm-leaf manuscripts and a stylus were neatly arranged. Startled on hearing Gnani's voice asking, "Have you come dears?" Adithya looked around searching for him. He was nowhere in that cave. Just then, Princeling looked in the direction pointed out by Mandagini. The small gap seen in the centre of the rock was very narrow. They could only crawl through it. There, seated on the other side on a stone seat, was Vajragnani, the fountainhead of knowledge.

"My son, several changes are taking place in the world. Even when the Mongolian Emperor ruled the world, Cambodia had maintained its freedom. But now, if you are not alert, that freedom may be lost.

"After the death of Emperor Timur, Mongolian hegemony has begun to decline. Even before that, the Ming dynasty has come to rule in China, having driven away the House of Yuan who were from Mongolia. Though the Ming dynasty is strong, there are possibilities of its weakening, due to internal squabbles.

"In Siam, Ayutthaya appears to be strong. In Lanka's south, King Parakrama Bahu VI, has been ruling with the help of a powerful naval force. Nevertheless, in the north, the Tamils rule the land under the leadership of Gunaveera Singai Ariyan.

"If you take India, Islam is spreading fast. In North India, many states have come under Islamic rule. In central India, the Vijayanagara Empire established by the Harihara and Pukka, stands guard preventing the Muslims from overwhelming south India. The Chera, Chola, Pandya and Pallava Kingdoms have been long gone.

"More than this, if you consider the western countries, after being in the iron grip of the Church for a thousand years, a renaissance of sorts has slowly begun to spread its roots. Because of this, novel methods are being devised to use and improvise Chinese inventions like explosives as weapons in war.

"In our neighboring states like Sri Vijaya too, Islamic dominance has begun spreading. A Shailendra Prince has converted to Islam, and is governing the port city of Malakka.

"Thus, many changes are taking place in the world. We, who are living in this changing world, should also adapt ourselves in accordance with these changes; otherwise, we'll be destroyed.

"If a cat closes its eyes, the world will not turn dark. On the contrary, if we are alert and act according to the situation we are in, we can safeguard our culture, religions, and lifestyles. More than all this, we can preserve these wonderful, artistic creations from destruction."

Ezhuth Aani

"What should we do now?" asked Princeling.

"Your immediate danger lies in an invasion from Ayutthaya. To counter this, you need an army, arms, and funds to recruit the army. In international politics, an enemy's enemy is considered a friend. On this basis, you can develop friendship with many countries. Your king has planned to send you as a messenger with this mission. It is his request, that using my worldwide network of friends, I should guide you.

"There are several reasons why he has selected you. Your bravery and martial skill are known all over the country. But that alone is not enough. Because in your childhood you lived in Vijayanagara and acquired mastery in various languages; because your cordiality and leadership qualities enable you to make friends easily; it is your king's opinion that you are the best person for this job.

"Diplomacy is not your only responsibility. You are also being sent so that you can visit various countries, study the technological advancements there, and invite the technical experts and bring them here.

"Technology has progressed not only in the art of warfare. It is also a solution to another big problem" said Gnani.

"What is that other problem?"

"As I said earlier, for Angkor city to have expanded to this extent, and for it to be ranked as one of the biggest capitals in the world, it is our ancient engineers' far-sightedness and technology that is responsible. The River Mekong, which originates from the snow-capped Himalayas, does not dry up at all. It is the waters of this River that fill up the inland sea called Tonle Sap. During the monsoon for at least four months a year, this Tonle Sap floods vast areas of land and appears as a great inland ocean. Fearing that if the capital were to be built on the plains, it may have to face the fury of a flood, our forefathers built Angkor city on comparatively higher ground.

"Water supply to Angkor city and its surrounding agricultural lands was arranged from rivers like Siem Reap that originated from the Kulen mountain range. In addition, reservoirs called Barays were constructed to collect the rain water. To further augment the water supply to these, water was diverted from the rivers by means of canals.

"But ... for the past three decades, there has been no rain. Even if it rains, it is only in the form of a deluge. This is because of environmental changes that have affected the whole world. In the northern countries, for several months there is cold, snowfall and rain, with the result that spring, summer and autumn have been shortened. At the same time, in our country, drought and monsoon failure have been recurring every year. Moreover, the sporadic floods have caused the dams and canals built by our forefathers, to be broken or silted. At a time when devotion and service to the king have decreased, the people too are indifferent. Because of all this, there is famine in the land."

"What is the solution to this?" asked Princeling.

"The solution to all this is water" said Gnani. "My son, the River Mekong will not dry up easily. But, both the River Mekong and the Tonle Sap Lake are in the valley. If water is to be supplied to Angkor city from these sources, huge machines that can pump water from a lower to a higher level are required. Such machines have not been invented in our region. Even in China, which has seen many innovations, the technology that can be used for this has not been perfected. Similarly, in India too, such machinery has not been invented. But many researchers have involved themselves in producing such things.

"However, in the western countries which are modern manifestations of the Roman Empire, there is a renaissance blossoming. New gadgets are being created. According to my calculation, the technology to be used for this has already been found. But the western scientists, who are caught in the tight grip of the religious leaders, are afraid of publicizing it.

"If we acquire this technology, we'll be able to pump out water to our fields not only from the River Mekong, but also from the underground."

Adithya interrupted Gnani, asking "What do you mean by the water underground?"

"During meditation, I've come to know that there is enough water under our soil to make a huge Lake. When it rains, the water absorbed by the earth goes down through small pores and remains there. As it is protected from the sun's heat, it does not evaporate. Thus, the water saved every year forms into Lakes and streams underground. Perhaps this is what our myths referred to as the Nether Ganges. Right from ancient days, man has dug the earth and used this water. On the seashore, if you just remove the sand a little, you'll come across good water underneath. I quote the ancient Tamil poet Thiruvalluvar:

The deeper you dig, the more water you get;
The more you learn, the more knowledge you glean.

"In a rocky place like ours, if we dig deeper we can access this water. Though there are deep wells here and there in our land, since we had sufficient water, we didn't feel the need to use these wells.

"However, now that all the water above the earth's surface has dried up, we need to use the underground aquafers. But we don't have the technological expertise to pump the water from a lower to a higher level. Although we have machines operated by men and oxen, the water thus obtained is not sufficient to meet our demand. Moreover, we don't have the tools to dig very deep wells of large dimensions.

"In Persia, engineers have found a method of drawing water by means of windmills. Western countries are trying to develop that method further. It is not enough for us to have the machines to draw the water from a depth. We need metal pipes and one-way valves to carry the water to long distances."

Gnani asked, "How does lightning appear?" Adithya replied, "Is it not Vajrapani's weapon?"

"Yes. We believed that thunder and lightning were the weapons of Indra or Vajrapani. But there are forces in Nature which we are not aware of."

Saying this, Gnani took him to another cave. Mandagini followed. This series of caves connected with one another by means of caverns, tunnels, small gaps and holes, appeared like a small town built with stones by Mother Nature. In some places man-made openings and vents could be seen, so positioned as to provide ventilation for the people living there. Adithya knew that as one ascended a mountain, it became more difficult to breathe. He was surprised to note how the Buddhist monks had adapted for their use this series of caves, taking into consideration every little aspect.

In this new cave, various things were arranged on stone shelves. They protruded inwards from the wall of the cave. From another place, Gnani took an object that resembled a small clay vessel. "This is from Baghdad city. One of my Muslim friends gifted this to me."

Ezhuth Aani

Inside that very thick clay vessel, there was a copper container. In the centre of the clay lid, an iron rod was fixed pointing inwards. When the lid was placed on the copper vessel, there was no contact between the copper and the iron metals; the object was so well produced.

While he was observing the structure, Gnani filled the vessel with lime juice. He then closed the lid again. Subsequently, he placed a copper wire on the vessel's lid, and another inside the copper container. And he connected both to a metal coil. What a surprise! The metal lit up suddenly and the whole cave became bright. Gnani then removed the wires, saying "If these are left connected for more than a few seconds, this coil will heat up and be burnt."

"My son, this is like Vajrapani's weapon, but very small. Nevertheless, it is my belief that lightning occurs by some such force. Man will invent, step by step, many such things. Even now, research is being conducted in many countries. A time will come, when we may use a sufficient amount of this lightning-like power for a sufficient duration of time. In fact, in some countries people may be using this power even now. If you can find out such things, and bring those scientists or their knowledge to our land, we can soon reach a solution to our water problem."

It took Adithya, who had scaled the peak of wonder, some time to regain normalcy.

Before his astonishment could subside, Gnani took them out of the series of caves, and led them once again some distance along the side of the mountain, on a path of rocks and steps. It was a very narrow path. On the way, a waterfall cut across the path and flowed down. They crossed this, getting wet in the water, holding on to metal handles fixed on the rock face, in a beeline sideways. Though there was not much water because of the drought, they had to be very cautious in their steps not to slip on the moss-covered stones. They knew quite well that if they were to stumble even a little, they would fall into a deep ravine. When Gnani and Mandagini, themselves familiar with the path, found it difficult to proceed in that darkness, need Adithya's condition be described? In addition, it was necessary to see that the lamp in the right hand did not get wet in the water and be blown off. Eyes accustomed to darkness, could see things at a little distance in moonlight. Adithya thought that it was better he could not see the valley below in the darkness. Otherwise, he thought that looking down into that abyss would make him dizzy and lose his balance and fall into it.

Having crossed the waterfall, they reached another cave that had been carved out of the mountain. The entrance to this cave was fitted with iron doors and closed with a huge lock.

With the large key which he had kept safe at his waist, Gnani opened the door and the three of them entered. When they descended some steep steps, a wonder world spread out in front of Adithya's eyes. A small hall had been built inside the cave. In the centre, a statue of the Buddha had been installed. It was not an ordinary Buddha. It was made of what appeared to be emerald and was gold-plated. Even in the light of their small lamps, this idol shone brightly.

"Have you heard of the idol of the Emerald Buddha?" asked Gnani.

"Yes. It is believed that many kings are searching for it. But people also say that there is no such idol" said Adithya.

"What you see before you is the Emerald Buddha. This has been carved out of a green-colored rock, not emerald" said Gnani.

Ezhuth Aani

"The one who sculpted this is Nagasena. It was chiseled in the city of Pataliputra about 1500 years ago. After several centuries, to safeguard it from a civil war, it was sent to Lanka. This Emerald Buddha was in the custody of the Lankan kings for many centuries. Later, in response to a request from the Myanmar's King Aniruddha, it was sent to that country by ship. But, on the way the ship was caught in a storm, and ran aground in Cambodia. The Buddha too became the property of the Cambodian kings.

"This Buddha idol has been in this cave hall for many years. All the workers involved in the construction of this hall were killed as soon as the construction was over. In those days, the task of maintaining and preserving this idol was handed over in every generation, to a hermit who lived in the forest. Every guru would pass on that responsibility to his most important disciple, before he passed on. That is how it came to me. Even the present king of Angkor does not know this secret."

Saying this, Gnani thrust a small compact Buddha idol into Adithya's hand. "My son, this is a replica of the Emerald Buddha, made of real emerald. If you show this to any Buddhist king, he will entertain and protect you. That is because it is believed that whoever carries this small Buddha knows where the real Emerald Buddha idol is.

"Kings believe that if they possess the Emerald Buddha, their reign will last long. It will also enhance their standing in the Buddhist world. Hence, take this small Emerald Buddha with you. May success crown your efforts."

The three of them then meditated before the Emerald Buddha. Afterwards, locking the cave again, they returned to the cave where they first met. "You can stay here and leave tomorrow morning. Mandagini will take you to one of my friends. Later, you must first travel by sea to Lanka. I shall write out a message to my friend. You can collect it in the morning."

So saying, he got up and went into another inner cave. Princeling and Mandagini had to spend the rest of the night in the dark cave.

"Mandagini, have you come here often?" asked Princeling.

"Yes. Right from childhood I've come here often with my father. But, he had never allowed me to go beyond the waterfall. Only today I've learnt the reason for it" she said.

"In that case, don't you know about the presence of the Emerald Buddha here?" asked Princeling.

"Not only me; nobody alive knows it except my father" she said.

"In that case, why did he inform us now?" asked Princeling.

"Father will never do anything without a proper reason. You are being sent on a mission to save this civilization from destruction. But, I don't know why he told this secret to me also. There is a big mystery behind my birth. As long as I can remember, I have known him as my father. He has also been a mother and guru to me. However, he has assured me that he would divulge my real identity at the right time. I suspect that the time is now ripe for that revelation" said Mandagini.

She then said, "O' warrior, we must begin our journey at dawn tomorrow. Let's sleep for a while."

So saying, she lay flat on her back on the stone floor. She gestured to him to lie down beside her. Both of them closed their eyes. Some time passed like this. He could not sleep at all. Tossing and turning, he finally asked, "Mandagini, have you slept off?"

"Have you too not fallen asleep?" she asked and continued: "Though I have learnt meditation and yoga extensively, tonight I'm not able to control my mind."

"Are you afraid to be near a man, alone?" asked Princeling.

"I'm not afraid of you. On Kulen hill, when we fell on each other and rolled down, you did not try to misbehave with me. Hence, I'm not afraid of you. I'm afraid of myself."

"What is your fear? Why are you afraid of yourself?" said Princeling. "O' warrior, till now I have fought on equal terms with ever so many men. I've done exercises standing shoulder to shoulder with them. I've never thought of myself as a lady on those occasions."

"For the first time in my life, my body tells me that I'm a lady. When I see you, instead of feeling that you are my rival, I feel as if you are my protector. At the same time, I'm concerned that you should be safe. Somehow I am afraid. At this time of difficulty and danger, I don't know what plan father has for whom. Having asked you to go to Lanka, I don't know what orders he has for me. You have come at such a crucial juncture in my life, to make me realise that I am a woman."

He did not make any response to this. Gradually, both fell asleep. On rising in the morning, Adithya took the miniature Emerald Buddha, and the message written by Gnani, and descending the hill with Mandagini, reached his place of stay. Finishing their morning ablutions, both of them set off to see the friend Gnani mentioned. As Mandagini had gone there a few times, they travelled along familiar paths.

Chapter 6

The small town called Prey Nokor was situated at the estuary of the River Mekong. Before reaching it, one had to cross the city of Phnom Penh. This city had begun to develop into the second largest city of the Cambodian kings. If one were to approach this city, located on the banks of the River Mekong, by boat, there was a danger of being intercepted by the spies of Ayutthaya, who had intruded into this area between Angkor and this city. Hence, they approached the west bank of the River Mekong, by going along the side of Lake Tonle Sap, which was filled by the waters of the River Mekong.

Both rode their horses, he on his Vibhanji and she on hers, and travelled for many hours. As the path was narrow in some places, they had to proceed in single file, one behind the other. They were both armed with long swords and small knives, worn at their waists. Though the path ran mostly along the river bank, in some places as the river bank was marshy, they had to enter the forest, and then return to the river again.

As they travelled side by side, they spoke to each other. They exchanged information on their respective lives. Then, he said, "Mandagini, though I have interacted with you only for a few days, I feel as if I have known you all my life. And I would like to spend the rest of my life with you."

"Oh warrior, let us first finish our duties. Then we shall think about our personal lives." The tone of Mandagini's voice as she said this left no doubt that she herself did not believe what she said. No matter how much her intelligence cautioned her, her emotions were engaged in a revolt against that caution. Yes. Her body and heart had begun to yearn for his intimacy.

Both of them travelled the whole day. Due to drought, the dimensions of the Tonle Sap had shrunk; however, because the areas

Ezhuth Aani

formerly covered with water were still slushy, the horses avoided them, and trod only on firm ground. The dry trees, and the leaves and twigs that had fallen from them, bore witness to the famine prevailing in the land. The sun too, had finished his journey for the day, and was preparing to take rest.

"We can't travel any more today. Let us rest and continue tomorrow" said Adithya, and pointing to a houseboat at a distance, he said, "Let us ask for shelter for the night in that house." Both went towards that house. The house made of bamboo and propped on stilts on a boat, was anchored in the middle of the river, and swayed gently due to the waves in the water. In the evening sunlight, the shadow of the bamboo sticks appeared like a prison in the water. Yes; the shadow looked like a prison door with bars.

To reach the boat, one had to wade through water and cross a few yards. Princeling asked Mandagini to hide behind a tree, gave his sword also to her, and taking only a small knife for company, stepped into the water slowly. Gauging the depth of the water with his toes first, he approached the houseboat. There was no sound at all. Planting his hand for support, Princeling got onto the boat, and proceeded cautiously looking out for any human presence. The house, with the roof made of tall bamboo poles outside, had a space in the centre hidden by a bamboo screen on all four sides. He opened it on one side and slowly went inside. There was nothing there, except a few steps in the middle, descending. Going down, a surprise awaited him. Yes; there were many rooms there. Seated in the room in the centre, was a middle-aged man.

"Sir, is this your house? May we stay here?" asked Adithya.

"This is a travel inn set up during King Jayavarman's time for travelers. You may stay here by all means. Have you come alone, oh warrior?" asked that man.

Only then, Adithya observed him clearly. Appearing to be around fifty, the man was bald and had a paunch. Though the head was bald, his moustache was oversized. Some of the hairs in the moustache had begun to grey. Even his eyebrows had shades of grey.

Adithya's instinct warned him that there was some mystery behind this man. He knew that King Jayavarman VII had constructed hostels all over the country for the sick, the aged and travelers. But, though he had heard of hostels on land routes, this travel inn in the middle of a forest was something new. However, reassuring himself with the thought that this lone man could not harm him much, Adithya said, "My wife has come with me."

"Bring her also. I shall prepare food for you" said the man, again engrossing himself in writing his palm-leaf ledger. As a second thought, he added, "Oh warrior, take the small rowing boat tied on the side."

Adithya took the boat and reached the bank. He discussed the situation with Mandagini. They tied their horses separately in two different hidden locations, gave them fodder, and hiding their long swords on the embankment, took only their small knives, and returned to the houseboat.

"O' warrior, your wife is very beautiful" said the man. Adithya replied, "I'm not a warrior; only an ordinary citizen." The man asked, "What's the reason for your travelling so far at such a difficult time?"

"We're going to Phnom Penh where my father-in-law lives, to escape from the famine here" said Adithya.

"Don't you have children?" asked the man, following it up enthusiastically with questions about his ancestry. To cover up one lie, a thousand more will be needed, they say. But, for Adithya, who had never before lied in life, it was difficult to pile it on thick.

Ezhuth Aani

Uneasily, he uttered a few lies, and then said, "My wife is tired; we shall talk later."

After that the man gave them enough food and water, and showed them their room.

"I have a feeling that this man is a spy" said Mandagini.

"We need food and shelter. At this time of the night, where can we go?" asked Adithya. But her doubt persisted. Adithya ate the fish and fruits given by that man. Mandagini ate only the fruits and avoided drinking even the water.

As soon as they finished eating, he invited her to sleep. As she lay beside him, he hugged her saying, "He thinks you are my wife. So, tonight I am going to make you my wife", and kissed her hard. "This is wrong. Please control your emotions" said Mandagini, as she struggled, unable to prevent him and not willing to do so at the same time.

As they lay in a close embrace, forgetting the world around, Adithya fell asleep.

"Oh warrior, warrior" she called, shaking him vigorously; but he did not wake up. She realised that his food had been drugged. As soon as she was aware of the danger facing them, she let him sleep, and taking a knife in each of her hands, she moved towards the central part cautiously. There she found a second person now, apart from the one she had seen. They were talking something seriously, pointing to the room which Adithya and she occupied. In their hands, both had huge swords, unsheathed.

The newcomer said, "No doubt at all; he is Adithya. If you kill him, our king of Ayutthaya will give you a huge amount of gold as a reward." Mandagini realised that if she did not act immediately, things would go beyond their control. She gauged the situation mentally. For some more hours, Adithya would sleep like a log. If they were to attack, she was a lone lady. And she had just small knives in her hands. Under the circumstances, surprise was her only friend. Though she was reluctant to commit two murders, she recollected the verse in the Bhagavad Gita, which says that even if a cow were to attempt to kill you, it was not wrong to kill it in self-defense, as her father often reminded her. A few minutes' delay could turn the tables upside down. Hence, she took a firm decision.

The next second, the two enemies fell to the ground screaming. Yes; her knives had penetrated deep into their chests. She took possession of the swords in their hands, and wrested the knives that were buried in their chests. Soon, their hearts ceased beating due to the haemorrhage.

At that time, Vibhanji's neigh shattered the silence of the forest. Mandagini realised that if Vibhanji was in danger, they would be in a quandary in the middle of the forest. Wondering whether to leave Adithya in the boat, she decided that saving Vibhanji was her first priority.

It is time that determines victory in such situations. Hence, taking a sword in her hands, she leapt into the water. For Mandagini, who had learnt to swim like a fish, it took only a few seconds to reach the shore. As she quickly neared the place where they had tethered Vibhanji, what she saw shocked Mandagini. Yes; two armed men were trying to bring the horses under their control. One of them had mounted Mandagini's horse. But Vibhanji would not allow anyone except her owner to mount her. Therefore, a war was going on between the man and the horse. Mandagini reached there just then.

Realising that danger would follow if the men were allowed to escape, Mandagini first faced the man who had mounted her horse. Though both fought fiercely, was it possible for that ordinary soldier to defeat Mandagini? As his sword flew up in the air, hers descended on his neck. Just then, the other man turned in her direction to attack her. His sword fell on her horse, which dropped down with a loud neigh. As Mandagini turned towards him, he tried to flee. She leapt on to Vibhanji and followed him. She then flung her small knife at him. As it pierced his back, he dropped to the ground.

Understanding the urgency to return to the houseboat, Mandagini took the weapons which they had hidden as well as Vibhanji, and reached the boat walking and swimming along with the current. Vibhanji too climbed into the boat.

Though she was saddened about the loss of her horse, she decided that this was not the time for sentiments. Similarly, though she was sorry that she had killed four men, she consoled herself with the thought, that if they (Adithya and herself) had been captured, it might have affected the future of their country. Gratefully, she thought of her father, who had taught her to fling knives with both hands at lightning speed.

Adithya was fast asleep in the boat. As he was not likely to wake up until dawn the next day, she decided that it was better for all of them to leave the place immediately and move away. Thinking how all of them could leave the place quickly and safely, with her lover being in deep slumber and her horse lost forever, The girl took a firm decision and raised anchor.

As the water flow in the River Mekong was quite swift that night, the boat began to move. As her father had taught her rowing also, it was possible for her to row the boat from the bank to the middle. Although the water was sufficiently deep there, she knew that there would be small islands and sand dunes in the middle of the river. She had travelled by boat with her father on a few earlier occasions along this river; but what had been a familiar landscape then, appeared quite strange now. Under such circumstances,

Mandagini understood the necessity for her to remain wide awake that night. Vibhanji stood guard at the rear of the boat. As the boat moved, she dragged the two dead bodies and threw them into the river. Their blood had flowed to the middle of the boat. As she had determined that as soon as Adithya woke up, they would leave the boat, she did not wish to waste her time washing off the blood.

With the incidents of the night having taken place at great speed, her mind was still in turmoil. Her heart beat had not returned to normalcy. Hence, she had no thought of sleep at all.
The entire night having passed in this way, the morning sun began to raise its head in the eastern sky. Soon the whole sky was red and the sun looked like a ball of fire. With the arrival of the sun, she could see her surroundings clearly.

Going back to their room, she shook Adithya awake. This time he moved a little. Encouraged, she pinched him on his neck. Princeling sprang up with a start.

"What are you doing, lady?" he asked angrily. "Do you know how painful it is? If only you had not been a lady, do you know what I would've done to you?" he said.

"Do I appear to be a lady only now? You expect me to act like a man just to protect you, is it?" said Mandagini.

"What do you mean?" he asked, and listened with surprise to her account of the night's incidents. "You are truly a wonder-woman. How fortunate I am to have acquired your friendship!" said Adithya.

"Now tell me. Had I not been a lady, what would you have done?" she asked, with a chuckle.

He hugged her tight, and said "This is how I would have hugged you."

Ezhuth Aani

"Only now I understand that you are that way inclined" said The girl, laughing.

Realizing the real import of his words and his subsequent action, he said "You have succeeded in cornering me. You not only have beauty and courage but also great intelligence."

"Okay. We'll see that later. Right now, the first thing we have to do is to reach the bank. Men will certainly come searching for the boat" said Mandagini.

Immediately they rowed the boat towards the bank. Going from there also posed a problem. Having lost a horse, they were both forced to ride on Vibhanji. Without any other alternative, Adithya sat in front and Mandagini behind him. It was necessary too for her to hold on to his shoulder. Though it was a necessity, it gave her pleasure. Vibhanji too appeared to be very happy to carry her owner and his beloved and gleefully began galloping.

Adithya reckoned that having travelled one whole day by land   and one night by the houseboat, another day's journey should take them to Penh hill, also called Phnom Penh.

As the two of them were seated too close for comfort, every time Vibhanji leapt forward, her breasts pressed against his back, giving both of them a pleasurable pain. As she had not slept the previous night, her eyes closed automatically; their physical intimacy added to her drowsiness, and she forgot herself having entered another world altogether.

Suddenly, realizing that her hands which had gripped his shoulders were loosening their hold, Adithya stopped the horse, and bound her waist with his. By this she was protected from falling off in her sleep. But this move served only to bring them closer. As her proximity increased, his manliness was roused. As his strong and robust back came into contact with her soft breasts, both yearned for a physical union. Mandagini, who was half awake and half asleep, wondered whether she was in Cupid's world in dreamland.

How they controlled themselves is not known. But before night set in, they somehow reached the town of Phnom Penh.

Chapter 7

Until recently, Phnom Penh had been a wasteland. But, one day an elderly lady saw a tree being carried towards her by the River Mekong. Inside the tree were two idols: of Lord Buddha and Lord Vishnu. She had them consecrated in that place. In her memory the area came to be known as Penhhill (lady's hill). Initially, there were only small houses and plots there. But, as drought and famine increased in Angkor city, more and more people had begun to migrate to Penh hill.

Where there had been a hill and dense forests, small plots of paddy fields had begun to appear. Arable lands and forests vied with each other. It is natural for forests to shrink when human habitation increases and vice versa. That is, it is Nature's law that when people migrate from their places they encroach upon forests. When civilisation dies the forest reclaims its lost territory. When one species declines, another prospers; this is Nature's unchanging cycle, thought Adithya. If Angkor, which is on the verge of destruction, is destroyed, Ayutthaya will flourish.

Adithya wondered what changes his efforts could bring about, when the fate had already been decided; at the same time, he recollected Gnani's teaching that one could change one's destiny through his or her intelligence. Had there been no human effort at all, invaluable creations like Angkor would never have come into existence.

The girl said, "An elderly lady known to my father lives here. Her son was my father's student. On a few occasions, I've come with my father and stayed here.

By the time they both reached that house, it was quite dark. It was Mandagini who knocked on the door and spoke first.

"Mother, I'm Mandagini, Vajragnani's daughter" she said.

Opening the door a little, the elderly lady held the small lamp which she had brought, level with Mandagini's face. "Oh my! You have grown a lot" she said, and asked "What brings you here?"

"This is one of Vajragnani's disciples. My father requested me to take him to Prey Nokor for a sea voyage." She then stepped aside, and Adithya came forward. "What is the reason for your sea voyage, my boy?" asked the lady.

"Mother, I wish to go to Lanka and learn about Lord Buddha's preachments. Tripitaka in its pure form is followed only there, is it not?" said Princeling.

The lady said, "May Lord Buddha bless your journey with success", and added, "It may take you a couple more days to reach there, I think."

"Yes, mother. On our way here, we lost a horse. We have to acquire another one somehow" he said.

The lady then said, "Boats come from Prey Nokor carrying fish and other commercial goods. When they return you can hire them for your use. Tomorrow morning, if you go to the boat jetty and enquire, you can find out when the next boat will leave from here."

After that, the lady made arrangements for their food, bath and ablutions. The old lady allotted two separate rooms to them. When he tried to enter her room, she prevented him. She did not wish to tarnish her reputation in the presence of the lady who was known to her father.
Exhausted after a whole day's travel, and confident that the lady would safeguard them, both of them slept soundly.

Ezhuth Aani

The next morning, finishing their chores they wore fresh clothes given by the lady, and went to the jetty. Vibhanji too, had slept well, eaten her fill and refreshed herself with a bath in the River. As the lady had said, a boat was preparing to return to Prey Nokor. Except for a few bags of rice, the entire boat was theirs. Parting with some money as the fare, Princeling hired the boat exclusively for their use.

The lower deck of the boat was allotted to them entirely. Vibhanji alone stood guard on the deck near the steps. One had to cross Vibhanji to enter the hold of the ship. When Adithya thought of the two of them and Vibhanji travelling in the same boat, he was reminded of his childhood puzzle of a tiger, a goat and a bundle of grass. The condition was that the boatman could take only one thing at a time in his boat. How he got all the three across, formed the puzzle.

If the tiger and the goat were left on one side, the goat would be eaten by the tiger. If the goat and the grass were left together, the grass would disappear. The solution lay in the fact that one item taken during the first trip could be brought back on the return journey of the second trip. This puzzle was given to children, to induce them to think out of the box. That is, if the children found the strategy that an item could be brought back to the same side, they could solve the puzzle easily. This holds true in real life too. Many problems can be solved if one could think laterally.

Mandagini found out the solution to this problem. And she said, "Here too, the boatman is taking a tiger and a goat."

"It's not a goat; it's a horse" said Adithya. "I didn't refer to Vibhanji, but the two of us" said The girl, with a smile.

During the past few days, they had been quite intimate; several times they had had the opportunity to indulge themselves, but had not done so. The resulting pent up frustration and the overwhelming desire for physical union which they experienced during the past two days – all this found an opportune moment now.

A mere embrace was not enough to stop the torrent that had been dammed all these days. They frolicked like tadpoles in a flash flood. All thoughts of tradition and custom were thrown to the winds, and The girl became one with him.

How many days can cotton wool and fire be separated? How long can hungry hearts be allowed to yearn for a union? Who can prevent Nature's law from operating? The next two days were like a honeymoon for both of them. Yes. Will they waste such an opportunity? The boatman too, did not disturb them. He treated them as husband and wife. Even Vibhanji revealed her joy through her body language.

Two days passed. The boat passed through the Mekong River estuary, reached the ocean and travelling further in the bay, reached Prey Nokor. Prey Nokor had a small fishing harbour, and a boat jetty for small ships to anchor. Though it was close to the path taken by large Chinese ships this harbour had not been developed to accommodate big ships. Hence, ships were anchored in the middle of the sea, and small boats served to transport passengers and goods to and from the shore. Apart from this, when small ships arrived, they would drop anchor in Prey Nokor, rest awhile and then leave. Fishing boats also left this jetty every night, and went to sea. Though only a small town, it served as a stopover for sea commerce between China and India.

The Mekong River branched out like the fingers of a hand at the estuary where it ran into the sea. Although Prey Nokor, situated close to this estuary, was blessed by Mother Nature with abundant land and water resources, it had not been developed into a big harbor, because of the occurrence of frequent floods. Nevertheless, with a sizeable population and surrounded by fertile lands, it had begun functioning as an important commercial centre.

Many houseboats remained swaying in these rivulets. On land too, many tall houses built of bamboos could be seen. On the outskirts of the town was a small vihara. Around this was the Buddhist monastery. This was Adithya's destination. Vajragnani's friend Rathinakaara, also called Rathina Thera, was the head monk here. As soon as he saw Vajragnani's letter and its message, he received them very lovingly. Having seen Mandagini as a child, he said with joyous pride, "You have now become a young lady." He allotted rooms for them to rest. A separate place had been assigned to female monks in the ashram. Mandagini had to stay there. Another place was given to Princeling.

Rathinakaara took both of them to a secluded room in his monastery. "My son, Vajragnani has asked you to go as a messenger to King Parakrama Bahu. There are two reasons for this. First, a long-standing friendship exists between the kings of Lanka and Ayutthaya. In the war that is going to take place, if Lanka remains neutral without helping Ayutthaya, that itself will be a big victory for you. This is the first request.

"Second, there is information that King Parakrama Bahu has gathered cannons and firearms. Western and Islamic engineers have begun to convert Chinese explosives into hand held and mounted cannons that can be used in war. If an army has these and other fire arms, it is difficult to conquer it. Hence, you must request and acquire such weapons and shells necessary for them."

So saying, Rathinakaara looked at Adithya closely. The well-built Rathinakaara was quite tall. His head was shaved, but his sharp eyes shone brightly like real gems (rathna). Perhaps, it was because of this that he was called Rathinakaara!

"My son, I know that you are not a Buddhist. If you approach Parakrama Bahu directly as a messenger of the Angkor Empire, he may not give you a favorable response. But, if you go there disguised as a Buddhist monk, you will have more opportunities to get closer to the king. Subsequently, by means of your diplomacy and negotiating skills, you can win his attention and friendship."

Adithya asked the monk, "How can I disguise myself as a Buddhist monk? Is it enough if I tonsure my head and wear saffron robes? When the others talk to me, won't they see through my disguise?"

"Of course you'll have to learn a lot about Buddhist monks. Otherwise, you'll be easily caught."

He added, "In a few more days, a big Chinese ship on its way to Malacca will pass by our shores. If you go with my note, you can travel to Malacca in that ship. From there many Buddhist messengers are routinely exchanged with Lanka. I shall see that you join one such group."

Chapter 8

From the next morning, his classes began. The girl said, "I would have taught you these details myself." Nevertheless, he learnt what Rathina Thera taught, very carefully.

The four noble truths are as follows:

All experiences in life lead only to sorrow; the reason for this sorrow is desire; the only way to avoid becoming sorrowful, is to eliminate desire; the practical way to achieve this, is eightfold path consisting of proper understanding, firm resolve, proper speech, action, lifestyle, endeavor, mindfulness and mental strength. Apart from the four noble truths everything else is transient.

There are many codes laid down for laymen. The Atta Sil (eight rules), is a tough set of rules. A simpler code to follow for all is the Pancha Sil (five rules), that is, to desist from murder, robbery, adultery, lying and alcohol.

Moreover, in Vinaya Pitaka, Lord Buddha has laid down many more rules for the monks. These rules specify what one should do and what one should not, in every aspect of life. Among these, some affected Adithya significantly; that is, not eating anything after noon-time; not demanding anything; not talking to ladies in private; and not sleeping with a lady under the same roof. Celibacy was important for Theravada monks while Mahayana allowed monks to marry. Consumption of meat varied according to local practice.

Rathina Thera did not implement these rules immediately. This was because, Adithya was merely a monk in disguise; he did not ask him to tonsure his head either. Rathina Thera also taught him that it was better for monks to observe silence. Adithya realised that this could be used as a shield to cover up his disguise.

Adithya prepared himself for his new role in earnest. At the same time, The girl too made arrangements to return to Angkor city. In the next few days, a group of traders was to travel to Angkor; the monk made arrangements to send her along with them. Simultaneously, he arranged for Adithya passage in a passing Chinese vessel.

Finally, the day approached for both of them to leave. From the day they had left the boat, it had become difficult for them even to see each other. Under such circumstances, they longed to spend at least some time in private. They wondered whether they would ever meet again. It was at this time that his head was tonsured. He decided that somehow he should meet her in his new avatar!

After reflecting for a long time, he came up with a plan. He informed Rathina Thera that, as he was going to take leave of Vibhanji he would like to ride her for some time, bathe her and then return.

With a smile the monk said, "Take The girl with you."

Realizing that it was not possible to deceive the Elder, Adithya did not try to conceal his love any more. Early in the morning, both of them mounted Vibhanji, and travelling through areas of alternating paddy fields and bamboo clusters, they reached a forest. There, Adithya leapt on to a low bough, and made Mandagini to sit beside him. For several minutes, both sat holding each other's hands, silently.

"When will we meet again?" he asked.

"When we will meet I do not know; but certainly it will be when there is a lot of hair on your head" she said, smiling.

Ezhuth Aani

"Stop making fun of me, at a time when I am saddened about our parting!" said Adithya.

"You look quite handsome even with your head shaved. But I prefer talking to you stroking your hair" she said.

"Mandagini, you are talking childishly, without knowing my sorrow," said Adithya angrily.

"Hmm Adithya! What do you know of the sadness in my mind?" she asked, addressing him in the singular (without the honorific).

"For years I have debated and fought with any number of men on an equal level, forgetting that I am a lady. But you have transformed me in to a helpless coward Adithya," she said.

"You, a coward?" he asked.

"I have never been afraid in the presence of others. But, for the first time in my life, I'm apprehensive about your safety" she said, wiping a tear at the corner of her left eye.

He now understood that she spoke humorously only to forget and conceal her sorrow and that it was she who felt their parting more intensely.

"My father often used to say that if you want to achieve something great in life, you'll have to relegate your personal joys, sorrows and desires to the background. Tears will benefit none. Your mission will somehow end in victory. So, return triumphantly, request my father for my hand and marry me" she said.

He thought. The cause of all sorrow in life is desire. Why does man have desires? Do all unions end in partings? If so, why does man have such feelings and yearnings to be one with his lover?

Lost in thoughts like these, he was stirred by her voice. "Princeling, don't lose today in worries about tomorrow" she said.

Then, he held her waist and drew her towards him. As if she had been waiting for that she fell on him, and face on face and body on body, the whole day passed in their love –making. Was it rhyme and rhythm? Of the two which was upper and which lower? In Nature's dance which was the hand and which the leg? Joy and sorrow are two pages of the same emotion. While a corner of the brain experienced sadness at tomorrow's parting, they rejoiced at today's peak of intimacy and bliss.

The whole day having passed in this emotional roller coaster, it was time for them to return. At the ashram gates they played out their leave-taking. As they could not touch or embrace each other there, Adithya held Vibhanji close and kissed her on her cheek. "Take care of your mistress. I shall return victorious" he said, looking at her.

"Tell him that you'll wait till he returns" she said.

Rathinakaara, who was standing there, smiled seeing them. "Everything is transient. Parting is also impermanent. May your separation come to an end soon" he said.

Vibhanji and The girl then went their way. Rathinakaara sent Adithya with a trustworthy young monk during the night to a place called Tam Thang. Tam Thang means three boats. From ancient times, this point jutting into the South China Sea had been used as a small port. During adverse weather conditions, this port served as a sanctuary for ships, and at other times it served as a stopover for small boats engaged in trading activities with Chinese and Arabian ships crossing the sea. Adithya's next phase of travel began in this peninsula, surrounded on three sides by sea.

Ezhuth Aani

Chapter 9

With his head completely shaven, wearing saffron robes, and carrying his few possessions in a bag slung over his shoulder, Adithya looked every inch a Buddhist monk.

His possessions consisted of the small idol of the emerald Buddha, and Vajragnani's missive to Parakrama Bahu, in a secret compartment in his bag, and Rathinakaara's letter to the Buddhist hermit in Malacca. Apart from this, he had also kept a small knife hidden in his waist band.

The two of them travelled on horseback and sometimes on foot through marshy land for several hours, and reached their destination just around dawn. The shore was dotted with rocks. These rocks served as a barrier to huge waves, and formed a sort of natural harbour.

The rising sun was painting the coast red, giving it the appearance of a sea of blood. The smell of the beach, the gentle breeze, and the vast expanse of sand made the whole scene very picturesque and serene. The occasional shrieks of the sea cranes and gulls, and the rhythmic lashing of the waves, produced a soothing effect on the mind. However, all this beauty and calm was not sufficient to heal the wounds in Princeling's mind.

Without talking much to the monk who accompanied him, this pseudo monk copied what the other did, and escaped being found out. Within a few days of his pretense as a monk, Adithya was surprised to find that even his thinking had become monkish. It is true that one's personality consists of 'half man and half garb'. Just as actors transform themselves into the characters they portray, he felt a kind of transformation within himself.

However, no matter how truly refined his thoughts were, he could not control his mind on one aspect. Yes. Mandagini was always in his mind. Never before had he felt such a desire for any woman. He felt a new energy. When he thought of how within a few weeks she had taken hold of him completely and occupied his mind wholly, he was surprised and puzzled. Was this love? A painful sorrow and at the same time, a tingling sensation of joy and elation! Only now he understood what love for a woman was!

He loved his mother very much. But that relationship was different from this. A mother's love was unconditional. But this love was not exactly unconditional; it had a tinge of jealousy mixed in it. While he was here, the group with which she travelled would have the opportunity to see her beauty, admire the sweetness of her voice, and wonder at the greatness of her intellect. When he thought that he could not enjoy all these, a feeling of helpless darkness seized him. But the very next second, he consoled himself saying that he should not lose his resolve by such thoughts.

They went to a hut that served as boathouse. The owner of the hut spoke a few words to Adithya's escort, then took them in very cordially and respectfully, and brought food and other necessities for them. He said:

"Large ships, under the leadership of the Chinese naval admiral Zheng He, established trade and diplomatic relationships between China, and India and the Arabian countries. But the Emperor suddenly stopped these expeditions. For the past few years, convoys of large ships do not take this route; but individual traders have been sending trading vessels by this route. One of these is expected to pass by here soon. Our spies have seen from the hill top some ships far away. Gauging their speed, we can expect them here tomorrow night or the morning after. Usually, our boats meet them in the middle of the sea and exchange goods and passengers. We can send Sadhu (Adithya) along with them."

Ezhuth Aani

These junks were huge. They were 100 yards long, 50 yards wide and 50 yards high above the water level. Made of wood and iron, these ships had heavy iron anchors let down partially, to balance and prevent them from tossing in the waves. Four or five sails were attached to the masts on the upper deck. These ships were capable of using the seasonal wind power to advantage, and travel comparatively fast.

In these ships more than a thousand people, consisting of sailors, navy personnel, their courtesans, nurses, cooks, and conservancy workers travelled. On the lower decks, food items, animals for meat and fodder for them were also taken. Similarly, in some of the lower decks, there were series of doors that could open and close, allowing the sea water inside so that the fish in it could be caught. More than all these, drinking water, man's dire necessity, was stored in huge barrels. In addition, perfumes, silk clothes and gems were also carried in some of the locked rooms.

As this port was located in a corner of the Cambodian peninsula, it was possible to see ships approaching from both sides, even when they were far away. Moreover, swift messengers carried this news to the ports en route. Because of this, those interested in trading with these ships could travel in small boats from the shore and meet these ships mid sea. As large ships would take several days to go round the peninsula, this swift dispatch of news enabled the small boats and ships on the shore to establish contact with the trading vessels.   At the same time, if enemy ships were to attack, it was possible to detect them easily and take counter measures.

It was on one such ship that Adithya was made to embark. His escort had said that his name was Dharmaaditta Thera, and that he was a man of few words. Therefore, no one attempted to speak to him much. A separate room had been assigned to him. It was difficult for him not to eat after noon-time. But, he followed this rule to avoid any suspicion in the minds of the others.

Life in the ship was rather difficult for Adithya. On land, he could go to any place at any time; accustomed as he was to such a life, this 'imprisonment' in a ship was quite painful. Luckily, as his room was on the upper deck, he could at least see the sky. Adithya's days were spent staring at the sea and the sky, and exploring the ship.

The more he looked, the more he was amazed at the wonderful ingenuity of the Chinese maritime explorers. On the masts to which the sails were attached, small trays were fixed in which herbs were grown. On the lower decks, musicians and dancers were taken for entertaining the affluent passengers and military personnel. They did not engage only in cultural entertainment. They also took care of the sexual needs of the passengers. Some of the sailors and navy personnel had been castrated. They were not interested in women.

The practice of transforming slaves into eunuchs was quite prevalent among Chinese Emperors. Zheng He was also one of these. A Muslim, he was captured when the Mongolian Yuan dynasty fell. But, as he developed a friendship with the future Chinese Emperor from childhood, he became his confidante and the leader of the group of sea expeditions.

In the Chinese Empire, there was always a power struggle between eminent eunuch generals and the bureaucrats who were in the soveriegn's service. As a result, the more dominant faction of the two exerted a greater influence on important decisions taken by the Emperor. When Zheng He was in the sovereign's favour, the latter supported whole-heartedly the far-sighted schemes mooted by the former. Therefore Chinese commercial ships travelled to various parts of the world at great cost, and established trade and diplomatic ties with the countries there. The other purpose of these sea missions was to collect tributes and in exchange offer protection and gifts from the Emperor to them.

In some countries, the host kings had set aside land adjacent to the ports for the use of the Chinese visitors. These places were used as warehouses for Chinese commercial products, dry food used during travel, and drinking water. Chinese officers had been appointed to maintain these places. Although they married the local girls and lived there, the agents remained faithful to the Chinese Emperor. Many of the danseuses taken in these ships were gifted to the kings of various countries. Similarly, the local beauties were employed to work in the ships and were taken back to China.

Although he was surrounded by music and dance, Adithya's mind was occupied fully by Mandagini. She was everywhere. She was in the moon in the sky. She was in the reflection of the moon in the water. She was the twinkling stars. She was the distant lightning. She was the raindrops in the drizzle.

In the garb of a Buddhist monk, he was scared to look at the ladies around him. He had taken a resolve not to be unfaithful to Mandagini even in thought. In addition, he was apprehensive that if anyone were to see through his disguise, his mission would be doomed to failure.

After many a days' travel in this manner, early one morning he saw land. One of the sailors beside him said, "Swamini, this is the Gulf of Malacca." On either side of this narrow gulf was land. On the east was Kedar (Malaysia) and on the west, Swarnabhoomi (Sumatra). The ship travelled in the centre of this narrow strait. Tall mountains could be seen close to the shore. The sky, which was frequently filled with smoke from volcanoes and forest fires, was a clear blue without even a streak of a cloud, during their passage.

It was a time when the Srivijaya Empire had disintegrated and the dominance of the Shailendra kings had declined. A prince called Parameswara had embraced Islam, and established a kingdom with Malacca city as its capital. He chose a spot where a deer turned back on its tormentors and chased the hounds back. The name Malacca comes from the Malacca tree.

As Malacca was located in the narrowest part of the strait, the one who had control of the city could also wield his power over the passage of ships through this strait. Very soon, Malacca attained the status of an important commercial centre. King Parameswara changed his name to Sikkandar Shah after he embraced Islam.

A Chinese outpost had been set up in Malacca. As this country had accepted Chinese hegemony, military protection was provided by China. Horses imported from Arabian countries, perfumes from India, ivory from Lanka, and Chinese silk were all brought to Malacca regularly by ships, and then exchanged.

When Adithya's ship reached Port Malacca, worship was first offered to the Sea Goddess, Maasu. Goddess Maasu would protect sailors from storms, and thunder and lightning. Buddhists believed that the Maasu was an incarnation of the Bodhisatvini called Quan Yin. And Quan Yin in turn was considered as a variation of the Bodhisattva, Avalokateswara.

Mention has been made about the Bodhisattva, Avalokateswara, in one of the important sutras of Mahayana Buddhism, called the Saddharmapundareeka sutta. According to this, Avalokateswara is said to be capable of assuming male or female forms to shower His blessings. It is in Saddharmapundareeka Sutta that the word Mahayana (large vehicle) is used for the first time. Moreover, just like the Mahaparinirvana sutta, this stanza also asserts very emphatically, that the seed of Buddha (Buddha Dhatu) in every living organism is immortal and indestructible.

Ezhuth Aani

After worshipping goddess Maasu, Adithya was taken to a Buddhist temple situated on an elevation referred to as Chinese Hill. The chief priest there was called Sankrama Paraakrama. In this temple, both Mahayana and Theravada Buddhists offered worship. This place served not only as a commercial hub, but also as a centre for social gatherings for all Buddhists, including the Chinese and those from Myanmar to Cambodia, whenever they travelled through Malacca.

It was the Chinese naval captain Zheng He and his assistants who helped to dig seven wells, and obtain fresh water for this city located north of Malacca. Sankrama Paraakrama welcomed Adithya and hosted him well. As soon as he read Rathinakaara's missive, he said "You have come at an opportune moment. In a few days, a Buddhist delegation of monks from Ayutthaya will be leaving for Lanka. Uththama Panna, one of those who, a few years ago had gone to Lanka and had the higher ordination called Upasampada, is leaving again with some young monks to visit Vanarathna Maha Thera's pirivena. They are going to meet the Buddhist monks in Karakkal on the banks of the River Kalyani, learn the nuances of the Tripitaka from them and return."

Sankrama did not know that Adithya's goal was not the study of Buddhism. That secret was known only to Vajragnani and Rathinakaara. The next day, Sankrama introduced Adithya to the others who were to travel with him to Lanka. Of these, Silaavi Sudhdhi, and Satthama Govida were of a slightly higher rank. They held responsible positions next only to Uththama Panna.

The next day, Uththama Panna gathered all of them and conducted a discourse. In total, there were twenty monks including Adithya, going to Lanka to take the initiation vows there. "Swaminis, we are now living in an important period. The real preaching of Lord Buddha has been maintained unadulterated, only in Lanka. In other countries, the worship of several Bodhisattvas has become commonplace. The worship of Avalokateswara in various forms has increased everywhere. Because of this, there is a risk of Buddhism declining in our countries. There are very few Theras here, who are eligible to administer Upasampada elevating Theras to Maha Theras. That is why we have decided to go to Lanka, acquire the necessary training there, return with the legitimacy and bring about a renaissance of our religion.

"Earlier, the worship of Avalokateswara did not exist in Lanka. But, when the Prince of Java called Chandrabanu captured that country he introduced it there. It was the Pandya king who helped to remove him and reestablish the reign of Sinhala kings. Nevertheless, from Polonnaruwa, the capital of the Sinhala kings moved gradually from the northeastern region to the southwest. Different princes competed with one another, and established various kingdoms. King Parakrama Bahu II, who tried to unify these kingdoms, revived the worship of Avalokateswara, introduced by King Chandrabanu. He introduced to the Sinhala people, a Bodhisattva called Lokeswaranadha under the name of Natha Deiyyo. By reviving the tradition of Mahayana, he paved the way for people to worship the king as the incarnation of Avalokateswara the Bodhisattva, in an attempt to gain currency among the warring factions.

"In the southern city of Devinuwara, he built a temple for Lord Vishnu under the name of Uppuluvan. He encouraged the people to worship Hindu gods like Vishnu and Subramanya as Bodhisattvas. "Parakrama Bahu I, called Maha Parakrama Bahu, crushed the Mahayana tradition, and acting on the advice of the heads of the Mahavihara, enthroned Theravada.

"However, unfortunately, to retain his authority, Parakrama Bahu II, allowed Mahayana to grow once again. But the present king of Lanka, Parakrama Bahu VI, is projecting Theravada as the main religion again. He is the one who has arranged this trip for us.

Ezhuth Aani

"From the time Dambadeniya (Gampola) was the capital of the country, work has been going on to revive Buddhism in the Kaarakkal area near it. The present King Parakrama Bahu continues to patronize this work. Every one of you should go there, and bring back to our countries Buddha Dharma in its purest form. A majority of us belong to Ayutthaya. The day is not far off when we shall invade Cambodia. After we capture that country and enslave its people, we must administer the noble initiation of Upasampada to the monks there. And we should destroy the vestiges of Mahayana there" he said.

They then retired to their respective places. All the ascetics from Ayutthaya stayed together. Nobody cared much about Adithya. He too, restricted his communication to a smile and a greeting. If he were to talk at length, his identity would be revealed. He thought that if he did not speak anything, he would not be exposed.

He felt that a monk called Satthama Govida eyed him with suspicion. Hence, he decided to avoid the latter. He made sure that the emerald Buddha which he had brought with him was in his bag.

The rest of the day was spent in going round Malacca. Many of the Chinese had begun to live here. They married the local girls, while the dancers travelling in Chinese ships married the local men, and thus many Chinese lived in Malacca with their families.

The banks of the River Malacca and the lands near the sea shore had plenty of coconut groves. Many of the buildings here were made of planks, thatch and fiber obtained from the coconut trees. The coconut palm played an important role in the lives of the people here. From tender coconut to grated coconut, the Malaccans used coconuts extensively in their food.

The city was situated close to where the River Malacca ran into the sea. Hence, the water in this river was salty. Therefore, the drinking water obtained from the wells dug by Zheng He's assistants was indispensable for people's use. Adithya was made acutely aware of the truth referred to by Vajragnani that the problem faced by many societies was, how to bring up the ground water to the surface for people to use. It was one thing to draw the drinking water from deep wells manually; but supplying water to cultivate three or four seasonal crops a year to fill the granaries of the Angkor Empire, was a totally different matter.

Chapter 10

Having spent the day sightseeing and idling Adithya slept soundly until he was awakened by Sankrama the next morning. Finishing his bath and ablutions, he took part as a silent spectator in some of the religious rituals; then, as one among twenty young monks called samaneras he was put aboard a ship, with the blessings of Lord Buddha.

The junk from which he had disembarked having to wait for favourable weather conditions for a few weeks more, he was put into a smaller passenger ship going to Lanka. As the huge Chinese junk had to go to Kozhikode, a Chera port on the western seaboard of the Indian sub-continent, and from there to Arabia, it was decided that it should wait in Malacca for favourable monsoon winds and also for merchandise to arrive from various other places.

Moreover, in recent times there had been an increase in pirate activity in the Malaccan strait; hence, it was decided that it was better to wait until escort ships arrived for help before risking a treasure ship in those waters.

As the waterway consisted of hundreds of tiny peninsulas and inlets, it was an ideal hideout for pirates. The Srivijaya Empire of the Shailendra kings which had been strong for several centuries, had of late, begun to lose its strength and importance and started to break into many fragments. With the waning of the Srivijaya naval power, the condition was favorable for the pirates.

The Srivijaya navy had retained its control over the peninsula for many centuries. For a short interval, the Chola and Myanmar kings wrested this control; however, the Shailendra kings regained their hold and tightened it.

It was a Tamil Prince, a descendant of the Shailendra kings of this region, who staked claim to the Angkor throne as his maternal right, and became the Emperor under the name of Suryavarman II. Steeped in such thoughts, Adithya was rudely shaken by the alarm sounded in the ship.

From the observation post atop the mast, a man had sounded the alarm. "Danger! Danger! Pirates are approaching us from both sides! All the men come to the upper deck! The women go down to your rooms and remain there," he shouted.

Of all the ascetics who had traveled with Adithya, Satthama Govida alone came forward to take up the task of protecting the ship, and advised the others to go down to the lower decks, and remain calm. Satthama Govida addressed Adithya: "Swamini, please go down. I have had military training. Before becoming an ascetic, I was a general in the Ayutthaya army. But a spiritualist like you need not be involved in this conflict. Even if the pirates capture this ship, they will disembark the ascetics somewhere. Hence, you too can go down peacefully."

Adithya knew that if he displayed his military skill, it would arouse suspicion regarding his identity; at the same time, if the ship were to be captured by the pirates, his journey would be delayed, and this might affect his mission adversely. He asked very humbly.

"Swamini, I request you to permit me to ascend the mast and watch out for their arrival. Long ago, I have served as a weather forecaster in Annam (Vietnam)."

Accepting his request, Govida gave a pep talk to the frightened sailors and the guards. "They are in two small vessels. Only a hundred people - fifty in each ship - can travel in total in those vessels. We have double that strength. Speed is their weapon. If we can slow them down, they will lose that advantage. Our weapon should be a surprise attack. So, we should pretend to surrender and when they are close enough we should attack them.

"Pirate ships are usually equipped with flame throwers. If we try to run or appear to attack, they will not hesitate to lob their fire balls at us. Therefore, we should first reduce our speed."

Immediately, the ship's captain ordered the sails to be lowered. In addition, anchor was dropped and the ship remained static in the middle of the sea. There was a rock beside it on the left side. As an indication of their surrender, Adithya was ordered to hoist a white flag on the masthead.

Satthama Govida divided the men into two groups, and asked them to remain hidden on the lower deck. Swords and spears were distributed to all of them from the ship's armoury. Down below, the cries and screams of the women could be heard. They knew only too well the fate of the women captured by pirates.

As the ship's captain knew this area quite well, he had anchored the ship close to a rock that rose vertically from the deep sea. If any other ship were to approach this one from the side of the rock, it would run into the rocks. With the rock on one flank, the pirate ships could not approach their vessel from both sides, and could approach it only from the right. The two pirate ships had to come in single file. If this had been a war situation, they would have started attacking immediately. But, as this ship had indicated surrender, the pirates were hesitant to attack. When the goal could be achieved easily, why cause unnecessary destruction and waste of energy and resources, they thought.

Moreover, as their ship had come quite close, they had lost the opportunity to hurl their flaming balls. In life, many problems belong to this category. Strategies which may be used from a distance become useless at close quarters.   Under   these circumstances, imagining that they had achieved victory very easily, the pirates approached the small ship with arrogance.

Their captain's name was Agni Gunda. Tall and well-built, he had a huge moustache and a scar on his forehead, giving him a fearsome appearance. As he was bare chested, one could see curly hair on his chest and back. His paunch shook visibly when he walked. In his hand was a huge sword.

As soon as their ship neared their quarry, some of the pirates leapt onto the latter, and tied both the ships together with a large rope. Moreover, to climb from their shorter vessel into this taller one, they let down rope ladders.

On the upper deck, only Satthama Govida and the ship's Captain were standing; Agni Gunda and his associates got on to the upper deck with sounds of triumphant glee. Their breath reeked of alcohol. As this region was full of coconut palms, it was not surprising to find them drunk. Nevertheless, though they were pirates, should they not have been sober when at work? Adithya thought that whatever work they did it was poor work ethic on their part to have been drunk when they were engaged in their occupation (robbery). He was sure that they were going to pay the price for their indiscretion.

"Where are your cowards? Have they jumped into the sea knowing that Agni Gunda was coming?" he said, and thinking that he had said something very humorous, he laughed uproariously. Adithya thought those who laugh at their own jokes are fools.

At this time, Satthama Govida shouted, "Begin the war! Start fighting! All hands to the upper deck!" As they were ready and waiting for his signal armed sailors and guards rushed up from the lower deck. Many of the pirates also got into this ship and began fighting in earnest.

Ezhuth Aani

With the clashing of swords, the entire seascape reverberated with the sound of metal on metal – cling, clang. In addition, with some men being pushed into the sea, and some compelled to jump into the sea, the wails of the wounded the drowning and the dying could be heard everywhere, indicating human agony at its peak.

For Adithya, who had been taught from childhood that war was a wonderful activity, and who had participated as a front-liner in many battles, this was not a scary event at all. What pained him was the fact that instead of taking part in the game, he was forced to remain merely a silent spectator. His plight was similar to that of the pancha pandavas the heroes of Mahabharata, who during their term of exile, came across many people who bragged about themselves even though they were far less talented; however, to avoid being recognized they were compelled to remain silent.

At this time, the battle seemed to be totally in favour of Govida's men. Some of the guards leapt into the pirates' first ship, and brought it under their control. To carry out a fire attack, the second pirate ship moved away from Govida's ship. But some of the guards hurled fire balls from the pirates' first ship on to the second and set it alight. At that time, one or two burning debris happened to fall on the first ship, but they managed to put out the fire and prevent it from spreading.

It was then that Agni Gunda's voice was heard loudly. "Stop fighting and throw down your arms. Otherwise, your leaders' lives will leave their bodies this very second."

Yes. Realizing that the odds were turning against them, Gunda and his associates had surrounded Satthama Govida and the ship's Captain, disarmed them and had them in their hold. Agni Gunda, who held Satthama Govida from behind tightly, also had his long sword at the latter's neck. In one second, he could have severed the man's head. Similarly, his associate held the ship's Captain.

There was a sudden calm. Having stopped fighting, they were waiting for the next order from Satthama Govida.

"Hmm! Tell your men to throw down their arms; otherwise, I will sever your head, unmindful of the fact that you are a monk" said Gunda. Though Satthama Govida did not care about his life, he was worried about that of the Captain, and hesitated.

All those who had stopped fighting waited for his order.

Govida and the Captain waited to breathe their last.

For a few seconds nothing happened. Everybody waited with breathless silence.

Suddenly, a loud thud was heard. Govida and the Captain fell down. But, why have Gunda and his associate also fallen down? Their swords too were on the ground. None knew what was happening.

Only then did they notice Adithya calmly descending from the flag mast and walking towards them. The saffron-clad, well-built monk Adithya wrested the knives from the chests of Gunda and his associate slowly, and wiped the blood off them.

Yes. The knives which he had thrown at Gunda and his associate simultaneously and at the right time had killed them, and as Govida and the Captain had been in their hold, they too had fallen down. As he realised that he could not participate in the fight, Adithya had taken another knife along with his, and waited on the mast watching the goings-on, and waiting for the right moment. Then, when he thought that it was a matter of life or death, he had to display his skill.

Ezhuth Aani

Everyone looked upon him with wonder and respect; the pirates surrendered, and their voyage continued. "Swamini, I have never seen anyone flinging two knives so dexterously, simultaneously. Where did you learn this skill?" asked Govida.

He thought within himself: Mandagini's skill was, in no way, inferior to his. Nevertheless, without revealing any emotion, he said "I just flung the knives. Luckily they were on target."

"Swamini, there is some mystery about your past. However, you have saved my life. I shall recompense for this at the right time" said Govida.

After this, their voyage continued without any further hitch. Following that incident, the younger monks considered him as a leader. But his objective was not to become their leader. On the contrary, he was apprehensive that if he interacted with them more freely, they would see through his disguise; he spoke sparingly and kept to himself.

A kind of respect mixed with gratitude towards Adithya, arose in Satthama Govida's mind, for having saved not only him but also his group and ship, although he had a slight suspicion about him.

After many days' voyage, a huge rock could be seen at a distance. "Swamini, we are approaching Devinuwara port" said Satthama Govida.

In that delightful evening, Devinuwara, the city which formed the southernmost point of the island of Lanka, gradually spread itself before their eyes. The gold coloured roof of the Uppuluvan temple glittered in the light of the setting sun, giving the city a magnificent aura. Adithya wondered, 'Is there a more beautiful island in this world'?

PART –II

Chapter 1

The huge walls of Beijing city beckoned him. With the work of constructing the new capital still unfinished, many buildings remained incomplete. Wondering if this were a new creation of Viswakarma the heavenly architect, Mahendravarman was suffocated for a few seconds due to the dust raised by the stone-masons and the land drills.

The western mountain range was covered with a white blanket of snow, decreasing the temperature to near freezing point, and making the people remain indoors. Proper houses and other amenities had not yet been provided for many of those who had been forced to migrate to the capital.

As the Yongle Emperor passed away before completing the work of building the capital, Hongxi Emperor, Zhu Gaochi, who succeeded him, undertook measures contrary to those of his predecessor. One of these was shifting the capital once again to Nanjing. Because of this, there was an air of uncertainty in the capital. Hence, construction work proceeded slower than before. However, within two years of his coronation Hongxi Emperor died of cardiac illness, and the process of shifting the capital to Nanjing stopped abruptly.

Mahendra had never even dreamt that things would come to pass like this. His memories went back to the incidents that took place when he first came to China six years ago. Will those days ever return? Oh God! What opulence! What ostentation! It was the time when Yongle proclaimed that he was the Emperor of the entire world. The leaders of all the countries of the modern world bowed their heads and paid their respects to the Emperor. The occasion when his own father paid obeisance to the Emperor, had been imprinted in his mind, and was as fresh as if it had happened just the day before.

Mahendra's father had come to China then, as the ambassador of the Cambodian king. Was he the only one? No. Representatives of all the countries had gathered there. Under the leadership of the navy general called Zheng He, large convoys of ships had gone many times to all corners of the world, to bring these leaders to China. Mahendra too, had come on one of those ships.

Twenty years ago, his mother had come to Cambodia on a large ship captained by Zheng He. She was also a relative of Yongle Emperor. By sending Chinese ladies to other countries, and by having Chinese men marry ladies from other countries, the Emperor developed relationships with various countries by means of marital bonds.

In a 'never seen before and never seen again' number of large ships, Zheng He travelled to many parts of the world. During every voyage lasting long periods, Chinese merchandise and exclusively Chinese goods like silk and ceramics were sent to different countries. On their return journey, these ships brought tributes and other gifts from the respective feudatory kings to the Emperor.

The main objective of these voyages was to make the other countries accept the overlordship and protection of the Chinese Emperor, rather than profit motivated trade. The feudatory kings who paid tributes to the Emperor, were drawn into China's security zone, and received the guarantee that at times of danger and need, they would be provided the necessary aid. Moreover, the Chinese Emperor bestowed them with awards and titles. By such means, he intended that the whole world should acknowledge Chinese hegemony. When China brought under its control countries like Annam (the northern part of modern Vietnam) and Manchuria by means of direct military invasion, it had to face very strong opposition. However, when Chinese supremacy was established through peaceful methods such as those mentioned above there was not much opposition. Because of this, Yongle Emperor had established his fame and honour worldwide.

However, this international diplomacy of his was contrary to the policies of his father and the founder of the Ming dynasty, Hongwu Emperor. Hongwu Emperor was the freedom fighter, who liberated China from Mongolian rule. China, reeling under assaults by Mongolian warlords like Genghis Khan and Kublai Khan was ruled by the Yuan dynasty installed by them for seventy-nine years. Not only China, but one thirds of the then known world had been captured by the Mongols. The man who led the peasants' revolt against that rule later came to power under the name of Hongwu. Wearing red head bands, his soldiers scattered the Mongolian dominance. Although the Mongolian Empire had begun to disintegrate, powerful kings like Timur still held large portions of the Empire. Hongwu focused his attention consolidating his position, securing his borders, and neutralizing his local opponents.

Although the Chinese emperors generally favoured foreign trade, Hongwu looked upon the traders with hatred and suspicion. He implemented policies which prohibited foreign trade. His aim was that China should be an agrarian based country. If the country were self-sufficient, where was the need for foreign trade? Due to such policies, China concentrated on internal development for a long time. It had become difficult for individuals to earn profit through trade due to high taxes.

Coming to power under such circumstances, Yongle Emperor had policies opposite to those of his father. He had determined that world-wide recognition and co-operation were indispensable for China's growth. Because of this, China had thrown its doors open.

To facilitate the expansion of sea trade, huge ships were built. Close to Nanjing port, dry docks that could accommodate seven ships at a time were constructed. Many huge treasure ships were built. Each junk carried highly valuable goods.

To build one such treasure ship, trees in 75000 acres of teakwood forests were cut down. On every voyage, a convoy of more than 60 treasure ships and others to protect them - 300 ships in all - sailed. Because of these expensive voyages, there was an acute shortage of funds in the treasury. Having commissioned six such expeditions, Yongle Emperor was forced to suspend these world-wide projects temporarily. Money was needed to counter the annoying intrusions by the Mongolians in the north, and this necessitated the imposition of exorbitant taxes which naturally incurred the people's displeasure and disquiet.

Mahendra reflected. Yongle Emperor died, and his son Honxi became the Emperor. Just as Yongle followed policies contrary to those of his father Hongwu, the next Ming Hongxi Emperor changed his father's policies. He not only stopped all sea expeditions, he ordered that the ships anchored in Nanjing port be burnt down. Subsequently, the attention of the Chinese emperors was concentrated only on defeating the Mongolian armies from the north.

Mahendra still could not believe it. Yongle, who had been crowned as the greatest king in the world, was no more. Not only that! His successor Honxi too was not alive. Within two years he had died of cardiac illness. After him, Emperor Xuande had ascended to the throne. But, ever since he came to power he had been engaged in a battle to assume control of the government against Zhu Gaoxu, his uncle and Honxi's brother.

Not only kings but even emperors die. And their big schemes die along with them. Oh God! How many were the schemes envisaged by Yongle! Was the organization of a strong navy his only achievement? He had achieved much greater things! His going with his father to the coronation of Yongle in the Palace City, referred to as the Forbidden City, was still fresh in Mahendra's memory.

Yongle decided to shift his capital from Nanjing to Beijing, also called Beiping.   Yongle came to power only by overthrowing his nephew, Jianwen Emperor. Hongwu, who had ruled for thirty years, had proclaimed his eldest son as his heir. The latter died very young, and his son and Hongwu's grandson, Jianwen, came to power in 1398. He ruled only for four years; during that time he had to face a lot of opposition from Hongwu's younger son and a strong warrior, Yongle. Later, Yongle surrounded Jianwen Emperor in Nanjing city. When Yongle attacked, some of the ministers indulged in sabotage work against Jianwen, from within.

Suddenly, there was a fire in the palace, and the burnt bodies of the empress and the prince were found. But that of the Jianwen Emperor was not to be found. It was officially announced that he had set fire to the palace and committed suicide. Chroniclers of the Ming dynasty were ordered to write about the incident thus in their records. However, Yongle feared that Jianwen had escaped alive, and that one day he might return to claim the throne that was his rightfully. Therefore Yongle made preparations to shift the capital from Nanjing to Beijing, which was his supporters' bastion.

The culmination of this very expensive shift was the celebration in which Yongle declared himself as the Emperor, in the presence of the world leaders. Mahendra's father had come to witness the event as the representative of the Cambodian King, and subsequently settled down there as the king's permanent ambassador. It appeared to him that all this had happened the day before. When these events took place six years ago, he was just fifteen. Even though the main palace complex had been constructed, work on houses and facilities for ordinary citizens, was still continuing to this day. There was mass displacement and forced migration of the citizenry to populate the new capital.

As one of the future leaders of Angkor, he had undertaken training in Vajragnani's school. In addition to fencing and archery, he also learnt various other skills, including wrestling, horse-riding, elephant-riding, and the art of leading an army. Tall and well-built, Mahendravarman had also taken part in small battles against Champa.

When they came here, the king ordered his father to settle down in the capital. The Cambodians knew that the friendship and patronage of the strong Chinese Emperor was indispensable for them. They believed that, as his wife belonged to the Chinese royal family, it would be easy for them to stay there and expand their diplomatic ties.

How splendid that palace city was! This was a complex of palaces designed according to the law of the confluence of Man and Nature, referred to in the Book for Change, written by Confucius. As ordinary people could not enter it, it was called the Forbidden City.

The Forbidden City occupied 180 acres of land and was surrounded by high walls. A moat, about 2.5 miles in length, was built around the perimeter. This city was a thousand yards long and eight hundred yards wide. It extended south to north. Around the Forbidden City was the Imperial City, also enclosed by a wall. Higher officials of the government lived here. Mahendra's parents also lived there. Outside this was the inner city. South of the inner city was the outer city. The ordinary workers lived here.

It was rumored that inside the palace city alone there were 900 buildings, and that there were more than 9000 rooms in them. Mahendra was sure that this was the largest palace in the whole world. He had been to the palace only on a few occasions. One of them was the coronation of Yongle Emperor. He had heard that in ancient India, 'Aswamedha yagas' had been performed. Messengers would go with the king's horse to other countries. On such trips, if an enemy king were to challenge the king claiming to be the emperor, the latter would wage war against the enemy, defeat and subjugate him. Those who did not wish to take the risk would offer a tribute to the king. When a hundred kings had been subdued, the Aswamedha would be performed. Only after that would the king be proclaimed as an emperor. Similarly, by means of Zheng He's voyages, the co-operation and submission of the kings of many countries had been obtained. Yongle's grand coronation took place after that.

Could Mahendra enter this fortified city by stealth? No! The moat surrounding the palace city was six yards deep and sixty yards wide. If one crossed that, there were walls eight yards high. These walls were seven to nine yards thick. The walls contained chambers for the soldiers to defend any attacks from outside as well as to keep watch on the inside. Built of brick, clay and mortar, they were strong enough to withstand heavy attacks.

Tall watch towers had been constructed in all four corners. The north south axis, along which the main buildings were built, extended from the front entrance in south to the back entrances facing north. The entrances on the eastern and western walls were closer to the front (south). Outside the front (southern) entrance was an enclosure surrounded by walls on three sides. The southern gate was the largest of the gates and was called the Meridian gate. It had five arches. The central section was the emperor's path. Only the emperor could enter through this.

Chapter 2

When Mahendra reached there, the sun had begun to set. Torches were being lit. He approached one of the smaller gates on the southern wall. Mahendra gave his missive to the guard. The sealed letter was addressed to the Chief Censor, Liu Guan. It was a paper note.

As soon as he saw the name of Liu Guan, the guard treated him with great fear and respect. The Chief Censor supervised the imposition of taxes and the collection of tributes from the citizenry and landed gentry. He was in a very powerful post. It was his responsibility to arrange the funds for the Emperor's development and war budgets. One who came to see him could not be an ordinary man.

The guard told him, "The Censor will come only after midnight. Hence, you can go elsewhere and come sometime before dawn." Yes. The only male who lived in that palace was the emperor. All those who governed the palace city, including the guards, were eunuchs or women. All other men, including the ministers, lived outside, and went in only for work. And the official work was done mostly in the nights.

Every day, only after midnight would the emperor present himself behind a screen. The VIPs, who came to see him, would explain the purpose of their visit, and wait for the emperor's order. Finally, after the sovereign had taken a decision, the order would be recorded by the official scribe, the words inscribed on wood and printed on paper. The order would be gazetted before dawn and sent to every nook and corner of the empire. A separate department had been set up to affix the seal of authority on these orders.

Those who administered this large empire from within the palace city were ladies or eunuchs. All the others, including the army

Ezhuth Aani

personnel, those in government service and the ministers, lived outside the palace city. This was done to ensure that the emperor was the sire of all the children born to the ladies in the harem.

To get close to the emperor, one had either to be a beautiful lady or a eunuch. To govern the large empire, an extensive administrative service had been established. Many training schools had been set up. Only those who studied the book of Confucius, passed an examination, and then cleared the government service test, could join this service. If ordinary people from the villages wished to come to Beijing city, the heart of the Chinese Empire, and get close to the corridors of power, joining and advancing through the ranks of civil service was the only way. Even if they managed to come to the capital through their merit, getting close to the emperor was nigh impossible.

There was frequent rivalry between the eunuch generals faithful to the emperor and the government civil service. Yongle Emperor trusted his eunuch chiefs. However, after his death the civil service had become more dominant. Liu Guan was a powerful man in this set up.

There were many men, who with the sole aim of working in the palace city and entering the inner circle voluntarily castrated themselves. Though these men lost the opportunity for procreation, their social status increased. This raised their own and their families' stock.

Similarly, if the ladies succeeded in winning the attention of the emperor by their beauty, they were accepted into the harem. Subsequently, their parents and relatives would be given several concessions and positions.

Thus, the Emperor was the centre of the universe. For the beauties and the eunuchs, once they entered the palace city losing their freedom or their manhood, the future of their families was sure to be prosperous. They deprived themselves to make their families rich and happy.

As advised by the eunuch guard, Mahendra left the place. He mounted his thorough bred black Arabian horse called Khan, and went to the suburbs. Night lamps had been lit in the streets there. To protect them from the snow and rain, they were enclosed in small metal mesh. Sitting in a small shop there, and eating his dinner, he reflected on the reason why he had come to meet Liu Guan.

Having come to Beijing to attend the coronation of the Emperor and then remaining there, he studied in the schools of that country. There was a much disciplined educational system in China. This curriculum had been in practice for the past 800 years, since the rule of the Sui dynasty, and was framed on the basis of the doctrines of Confucius. As Mahendra was a foreign citizen, he could not attend the exclusive schools which the children of the Chinese aristocrats and landlords attended. Here, military training was given to the ruling class.

The education which he received in Angkor city gave him the knowledge that was essential for a warrior. But here, greater attention was paid to the strengthening of the emperor's administrative service. Could one belonging to the royal family of Cambodia be satisfied with mere rote learning geared to prepare civil servants? However, in this foreign land, he had no identity and no access to education commensurate with his royal status.

He had a longing to return to his motherland. Drudgery and frustration had set in having to lead an uninteresting life in a foreign country. Perhaps destiny intended to bring to an end this state of affairs. One fine day, a messenger from Cambodia came searching for their house.

Ezhuth Aani

The messenger came in the night. He spoke at length with Mahendra's father, Jayendravarman. He explained in detail the danger facing Angkor. He pointed out that military aid, arms and technological knowledge were urgently needed from China.

After the death of Yongle Emperor, China had decreased its foreign ties significantly. The emperor no longer engaged himself in entertaining, or holding regular meetings with, foreign dignitaries. The usual diplomatic network had been disbanded. Hence, Jayendravarman could not offer any help, living in Beijing. Instead, King Sri Suryavangan's order was that Jayendravarman, who was experienced and skilled in leading an army, should return to Angkor and help in preparations for the final war. At the same time, the king had sent a missive to the powerful official, Liu Guan. The messenger's advice was that somehow the message seeking military aid should be handed over to Liu Guan.

It was a time when the great Chinese Empire had encroached upon the country called Annam (the northern part of Vietnam), and then struggled, unable to face the rebellion launched by the enemy. In that war, Annam had requested neighboring countries like Champa and Ayutthaya to remain neutral. It was doubtful that the Chinese armies would come to the help of Angkor against the wishes of all those countries. Nevertheless, China could offer indirect aid. In addition to providing arms and ammunition, Chinese military advisors could come to Angkor and offer advice on the latest battle arrays. Great empires were all engaged in the game of rocking the cradle and pinching the baby simultaneously. By means of such diplomatic tactics, they retained their status as empires.

Moreover, in every government there would be various power lobbies. The friends of the one which was dominant would have ascendancy. Given the fact that it was impossible to approach the emperor for the time being, the Angkorean King decided that it would be best to seek the friendship of a powerful man like Liu Guan. In a horse race one had to bet on one horse. Among the present Chinese officials, Liu Guan appeared to be the winning horse.

Although the emperor was the head of the Chinese Empire, he could not function as he liked. In Chinese society, from ancient days, there has been a disciplined order of governance.
On one hand, there was the army and its officers; on the other, the powerful Chinese administrative service. In addition, a vigilance department, directly under the emperor, watched all employees.

The Chinese had a much disciplined social structure. Confucius's basic philosophy that one should first be loyal to one's family, society and the emperor was implanted right from childhood. Government administration was divided into provinces, districts and sub-districts, so that power delegation became easy. In every division, employees were appointed, for tenures of three years, renewable. Military service was also on par with this. Army officers were those born in the military families, or relatives of the aristocrats.

While the army and the vigilance department were under the control of the emperor, the governance of the people was in the hands of the administrative officers. These officers had an important role in allocating funds for the emperor's grand schemes such as waging wars, and in settling issues of succession. When Yongle Emperor superseded his nephew usurping power, he had to justify his deed to these officers.

Amidst this well organized power structure, the ones closest to the Emperor were the palace officials. They were either ladies or eunuchs. Eunuchs played an important role in imperial China. Even in the army, many officers were eunuchs. As they did not have children of their own, these eunuchs were very loyal and dedicated in their work. Though others wondered how it was possible for a person to love one who had deprived him of his manhood, the fidelity of the eunuchs to the emperor was unsurpassed.

In such gigantic government machinery with multiple power centres, various foreign governments approached the officials holding responsible posts. Though it was difficult to get their work done by these officials without attracting the attention of the omnipresent vigilance department, the small neighboring countries of China each managed to safeguard its own interests through powerful friends among the officialdom. As Liu Guan had a Cambodian lady as his mistress, the Angkor government considered him as its best potential supporter. Liu Guan would visit that lady, who lived in the suburbs, only rarely. It was difficult to approach Liu Guan directly; especially because, Jayendravarman being a foreigner would be constantly watched by the spies. But the chances of young and relatively unknown Mahendravarman being spied upon were slim. Mahendra was assigned to befriend and win the confidence of Indraveni the paramour of Liu.

Mahendra sought employment in the house Indraveni. She appointed him as her bodyguard. She had already known Jayendravarman as the Cambodian ambassador. During the times Liu Guan visited her, Mahendra was not allowed to be there. But at other times, he was able to win her trust and support. Who would not like a youth full of vigour, vibrancy and a sharp intellect? After a short time he approached her and explained his purpose. Indraveni too, because of her patriotism and her sympathy for this energetic young man, agreed to help him.

It was common for Chinese courtiers to have several mistresses. They would come to their houses only occasionally. However, financial help and a luxurious life were assured to them. If a lady, who could not enter the emperor's harem, managed to attract a courtier's attention, her life would become prosperous. Although the place of women in that society was considered inferior, many matters were decided by the women in the administration of the king's palace and in the lives of the important courtiers. Mahendra tried to enter the palace fort with Indraveni's recommendation.

"Young man, have you finished eating?" asked the owner of the eatery. "Those who are out at this time of the night should be either government employees or spies."

"Spies? There is no war in the country" said Mahendra.

"Do you think that spies will be moving around only during times of war? Have you not heard of the Emperor's vigilance squad?" asked the elderly man.

Though he was all alone in the shop, his voice was quite low. In a whisper he said, "Not only the Emperor, but his advisors, mistresses, and courtiers like Liu Guan also have their own personal spies."

At the mention of Liu Guan, Mahendra pricked his ears. "Who is Liu Guan?" he asked.

The old man said, "Are you new to this place? He is the most powerful of the officials here. Even the emperor will not ignore his opinion."

"Is that so? I have come from the eastern region Honshu. I have come to complain about the corruption of the authorities there. They have dismissed my father, and appropriated our lands" said Mahendra.

"Which place is corruption-free? If you wish to present your problem and find an immediate solution, Liu Guan is the right person", said the old man.

Looking at the man - short, stout, and with a huge paunch - Mahendra wondered whether he ate all the food in his shop himself. He had a grey moustache; bald in the middle, the few grey hairs on the fringe had been plaited into two. Thinking that this man himself may be a spy, Mahendra decided that he would not reveal the truth about himself.

Inside the shop, there was a fire for warming. Around it were seats for the diners. In the centre of the square building there was a courtyard. As the night progressed, it began to snow. It appeared to Mahendra, as if the whole courtyard was strewn with white flowers. The building was on four sides of the courtyard. In the front was the shop; the rest of the house was occupied by the owner's family apparently.

"Young man, during times of snowfall, not many men move around. But, the Emperor will meet his officials only around midnight. The decisions taken therein will be recorded overnight and sealed. Hence, those moving around at this time will be the officials and the spies following them. You have come with a horse that is of high breed. That is how I gathered that you were not an ordinary citizen", he said.

"Sir, you are right. I must present my case to Liu Guan. How do I meet him?" asked Mahendra.

"You can leave your horse here and go" said the shopkeeper, pondering. "Liu Guan has his own weaknesses. He is slave to wine and women" he added.

"How do I travel without the horse?" asked Mahendra.

"I can take you on my mule. For use in winter, the mule is the best" said the shopkeeper.

It appeared to be the right thing to him. If he rode an expensive horse like Khan, he would be easily exposed as a noble. When visiting dignitaries in this environment of political intrigue, it was better to be anonymous. So, he left his horse in the shopkeeper's house and travelled with him on his donkey. He gave him some silver as a gift.

The shopkeeper ensured that Mahendra shaved his face clean before he took him to the palace. He gave him a shaving knife and a mirror made of brass and lead. In a fortress city ruled by eunuchs and ladies, anybody moving around with a moustache and beard would appear different. They would attract the attention of the detective force. Hence, it was better to go about without displaying any signs of masculinity, he said. He left him at the gates of the fort; that is, at the gates of the imperial city. After that, Mahendra walked up to the palace entrance.

The security there was very tight. He had a tough time in convincing them that he had come there only to hand over Indraveni's letter to Liu Guan. Having managed that, he entered the fort. It was still snowing. However, the government servants continued with their work through sunshine and snowfall.

Torches had been lit throughout the palace making it seem like daytime. Apart from this, the moon too shone its silver light through the clouds. With the whole ground covered with snow, and the silver beams of moonlight scattered on the snow, the entire area was drenched in a whitish glow. Wonder-struck by the external grandeur of the palace, Mahendra was stunned even more by its beauty when he went in.

The white snow strewn in patches on the roofs of the grand red and yellow wooden buildings, presented an enchanting scene. On entering the gate after crossing the outer area, a huge ornate gate called the Gate of Supreme Harmony confronted him. The buildings were all made of wood, and rested on a highly polished floor made of clay. On crossing the Gate of Supreme Harmony, he found himself in the Hall of Supreme Harmony. It was in this huge building that the emperor would grant an audience during celebrations. On the ground in front of the ornate gate, an artificial canal called the golden stream snaked around the compound. Bridges had been constructed in five places to cross this stream. In the section between the ornate gate and the hall, was a three level terrace of white marble.

Mahendra realised that most of the important buildings were in the central north-south axis, with the front (southern) part containing the buildings accessible to officials and the back (northern) section containing the living quarters of the royal family. The southern and northern sectors each had three palaces built in the central axis, one behind the other.

On crossing the Hall of Supreme Harmony, as a continuation of its central part but much smaller, was the Hall of Complete Harmony. To its north was a broader Hall of Protective Harmony, the third of the halls on the front portion of the campus. All these were built in accordance with the Chinese building laws of Feng Sui.

The Hall of Supreme Harmony was the biggest building in the whole complex. This rose to a magnificent height of about 90 feet, from the marble floor surrounding it. In the centre of the roof of this hall was a large chandelier. From the middle of this a huge dragon appeared to leap down. From the mouth of the dragon, five bright metal balls hung down.

Important functions were held mostly in this hall. The Hall of Complete Harmony behind this was meant for the emperor to rest during the ceremonies. In the Hall of Protective Harmony further behind this, rehearsals for the festivals took place. Bisecting these halls from the south to the north was the royal path.

There were two halls on either sides of this central building complex. On the west was the Hall of Martial Victory. It was here that the Emperor sometimes met the ministers and army officers and discussed matters with them. On the east was the Hall of Literary Glory. Here, discourses by famous intellectuals would take place from time to time. Here too, was Liu Guan's office.

There were many more buildings built to the east and west of the central palaces. The whole site contained many parks and gardens.

Government employees and their assistants could move about in these palaces in the front. But the buildings behind these palaces were inaccessible and included the emperor's private chambers and his harem. Outsiders could not easily enter here. This was the inner sanctum.

In this section too, there were three buildings similar to the ones in the front part. But only they were smaller. They too were built sequentially along the central axis. The one in front, that is, in the south, was the Palace of Heavenly Purity. This was the emperor's living chamber. The one furthest behind that was the Palace of Earthly Tranquility. This was the empress's abode. The hall in the middle between the two was the Hall of Union. According to Chinese belief, the world functioned due to the union of two natural forces Yin and Yang. This could be compared to the Hindus' Siva and Shakthi. It was believed that the emperor represented Yang and the empress Yin. And when they came together, there was peace, prosperity and harmony.

In this building complex, which evoked wonder and astonishment, there were some places here and there, which had been burnt down; he felt sad on seeing them. Yes; within a short time after completing the building, some of the large structures were destroyed in a huge fire. Though it was said that a lightning struck them down people had their own stories to tell. There were rumours that a friendship developed between one of the mistresses of the emperor and a eunuch guard, which later blossomed into love; the enraged Emperor murdered more than 2000 of his harem's women in a single night, and lightning struck as retribution.

The relationship between the eunuchs and the ladies in the harem was unique. The harem was merely a gold-plated prison. In it, there were hundreds of heroines vying for the attention of one single hero. Though their being part of the harem brought social status and money to their families was there any chance that the women's physical and psychological needs could be satisfied in this environment?

Although there were various means of entertainment such as music, literature, drama, and libraries, how could one satisfy one's physical cravings? There were rumours that these ladies secretly indulged in lesbian affairs. However, sometimes it may be difficult for ladies to have such a relationship, because, they were all rivals in trying to attract the emperor's attention. How could they trust anybody? If a lady catches the fascination of the emperor, her status and facilities would be enhanced. But her hold would mostly be temporary. Once the emperor got tired of a lady, his gaze would shift to another. If a lady succeeded in mesmerizing him for a long time, she would receive titles and other benefits. Only one lady could be the empress at any one time. But in the second rank, there were many who were considered as mistresses. Even these were not permanent. If the empress incurred the wrath of the emperor, or if she failed to yield a male heir, she could not hold on to her position. In such a competitive world, the only lady who had no worry about her position was the emperor's mother. As a widow, she was given the status of dowager empress, and wielded great authority. Even in this, there was a danger. Sometimes, when an emperor died, his wives too would be killed and buried along with the emperor. This was to prevent them from having a relationship with another man, and losing their purity.

It was inevitable that several ladies were friendly with the eunuchs. Though they could not have conventional sex, a eunuch could satisfy a lady in other ways. There was also no necessity that these friendships should all end in physical relationships. As some of the ladies felt that they could open their hearts freely only to the eunuchs, they were friendly with them on a platonic level. However friendly another lady of the harem was, she was ultimately their rival.

Mahendra was taking in the structure of the complex as well as the beauty of the buildings. Though he could not go north, he knew that beyond all these buildings and before the northern gate, was a royal park. The northern gate was called the Gate of Divine Prowess. The golden stream entered the complex at the southeast corner, and wound its way along the southern part of the complex, and ran parallel to the western wall to exit at the northwest corner. As soon as he entered, it became clear to him that it was a prison. Yes. It was difficult for an enemy to escape from this fort. Even if he did, he could only go as far as the Imperial City. How could one escape from there? Even if he did, there was the inner city...

He was surprised when he wondered why he was thinking of escaping even as he entered. A strange feeling of foreboding overcame him. Though he asked himself, 'Am I a fugitive?' having been trained as a warrior, he did not fail to assess the security measures taken in the fort. He could not help looking for potential weak points.

The entire harem was governed by ladies and eunuchs. There were thousands of eunuchs working in the palace. As Mahendra was clean-shaven, the onlookers may have mistaken him for a eunuch.

After scrutinizing his documents, the guards asked him a couple of questions, and sent him along with one of their men to Liu Guan's office. On mentioning that he was Indraveni's messenger, there was no further checking. All of them knew about Liu Guan's beloved.

Close observation was made of those who entered and left that building. Every minor activity was documented. Important information was replicated with the help of wooden blocks, several copies taken and these were sent to different parts of the country. Hundreds of workers were engaged in this work of information gathering and exchange. Mahendra's presence was also registered. Instead of his real name, he gave a Chinese name to them.

Chapter 3

He was taken to Liu Guan's office located in the Hall of Literary Glory on the east. The former had gone to meet the empress when he went there. He was made to wait in a room. The eunuch guard on duty there observed him carefully. As his mother was a tall northern Chinese lady, Mahendra was more than six feet tall and well-built. He was fair in complexion, and his dark hair had been plaited in typical Chinese fashion. His wide eyes were exactly like his father's. Though he looked different to ordinary Chinese, his appearance was not out of place. It was quite common for people of various races from all corners of the Chinese Empire to visit the capital. Many of them were of mixed origin.

It was in the darkness of the night that many of the government transactions were carried out in a hectic manner. This was common in China. He had to wait for quite some time for Liu Guan's arrival. While he was wondering what the next moments were going to bring, Liu Guan entered the room hurriedly. Two others came along with him. Tall in appearance, he sported a moustache and a long beard, in accordance with the Chinese tradition. Traces of grey could be seen in them. He had also plaited his hair. In addition to high quality Chinese silk clothes, he wore a band signifying his status around his waist.

On entering the room, he ignored Mahendra and taking his guests into another room, bolted the door. After some time, the door opened and the two guests came out. Appearing to notice him only then, he called Mahendra inside.

As soon as he entered, he bolted the door and said, "Did Veni send you? It's two weeks since I saw her."

He then took him into an inner room. He learnt all the details about the latter. Realizing that it was futile to conceal anything from him, Mahendravarman revealed to him the whole truth - from beginning to end. Having listened to him patiently, Liu Guan extended his hand, raising his brows. When the young man looked at him in confusion, he asked, "Where is the missive?"

Mahendra realised that he was standing before a man with a fine understanding and a sharp intellect.

On receiving the letter from him, Liu Guan read it silently for some time. He then said, "Your king seeks our assistance. Chinese aid is not easy to come by. There are several mandarins here with different aims. Each of them is trying to achieve his own individual goal through the emperor."

"During Yongle Emperor's period, China was actively engaged in developing its ties worldwide, with a global perspective. Though it was very expensive, our suzerainty and influence extended far beyond our shores. But, Hongxi Emperor, who succeeded him, has followed the policies and objectives of the first Ming, Hongwu Emperor. His schemes were directed towards making China a self-sufficient agrarian country. Current policy is to retract inwards. Also rebellion has broken out in Annam against the Chinese army, which is stationed there. In Annam, our army needs the assistance of those of Ayutthaya and Champa. At least they need to be neutral. Under such circumstances, it is not easy for us to offer military aid to Cambodia."

Saying thus, he looked at the young man keenly.

"Will you do anything for your country?" he asked, and expecting an answer he peered at him.

"I shall certainly do everything within my power to save my land and its traditions from destruction" said Mahendravarman.

Taking him to another room, Liu Guan locked the door and gently rolled the floor carpet. The red Persian carpet, woven with intricate designs, was flush with the floor. But, once he removed the two nails fixed in two corners on the right side, it was possible to roll it. On removing some more nails, half the carpet could be rolled back from the floor.

In the centre of the plastered floor, a square patch, one yard long and one yard wide, could be distinguished from the red floor by its lighter shade. On observing it carefully, there was a small depression on one side. Inserting two fingers into it Liu Guan raised it. The central square began to move slowly. Yes. It was the entrance of an underground tunnel. Lifting the door a little, Liu Guan ordered him to help. Mahendra too knelt down, and inserting his hands raised the trap door, revealing a big square opening on the floor. A ladder could be seen resting below.

Taking a lamp with him, Liu Guan gestured to him to follow. Then, making sure again that the room door was firmly bolted, he stepped down the ladder.

Mahendra too followed, and they reached a small underground room. On one side of that room, was a narrow tunnel. In this, an adult could only crawl. First Liu Guan and then Mahendra crawled and reached another room. There was a bed in that room. In one corner water and in another some fruits were placed.

Liu Guan said, "I have an important task for you. But it's not the right time yet. You may have to stay here for a few days. I shall fetch the water and food you need myself. There are no toilet facilities here. So, you'll have to collect your waste in this pan. I shall remove it every day."

Ezhuth Aani

Mahendra realised that he had been caught in the grip of Liu Guan. He knew only too well that not only his life, but the future of the people of his country too, was now in the hands of this man. Having taken a bet on the horse called Liu Guan, he had no other alternative but to obey and please him.

Mahendra wondered what would happen to him, if Liu Guan forgot all about him and became engrossed in other work. According to the Cambodian King's order, requesting the Chinese Emperor for aid was not his only allotted task. Subsequently, he had been given the important work of acquiring the latest technological knowhow of pumping water from under the ground, and the manufacture of explosives, from the Chinese scientists and experts. Though he knew that lying helpless in an underground cell in the palace fort would be of no benefit either to him or to his country, not having the capacity to change the course of events, he spent his time ruing his state. In life it is the feeling of helplessness that really saps the vitality from a person. Mahendra was in this state of mind and thought he would probably die in this clandestine room unknown to any of his friends or relatives.

Two days passed in this manner and Mahendra had lost all hope. Liu Guan did not appear as promised; but he had sent a trustworthy eunuch. He too did not speak much, but left after catering to his needs. There was light in the room only when he came; otherwise Mahendra had to spend his time in total darkness. Once he became accustomed to the darkness, he could see just a few things around him. How long could he go on like this? With the help of the methods of meditation taught by Vajragnani, he was able to while away his time to a certain extent but even that was becoming progressively difficult, as anxiety built up.

Mahendra got angry, asking himself repeatedly, 'What a plight to be in, for one belonging to the Cambodian royal family?'

For his father to return to Cambodia and lead a royal life, should he alone languish in an underground cell uncared for by anybody, wondered Mahendra.

While he was engrossed in such thoughts, Liu Guan appeared there suddenly. He took Mahendra to his private room again. "How are you?" he asked. Mahendra understood that he was not really interested in his welfare, but was merely following a formality.

Before he could answer, Liu Guan said, "An important task awaits you. If you fulfill it well, I can guarantee that I will personally arrange Chinese aid to Cambodia."

"What do you expect me to do?" asked Mahendra. In reply Liu Guan looked at him intently for some time. Then he spoke slowly, almost in whispers. "The world knows only about the Chinese Emperors. But every emperor has an empress. The outside world does not know much about her" began Liu Guan, with a preamble.

"But in our culture, the position of the empress is also important. People believe that when the two natural forces of Yin and Yang come together, there will be peace and prosperity in the world. It is on this basis that this palace has also been built. If something goes wrong in this, people will be dissatisfied. Only by maintaining this balance, can we control the people."

He added: "The emperor's status is his until his death. But the empress's status does not carry such a guarantee. At any given time, next in rank to the empress will be many wives such as noble consort, imperial concubine, consorts, and beauty ladies. All of them will have an eye on the empress's position.

"If the empress fails to yield a male heir to the emperor, the wife next in rank will carry out that task. Then, as the mother of the prince, she will take over as the empress.

"The current empress, Gong Rang Zhang is a relative of mine. Though she tried her best, she has not produced a male heir. At the same time, the next wife, Zhu Disen is rumored to have conceived. If this is true, and a boy is born in ten months, Gong Rang Zhang's plight will become precarious."

"In that case, what do you want me to do? Do you want me to kill Zhu Disen? I am not the right person for such a task. I have not committed a single cold blooded murder in my life" blurted Mahendra.

"I have not brought you to kill. On the contrary, I have brought you here to give life" said Liu Guan.

"I can't make out anything" said Mahendra.

"The empress's post depends on her begetting a boy. Only if she retains her position, people like me can wield our influence. And only if I have authority can I help Cambodia."

He then looked at him and said loudly, "Only if my plan works out well, will yours too work. For this, the empress should conceive. She has not succeeded despite her having sex with the emperor. In view of this, the emperor has also shifted his attention to the next lady.

"If you can make her conceive, my influence will continue. Do you understand what I'm saying at least now?"

Mahendra was shocked. Until then he had not even thought of sex. How was he to undertake such a task? "I have no experience in these matters" he blabbered.

"You don't have to do anything. Your co-operation is all that we expect from you. She will take care of the rest" said Liu Guan, and indicated that it was time for him to leave.

Mahendra then asked, "Right. Let us assume that she conceives, as you say. Won't the Emperor suspect how she conceived without having had sex with him for a long time?"

"We have thought it all over. We shall make sure that she has sex with him before such an eventuality occurs."

An overwhelming sense of shame over took Mahendra. He was supposed to be a warrior who would be leading the armies of his nation from the front. But here he was, being used as a stud to impregnate an unknown woman. What a come down! But he also understood that he was firmly in the hold of Liu Guan. He had no choice.

With these words, Liu Guan took him to his assistant. He was also a eunuch. He helped Mahendra to bathe, eat and get dressed in smart clothes. Yes. He was treated royally. For that day, he was the emperor of the world! The one who was to rule the empress was the emperor, was it not? He was disgusted with his plight. Like the adage, 'On digging a well a genie appeared', what had begun as a noble quest had now come to such a pass, he thought.

That eunuch again took him through another tunnel to the empress.

Chapter 4

The inner walls and the sloping roof of the mansion were very beautifully done with intricate workmanship. With yellow and red decorations the interior of the mansion glittered in the light of the lamps. But the room, to which he was taken, was dimly lit. In the centre of the room was a large couch with a soft mattress. Silk cloth was spread on it. High quality carpets enhanced the beauty of the floor. The eunuch, who took him, left him and waited outside.

In a short while, the empress entered. Looking like a celestial goddess, she asked him, "What is your name?" He told her the truth. She was happy when she knew that he belonged to the Cambodian royal family.

Subsequently, the night prolonged. She became his teacher. She taught him things which he had not hitherto known. Then she became his slave. Thus, the whole night was spent, drenched in the enjoyment of their senses.

He knew quite well that she was exploiting him. It angered him. But who would not be excited on seeing such a beauty? Only the most beautiful women in the whole empire were selected and taken in to the harem. And if she were to attract the attention of the emperor and become the empress, must her beauty be described? Her face fair in color, she had combed her dark hair and knotted it into a bun high above. Her long narrow eyes and arched eyebrows, reminded him of the crescent moon. With small nostrils and mouth, her triangular face drew the onlookers like a magnet. When her lips moved, he had the illusion of a flower speaking.

Her body was like a beautiful doll created by Brahma under the direction of Cupid. Curved where necessary and lean in other places, she was the very definition of the female form.

The ladies in the harem of the Chinese Emperor were well-versed in the art of love. When she approached him, how could he desist? Even if he were a hermit, when an angel-like lady offered herself to him, how could he hold his penance?

Although he was disgusted initially, he too had his own bodily cravings. He indulged himself wholly in that night's game of love. As soon as it dawned, the guard came and took him to another private room. With a smile he asked the youth, "How was her love-play?" Mahendra then asked him, "Do you know what is happening?"

"Hmm. You are the third person" said the guard. "What do you mean?" asked Mahendra.

"For the past two months two different males have been engaged to somehow make that lady conceive during her fertile period. But so far she has not succeeded. Only if she conceives can she retain her position" he said.

"Where are they then?" asked Mahendra.
"Aahaa! How can you be so naïve and innocent?" asked the eunuch.   He then said, "After having been intimate with the Empress, can you be allowed to move about freely outside? If this news is leaked out, the entire royal family will be disgraced. Hence, every month during her fertile period a man will be chosen, and once his work is over he will be put to death. This is Liu Guan's plan."

"How do you know for certain?" asked Mahendra.

"I was the one who severed their heads" said the guard. He then continued: "You seem to be a good man. But I'll have to kill you also, in another three days."

Mahendra laughingly told him, "Don't feel sorry for me. Feel sorry for yourself. My friend, both of us are sailing in the same boat."

"What do you mean?" asked the guard.

"Let us assume that by chance the empress conceives. The big secret about the next heir will be known only to you and Liu Guan. Do you think he'll allow you to live? Someday if you happen to leave and leak out the secret, what impact will it have? It is absolutely necessary that wrongdoers eliminate all the incriminating evidence against themselves. You are an important piece of evidence."

When Mahendra said this, the eunuch began to think. After mulling things awhile, "What you say is also true" he said.

After that, the two did not talk. The next two days passed like the first - enjoying the night with the empress and sleeping the next day.

During this time, the two of them conversed. Initially, they spoke with some reservation. But, in course of time they began to trust each other and speak more freely. The guard told Mahendra his story. He was a Mongolian. Yongle Emperor waged war several times on the Mongolian border. It was on one such occasion that his village was overrun and ransacked by the Chinese.

His name was Boloma. When he recollected that incident, his voice faltered and his eyes filled with tears. It was a summer night. The Chinese army which entered their village killed all the men first. They burnt the crops and houses. They raped the women and turned them into sex slaves. They threw the babies into the fire. They forced the children to come with them. Ten year old Boloma too, was taken away in this manner. They were castrated and turned into eunuchs.

Some of them died bleeding; the others were taken as slaves to China.

Incapable of reproduction, these young eunuchs became trustworthy workers. Totally dependent on their owners for every need of theirs, they became very honest and hard-working servants, in course of time.

It was in this manner that Boloma became Liu Guan's slave. Not knowing any other life, his thinking too was circumscribed by the circle drawn by Liu Guan. Even the mere thought of stepping out of that circle, produced an unknown fear and apprehension in him.

On hearing about his past, Mahendra asked him, "My friend, it is certain that both of us will die. But, would you like to die a slave, without fighting for freedom? Or would you rather make a dash for freedom, knowing well that you may die doing that?"

Boloma said, "Do you know how strong the protective walls of this fort are? It's impossible to escape from here."

Mahendra did not answer him immediately. After some thought, he said, "My friend, they say our body has nine portals. It's not necessary that we should use only the seven portals on our face to enter or leave our body. On the contrary, it's easy to use the backdoors. Similarly, to enter this city or the palace fort, it is not necessary that we should use only the main gate or the walls in front."

"A city is like the human body. For water to be brought in and to remove the waste from here there will certainly be other gates unseen by people. These may not be guarded so zealously. These are the chinks in the city's armour. If we target these, we can find a way out. Think seriously, my friend." Although Boloma had been working for a long time in this palace fort, he had failed to observe what Mahendra had, within a short time of his arrival. Only if Boloma had any intentions of escaping, would he have tried to find the ways to do so!

But when Mahendra's sharp intellect and Boloma's detailed knowledge of the palace were combined, it was easy to find a means of escape.

The artificial waterway, golden stream, running across the city ran into the Forbidden City from the moat at the south eastern corner. In this place, there was an opening in the rampart for the water to enter. The hole just below the water level was not visible to the untrained eye.

As far as Boloma knew, vigilance here was not very strong. Once they reached the moat, they could swim across. But Liu Guan had told him that there were dragons and crocodiles in the moat. He informed Mahendra about this.

"My friend, the dragon is an imaginary animal. There is no such thing in the world. It is doubtful whether crocs would survive in cold regions. They live only in the warmer climes of Cambodia and such places. Moreover, even if there are crocodiles here, it is better to fight with them and die, rather than be caught by human crocs" he said.

Together, they planned. If they cleared the Forbidden City, the next was the Imperial City. This too was surrounded by walls. But in the Imperial City, running south to north and parallel to the Forbidden City on its west was a continuous water body consisting of lakes, canals and ponds. This water body cut across the northern wall of the Imperial City. Even if they crossed the walls of the Imperial City, there was the inner city. This was also a fort, surrounded by walls. But these water bodies cut through the wall, and eventually joined the Yongding River. They decided that their means of escape lay in these water ways which traversed through the huge walls.

They thought that if somehow they crossed the inner city, they could find a way of escape and go into hiding. Boloma had a sedative drug. This was to be used to immobilise the empress's lovers when their throats were slit, to prevent them from struggling. Liu Guan had given him this. Both of them prepared to take leather jackets to protect themselves from the cold of the night.

That night, once again Mahendra was taken to the empress. This time, after a little play he mixed the sedative with the empress's drinking water. As she slept off before midnight, they took her insignia ring and left the place. The empress's seal was affixed on a letter, prepared earlier. This was an edict that all arrangements should be made for its bearer to travel without any hindrance.

Through the tunnels known to Boloma, both of them went out hurriedly. This left them near the Hall of Literary Glory, south east of Liu Guan's office. Being the New Moon's night there was darkness everywhere. Besides it was snowing too, making the visibility poor. That night the snowfall was unusually heavy. Because of this, the sentries' torches were extinguished frequently. Patrolling had also reduced as the soldiers struggled to cope with the weather. It was a snowstorm! The snow which fell like white flowers from the sky covered the roofs of the buildings with a canopy of white. But it kept coming unceasingly. The snow on the ground was at least one foot deep. It still continued to accumulate. The weather was bitterly cold.

When they reached the place where the golden stream joined the moat outside the wall, "My friend, the stream has frozen unexpectedly" moaned Boloma. Yes the stream and the moat had frozen due to the sudden drop in temperature!

Ezhuth Aani

"Don't worry! Only the surface of the steam has frozen. Underneath there'll be water." Saying this, Mahendra took the sword given by Boloma, and pierced the surface of the golden stream near the wall. About half a foot below, there was water. Mahendravarman then expanded the hole which he had made, big enough for a man to enter. Though there were warriors in the watch tower nearby, their vigilance was not very strong in the midst of the snowstorm.

Despite the leather clothes which they wore, their faces and hands had become numb. Their hands, lips and tip of the nose seemed to be lifeless and felt like wood. The corners of their mouths had begun to crack. Boloma asked how it would be to get into the water, when they were already half-frozen.

"My friend, the water underneath will be warmer than you think. That is why it has not frozen yet" said Mahendra.

He continued: "You'll have to hold your breath and swim under water. The wall is nine yards broad. If we cross it, I shall break the ice for us to surface again. If the moat is frozen we can crawl over it. Otherwise, we'll have to swim. The moat is fifty yards wide. We can cross it in a few seconds by swimming. Don't make a noise under any circumstances."

Mahendra recollected the breathing training given to him by Vajragnani. The guru had taught him how to be under water, holding his breath for several minutes. But the situation here was different. The waters of the Mekong and Siam Reap Rivers were warm. Here, they had to swim in near freezing water. However, when it's a matter of life or death, the body changes its metabolism somehow, and preserves its functions.

He replaced his sword in its sheath, and jumped into the water. It was pitch dark under the water. With faith as his guiding light, Mahendra swam forward. Boloma followed him and jumped into the water.

After swimming for many seconds, Mahendra tried to come to the surface. Oh oh! The frozen ice block above him was not yielding! In the freezing water, he could feel his pulse slowing and muscles losing their power. "Why can't I rise to the surface? Are we, perhaps, still under the wall? Not likely. Certainly I should be in the moat outside the rampart!" Confused with such thoughts, Mahendra struck his sword above his head with all his might. Uhum! Nothing happened. Twice he tried and failed. He needed to take his breath again, urgently. But, how could he, under the water...He thought he is going to die. But his survival instincts kicked in.

Finally, he swam forward a little, and as a last attempt swung his sword over his head with all the power he could muster. What a miracle! With a crackling sound, the ice gave way and the water gushed out of the crack with a hiss. He had done it! Mahendra widened the crack. He managed to raise his head above the water and take a deep breath.

Just as he was inclined to relax, the realization that not only he, but Boloma behind him too was struggling to hold his breath hit him. This induced Mahendra to work again desperately. He had been taught that a leader should never unnecessarily sacrifice the lives of those who follow him. Even if he did not value his own life, he was duty bound to save Boloma. Mahendra reminded himself that, at that point of time, Boloma's life was more important than his own. Even in a sinking ship, the captain should leave last, only after all the others had been saved. But here, he knew that only if he paved the way, his friend could escape. He had to get out of the hole first if he were to save Boloma. Having raised his head above the water, Mahendra breathed in much-needed oxygen. Thinking that Boloma could also come out only if he emerged from the hole, he left the hole and lay on the frozen surface of the moat.

Ezhuth Aani

He could then hear Boloma struggling inside. In total darkness, unable to see anything, Mahendra extended his hand into the hole. Struggling to hold his breath, Boloma caught the former's hand and pulled it. Mahendra tried to lift Boloma, but the latter's weight was too much for him; thus, with both of them pulling each other, the ice on which Mahendra lay cracked and he too fell into the water. This was actually helpful as the hole which he had made became many times bigger. As there was a huge gap in the ice, Boloma was able to raise his head above the water and breathe freely.

Both had managed to escape certain death in the nick of time. Luckily for them, their noise was unnoticed because of the snowstorm. Mahendra egged Boloma on and encouraged him not to relax. They had no time! Both crawled over the frozen moat and crossed it. On the other side, there was a dense forest. For the time being, both felt relieved that they had reached a safe place. The snow continued to fall.

Suffocated and saved at the last minute, Boloma was completely unnerved. In addition, his pulse too was unsteady. His teeth chattered and his tongue parched; he couldn't speak. When he could mumble, he complained that he had nearly lost his life, trusting Mahendra. He could have stayed within his comfort zone.

"My friend, was your life as a slave worth living? What was there in it, to be lost? As soon as the empress's pregnancy was confirmed, they would have put an end to you. If you come with me, you have the chance to become free.

"If you were to surrender yourself to them now, they'll certainly kill you. So, remain silent and come with me. Had I wished, I could have abandoned you when you struggled in the water! But I shall never betray one who has reposed his faith in me. Let us proceed on our way with determination. We are in this together" said Mahendra.

In life, at various stages, we are given choices. Once we have chosen a path, we should never falter and think of other ways. That will not lead us anywhere. It was clear to Boloma that it was better to trust Mahendra and follow him. He made a resolve and summoned his strength and began to walk. Both of them knew that they would have some chance of survival only if they left the Imperial City soon. It was also clear that as soon as it dawned, a search warrant would be issued and a dragnet cast for them. They would be caught. Taking advantage of the snowfall, they walked along the water on the west of the Imperial City.

Snow was everywhere; on the lakes, and on the banks. And darkness was everywhere. They reached the place where the lakes cut across the inner wall of the Imperial City. Walking along known paths for some distance and through dense woods on hearing footsteps, they reached the northern wall. Luckily, the water here had not frozen. They could swim and cross the wall. Next was the inner city. Following the water they reached the outer wall of the inner city. Here, the snowfall was not heavy due to direction of the wind.

They crossed this wall too by their usual method of swimming. Now they had to reach the suburbs on the south, because Mahendra's horse and the best possibility of a hideout was there. He had developed a trust in the shopkeeper who had helped him. He realised that the latter was the only person who could help him at this stage. They decided that they should meet him and seek refuge before dawn.

The house was in the southern quarter of the inner city, while they were in the north of that city. If they were to walk the distance, it would be sunrise by the time they reached there. As they were pondering their options, a patrol party approached them.

Ezhuth Aani

"Where are you going? Who are you?" they asked. The patrol party consisted of three mounted soldiers. Boloma introduced himself. "I am the empress's personal assistant. We were on an urgent mission when we were caught in the snowstorm. In the confusion, our horses ran away."   So saying, Boloma showed them the letter with the imperial seal.

He refused to answer their question, "Where are you going?" Instead, he asked the warrior, "Will you obey the empress's order or not?" The warrior bowed his head in respect and said, "It is my duty to offer whatever assistance you require."

Immediately, Mahendra said, "Give us one of your horses." Once they mounted the horse, first, they pretended to go north, but after ascertaining that they were not being followed, they proceeded towards the south.

The shopkeeper was surprised and frightened when he saw them. But, realizing that it was not humane to let the shivering men stand outside, he invited them in. Boloma, who had all this while endured the cold, began to manifest its full impact as soon as he went inside. For hours, he ranted to himself deliriously.

The shopkeeper was a nice man. He allowed them to rest in a room, and provided a fire and hot food.   He then said, "I don't know who you are. But if I don't help you while you are struggling in this cold, I am not a human being."

Mahendra had been greatly affected physically and mentally, by the twists and tribulations of the past few days. He was happy that humanitarianism was still alive when he saw the generosity of the shopkeeper. In the royal palace, when each individual functioned with his or her own agenda, human life and humanity had been relegated to second place. When he saw the shopkeeper helping them without expecting anything in return, he was overwhelmed. Tears rolled down his cheeks. A man should not cry. But this was not the usual weeping. A man normally cries when he laments his losses and pities his own plight. But the tears that one sheds on seeing the deeds of selfless love for others do not belong to this category. These tears were the result of the feeling of oneness with the universal force. Gratefully, he narrated all the incidents that had taken place, from the beginning till the end. He needed to unload the burden in his heart by pouring out his grief to someone. The shopkeeper too, listened patiently to what he said.

Having heard how Mahendra set out on a mission to serve his country, how he got entangled in Liu Guan's unholy plan, how he was used as a reproductive bull and how he escaped from it all, the shopkeeper said, "You are lucky that at an early stage in your life, you have acquired such an experience."

"Every experience in life teaches us a lesson. The one who learns from it is intelligent. The others are fools" he added.

"You are now on the 'wanted' list of Liu Guan and the empress. In addition, if the emperor comes to know of this, not only you but they too will not be alive.

"You have two choices before you; one is to escape from China and go to Cambodia. If you choose this, you'll have to forget about Chinese aid to Cambodia. The other choice is to seek shelter with the dissidents of the regime in China. By means of this, not only can you save your life, but can also receive the aid you require for your country, provided they win..." he said.

He then advised them to take rest. Boloma had high fever with shivering, and kept mumbling incoherently for two days. When he regained his senses on the third day, he realised the magnitude of his achievement. He had laid the foundation for a life of freedom, something which he had never even thought of all his life. Having tasted freedom could he now retreat and go back to slavery? Never. He realised that if ever he went back, death was certain.

Leaving both of them inside, the shopkeeper went out on a reconnaissance mission.

"Is the security strong?" asked Mahendra. "Oh no. They will not search for you openly. That is because, if the plot lain by the empress and Liu Guan came to light, their own lives will be in danger. But, Liu Guan's spies may be anywhere. Therefore, you can never afford to slacken your vigil."

He then served them lunch. It consisted of roasted meat, rice and bean curd which they ate with chop sticks. He then told them, "In Chinese politics there'll be frequent clashes between uncles and nephews. After Hongwu Emperor died, Jianwen Emperor was overthrown by his own uncle Yongle. It is believed that Jianwen Emperor is still alive. In fact, many people believe that one day he will return and reclaim his throne. I am one of them."

He then said: "When Yongle died Honxi came to power; when he too died within two years, Xuande took over. But Honxi's brother Zhu Gokshu has begun to revolt. These rebels have chosen Shandong area as their centre and are raising and training an army. If you succeed in going to Shandong region, you can be sure of your safety. Moreover, if Zhu Gokshu's men capture the throne, you can certainly get aid for Cambodia."

"If we go there, will they not suspect us?" asked Boloma.

"If you go with my letter, they'll definitely receive you" he said.

"Who are you?" asked Mahendra.

"I am a loyalist of Jianwen Emperor. But right now I have work here. I shall join the rebels at the proper time" said he. He then went away on his business. The two of them conversed like long-standing friends.

Chapter 5

The next day, he dressed them up as traders. "It's fortunate that the temperature has risen. Otherwise the Grand Canal would have been frozen. It will then be difficult to travel through it."

Mahendra understood that he was trying to send them by boat. They went to the port near Beijing. There, the shopkeeper handed them over to a boatman known to him. He introduced them as silk merchants, who wished to go to Shandong. Mahendra's horse Khan was also sent with them. But as it was laden with bundles of cloth, it looked like an ass, and not the majestic high breed horse that it was. Yes. This disguise was to prevent anyone from suspecting from the look of the horse that they belonged to the royal family.

He knew that the long, broad Grand Canal was more than 1500 years old. More than 1,000 miles long, this canal connected five rivers including the Yangtze and Yellow Rivers. The Grand Canal was an engineering marvel. Various Chinese dynasties had renovated and extended this canal at different times, and changed it into the longest canal in the world. When the Mongolian Yuan dynasty chose Beijing as the Chinese capital, the canal was dredged and extended. Because of this, ships were able to navigate to Beijing city directly from the East China Sea. This canal had become a 'bridge' that connected north and south China. It helped to develop commerce and cultural ties and unify the country.

Yongle Emperor first made the Grand Canal deeper and wider, before implementing his ship-building project, and the construction of Forbidden City. This paved the way for timber and food such as grains and pulses for the workers, to be brought easily. It was necessary for the millions of workers and the soldiers who supervised them, to be fed.

They travelled through this marvelous Grand Canal. The journey lasted two days. They did not speak much with anyone. But, an elderly looking person came near them and repeatedly smiled at them. Mahendra too felt he was very familiar to him.

He began conversing with them. Tall and slim, he had tonsured his head. His moustache and beard, salt and peppered, were evidence that he was around fifty years of age. This appearance gave him a scholarly and respectful look. As he wore a light red dress, Mahendra thought that he must be a religious leader. His high cheek bones and narrow eyes identified him as of north Chinese descent.

He said, "This Grand Canal is evidence of the excellence of Chinese engineering. Nowhere in the world has such a canal been constructed. In the Shandong region, there is another marvelous innovation. Here, as the ground level rises, there will not be sufficient water for ships to pass, and they may run aground. To prevent this, pond locks have been built on both sides and the water level is made to rise when ships need to pass. Every day, this will be done a specific number of times to allow ships to pass. Those coming at other times will be made to wait.

"This engineering marvel, set up by the Chinese experts, was the first of its kind in the whole world. This was done by us 400 years ago."

He added, "You appear to be traders from outside."

Boloma then said, "We are working for a huge commercial establishment in Beijing."

He enquired more about them. Mahendra regretted ever having spoken to him; it was because, having uttered one lie it was now necessary to utter a hundred lies to cover up the first. As they did not know much about the silk trade, it was difficult to keep up

Ezhuth Aani

the conversation with him. At the same time, they were scared also to ignore him altogether. If they did so, they might invite suspicion not only from him but from the others around.

He understood that they were fake traders. But, he did not expose them. After that, to relieve them of their discomfiture, he spoke about other things. The ship reached a port in Linqing city. This was a commercial centre. Huge warehouses had been built here. Grains and clothes were stored here, and later distributed. There was also a granite quarry nearby and a store here. The stones and other building materials produced here were used for constructing large structures like the Forbidden City and the Great Wall.

As soon as the ship anchored, the passengers were disembarked. It was a levy point. Under the security of the armed guard, the employees of the customs department weighed all the goods and levied taxes.

Mahendra and Boloma faltered when answering questions such as "Where are you going?", "What goods are you taking?", and "Where will you stay?" Immediately, the elderly man intervened, and said, "These are my agents. I have had these goods brought for my shop in Shandong." He then thrust the insignia ring on the ring finger of his right hand in front of the official's face.

The moment he saw it, the official trembled, stood up and greeted him with great respect. After that the official stopped interrogating them. He then asked, "Did Liu Guan's men come here?" The officer said, "Yes. For the past two days they stayed here and searched all the boats. They left only this morning."

He then ordered, "Get ready two more horses for our journey. You can take the silk clothes that we've brought."

"Yes, Sir" said the official, and within three hours he made their travel arrangements. The ship left them and continued on its journey. "Who are you? Where are you taking us?" asked Mahendra. The latter said, "This is not a moment to waste time. Listen to me! Where is the empress' ring?"

Realizing that nothing could be hidden from him, Mahendra asked, "Are you Liu Guan's spy?" To that he replied, "Had I been so, I'd have arrested you right at the beginning! I'm on your side. Trust me."

The youth trusted him, and gave him the ring. The man said, "Though this place is under the control of the emperor during the day, in the night it'll be in the hands of Zhu Gokshu's rebels. The emperor's army is confined to its barracks at night. These officials come from the villages and perform their duties, but should they not return home to their families for the night? At night the villages are run by Zhu Gokshu's men. And my ring carries some currency here."

"Are you one of the rebels then?" asked Boloma. He had an unknown fear of this man and at the same time respect for him too. "No, no. I don't belong to their army. But I know Zhu Gokshu well."

He added, "If we travel five or six hours, we can reach Shandong. It is ruled by the rebel army. Liu Guan's men can never come there."

"I know that you are fleeing from Liu Guan. But, only if you tell me what you are going to do next, can I help you as best as I can."

The three of them raced through the forests on horseback while talking.

As they travelled it became dark. On the forest tracks, the snow began to fall. Suddenly, they realised that a tree lay across their path. Becoming aware of the obstacle on their track, the horses stopped abruptly, neighing loudly.

Ezhuth Aani

That very moment, a man fell from the tree. The elderly man who had jumped from his horse, rushed to the fallen man. He asked him, "Are you alone, or are there others with you?" A knife had pierced his throat. He kept moaning, without answering the former's question.

Losing his patience, he kicked the man in his groin. To the man who screamed "Ah", the elder said, "Will you tell me the truth or shall I…" As he raised his leg again, the man said, "Don't beat me! I'll tell you everything."

"Altogether ten people came with me. On our way it started snowing. Leaving me on guard on the tree, they have gone to a hut nearby."

"Who sent you?" asked the elder. As he remained silent, he raised his leg again. Hurriedly, the stranger said, "Liu Guan"!

The elder wrested the knife from his chest, and in a few seconds he lay still. Only then he noticed that another knife had pierced him.

"It is dangerous for us to remain here" he said. Immediately, going round the felled tree, they sped on their way on horseback.

A while later, the elder asked, "Who threw the other knife?"

"Myself" said Mahendra. The other said, "There are very few men who can throw a knife right on target in the dark, calculating sound and movement."

"This is one of the arts taught by my guru" said Mahendra.

"What is the name of the guru who taught you?" asked the elder.

With great reverence, he said, "Vajragnani." The elder leapt down from his horse, as though nearly falling off.

"Do you know my guru?" It was now Mahendra's turn to be surprised.

"Know? We are students of the same master! Not only that. Some of the most important secrets of my life are buried in his heart."

The youth asked him who he was. "I shall tell you who I am at the opportune moment. Right now I'll say only this. The person both of you stayed with, in Beijing, is one of the leaders of the rebels. Somehow he happened to like you. As I was also travelling to Shandong at the same time as you did, he asked me to watch over you. You know the rest."

After this, they journeyed silently. Travelling the whole night they reached a small cave. The elder said, "I know this area like the palm of my hand. This cave is several miles away from the main road. Nobody will come searching for us here. But, this is not my home. If you have faith in me, I shall take you with me and help you to the best of my ability."

The snowing had stopped, and the sun was sending his hot beams to the earth. The sky was clear blue, without a single streak of cloud. But the cold was still unbearable. Inside the cave, they lit a fire and warmed themselves. From a Lake nearby, the elder caught a fish using a spear and brought it to the cave. Roasted fish and a herbal drink drove away their fatigue in no time.

When they resumed their journey, they had to traverse a mountainous region. The ground gradually rose as the landscape

Ezhuth Aani

was dotted with rocks and hillocks. As they went north to south, the level kept rising. Both sides of the path were dense forests with trees with needle shaped leaves.

"This is the Tai mountain" said the Elder.

Then Boloma said, "People say that the Emperor and his family come here frequently on pilgrimage."

"Yes, my son. For those who follow the Tai religion, this is a sacred mountain. This is in the east of China. We consider five such mountains as sacred" said the Elder.

The ancient temple for the Tai mountain God, situated at the foot of the mountain was big. It was constructed on a 23 acre plot of land. There were five big halls and other rooms, with pillars the bases of which were shaped like turtles. The walls were decorated with paintings. They depicted exploits of the Tai mountain God.

From behind this temple 6000 steps led to the top of the Tai mountain, where there was another temple. From some places in the temple one could see the sunrise.

At the foot of the mountain too, there were many temples. As this area had been declared sacred, there was no armed presence here. Though the surrounding areas were under the control of the rebel army, there was no sign of them here.

The Elder said, "Though no armed men go about in this area openly, there is surveillance by all parties. So, let us not linger long here." They then went through the forest along the mountainside and reached another temple, and a monastery adjacent to it.

"This is my residence" said the Elder. They were then allotted a room.

All around the Tai mountain, there were temples, steps, festoons and arches, making the whole place appear sacred and worthy of worship. In the Elder's monastery too, many hermits were meditating.

When they were alone, Boloma asked, "I cannot understand you at all. You are a religious head. But, in the forest you did not hesitate to kill the spy; why?"

Laughing, he said, "Which was the knife that killed him — mine or Mahendra's? If I had not thrown my knife, would he have lived? Every time, every second, we must do what we have to do. There is no place for second thoughts here."

The Elder then gave them an explanation about the Tai religion. "The Tai religion is more than 2000 years old. It was widely prevalent here, even before the book called Daavodijing was written. This book was written by Lao-tzu. The basic belief of this religion is that all living things, from the insects to the gods, originated from one primordial force.

"This is similar to the Hindus' belief in the Brahman and the Mahayana belief of Buddha Dhatu. Several forms of this divine power are worshipped. Various rituals have become incorporated in course of time. Viewed from another perspective, the basic Tai beliefs are more about the way of living than about religion. Lao Tzu's writings tell us not only the philosophy of life, but also how to conduct wars, trade and so on. They deal with our way of living on earth, and do not pay much attention to life after death."

"In that case, what is the difference between the philosophies of Confucius and Tai?" asked Mahendra.

"Qufu, the birthplace of Confucius, is not far from here. The Tai religion focuses on how a man can ennoble himself by meditating on his inner self. Meditation does not mean being lost from the world. We call it poised awareness or mindfulness. Though the mind is focused, it observes things happening around us. It was because of this power of observation, that I was able to notice the man on the tree. Many of the wonders in China were made possible only by means of this 'self-observation'. Branches of knowledge such as acupuncture were formulated by those who had mastered themselves by these means.

"At the same time, Confucius teaches us how if each one of us performs his/her duties properly, the entire society can progress. That is, the Tai religion encourages individual upliftment. Confucius's philosophy is a treatise on how a disciplined society can progress well. The two of them teach us two different things. But they are not contradictory to each other. If China is a super power today, it is because of the social structure and organization taught by Confucius.

Boloma asked, "What place does Buddhism have in this?"

"A good question indeed. Buddhism talks about our destination after death. Tai philosophy talks about how man should conduct his life on earth. When Buddhism came to our country, it was easily assimilated into the existing beliefs. Mahayana's Buddha Dhatu, Tai religion's Chi and Hinduism's Brahman are all the same. Hence, Buddhism was easily adapted to the local Chinese customs and integrated with them. Therefore, there is no contradiction between these" said the Elder.

He then added: "I shall introduce you to many of the technologies that you need, in Shandong area itself. But, you cannot expect to receive Chinese military aid from the present government, because Liu Guan has now become your enemy. However, there are possibilities of a change of regime. Even otherwise, Liu Guan may lose his post and power. So, set aside that and focus on other work.

What you want is the knowledge of where to acquire explosives from, how to convert them into arms, and pumping water from a lower level to a higher one. I shall arrange for these technologies to be made available to you."

The next day, with Mahendra and Boloma in tow, he travelled many hours through hilly regions and reached a small building complex in the forest. That place had been cleared of many trees in the middle of the forest. With tall mountains on one side, and forests on the other, the complex was so positioned that it was not visible to outsiders.

Introducing himself to the guards there, the Elder took the youths to a small hut built inside. He introduced the man there, as the chief engineer.

Chapter 6

It was a fire arms factory. The cannon balls produced here, would supply the rebel army. The Chinese Emperor had several such huge factories. The rebels had just a couple of them. However, small armies that specialized in guerilla warfare and blitzkrieg, did not require as many arms as a traditional army would.

The Elder said, "There is a Chinese proverb. 'It is better to teach a man how to catch fish, rather than give him a fish to satisfy his hunger'. This will enable him to fish all his life, and not depend on others for a livelihood. Similarly, instead of supplying arms to you, I think it is better to teach you how to produce them."

He then took them to a long and high roofed shed nearby. There, several workers were busily engaged in combining various components of gun powder, mixing them with water, drying the mixture, stuffing it in metal tubes and then drying them again before sealing the tubes. A wick was also placed in the metal tubes containing the explosives. After showing them how the fire arms are made, he took them outside.

There, in the middle of a vast open ground, a huge brass tube had been placed. It was mounted on a platform in a slanting position facing the sky. He loaded a shell filled with explosive into the tube, lit the wick and ordered all of them to close their ears and lie on the ground. In a few seconds, with a loud 'boom' the shell flew into the sky burning, and crashed into the side of the mountain in the distance. The sound echoed repeatedly. A fire broke out at the place where it had landed on the mountain, lasted for some time and then went out.

When he asked them, "Have you seen such a weapon before?" Mahendra said "No" and Boloma said "Yes." Boloma was somewhat familiar with cannons. Explosives had been invented in China several centuries earlier. Chinese alchemists were experimenting with combinations of various medicines to find a way to immortality, when suddenly a medicinal mixture caught fire and exploded; only then did they realise that this was a new find. They also realised that this new product could be used not only for making fireworks, but also for military purposes.

During the rule of the Song dynasty, information about explosives was detailed in a military manual called Wujing Zongyao. Later, when the Mongolians over ran many parts of the world, there were several Chinese weapons experts in their army. The technology which they took with them began to spread to different countries. Islamic kings, and going beyond them, even kings in western countries, began to learn about this new military innovation and these deadly weapons. Due to this, revolutionary changes took place in the traditional methods of warfare. This technology had not reached Cambodia yet. There were rumors that King Parakrama Bahu VI, who ruled Lanka, had these arms.

"If saltpeter, sulfur and charcoal are mixed in a particular ratio, it becomes a powerful explosive. If it is ignited, it will explode with great force. There are some problems in this work. First, when we are preparing these, they should not explode amidst us.

"Because of this, some manufacturers mix these in water or other liquids to form a paste, place it in individual containers, and dry it again. Later, they would bury a wick in the centre of that container. When the wick was lighted, and the fire reached the container, it would explode. By this technique, we have time to escape."

"Initially, we fixed the explosive on arrows, lit the wick and shot the arrows. In course of time, we understood that with the impetus produced by the explosion within the container, it was possible to propel it to a great distance. If the brass tubes are fixed on the ground so that they do not move backwards, the impact will propel the shell forward. Due to this impetus, the shell will hurtle towards the target without the help of an arrow. Cannons are made in this way."

"Another step of progress in this is that, by using a small wick to produce an initial explosion to propel the shell forward, and then using that blast to ignite the main payload, we can make the shell strike the distant target with precision and explode near the target."

"Before manufacturing any dangerous weapon, you must understand one thing. Destruction can be wrought easily by anyone. But reconstructing damaged lives, relationships, and buildings is a far more difficult task. Hence, you must give me an assurance that you will use such weapons only for self-defense" concluded the Elder.

"Certainly! We are fighting only to preserve our lifestyle, culture and values, and not to enslave other races or countries", assured Mahendra.

He then asked, "Where do we get saltpeter from? Similarly where do we get sulfur from?" The Elder said, "We get saltpeter from the caves nearby. In these mountain caves, there are millions of bats and other mountain birds. Their droppings have solidified as deposits. From them we get the saltpeter. In the Battambang bat caves in Cambodia there are large deposits of saltpeter. Don't you know that?"

"Where are they?" asked Mahendra. He answered, "There is plenty of saltpeter in the caves in the Pnom Sampieu Mountain, also called the boat mountain near the Sanke River, west of the Tonle Sap Lake." Mahendra then asked, "How do you know this?"

For a long time, he was silent. His eyes seemed to roll upwards. It was clear that he was in the 'flashback' mode. "Those days... Then, Vajragnani and I used to go places together. How many secrets between us... how many memories..." said the Elder. His eyes moistened.

"Tell us at least now, who you are" said Mahendra.

"I'll tell you soon, my son."

He then added: "You are going to ask me where the sulfur deposits are. Wherever there is a volcano, there'll be sulfur. We can get sulfur at some distance from here. In Cambodia, there is a lake called Yeak Laom; it is the mouth of a volcano. On the banks of that lake there are plenty of sulfur deposits."

"If you manufacture these weapons in Cambodia, you can ensure a continuous supply of weapons. Initially though, removing and refining these deposits may appear difficult. But in a short time you can set up a continuous chain of production.

"Charcoal is obtained by burning trees under specific conditions. This can be acquired very easily." The Elder added, "One of you can stay back here, and learn how to obtain and purify these raw materials, and how to make weapons. The other can come with me, and I'll teach him details of the Chinese water management schemes."

Boloma said, "I'll stay here and learn about the production of explosives."

Mahendra said, "My friend, are you coming with me to Cambodia? So far we've not spoken about that. You are a Mongolian. Who is there in Cambodia for you? When we escaped, both of us had only one goal; that is, escaping from Liu Guan's custody. Now there is no compulsion that you should come with me. If you wish you may go your own way."

Ezhuth Aani

"Where will I go? I don't have anybody" said Boloma.

Mahendra said, "You are not slave to anyone. You don't have to be submissive to anybody. You have complete freedom to take the path you wish. You can return to Mongolia and live with your kin. If you come with me, all I can offer you is only war, and more war. At the end, my whole race may be annihilated. Would you like to be part of such a future?"

Boloma replied: "My friend, I was separated and taken away from my family in my childhood. They also destroyed my whole family. They deprived me of my manhood. Even after all this, I lived as a slave of my oppressors. Scared even to think of what was outside the circle they drew around me, I lived a boring, dry and meaningless life.

"Had you not opened my eyes, I would have fallen prey to Liu Guan's conspiracy and died. You saved me from this degenerate existence and enabled me to breathe the air of freedom. Accept me as your slave! I shall serve you all my life. Don't ask me to go back to my country. I shall come to Cambodia with you. I shall stand shoulder to shoulder with you and fight. If I die in the process I will embrace death willingly. Please accept me" said Boloma excitedly.

Mahendra too became emotional. He hugged Boloma. For a while, they remained silent, shedding tears. Then Mahendra said, "I'll be very happy to take you to Cambodia with me, on one condition."

"What is that?" asked Boloma.

"My friend, if you wish to come with me, you must come as a free man, as an equal, and as my dearest friend! You are not a slave to anyone. We shall get rid of this pernicious practice of one man being a slave to another! Though we were born in distant lands, fate has brought us together. Now you are my friend; my dearest friend! If you are prepared to accept this status, you are welcome" said Mahendra.

Overcome by emotion, both did not speak for a while. It was the Elder who broke the silence. "In that case, let Boloma stay here and learn the art of modern warfare. We'll go and attend to other things" he said, rising.

Both of them returned to his monastery, while Boloma stayed back.

The next day, he travelled with Mahendra again. After a whole day of traveling, they reached a river bank. They went some distance along the river. He said it was called the Hui River. The river snaked its way between mountains. When they crossed a bend in the path, what unfolded in front of Mahendra's eyes was a sight to behold!

On one side of the river, the setting sun reddened the sky, and the hills on that side along with the trees on them and their leaves, all shone with a reddish green tinge. The red sky was reflected in the waters of the river. Against this background, on the other side of the river, on the banks were huge windmills arranged in a long line along the River. As it was a valley, the wind always blew fast due to the funnel effect.

On a tall vertical pole, huge horizontal sails were fixed in all directions like the sun's rays. These sails, similar to the ones used in ships, were made of cloth and were fixed to wooden frames. They were so shaped that they were narrow near the center and broader as they neared the periphery. They were angled to make them bear the full force of the wind. The vertical axle kept rotating all the time, either clockwise or anticlockwise, depending on the direction of the wind. However, this axle was connected to another horizontal axle by toothed wheels in a transmission joint in a way that no matter which direction the vertical axle rotated, the horizontal axle always rotated in the same direction. A huge wheel was fixed to the horizontal axle which protruded out till the centre of the river, and many buckets were fixed on it. When the buckets came down they scooped up the water from the river, and discharged it when they went up. To receive the water thus hauled up, there was a funnel fixed at the top.

The water scooped up by each such wheel of buckets flowed through a channel into a central duct. This duct was placed on pillars constructed in the middle of the river and high above it. Running several miles, this duct was constructed with a gradient, by making the pillars progressively shorter. Even so, the shortest pillar too was several yards above the level of the river. Extending as far as the eyes could see, small outlets were built on both sides of the duct, and they carried the water to a network of irrigation canals on the banks of the river, taking the water towards the fields. Flaps were provided to open and close the outlets on the sides of the central duct. The entire system could be operated from ground level.

The water carried by these canals helped to make fertile the paddy fields that stretched as far as visible to the naked eye. "What do you think of this method?" asked the Elder.

"This is a world wonder!" said Mahendra.

"It is not a wonder. It is something which we had set up to fulfill our needs. It is a method we have adopted to irrigate lands that are on a higher level than the river. We have been able to complete such large schemes only because of the social ethic of Confucius. Right from childhood, we've been taught to value social needs above our own individual likes and dislikes. That is why we have been able to implement such schemes.

"In your Cambodia also large irrigation schemes had been built. This was possible only because people considered the king as the Bodhisattva according to Mahayana Buddhism, and as an incarnation of Lord Vishnu according to Hinduism, and therefore whole-heartedly undertook the king's service as their own. But now, people have become confused with the spread of Theravada Buddhism."

"Why didn't our engineers use wind power?" asked Mahendra.

"The method of pumping out water through windmills using wind power was followed not only in China but also in countries like Persia and in Harshavardan's Kushan Empire. The Hindus worshipped wind as the God Vaayu. But we consider the wind as a natural force.

"Your engineers had worked out the process of supplying water to Angkor city from the Kulen Hills through rivers like the Siam Reap. As the Mekong River was frequently flooded, they established their cities on land that was on higher ground than that river. They would not have envisaged that a severe drought such as the one that prevails now would occur."

"If water can be raised to a very high level by the thrust of the wind power, it will then become very easy to irrigate lands that are on a higher level than the river.

"Necessity is the mother of invention. Details about the scientific progress made in various places can be collected and exchanged only when people travel to different parts of the world. It is by means of such exchanges that mankind is able to progress collectively. Otherwise, we would still be hunting in the woods!" said the Elder.

He then took him to a village nearby. The workers, who operated these windmills and regulated the irrigation of lands, and their families, lived there. In one of those houses lived the chief official. Facilities were made for Mahendra to stay in that house.

The Elder said: "The government pays these workers, from the tax remitted by the farmers who are benefitted by this scheme. In your country, tanks and canals have not been maintained properly; they have been silted because manual labor has been obtained voluntarily in the name of the royal service. Every time there is a flood there is erosion of soil and subsequent precipitation in the canals."

Later, that official taught him minute details regarding wind technology. Mahendra stayed there for about a week and learnt all that he needed to know. Until they returned to the monastery, Mahendra and the Elder interacted as though they had been friends for a long time. In life, on many occasions friendships develop despite age differences, because of mutual understanding. They engaged in prolonged discussions several times. On one such occasion, Mahendra said, "You have been very friendly with me. But you have not disclosed your identity yet." The Elder gazed at him for a long time and then asked, "Do you know how Yongle Emperor came to power?"

"No" said Mahendra.

Chapter 7

"**H**ongwu Emperor drove away the Mongolian Yuan dynasty and established the Ming dynasty. Before he died, he declared his elder son as the Princely heir. Unfortunately, the prince died, and the emperor appointed his grandson as his heir.

"The grandson Jianwen ruled for four years. One night..."

His eyes rolled up, and his facial expressions changed dramatically, indicating that he was recollecting a very tragic experience again. His voice too was feeble, sorrowful to listen to, and came from afar as though he was in a dream world. Every word was measured and uttered with long pauses in between.

"Yes. That night! The incident took place twenty five years ago; but is still evergreen in my mind. A man was asleep; everything around him was on fire. Because of the heat he rises, disturbed from his slumber. Only then does he realise that the fire had spread all around him! He realises that he would have to leave the place immediately, if he wanted to save himself. What about the two lives beside him? It was too late for them! Yes; they had been charred in the fire. The flames had consumed them before they could wake up. He was compelled to flee, leaving his two beloveds behind! Why didn't he kill himself? Why didn't he die along with his family?"

When he said this, his eyes moistened. Tears rolled down his cheeks. After a minute's silence, he sobbed like a child. Mahendra, who had all this while seen him as an elderly scholar, now for the first time saw him as an ordinary sensitive man prone to human emotions.

He said, "In the Nanjing palace there was a mysterious fire. The world believed that Jianwen Emperor, the empress and their child died in that fire."

Ezhuth Aani

"But all three did not die. The emperor escaped with minor injuries. Subsequently, the emperor's uncle who usurped power came to rule under the name of Yongle. What happened after that, you know."

"In that case you are...?" asked Mahendra.

"The wretched soul who could not save his family and his kingdom, stands right in front of you" he said. "You? Are you Jianwen Emperor?" asked Mahendra, and was about to touch his feet in obeisance.

Preventing him, the Elder said, "I am not worthy of this respect. I am a king without a kingdom." He then asked Mahendra, "You did not ask me for any proof that I am Jianwen Emperor?"

"I believe you implicitly" said he.

"Trust is one thing. Fact is another. Anybody can say that he is the emperor. You should verify what you hear and then only accept it" the Elder said. "Alright. I demand proof that you are indeed the emperor" asked Mahendra.

He showed him the insignia ring on his right hand. He asked, "Did you wonder why the soldiers who interrogated you in the port did not arrest you?"

"In that case, do they know who you are?" asked Mahendra.

"They know that there are many rebels here. These rebels are faithful either to me or to the present emperor's uncle. There is great respect for my insignia ring. But very few actually know who I am. Now you are one of them. I revealed the truth to you only because I happen to respect and trust you greatly."

"What happened then?" asked Mahendra.

"My grandfather had given me a small casket. He had told me to open it when I was in great danger. As soon as I escaped from the fire, I opened that casket. It contained a shaving knife, a monk's saffron dress, and maps indicating the tunnels through which one could escape from the Nanjing palace. I tonsured my head, wore the monk's dress and left the palace. My wanderings which began that day continue till today.

"Unable to determine whether I had escaped or perished in the fire, Yongle cast a net for me. As there were rumors that I had gone abroad, he sent spies wherever his navy went. But he was not able to find me. He knew that until he found and killed me, the sword of Damocles would hang above his head. Yongle Emperor, who ruled the world, had no peace of mind. He did not get this peace till his death.

"To escape from my shadow, he changed his capital from Nanjing to Beijing. He built the huge fortified palace. But, deep down in his mind he had the fear that someday I would return. During his last days, he suspected everyone around him. There was an accidental fire in the Forbidden City. Thousands of people, including several of his mistresses were killed in that fire or the rage that followed. Nevertheless, he died before he could find me."

"How did you escape the spies of the Chinese emperor and where did you hide?" asked Mahendra. "I knew that it was impossible to escape from Yongle's net and remain in hiding in China. That is why I went in search of my childhood friend, Vajragnani. We had studied under the same guru. Later, we went our own ways. I concentrated on ruling my country; and he, on ruling his mind. I became the emperor of China. He returned to Cambodia and set up his monastery and school there. His fame spread far and wide. Some of the princes from my own country had attended his school and returned. Thus, we had maintained our contact to a certain extent. When he learnt that I was in danger, he sent me a message. It was that any time I was welcome to stay with him."

"Initially, I was hesitant to leave my country. But, in course of time, I realised that it was difficult to survive in the midst of the military checks and constraints. I went to Cambodia and found Vajragnani. Even there, I had to avoid being seen by the Chinese spies. As per his advice, I hid myself in the Battambang mountain caves."

Having said this, he once again went into his dream world. "Yes. How sweet that time was! Having lost my Kingdom, and orphaned by the loss of my family, my mind had become a desert benumbed of all feelings. But, I realised only then that even in a dead tree there will be fresh shoots deep inside.

"Vajragnani had appointed a Cambodian princess to take care of me." Saying thus, he fell silent.

"My son, do you know what love is? Have you experienced love?" he asked.

"No, my lord! I fell a prey to the empress' lust. But that was physical hunger, lust! I have never experienced the tender feeling of love" said Mahendra.

"Only those who have experienced it will know! I had thought that it had died in me. But after I began to interact with that lady, gradually there was a change in me! Initially, I considered her as a balm for my loneliness. She too regarded me with sympathy and nothing more. But, as the days passed I changed even without my own knowledge. I, who should have spent my life as a monk, gradually began to yearn for her visits. Her mischievous speech and debating skill impressed me greatly. More than this, she was a divine beauty. I have never seen such a beauty in this world. There was a time when all the best women in the land were at my feet in my harem. But, this Cambodian princess had the combination of intellectual strength and physical beauty, which the ladies in my harem did not."

"What happened then?" asked Mahendra.

"She did not know who I was. She knew me only as Vajragnani's friend. She was ten years younger than me. Nevertheless, I do not know what she found in a destitute man like me. Feelings of love blossomed in both of us simultaneously. What next? When two minds unite, will there be any hurdle for physical union? Not at all. Hence, we became one, physically and mentally. However, I gave her nothing but sorrow. For giving herself wholly to me without knowing who I was, what could I give in recompense? Status? Money? I did not have anything! She suffered because of me. Having lost herself to me, I did not give anything to her. On the contrary, as a symbol of our love I gave her a child! What a wretch I am! Did I give her only a child? No. During childbirth I took away her life too!" He sobbed inconsolably.

"In that case, where is that child now?" asked Mahendra.

"I do not know! The child who is the heir to the thrones of China and Cambodia lives today as an orphan, ignorant of who its parents are."

Once again, the emperor began crying. For a few seconds there was an uneasy calm. Mahendra did not know how to console the Elder. He was a man; that too one elder to him. The youth had never seen a man crying like this in his life. The latter also felt uncomfortable for having forgotten his status and age, and for crying like a child in Mahendra's presence.

In a few seconds he collected himself and returned to normal. He then said, "In life, many incidents happen in spite of us. If we keep thinking of them we may lose focus on present and future events. Not only myself, but you too have several duties. To fulfill those duties, we must keep our personal emotions under control. Your country is teetering on the edge of destruction. Similarly, my land also is expecting big changes. There is the danger of not only the Mongolians in the north, but countries west of the Islamic world, turning their attention towards the east. To face these challenges it is necessary to build a very strong China. I have doubts as to whether the present emperor is capable of carrying out this task.

"For a long time, I had the desire to become the emperor again. But, as days passed I gradually acquired the mental maturity and the pragmatism to accept the ground reality. At my age, and being childless, I feel that instead of my capturing the throne again, it would be better for a youth who could carry forward my policies, to come to power."

"Who is the youth who has earned your trust and regard? You say you are childless. Where is the child born to you and the Cambodian princess now?" asked Mahendra.

"She is a girl. But I have no answers to questions like 'Is she alive?' and 'Where is she?' Moreover, history has no record of a lady having ruled China. Although the empress may have wielded power in a traditional, ceremonial way, they have never really had any authority."

He added, "There has been no other lady in the whole world better than my beloved, who possessed a sharp wit and beauty combined. I would not like the daughter of such a lady to be the slave of a man and remain a dullard fulfilling only his physical needs. I want her to be equal to men and share their life equally. Rather than be a dressed up doll called empress, she should be an independent lady even if she has no identity of her own." When he said this, his face lit up with pride about his beloved.

Mahendra then asked, "Who would you like to rule China?"

"Just as I was driven away by my uncle Yongle, the present emperor will also be driven away by his uncle, who will then rule the country! This is what is called *Karma*" said the Emperor.

"Yongle Emperor loved his younger son Zhu Gokshu very much. Just like him, the son had won several battles and proved his mettle; the emperor loved him. Later due to a minor misunderstanding, Zhu Gokshu was sent to Shandong. When Yongle died, Zhu Gokshu claimed his right to the throne and rebelled. Under the circumstances, he desired my recognition and blessings. I too favoured that. Now, the rebels faithful to both of us have come together. Soon, they will move towards the capital" said the emperor.

Chapter 8

He then detailed his dream. "When I came to power, I engaged myself in building a strong China and placing it on a pedestal in the world. Before my dream could materialize, Yongle came to power. To a certain extent, he followed my policies. The Chinese navy was expanded, and messengers under the leadership of Zheng He were sent in all directions by sea. But, he indulged in extravagant and expensive schemes. Having expanded the navy, huge ships were sent to various countries carrying gifts. Commerce is one thing. Exchanging gifts is another. His schemes could not be sustained for long. They would not be economically viable. They would empty the coffers. Not only that. He shifted the capital to Beijing. He built the Forbidden City at great expense. People were dissatisfied with his actions. These schemes were executed by using millions of people as slaves."

"After Yongle's death, his descendants have been engaged in activities quite opposed to his policies. Just as the tortoise withdraws its limbs into its shell, these descendants have been vigorously engaged in retracting China to within its boundaries. Though the consequences of this policy may not be known now, the impact of their foolishness will be understood by the future generations."

"It is rumored that Zhu Gokshu has passed away" said Mahendra. "He was arrested and imprisoned. What happened thereafter is not known. Our rebellion is not confined to individuals like me or Zhu Gokshu. This is a rebellion for China's heart; for China's future; for the well-being of the future generations. It is a rebellion that will decide whether China is going to shrink inwards, or whether, like the dragon, it is going to become a super power respected by the whole world. If our rebellion fails, its consequences will push China back 500 years in the world arena before it takes up its rightful place."

He continued: "China was once the most progressive country in the world. We were unsurpassed in science, medicine and military might. When we were a super power, the western world was in the iron grip of the Christian church, a descendant of the Roman Empire. But, because of the sudden invasions of the Mongolians, our scientific inventions were taken to all parts of the world. Thus, knowledge began to spread to the western world.

"Ideas of a renaissance began to appear among the people of those lands, who had hitherto lived in a dark period. They have started searching for paths come to the eastern countries. They are trying to improve upon our own inventions and produce better weapons and faster ships. Someday if not today, they will try to bring the whole world under their control. Are we ready to face these challenges? Because of the narrow-minded outlook of the present government, we will be totally unprepared to deal with the changes in the world that are going to take place. Prevention is always better than cure. If a cat closes its eyes, the world does not end, says the proverb. That is why there should be a change of government."

These passionate words kept echoing in his ears repeatedly. Yes. The plight of Cambodia was also the same. Any country that basked in the glory of its past and rested on its laurels would be in the same position. He understood very clearly, that in this changing world all cultures that did not engage and adapted to the events taking place in the other countries, and anticipate changes likely to occur in the future, would be destroyed unable to withstand the impact of foreign influences. He was happy that, though late, he had at least now understood the political changes taking place in the other countries.

The Elder then said, "As far as you are concerned, consciously or otherwise, you have become the enemy of the empress and Liu Guan. If you and Boloma are allowed to escape, they will lose their grip on a great secret of theirs. Hence, you cannot go back to Beijing seeking the emperor's help. And if you don't leave China soon, their spies will try to eliminate you.

"The only way open to you is to align yourself with the rebels. We've already shown you the technology you require. If we succeed in our mission, though we may not be able to help you by sending an army, we'll help at least by providing weapons."

Subsequently, both of them travelled along the mountain tracks for two days. The path had tall hillocks and forests on both sides. It later curved up a mountain. They journeyed on a narrow track, one behind the other on their horses. Though there was a slight drizzle, neither the men nor their horses paid any heed to it. Mahendra's horse, Khan had always been equal to any work given to it. The emperor's horse too, was equally good. They travelled through forests, along mountain paths and even over small streams effortlessly.

When they reached the summit of the mountain, the Elder said, "Mahendravarma! What do you see before you?" A wonderful scene presented itself before their eyes. In the valley adjacent to the mountain, were rows of tents stretching as far as the eye could see. Beside the tents mounted warriors were seen to be riding everywhere.

All of them were engaged vigorously in their own respective tasks. Discipline was seen everywhere! Order everywhere! Yes. It was a military encampment. On one side, mounted cavalry were engaged in their work; on another, the infantry was on a parade; on yet another side, the men in charge of the cannons were checking them; thus, everywhere military preparations were in full swing. On the surrounding tall hillocks guards were on duty watching in all directions looking out for approaching enemies. The spies in the forests around the area kept moving in and out of the barracks. Mahendra had never seen such a huge army.

"Do you know that they are aware of our watching them?" asked the Elder, surprising the youth.

"In that case, why did they not stop us?" asked Mahendra.

"I have already signaled to one of them. They know that I use this path" said the Elder. He then clapped his hands. From between the trees two men came and stood respectfully. He showed them his insignia ring and ordered, "Take us to the camp."

They were then taken down along the mountain path and admitted in to the camp.

"One can't keep such a huge army idle for long. The men will begin to move soon" said the Elder.

"Why not now?" asked Mahendra.

"An army does not consist merely of soldiers. It can move only after ensuring the supply of arms, food and water, and their transport. Moreover, it is easier to begin and conduct the offensive after the winter ends," said the emperor. He continued: "Some time back, we began fighting before we were fully prepared; as a result, we had to meet with failure and losses. We have regrouped. We are not willing to make the same mistake again."

Later, they were taken to the main barrack. On learning of their arrival, about ten men emerged from the tent and stood in obeisance. "Long live the emperor" said one of them.

"Comrades, here no one is king or emperor. All the leaders are comrades. Ours is a joint leadership. All important decisions are taken unanimously after debate and deliberation" said the emperor, and introduced Mahendra to them.

Ezhuth Aani

"This is Mahendravarman. He is one of the Cambodian princes. He has come seeking our friendship and support to protect Cambodia from the many dangers it faces. I have assured him of our help if we win. I hope to find my lost daughter through him. Friends, even if I happen to die in this war, you must keep my promise that I would help him."

"Thy will be done" said they in chorus. Though a joint leadership was their policy, Mahendra understood that the emperor's words commanded special respect. The Elder then took him to his abode. Boloma had already come there. The Elder took them to a separate room. "Tomorrow you shall leave for Cambodia. At an opportune moment, we shall send you the help you wanted" he said.

Mahendra then said to Boloma, "If you wish you may stay here. It is not too late to change your mind, even now. If you come with me I can give you only sorrow and suffering."

Boloma replied, "My friend, since the Chinese soldiers captured me, I have not had an identity or a life of my own. Only after my association with you, I acquired an identity for myself, and self-respect. Rather than being an anonymous slave here, it is better that I dedicate myself to the struggle to preserve a nation's independence, along with you."

The Emperor then said, "As soon as I saw Boloma, I understood that he had leadership qualities. At different stages in their lives, people are crippled by their circumstances. But, if they are given the necessary training and directions for their progress, they can become great leaders and realise their full potential. We have given Boloma training in producing fire arms and also in their use. Let him accompany you and set up the first Cambodian cannon battery. You will be surprised at his efficiency."

Mahendra embraced Boloma. "My friend, you should come with me and contribute your share to our struggle" he requested.

Chapter 9

The emperor then gave Mahendra a sealed envelope. "Mahendravarma, you should give this letter to my respected friend, Vajragnani, and do as he bids you" he said.

Mahendra kept the letter carefully. They then planned their journey. The emperor said, "Liu Guan's men would have intruded into many places. Hence, you will have to be disguised." He added, "If you travel by land through China, you'll certainly be caught. Therefore, I'll first send you to the peninsular country of Joseon (Korea). The influence of the Ming emperor does not extend to Joseon. From there, you can escape to Japan. Then, you can go to Cambodia by sea."

Subsequently, both of them tonsured their heads and were dressed as Buddhist monks. The time came for them to leave.

The Emperor knew that they would not meet again in their lives. But, what could be done? It is a fact of life that people need to go their own ways at certain times. However deeply they loved one another when they were together, they knew well enough that they could not be together permanently. The emperor's duty was to his country, while Mahendra's was to his own country. Though he loved the youth as his own son, he knew that it was imperative for him to allow the youngster to proceed on his own path. Similarly, though Mahendra considered the Elder equal to his own father and guru, his first priority was to fulfill his duty to his country. However much they tried to control their minds, they were not made of stone! They too had tender feelings in their hearts for each other.

If this was the case of these two, Boloma's state was worse. It was not easy to leave forever, the land which he had considered as his own from as far back as he could remember. Above all, it was very painful for him to part from the one Chinese man who had, for the first Mytime in his life, treated him compassionately as a human being. All three of them knew that the possibilities of one or even all of them being killed in the process of carrying out their duties were very high. However, life had to go on. They controlled their emotions, and hugged one another lovingly.

After a few minutes' silence, the Emperor said, "Wish you the very best, my sons. Dedicate yourself to fulfilling your duties. You will certainly succeed."

Then, along with two guides who were waiting for them, they journeyed towards Joseon. After several days' continuous travel through forest tracks, they finally reached the coast. The place which they reached was called Weihai. It was a natural port. There was a small island at the estuary of this gulf, which had a rocky shore. Their guide told them, "There is a naval base belonging to the Ming dynasty in this port. Therefore, we cannot approach it directly. We have to travel further north, along the coastline. People faithful to us are running a clandestine boat service there. They will take you to an island called Sudong. From there, our friends will take you to a place called Boryeong in Joseon. Then, go to a port named Busan, which is on the east coast of the peninsular country. From there you can board merchant ships, and reach Cambodia either directly or via Nippon."

The so-called friends of the rebels were in reality Japanese pirates. The Ming government had sent a special naval contingent to Weihai to eliminate these pirates. However, the pirates shifted their activities to the north of Weihai. The government and the pirates played a game of cat and mouse but it had no impact whatsoever on the smuggling operations.

Not having a navy of their own, the Chinese rebels fulfilled their maritime needs through these pirates. This was an uneasy symbiotic relationship. The pirates knew that, the moment the

Ezhuth Aani

rebels won power, they would turn against them. Nevertheless, they needed the support of the rebels to set up a base on Chinese mainland.

The pirates believed that Mahendra and Boloma were indeed Buddhist monks. About ten years earlier, the Joseon government had taken stringent action against them. Their headquarters located on an island called Tsushima, on the east of Joseon, had been completely wiped out. Subsequently, the pirates called 'Wokou' had shifted their activities to the west of Joseon. After the unexpected defeat, many of them had become Buddhists. They did not trouble Mahendra and Boloma who were dressed as Buddhist monks. On the contrary, they not only disembarked them safely at Boryeong, but took them by land to the port of Busan.

Huge merchant ships had anchored at the port of Busan. They were engaged in trade with India and the Arabian Gulf countries. As soon as they reached Busan, the two of them discarded their robes, and claiming that they had to go to Cambodia on business, procured their places in the ship that was to sail next. After reaching Angkor after several months of travel they went straight to Vajragnani's ashram.

Mahendra was stunned when he heard the latter's question, "Have you brought it?"

PART – III

Chapter 1

The port city called Thennaavaram or Thevan Thurai in Tamil and Devinuwara in Sinhala was decorated by the glitter of the sun's rays. The gold and copper roof of the temple, the most important structure in the city, scattered the rays of the sun in several directions. There were separate temples constructed for Siva, Vishnu and Ganesh. The temple for Vishnu, called in later years by some Buddhists as Uppuluvan, and considered by some others as the incarnation of Avalokateswara, was the centrepiece. A large rock jutted out into the sea in this place, the southernmost point of the island of Lanka. On the east side of the rock was the port. Adjacent to the port was a large commercial centre.

All the passengers were 'checked' at the customs post. A man holding the post of 'maha panditha' examined their belongings and levied tax. Goods brought for trading were taxed more. The twenty monks, Satthama Govida, and Silaavi Sudhdhi were exempted from customs formalities. Later, they were taken to the nearby Kihireli Pirivena. They were able to refresh themselves and rest there, after the long sea voyage.

The next day they travelled to the Kaarakkal Pirivena. The small town of Kaarakkal was on the banks of the River Kelani Ganga, also called Kalyani. Vibheeshana was worshipped as the guardian deity of the town, and a temple had been built for him. Many poets have mentioned the town of Kaarakkal in accordance with the literary tradition prevailing then, called Sandesaya or bird messenger. Many works had also been written, imagining birds like swans, peacocks, ducks, cuckoos, and so on, going as messengers of praise. The birds would fly over the towns in a particular route extolling the virtues of the town as well as the hero/ heroine. They had been written in the style of Kalidasa's Meghdoot.

They went to the Samandhakooda Mountain (Adam's Peak) on the way to Kaarakkal. As they went on foot from Devinuwara, this journey lasted several days. The natural scenes of the pleasant and fertile island of Lanka induced in the young monks a mixture of peace and expectation. As far as they were concerned, this was the sacred soil of Buddhism. Wherever they went, the place appeared like a hermitage to them. Hillocks, rivulets with water flowing placidly, waterfalls, luscious grasslands green as ever, rain forests and the colorful wild flowers – what a country! Everywhere was green. Different shades of green merged seamlessly to produce a collage of immense beauty. Isn't this Paradise on Earth? As they proceeded, hitherto unseen wonders captivated their eyes! Not only was this a feast for the eyes. The ears too were enthralled with the joyous sounds of nature, the bird songs, the trumpets of elephants, the bellows of deer, the screams of peacocks...and all the animals seemed to live in harmony. And the noise of the wind rustles of the leaves and the gurgles of cascading waterfalls seemed to add to the serenity of the land.

Walking all the way, they reached a tributary of the River Kalyani. From there, they could see the Samandhakooda Mountain. Satthama Govida asked, "Would you like to climb the hill?" Eagerly, all of them consented.

The Samandhakooda Mountain had significance for many religions. The Buddhists called it Samandhakooda in honor of Saman the Bodhisattva. They believe that Lord Buddha's left footprint could be seen at the summit of the hill. The Hindus call this hill Trikoodam or Sivanolipatham. There are details about this hill in the Ramayana. The Hindus believe that the footprint at the top of the hill is that of Lord Siva.

The monks climbed the hill with difficulty, starting in the afternoon and gradually scaling the heights overnight. It was a tiresome climb and they rested intermittently. But it was worth all the effort. As the next day dawned, they were wonder-struck by the sunrise. It was a glorious sight! Beyond the clouds, and behind the mountain peaks, the sun spread its red beams in all directions and decorated the entire sky. On the ground, the shadow of the hill was triangular. It was a sight to behold.

Having enjoyed the sunrise, they reached Ratnapura through forest tracks. In this city, famous for its gems since ancient times, gems could be found almost everywhere you dig! What natural resources this country had! As they travelled through forest tracks, they observed elephants bathing in several places. They had to cross six hills to reach Ratnapura.

Days passed in this slow paced heaven, enjoying nature's scenic bounty and meditating. As a warrior, it was a trying time for Adithya. Having set out to obtain military aid for his country, here he was with the other young monks, blissfully ignorant of the passage of time and wandering like this; he was surprised at himself. When he thought of why Vajragnani had sent him on such a futile mission, he was very angry and frustrated with him. At the same time, he was not unaware of the fact that the great man would not have sent him here without a proper purpose. Adithya was waiting for an opportune moment to approach King Parakrama Bahu. Will it ever come?

They next reached Vanarathna Thera's pirivena at Kaarakkal. The Kaarakkal Pirivena, situated on the banks of the River Kalyani, was on a rock near the river. More than a hundred young monks were studying here. However different his motive was, the spiritual peace of the Kaarakkal pirivena had begun to permeate him. The memory of Mandagini, which had possessed his mind fully, now began to decrease slowly. Time is a great healer that can cure the disease of love. But, spirituality and religion too, can be soothing balms to the mind. This was what was taking place in Adithya's life too. But the life of a trainee monk was not what he came here for. His main objective was to fulfill his duty towards his motherland.

Everything else should take only second priority, he kept telling himself often.

Chapter 2

It was then that unexpectedly he had an opportunity to meet the king. Vanarathna Maha Thera had been invited to preside over a celebratory event at the Sunethradevi Pirivena. This pirivena had been built in memory of the king's mother, Sunethradevi. As it received royal protection and patronage, it acquired a great reputation within a short time. Students flocked to it from all corners of the country, competing with one another to study there. It was common to find not only the students competing to go there, but even the others longing to receive an invitation to participate in the festivities taking place there. These periodic celebrations drew various sections of people, such as monks, princes, and soldiers. They used these festivals as a platform to exhibit not only their scholarship, but also their courage and skill in warfare. They came from all over the island. Education and skill have no language!

Several literary works were launched, not only in Sinhala but also in Tamil. Many poems in the Sandesaya tradition were published during such festivities. As the king had given equal importance to both Buddhism and Hinduism, both were honoured here without any discrimination. For the learned, education is the language, and skill is the religion. Vanarathna also travelled with his disciples to Sunethradevi, situated at a place called Pepiliyana.

For the Buddha Jayanti (Vesak) celebrations, the whole country wore a festive look. It was on the full moon day in the month of Vishaka that Lord Buddha was born, attained enlightenment and attained Nirvana. This is a very special day in the Buddhist calendar. Everywhere, the streets were decorated with festoons. Oil lamps were lit in all the houses. People thronged the Buddha viharas, day and night, to chant the Pirith and to worship.

In the Sunethradevi Pirivena, Buddha Jayanti was celebrated that whole week as a grand festival. There would be worship, cultural programs, and plays based on the Jataka stories every day. Ladies in white would hold lighted clay lamps in their hands, and go in a procession in rows before the statue of the Buddha; some would bring lotuses, and place them at the feet of the Buddha. The whole place would have a spiritual aura about it.

There was stiff competition among the various pirivenas on staging plays based on the Jataka stories. Though not one of the Jataka stories, Vanarathna Maha Thera had selected for the foreign students, a popular Theragatha story called Angulimala Sutta. Some weeks passed, with the students rising in the morning, finishing their ablutions, cleaning the place, attending the Tripitaka classes, and after meditation in the evening, rehearsing the play.

Noticing Adithya's dominant personality, Maha Thera cast him in the main role of Angulimala. Angulimala was a cruel robber. He killed mercilessly the citizens of a place called Savaththi, in the country of Kosala ruled by King Pasenadi. Fearing him, people from the neighboring villages evacuated and went elsewhere, and hence those villages were deserted. He had severed the fingers of the people whom he killed and wore them as a garland. Though the people, scared of him, travelled in groups of ten, twenty, thirty and so on, they still could not escape from his attacks.

It was under such circumstances, that the Shakyamuni Lord Buddha stayed in a monastery called Anatha Pindika nearby. As was his custom, he began to go around daily with a begging bowl seeking alms. Noticing Lord Buddha going along the path where Angulimala resided, the people advised the former not to go there. As he continued to go his own way, the people pleaded with him to return. But, he did not pay heed, and continued on his journey.

When he observed Lord Buddha coming towards him, Angulimala was furious. He took his knife, bow and quiver of arrows, and rushed towards the Buddha. But however fast he ran, he could not catch up with the Buddha. He then told the Buddha, "O' saint, stop. Though I ran very fast, I have not been able to catch you. I have stopped. But you are still going fast."

To this, the Buddha replied, "I stopped long ago. You are the one who is still running."

"How is that? You continue to walk. I'm standing in the same place" said Angulimala.

"I stopped long ago. I stopped harming other creatures completely long ago. You are the one who continues to rotate in the cycle of cruelty" said the Buddha.

The moment he heard this, there was a big transformation in Angulimala's thinking. From that day, he abandoned violence and changed himself into a monk dedicated to the service of the Buddha.

This is the story of Angulimala. This was dramatized by Adithya and the other student monks. On the day their play went on stage, they were in for a pleasant surprise. Yes! King Parakrama Bahu VI was to visit the Sunethradevi Pirivena that day. Along with the king, his family too attended the play.

As soon as the play was over, the king stood up. He lauded Adithya for his excellent performance, presented him with a saffron robe, and the Kaarakkal Pirivena with the documents for lands vested on the temple as gifts. He also requested Vanarathna Thera to come to the palace and bless them. On either side of the king were seated the members of his family. On his right was his adopted son, Shanbaga Perumal and on the left was his daughter, Visaka. As King Parakrama Bahu VI had no apparent male heir, he adopted the son of one of his generals, Shanbaga Perumal, as his son. Among his daughters, the younger one Visakadevi was so beautiful that she was the cynosure of all eyes.

Adithya too was lost in Visaka's beauty. Do saffron robes deprive the eyes of the power of appreciating beauty? His eyes turned towards her repeatedly. It appeared as if she too reciprocated his looks. As he was clad in a monk's dress, he had to act as one. Otherwise, he would stand exposed! He controlled himself. But he could not help glancing in her direction several times.

Whether the others noticed it or not Shanbaga Perumal observed Adithya looking at Visaka. It was unbecoming of a monk to cast such glances at a lady; in such a case, either he should have abandoned his vow of celibacy or he must be a spy in the garb of a monk. With these thoughts, Shanbaga Perumal made a mental note that he should be careful with this monk.

The king's adopted son, Shanbaga Perumal was the son of one of the soldiers who had migrated from Kerala in India. When the Tamil kingdoms fell and Islamic invasions continued to take place, many warriors left India and went to Lanka. Later, when the Vijayanagara Empire became a strong force in Central India, many of the migrants returned to their motherland. Many, however, remained in Lanka and carved out a career for themselves. Those who excelled in bravery joined the Sinhala King's army, and distinguishing themselves by their skill, occupied high positions. Marrying Sinhala women, and embracing Buddhism, they integrated themselves with the populace of the island nation. In those days, language and religion had not become forces strong enough to divide the people.

Shanbaga Perumal's father was one such migrant. He rose to become one of the important generals of King Parakrama Bahu's army and was prominent in the royal court. But, more than him it was his son who attracted the king's attention. From a very early age, Perumal drew the others by his sharp intelligence and military skill; no wonder then, that the king too noticed him. Distressed that he did not have a son of his own, the king adopted Shanbaga Perumal as his son, and proclaimed that he should be given all the respect and concessions due to a member of his own family. Even as an eighteen year old, Shanbaga Perumal proved that there was none in the land to surpass him, and earned great fame and reputation. He also nurtured hopes that he would be the next king. Participating in all the contests held in the king's court every year, Perumal established his supremacy in fencing, archery, flinging knives and other martial sports, again and again.

However, he was distressed at the reality which he could not forget, that no matter how capable he was, he did not belong to the royal family. He went out of his way to exhibit his fidelity and gratitude to the king. Naturally he was very protective towards the king's daughters, whom he considered as his own sisters. Therefore, on noticing Adithya's amatory glances towards Visaka, Perumal decided to bring him under his surveillance. Something about this monk did not add up he thought.

As soon as the plays were over, fencing tournaments were conducted. The best warriors in the country vied with one another to get noticed by the sovereign. The winners of one round progressed to the next; the losers stepped out. Some were wounded, while a few even died. Yes; it was such a brutal fight. If one won the competition, he would obtain the king's recognition and reward; this would elevate him from his mundane level of existence to a high social rank; with this dream all of them competed without any compromise. No quarter was given or taken. If they let go of this chance they would have to return to their boring eventless slavish life for one year more; hence, they decided that it did not matter even if they died. They fought ferociously. Several rounds of sword fights were conducted, until a single winner emerged as the champion. Finally, a warrior called Saliya was announced the victor.

Saliya was tall and well-built. The King praised him, and invited him to participate in the competitions and feast that were to be held in the palace the next day. Yes; the winners were invited to compete with Shanbaga Perumal and prove their worth.   Although he was considered as the prince, Shanbaga Perumal did not seek any concessions. He was sure that there was none to excel him in the land.

Saliya was delighted to receive a royal invitation. Though he was certain to be defeated by Shanbaga Perumal, he knew that his having reached this far was in itself sufficient to secure a comfortable future for him. Moreover, it was customary for the winners in such competitions to be appointed as the king's bodyguards or employees in the palace. Once he entered the king's inner circle, the chances of his becoming one of the military leaders would improve immensely. Saliya indulged in such dreams.

Adithya, on the other hand, was lost in another kind of dream. Visakadevi's eyes appeared repeatedly in his mind, and tormented him. On one hand, Mandagini's face, and on the other, Visakadevi's eyes, both produced in him a kind of confusion. He laughed at himself, thinking how despite having lived as a monk among monks all these days, his mind was still unsteady and full of lustful thoughts.

Chapter 3

That day also dawned. The king had sent many carriages to bring the monks to the palace. The truth was that, having travelled all these days on his own horseback or on foot, Adithya did not much relish the idea of riding in a carriage driven by someone else. In the battles in which he took part in Cambodia, he always rode on a horse or elephant. Riding on an elephant, even with its mahout, in the heat of a war, with tempers rising, emotions peaking, and heartbeats galloping was very different. It was quite another situation, to travel with many monks, in a carriage driven by somebody on a path chosen by somebody else. Nevertheless, he knew that if he wanted to keep up his disguise, he had to be one among them.

The king himself came to the palace gates to welcome them. The huge hall was supported by solid columns, on which were sculpted forms of the Lord Buddha, lions, elephants and lotus flowers. At the entrance, in front of the steps was a moon stone. On this semi-circular stone were concentric half rings of sculptures of various flower-bearing creepers, animals and other wavy designs. In the middle was a lotus. In the centre of the hall was a dais, and seats were arranged on all four sides of it. On one side of the dais, there was an idol of Lord Buddha and lamps were lit in front of it. Lotuses were also placed at the Buddha's feet.

First, worship was offered to the Buddha; following this were religious rituals such as the chanting of Pirith. Food was then served to all. This was followed by the staging of the play Angulimala once again. Later, with the Buddhist monks sitting on one side and the royal family on the other, the previous day's champion Saliya fought with Shanbaga Perumal. To prove his mettle, Saliya fought ferociously and with great speed and skill. But it was soon quite clear to the spectators that Shanbaga Perumal's fame was not without a foundation.

The young monks sat on the floor in the front row, while the elders sat behind on seats. Similarly, on the other side, the youngsters sat on the floor and the elders on seats. However vigorous the fight between the contestants was, and however well he analyzed the fighters' strategies in his mind, Adithya's eyes were repeatedly drawn towards Visakadevi's face. He had an illusion that she too was looking at him. He was lost in the thought as to whether it was real or imaginary, or whether his eyes were playing tricks on him.

A dusky complexion; long black hair; eyes that shone like diamonds; large curves in the right places; a waist so slender that made one wonder whether it was capable of supporting its burden or whether it would break in the process; feet light pink in color like lotuses; as she sat in Padmasana, cross-legged on the floor, all her features invited him to look at her again and again.

If this was his condition, Princess Visakadevi's mind too, had been impacted. Though she was surprised as to why a young monk was stealing glances at her, his well-built body, his strong knotty muscles, his sharp nose, and his eyes that seemed to penetrate her mind, disturbed her greatly. Questions such as 'Who is he? Why is he watching me?' arose in her mind and confused her. She had never experienced thoughts and desires like these before. She wanted to learn more about him. Though her thoughts were wavering, her mind kept reminding her that it was wrong on her part to view a monk in this manner, and returned her attention to the ongoing fight. But, in a few seconds, her mind and eyes returned to him. Visakadevi decided that he was not an ordinary monk.

As both of them were engrossed in their own worlds, suddenly with the sound of heavy metals clashing, Saliya's sword flew upwards, and descended speedily towards where the monks were sitting. The monks who saw the sword falling in their midst, scattered in all directions. At the same time, Adithya who returned from his dream world to the present did not panic seeing the sword coming fast towards him. Instead, he rose slightly on his knees and kneeling, extended his hand and caught the sword exactly on its grip. Whether the applause of the gathering was for Shanbaga Perumal's valour, or for Adithya's dexterity, was not clear. But Visakadevi's claps were certainly for the latter.

Then, King Parakrama Bahu addressed Adithya: "Thera, from the manner in which you held the sword, I can understand that you are well-trained militarily. What is your past?" Silaavi Sudhdhi interrupted and said, "This monk must have been a military captain. When the pirates attacked us also, we were able to overcome them only by means of his timely and skillful intervention."

The King asked, "O' Monk, who are you?"

"When the time comes I shall tell you, my lord. This is a moment when we should applaud Prince Shanbaga Perumal's valour. I do not wish to attract every one's attention towards me now and detract from the prince's achievement" said Adithya.

Shanbaga Perumal was enraged. When he should have been crowned as the greatest warrior in the country and feted, who was this man to attract the people's attention and dilute his fame? Furious at Adithya he said, "O' monk, if you are a real warrior fight with me and prove it."

But Adithya said, "Prince, I have no desire to fight with you."

Shanbaga Perumal's wrath increased manifold. "If you know your father's name, fight with me. Otherwise, accept that you are a coward and divest yourself of your monk's garb" he said. Adithya eyes searched for Visakadevi. As she too looked at him, their eyes met for a second. Her appeal to him 'prove your worth' was plainly written on her face. It was as though she was pleading with him to accept the challenge.

What little doubt he had as to whether he should take up the dare or not, vanished the moment he saw Visaka's face. Nevertheless, as a matter of respect, he said to Vanarathna Maha Thera, "If you permit me I shall take up the Prince's challenge." "Who am I, O' monk, to prevent you from proving your mettle? Both of you have my blessings. Exhibit your skills without violating the rules of warfare," the priest said.

Adithya then raised his sword and kissed it. He looked at Visakadevi as he did so. She too observed him keenly without batting an eyelid. When he realised that the time had come to discard his disguise, Adithya was very happy. Back to his old life! The heroic life that he had lived from as far back as he could remember! It was time for him to bid goodbye to the phase, when hiding behind saffron clothes he had to remain a passive spectator with folded hands watching others' exploits, and get into the arena and fight like a warrior! The time had come for him to reveal his valour in the presence of no less an august assembly than the king himself, the beautiful princess, and hundreds of others! What more could a warrior ask for? There was no time to waste thinking of his mission or his future. The only thought in his mind was his enemy; his sword. Nothing else mattered. He was not prepared to let his mind be distracted now.

The duel began! He was a knife addict! Just as people become slaves to drugs, they become slaves to swords also! If a warrior did not fight, his hands would itch. His mind would be distressed. That was Adithya's condition. As soon as he took up his sword in his hand, his joy knew no bounds. Nevertheless, he began steadily. Anger and haste, they say, blunt one's brain. Shanbaga Perumal gathered his full force and fought. Within the first few seconds, Adithya realised that his rival was no mean swordsman, and so engaged in defensive moves without losing his calm. While

Ezhuth Aani

Shanbaga Perumal whirled round and round, and thrust from different directions, Adithya moved just a few steps from where he stood, and managed to hold his ground.

Having lived a monk's life for several weeks without wielding his sword, his hands and legs had become a little rusty; but within a few minutes of the start of the duel, they regained their usual form. Habits die hard! Engaged merely in parrying his rival's thrusts, Adithya waited until Shanbaga Perumal's fury reached its peak, to match the latter's excellence. Perumal, who had never before met a man who so easily faced his thrusts, did not know what to do next. Many, who are the kings in their own limited circle, are not aware of people better skilled than they are, in the outside world. Imagining that there is none to surpass them, they go about strutting with pride! There is always someone better than you; this is Nature's law! One unerring fact of life is that the person who believes that he is the best will have to come to terms with reality sooner or later.

Seeing that Adithya was matching all his strategies effortlessly, and wielding his sword in all directions forming a kind of shield around him, Perumal did not know what to do. So far, none of his rivals had been able to withstand his fencing skills on an equal footing. This was a new experience for him. He had not been trained or prepared for an alternative strategy as he had never had to face a challenge of this magnitude. As he began to think of his next move, there was hesitation in his methods. Laymen's eyes will not detect these nuances easily. The spectators did not notice Perumal's confusion, as he was still wielding his weapon furiously. But, the experienced Adithya understood his rival's faltering very clearly. Using Perumal's weakness, he slowly changed his moves from the defensive to the offensive. Realizing that defeat was inevitable if the same trend continued, as a final attempt, Perumal gathered his full strength and holding his sword with both his hands, he lunged at Adithya.

Had ordinary warriors been involved in such a 'do or die' attack, they would have perished. But, Adithya who had been expecting that final thrust from his rival, simply moved slightly to one side with the result, Perumal having missed his target lost his balance and stumbled. Adithya could have wounded or killed him. But he did not wish to shed the blood of one younger to him, and a prince who could serve his country for long. Killing a prince of the host country was not going to serve his purpose in any way.

On the contrary, intending to end the duel, he struck Perumal's sword near its hilt, and by turning his wrist pulled it off. The already stumbling Perumal could not match this; as he loosened his grip on his sword, it flew in the air and fell far away. Simultaneously, Adithya threw his own sword, so that it fell on the ground just in front of Visakadevi.

For the spectators, who were unaware of the intricacies of warfare, it appeared as if the fight had ended in a stalemate, as both the contestants had lost their swords. But Perumal knew that this was the first defeat he had ever faced in his life. Just then, Adithya stood before the King as if nothing serious had taken place, and said "Thank you for allowing me the opportunity to fight with the Prince."

His humility endeared him to the king. But, Silaavi Sudhdhi shouted, "He is a fake monk! He has disguised himself as a monk and cheated us. He is a spy. He had disgraced Buddhism. He must be arrested and interrogated, my lord." The king liked Adithya very much. But, it was clear that there was some truth in Silaavi Sudhdhi's accusation. One who disrespected Buddhism in the presence of Vanarathna Thera could not be allowed to go unpunished! So the king ordered. "Arrest this monk. I shall interrogate him myself."

Adithya was also in a dilemma. One minute his mind had soared to the sky in delight; the next he had plunged into an abyss.

Ezhuth Aani

He knew only too well that it was futile in a foreign land to resist his arrest. Without showing any opposition, he co-operated with his captors.

He was handcuffed. He was disrobed and checked to see if he carried any arms. Then he was made to wear the white dress of the prisoners. He was taken to an underground prison. His guards were very respectful towards him, because they had seen the way he fought. In addition, they had seen him act as Angulimala. They knew that they were in the presence of an extra-ordinary human being. Whether it was due to this respect or not, his possessions were returned to him. He had coated his emerald Buddha with clay. Also it was in a secret compartment of his bag. They returned his bag along with his other belongings.

Chapter 4

For two days he was confined in darkness. He did not know whether it was day or night. There was no one even to talk to. This too was a torture. Adithya thought that this mental torture was worse than physical abuse.

As the days passed, he began to wonder whether the world outside had forgotten him. Initially water had been kept in a pot. There was no food. In course of time, his intellect began to dim because of starvation. On one hand, the total silence and all-pervading darkness; on the other, prolonged starvation. If things continued in this way, Adithya thought that either he would die soon or lose his mind. It was all because he wielded his sword, bemoaned Adithya. But how long could he go about in the guise of a monk, forgetting his mission? Somehow he had to reveal his real identity and approach the king; hence, he consoled himself saying that he had not done anything wrong. He recollected the incidents of the past few days a thousand times; however, Visakadevi's eyes alone kept haunting and agitating him. He comforted himself with the thought that even if he were to die in this dungeon, he had proved his valour to that lady.

Lost in such reflections, and confused as to whether it was sleep or dizziness, Adithya was surprised to see a small flickering light far away. He did not remember having seen that light before. Was it a light or a star? Had he already died? He began wondering if he was actually alive, as he watched that light. That small light seemed to descend gradually from above. He had heard soldiers mortally wounded in battle say that when they were in the grip of death, they were taken through a dark cave, and at the end they had seen a light. Not knowing whether this was a real experience or an illusion, Adithya wondered whether he too was approaching death.

Ezhuth Aani

That light seemed to descend gradually. Moreover, as it neared him, its dimension and brightness appeared to increase manifold. Only then could he see his surroundings. He understood that he was in a cell with doors made of iron bars, that the bearer of that light was a human being, and that it was descending from the steps towards him. He knew from its dress that it was a man. But the face was covered with a cloth. When the form came near, it opened his door with a key! Then, it signaled to him to follow. Though the question arose in his mind, as to why he should obey the person without knowing whether it was a friend or foe, he also realised that if he let go this opportunity, he may never again be able to leave this dungeon. Once he got out, even if he were in the midst of enemies, he could either fight with them and die, or escape. But, if he remained inside, there would be no chance of freedom. Thinking that he would have to take his chances no matter what, he followed that figure and ascended the steps.

Very steep spiral steps led upwards. He did not remember having been brought to the prison by this path. At the same time, as recent memories were appearing as vague shadows in the distance, he could not say with conviction that he had not been brought along this path. Having reached level ground, that figure rolled a stone and closed the entrance to the steps. Then, going out of the room it removed its mask. Ah! It was a lady! Though she wore a man's clothes, her long hair and hand and hip movements proclaimed her feminity. But, because she did not turn as she walked forward, he could not see her face.

From the manner in which those guards greeted her and stood aside for her to pass, he surmised that she belonged to the royal family. She left that building and got into a palanquin waiting for her, and gestured to him to get in too. The waiting workers lifted the palanquin and began to move.

Only then was he able to see for the first time the face of the lady seated next to him. Yes. It was Visakadevi herself! Many questions arose in his mind: why did she free him and where is she taking him? Then she said, "O' warrior! Pardon me for taking you like a lady in a palanquin. This is for your safety."

"Princess, why are you saving me?" asked Adithya.

"O' warrior! I do not know who you are or what your motive is. But I do know that you are a good man. That you are not a Buddhist monk and that you belong to a royal family I understood from your stride and demeanour. That you did not disgrace my brother but spared him shows that you are a responsible warrior. It was wrong to have imprisoned you. But escaping from the accusation of sacrilege against Buddhism is rather difficult. That is why I am freeing you clandestinely" said Visaka. "How do you know I spared your brother?" asked Adithya, feigning innocence.

"I am not an ignoramus. I know the nuances of fighting very well. If you had wished, you could have killed my brother. Instead you threw away your sword! That too so that it fell at my feet. Do you think I do not know all this?" said Visaka.

"It is my good fortune that the princess is merciful to me. But you should not have freed me against the king's wishes" he said. "It is with the king's permission that I have released you" she said. "In that case, he could have ordered my release directly."

"You do not know how authority is shared here. The king may be the sovereign of the land. However, if the Buddhist Sanga says that he functions against Buddhism the people will lose their faith in the king. According to tradition, whoever has the Buddha's sacred tooth has the exclusive right to rule the country.

"You were disguised as a Buddhist monk. You deceived everyone and therefore insulted Buddhism. If you are not punished

Ezhuth Aani

the Buddhist Sanga will rise in rebellion. After that there'll be a revolution in the country" she said.

Only then Adithya understood that it was the Buddhist monks who had supposedly renounced the world, who ruled the country in reality. He also knew that the status which the monks enjoyed in Theravada Buddhism was much higher than that enjoyed by the monks in Mahayana Buddhism. It was difficult to rule the country, antagonizing the Buddhist Sanga. When he thought that such a state could befall Cambodia also, he had goose bumps.

By then, the palanquin entered her palace, and she took him to her inner quarters. She then allotted him a room, and ordered food and other amenities to be provided. That room was next to hers. He understood that the princess kept him under her direct observation and protection. He also knew quite well that outside this place, he had no safety.

Not only Shanbaga Perumal but even king Parakrama Bahu himself could enter that part of the palace only after obtaining her permission. Visakadevi told him, "O' warrior! You rest today and recover yourself from the trauma of the recent events. We can think of our next move tomorrow morning. I guarantee you of your safety inside this palace. But do not go out."

She met him the next morning. Wearing a red dress she looked ravishing. He was confused as to which part of her to relish. After roving over her fully, his eyes returned to hers. They were so magnetizing.

She laughed heartily. "Being a Buddhist monk, can you look at me lustfully like this?"

"But I am not a Buddhist monk" he said.

"Nevertheless your look is not right. My brother has noticed you ogling me. You don't have any discretion" she said, and continued: "Eyeing the Princess lustfully is a punishable crime." "What punishment are you going to give me?" asked Adithya as he took her hands in his.

"Gradually you are losing your respect for me!" she said, without trying to extricate her hands from his. Adithya drew her close and hugged her tightly. Her cheeks and ears blushed in shyness. She then said, "When you are in danger of death, can you desire a lady?"

As he tightened his hold, he said "For the sake of this beauty I'm prepared to die a thousand times."

"O' warrior! Do not waste your time, forgetting your mission. I came here only to take you to my father. But, before that you must tell me who you are, without concealing any of the facts" said Visakadevi.

Somehow he trusted her. Sometimes, in life don't we trust near strangers? It feels like we have known them all our lives! Don't we confide in them our private affairs? That is how Adithya too wanted to unburden himself of all his trials and tribulations. He told her all the details of the state of Cambodia, his ancestry, and the reason why he came to Lanka, from the beginning to the end.

"You could have come directly as the messenger of the Cambodian king, couldn't you?" asked Visaka.

"Had I come as the Cambodian King's messenger, my journey would have been cut short long ago. Our enemies' spies are roaming everywhere. Moreover, countries like Ayutthaya and Champa, which were frontrunners in embracing Theravada Buddhism, are maintaining close ties with the Buddhist Sanga in Lanka. If I had come explicitly on behalf of Cambodia, my journey would have been futile. That is why I came in disguise. My plan was to somehow contact the king secretly, win his affection and talk to him. If you help me in this, I shall always be grateful to you" said Adithya.

"What then do you expect from the king?" asked Visaka. "I have learnt that the king has a cache of fire arms and cannons. We need arms, ammunition and military aid. At the very least, the king should be neutral without helping our enemies" said Adithya.

"I shall take you to the king. It is your responsibility to convince him and win his favour" said Visaka. Adithya was invited to have lunch with the king.

The king was very simple. Having gone underground for many years in the struggle for the throne, his needs had been reduced to a few.

Without any preamble, the king asked "Who are you?", and when Adithya revealed his real name, the former said, "Are you Adithavarma? Your fame has reached us over the seas! We have heard of your heroism through the Chinese ships and passing travelers. There is justification for your having come in disguise. Had you come as Adithavarma, your enemies would have attacked and eliminated you long ago."

The king then listened patiently to Adithya's demands, and said, "Countries like Champa and Ayutthaya have established close ties with us. Theravada Buddhism is the bridge that connects us. Under such circumstances, we may have to face several issues in helping you with military aid against them.

"Buddhism has become an integral part of Lankan politics. Though we may not dislike the other religions, the Buddhist Sanga's intervention and influence in the everyday life of the people, has increased greatly. In recent times, due to the competition between the royals, the capital has been gradually moving southwards. Parts of the island are not under our control. Due to the intervention of Javanese and the Cholas, the island's northern part is flourishing as a separate kingdom under the control of the Tamils. We have also been compelled to seek the help of the Pandya kings frequently. In such trying times, it is Buddhism that assists us in preventing the people from rebelling, and leading them in the right path.

"An aggressive campaign has been launched on the streets that you have disgraced Buddhism by disguising yourself as a Buddhist monk. Buddhist leaders of the higher ranks are very angry with you. Although I understand your difficulty, I am not in a position to give you due recognition and help you openly."

King Parakrama Bahu added, "Give me some time to think over this in detail." Subsequently, it was decided that Adithya should stay in the princess' palace as it was dangerous to go out in the open.

When they were alone again, Adithya said, "Must thank Lord Brahma for having created you."

"Ah! You'll say anything to flatter ladies, won't you?" said Visaka.

"Did I say anything offensive?" asked Adithya.

"You praised my beauty" said Visaka, with a shy smile.

"Who praised your beauty?" asked Adithya.

"Didn't you just say that you must thank Lord Brahma for having created me?" said Visaka.

"I said thanks; for the help that you rendered" said Adithya.

"Am I not beautiful then?" she asked in real anger.

Adithya began describing her beauty. 'A round moon-like face, hair like dark clouds, eyes like stars, long pretty neck' he said, and proceeded with the rest of her body.

"Enough, enough! The fake monk has now become an amorous poet. Are you an all-rounder? You have no equal in bravery. You also seem to excel in drama and poetry." said Visaka.

With both hands Adithya drew her near and hugged her. She made no attempt to release herself from his hold. It was a new experience for her. Having grown up without any male contact, his touch was both new and comforting. Her heart raced. When she felt his lips on her cheeks, they were hot. Deftly he turned her face and kissed her. As they remained in blissful oblivion, the seconds became eons. Will his hands be idle, given such a chance? They started feeling her all over. But, even as she was lost in his embrace, Visakadevi suddenly pushed him away and stood aside.

"O' warrior, if we fall in love it shall never reach fulfillment. Don't forget your duties to your country and lose yourself in your personal emotions. Like you, I too have my duty. I cannot come with you leaving my obligations. Continuing this will only end in sorrow. Hearts that come together will then become broken hearts. Please listen to what I say!" said Visaka.

"What is that duty of yours?" asked Adithya.

"I shall show it to you tomorrow" said Visaka.

"Don't you like me?" Adithya asked.

"O' warrior! Don't misunderstand me. Since the day I set eyes on you, I have lost my heart to you. But, can we allow our lives to follow our hearts blindly? Every man and woman has different likes and desires that appear and disappear. We all go through transient infatuations. We are attracted to so many people. Can we marry them all? Is it possible to carry on life like that? No, no! We must control our mental desires and give priority to our duties. Only then can we achieve anything in life. Otherwise, we'll be entangled in transient pleasures and be ruined" she said.

"What high philosophy at such an early age!" said Princeling; after that he refrained from eyeing her lustfully.

Chapter 5

On the following day, he was taken to King Parakrama Bahu again. Pacing up and down, the King said, "Adithavarma, I have considered your request for a long time." Visakadevi too was present there.

"Maha Parakrama Bahu ruled over the entire island of Lanka. That golden period has now given way to a split land. The Javanese and Tamils have together established the Jaffna Kingdom in the northern part of the island. Our capital has moved southwards gradually. If this continues, we'll have to leap into the ocean as Duttagemunu said."

From his long preamble, Adithya realised that the former's response would not be favorable. Nevertheless, he listened to the king patiently. The king added: "My first objective is to bring the whole island of Lanka under a single rule, and earn a place in history equal to that of Maha Parakrama Bahu. I have been preparing an army and collecting arms and weapons for this. I am expanding my navy as well, to prevent the Jaffna Kingdom from obtaining aid from the Indian sub-continent. Under these circumstances, it is not possible for our army to bear the loss of arms, materials and men that would result from our direct involvement in the war taking place in Cambodia."

Visakadevi then interrupted and asked, "Father, even if we cannot send an army, can we not help them with arms?"

"My dear, you do not understand our politics. Our royal dynasty and the Buddhist Sanga have been wielding equal authority over the people. According to tradition only the person who is in possession of Lord Buddha's tooth relic is the legitimate ruler of the land. It was specifically because of this, that when the Cholas invaded Lanka, with great difficulty we managed to save the casket containing the sacred tooth, with the help of the Buddhist monks. Every time there is a foreign invasion in the country, it is the Buddhist monks who infuse in the people nationalistic fervour and thirst for freedom. As this has happened many times, the authority and influence of the Buddhist Sanga have increased among the people gradually. In so far as conditions stand today, just as they cannot maintain their hold antagonising themselves from me, I too cannot carry on my rule without their support. This can be considered as a kind of 'power-sharing'. It is a fine balancing act and both parties tread carefully and try not to step on the toes of the other.

"In recent times, Buddhist delegations from countries like Ayutthaya and Champa have been visiting us. They have sought our religious leaders' assistance to enthrone Theravada Buddhism as a social framework in their countries. Because of this, the ties between our countries have been strengthened and become closer. Under such conditions, Adithavarma, how can I accede to your request? Though I like you personally, if I offer you military aid against the Buddhist Sanga's wishes, my position as the king will be in peril. Hence, please forgive me. Ask me for anything else; I shall consider it" said the king.

Visakadevi too looked at her father with great disappointment. As though he understood her inner mind, the king said, "My dear, I agreed to release Adithavarma at your request. Otherwise, the Buddhist fundamentalists would have torn him to pieces. If I were to function against them beyond this, I will be in danger myself."

Adithya then said, "Your Highness, will you give me another opportunity to change your mind?"

"What other argument are you going to put forward? Is there anything that you've not said so far?" asked King Parakrama Bahu.

Ezhuth Aani

Adithya took out the Buddha idol from his bag. He then struck it hard against the wall.

"What are you doing, Adithavarma?" screamed Visaka. She was worried that if his breaking the Buddha idol was known outside, his life would be in danger.

Then, the clay coat broke open and slowly the emerald Buddha began to appear. "The emerald Buddha" shouted the king in amazement.

"Your Highness, this is a miniature replica of the Emerald Buddha. The real Emerald Buddha is several times larger. He is safe in Cambodia." Saying this, Adithya took out the missive given by Vajragnani from the hidden compartment in his bag and gave it to the king.

The king read it slowly and took in its contents. He then said, "I've heard a lot about Vajragnani. I have not been lucky enough to meet him. But foreign traders who have been here have spoken of him with great respect. I have also heard that men from many countries have gone to his monastery to study, notwithstanding their political leanings."

He added, "Does Vajragnani have the Emerald Buddha?"

"Yes, Your Highness! I have seen the Emerald Buddha with my own eyes. The Emerald Buddha is enshrined in a very secret place. We have kept him very safely. Even if the Angkor Empire falls, the enemies cannot find out the place where we have hidden the Emerald Buddha. Only a couple of those who know that place are alive now. Although I have seen the Emerald Buddha, I do not know the way to reach it. Vajragnani asked me to tell you that he is prepared to give you that valuable Buddha as an offering. He has laid down only two conditions for that. First, we should escape from this situation without getting destroyed. Second, you should help us with arms and soldiers."

The king was lost in silent thought.

"Consider well, Your Highness. If you have the Emerald Buddha in your hands, your status in the Buddhist world will be elevated. Already you have Lord Buddha's sacred tooth. If you bring the Emerald Buddha also to Lanka, nobody can challenge your sovereignty over the Buddhists after that. It will give you a legitimacy that even Maha Parakrama Bahu did not have. The Buddha Sanga too will have to accommodate you. Otherwise, they will lose their influence over the people totally."

The king was pacing up and down. Some time passed in silence. Then, the king spoke first. "Adithavarma! Your arguments are sound and persuasive. I do not know if I am committing a serious mistake by helping you. However, within the next six months to one year, I shall send you two shiploads of cannon and explosives. It is your responsibility to take those ships to Angkor City through the Mekong River.

"Helping you with arms may itself land me in grave danger. Hence, I am not in a position to help you with an army. If you win this war, you will have to take the responsibility of sending the Emerald Buddha to Lanka. I'm doing this on the strength of Vajragnani's word. I pray that we may receive Lord Buddha's grace and blessings."

Hearing this decision, Adithavarma became very happy. His first aim had been achieved. He will now have to go to the Arabian countries and try and take their technological knowledge to Cambodia.

Ezhuth Aani

Subsequently, Adithya was again taken to Visakadevi's palace. Since her father had agreed to meet his demands, she was very happy too. She thought Cambodia will prevail and escape calamity. Adithya then asked her: "O' princess! Now tell me what is that duty that you have, more important than love? What is it that forced you to reject my love?"

"Adithavarma! I have not rejected your love. But, I cannot flee from my obligations. If you come with me I shall show you my duties in person" said Visaka.

She took him to another room. It was well decorated and painted in different colors. It did not have many items of furniture. In the centre of the room was a big cot, rather low in hcight. A small child was playing in the middle of the cot.

That beautiful child was about two years old. There was something different about the child, which was cared for by nurses. The beautiful eyes were narrow, and slanted from the sides to the centre. The ears were a little lower than normal. Between the small nose and the inner edges of the eyes on both sides was a fold. The neck was broad, and the folds of skin seemed to be more than usual. Some teeth had appeared. The child's tongue appeared to be larger in proportion. Though it tried to speak, the words were not coherent.

As the child waved its hands towards them and babbled something, Visaka embraced and lifted it. As she did so, the hands and legs of the child appeared to dangle. A deep line ran on the palms and soles. On the feet, there was a large gap between the big toe and the other toes.

"This is my sister's son. Vijaya is two years old. Do you notice any difference between ordinary children and this child?" asked Visaka.

"I do notice a difference, but I cannot specify what it is" said Adithya.

"My sister died during Vijaya's delivery. Since that day, he has been my world. As my father does not have a male heir, this child is the titular prince. My main duty is to bring him up. Now tell me if you understand why I did not accept your love."

Adithya looked at Visaka in surprise, as she said this. "There are ever so many servants in the palace to take care of the prince. Where is the need then for the princess to dedicate herself to the care of this child?" asked Adithya.

"Did you see how beautiful this child is? But it is different from the others. In Nature's creations, each one has its own beauty."

"But as he grew, I observed certain differences. His movements like turning over, sitting up, walking and so on were all delayed. Therefore, I spent a lot of time with him, and gave him attention and physical exercise. Now he has started walking like other children. My next aim is to make him speak. His lips and tongue get exhausted easily as his muscles are weak. So, I have begun to give training for the muscles of his lips and tongue. I have seen a lot of progress." As she said this, Vijaya called her "Amma."

Visaka gathered him in her arms and kissing him, said "How many types among us, how many varieties! Of these some are differently abled. The best that we can do for them is to train them properly and help them to attain their full growth and maturity. What they need is not money or sympathy, but quality time, understanding and goal-oriented training.

"Vijaya is the titular prince. Though he was born in a palace, all his potential cannot be realised completely, unless a lot of time is spent in giving him the right training. How many children are there like him! As timely proper care and training are not given, they are not able to lead independent lives. After the damage is done, what is

Ezhuth Aani

the use of being charitable towards them?" As she became emotional while asking this, her voice quivered and tears welled up in her eyes.

His eyes too moistened. "O' princess! You are a goddess. Your work is noble. It's my mistake to have looked at you lustfully, without understanding you properly" said Adithya remorsefully.

"Adithavarma, you have not done anything wrong. When young men and women see each other it is natural for love and lust to appear in them. But each one of us is a prisoner of circumstances. Your first duty is towards your country; mine towards my child. If we forget this, and give priority to our romantic feelings, what is the difference between animals and us? Nature has given humans the ability to think, for us to reason out matters and act accordingly.

"Thoughts occur naturally. There's nothing wrong in that. But when we allow those thoughts to lead us to act indiscriminately, mistakes occur.   Adithavarma! You have not committed any sin. Had these bonds not been there, I would have willingly been confined in the prison of your hands the very first time you hugged me. It is my good fortune to have received the acquaintance of a warrior and scholar like you. My life has been enriched by meeting you."

"I am lucky to have known you. When I realise that the world contains women of such sacrificial and noble nature, I am enthralled" said Adithya. The ardent love he had for her gave way to great respect. Instead of considering her as a woman and an object of sex, he looked up to her as a great human being.

"Adithavarma! Your duty beckons you. My duty has fettered me. It is fortunate that our paths met. Let us take an oath to carry out our duties with greater determination, inspired by each other. If we allow our individual desires to control our lives, we'll not be able to achieve anything.

"As far as I am concerned, my first and most important duty is to make Vijaya talk, to draw out his hidden skills as far as possible, and at the right time to enthrone him."

Having said this, she wished Adithya success in his future endeavors.

"Adithavarma! My father has given you his word. He will keep it. But it is not easy. There are many who will oppose it. Why, even if you were to go out of this palace alone, there are people waiting to pounce on you. Most importantly, from the manner in which he behaved towards you, I could make out my brother's hatred towards you. It is up to you to decide whether you'll return to Cambodia, or go to the Islamic countries or to India, and gather the technological knowledge necessary for you. But, first you must escape from Lanka. We must think carefully before drawing up the plans for this" said Visaka.

Chapter 6

The palanquin wended its way in darkness towards the River Kelani. Two boatmen waiting at the jetty on the river bank, untied the boat as soon as they saw the palanquin as though they expected its arrival, and prepared to leave. As a plank had been connected to the jetty from the boat, those in the palanquin were able to get into the boat without getting their feet wet.

Two ladies were let down from the palanquin. They got into the boat without a word. The leader of the group, who gave the boatmen money, gave instructions and left.

Due to the recent rains, the river was in spate. The wind was so strong that the boat swayed menacingly. But because of the boatmen's skill, it remained steady enough to prevent the two ladies from getting too wet. After a few minutes' journey, the boat reached the other bank.

It was the jetty of a commercial wholesale warehouse. It was a place for collecting and distributing goods for import and export. Grains like paddy and rice, spices like cardamom, and valuables such as ivory and pearls, brought from all over the island, were exported to other countries. At the same time, goods like silk clothes, ceramics and new equipment of various types imported from other countries were unloaded and stored in such distribution centres. Later, the local traders would buy these goods, take them to their towns and sell them.

The two ladies were disembarked in one such commercial centre. Hectic arrangements were being made for a convoy of vehicles to leave the next day from this place to a port called Maathottam. Though it was night time, many torches had been lit, so that the whole place was flooded in light, making it appear like daytime.

This place functioned as a distribution center where goods from various parts were loaded and unloaded. Though security men had been posted on all sides to protect the goods, they did not check individuals for their identification.

As soon as the two ladies were handed over to a trader, the boat that brought them left. One of the ladies spoke a few words to the trader and mounting the horse he gave her, disappeared into the darkness of midnight. The other lady stood watching the former, until the trail of light decreased gradually and merged with the darkness. The trader then asked her to come inside.

He was an Islamic man. His business was to bring from the Arabian countries rare precious items such as saffron, and artistic metal instruments to Lanka, and take from here ivory and gems to sell them there. As he was very affluent, he maintained contacts with the royal families. The other lady had given a bag of gold coins to the trader before she left.

"Please come in" he said, and taking her into his tent, said "Wear this." What he had given her was a dress called 'abhaya', which Islamic women wore covering their whole bodies and heads. Though the lady had covered her head and worn a scarf, feeling that the dress which he had given her would be more protective, she accepted it.

Their journey was scheduled for the next day. It was towards Maathottam or Maandhai, a port on the north western shore of Lanka. Goods and men were loaded into fifteen carts, which travelled as a caravan. Each vehicle was drawn by two mules. For security reasons, mounted soldiers were positioned in front and in the rear, as well as on the sides of the convoy.

Ezhuth Aani

Slowly their convoy reached Maandhai. In ancient times, Maandhai on the northwest coast of the island was a busy port used by the Cholas, to disembark their armies. Later, it was captured by King Vijayabaahu, and came under the control of the Sinhala kings. After the Tamil Kingdom was formed, Maandhai which was in the border area between the Tamil and the Sinhala kings often changed hands. However, to avoid any disruption to the traders, it had now been declared as a war-free zone. That is, although the port was under the control of King Parakrama Bahu, a guarantee had been given that the merchants who landed at the port could go unhindered to any part of the island.

With the king preparing for war, many of the traders had doubts as to how long this assurance would hold good. Goods bound for Jaffna were now being sent directly to the ports in the north of Lanka. However, rich traders from the Arabian countries landed at Maandhai, and sent their goods to both sides of Lanka. Neither the Sinhala nor the Tamil kings were willing to snap their ties with these affluent merchants. Both parties earned substantial customs revenue from the Arabian trade, and hence, did not wish to disturb the arrangement.

But on days when the war clouds hung dark over the island nation, both sides had placed their spies and ambush parties to roam around Maandhai. This trade convoy had camped near the Thirukeththeeswaram temple close to Maandhai. In those days, though the Buddhist kings followed Buddhism, they did not interfere with the Hindus' religious freedom. Lanka's five major Siva temples of Nakuleswaram, Keththeeswaram, Munneswaram, Thaandeeswaram, and Koneswaram enjoyed the kings' patronage and support, and carried on their activities without any hindrance. Of these, Keththeeswaram and Koneswaram were celebrated in the hymns of Saivite apostles of India. There was also the famous Murugan temple at Kathirgamam which enjoyed the veneration of all, irrespective of their religious leanings. Apart from these, to enable the Arabian merchants to trade freely in the land, mosques had been allowed to be built.

The trade delegation had encamped on the banks of the Paalaavi, a large irrigation tank near Maandhai. The lady who joined the team was allotted a separate tent. The lead merchant, Ahmed Lebbe, had set apart a tent for this lady close to the tents occupied by the ladies of his harem.

As Thirukeththeeswaram on one side, the Paalaavi Tank on the other, the canal constructed from the River Aruvi Aru to feed water to Paalaavi on yet another, were enhancing the beauty of the evening further, that lady who had covered her whole body with the black dress sat on a small rock by the wayside, lost in deep thought. Suddenly, a loud commotion was heard close by. She got up to see what was going on.

A group of soldiers were hurrying towards them from different directions. They soon surrounded them, cutting down the shrub bush around the open ground where the camps were. From their dress and dialect, it could be surmised that they were Sinhala soldiers. As the men on foot progressed, cutting down the bush in their path, behind them came the cavalry with their swords drawn. They not only surrounded the camps but intruded into them from various sides. Then, one who appeared to be their leader, shouted at the occupants of the camp to surrender or face death. Knowing that it was futile to resist, Ahmed Lebbe ordered his guards to lay down arms. He also demanded from the captain, "Who are you? I have King Parakrama Bahu's writ. If I complain to him about this transgression he will not spare you."

The captain of the soldiers said, "We belong to a division of the king's army. I am not going to trouble you in any way. Our aim is not to rob or hinder you. We have come in search of a foreign spy. We have surrounded not only you but all other traders too. Please co-operate with us. We will not harm you. As soon as we capture the man we came in search of, we'll leave."

Ezhuth Aani

Lebbe then ordered his men to abide by the captain's instructions. The Sinhala soldiers collected them all and separated the men and women. The Muslim women who had covered their whole bodies with black dresses and the Lankan women in ordinary dresses were made to stand in a line.

Out of respect, the soldiers examined the ladies one by one without lifting the head scarves that covered their faces. When they came to this lady they looked her up and down for some time. For a second, the ladies' eyes met the soldiers' through the small eye slit in the full body dress. That moment seemed like an age to the lady. When she observed the soldier peering at her, she cast her eyes to the ground. After a slight hesitation, the soldier moved on to the next lady. Only then, by chance he noticed this lady's feet. Oh no!

He could see some difference in her feet. Yes; they were not the soft small feet of a woman. Without any ornaments on the ankles or embellishments on the toes or nails, they were different from those of the other women. About to move on to the next in the line, he suddenly turned towards her and raised her head dress with his sword. Lo and behold! Wonder of wonders! It was a man. That too, a majestic man with a clean shaven head! Yes. It was Adithavarma himself.

Shorn of his disguise, Adithya tried to draw his sword, kept hidden at his waist. But his dress proved to be a hindrance, and before he could move, his hands were held from behind and bound tightly. With the same rope his legs were also tied and his mouth was gagged. No chance was given to him to struggle and free himself. On the contrary, he found it difficult even to breathe. Before he could gather his wits, he was pushed on to the ground, and two Sinhala soldiers stood on him.

Having found what they had come in search of, the Sinhala soldiers left the others from their hold and dragged Adithya alone with them. His guards took him to their camp, west of the Paalaavi Tank.

Realizing that he had no other alternative but to follow them, Adithya gave up the idea of resisting and went with them. However, he observed his whereabouts very carefully to see if he could get a chance to escape, as he followed them silently. With his hands and legs tied, he was confined in an iron cage, like an animal. Beyond that, nobody tried to torture him. There were many soldiers there, who had seen his valour and majestic personality. They felt awe mixed with respect towards him. At the same time, none of them had the authority to decide what could be done with him.

They appeared to be waiting for orders from a higher source. A few hours passed in indecisive hesitation. The sun too had set and darkness began to envelop the area. The soldiers began to light torches and make their camp and its surroundings well lit. They were scared of Adithya even with his hands bound, and caged!

Suddenly there was a rustle and murmur. And then jubilation! The soldiers began to move about in joy. That army unit, which had all along been like a headless torso, suddenly transformed itself into an active machine. Yes. The leader whom they were expecting had arrived!

The shouts of "Long live Prince Shanbaga Perumal" rent the air and echoed. The soldiers, who had so far been wondering what to do with Adithya, now took Shanbaga Perumal to the cage where he was confined.

Adithya was dragged out of the cage and presented before Shanbaga Perumal. Their eyes met momentarily. However much Adithya had downplayed his victory, he could not conceal the look of arrogance on seeing the vanquished. Having been defeated,

Shanbaga Perumal too understood immediately the import of Adithya's look. As he had been observing Adithya very carefully expecting this from him, the Prince was able to catch that stance at once. Because of this, his anger and jealousy increased manifold and made him furious. He wished to insult and disgrace the unarmed Adithya further, and then kill him. So, hiding his anger he asked with a smile, "When did the Cambodian warrior become a lady?" Adithya did not reply to this.

His silence infuriated Perumal. The hatred and malice which he had been controlling now burst to the surface. All his pent up emotions exploded. "I shall sever the head of this Cambodian spy and offer it to my father" Perumal shouted, and raising his sword he leapt upon Adithya.

As he thought that his life was over at that moment, suddenly several memories flashed across Adithya's mind. On one side, Mandagini's sweet face appeared and asked, "Is your life going to end like this?" On the other, Visakadevi's attractive face appeared and said, "Adithavarma! Your duty beckons you. There are so many things to be done before you die." Vajragnani, on his part said, "Is this what I sent you for?" Though these thoughts lasted just a few fleeting seconds, it seemed an eternity to him. Expecting the sword to fall on his neck any moment, Adithya waited with the peaceful feeling that everything was over. At some point in life, when all human endeavours fail, man gives up. And when one gives oneself up to the hand of fate a serene calm comes over that person. In Mahabharata, after the initial struggle, Draupadi gave up trying to hold onto her sari from her assailant Dussaadhana. She completely surrendered to Krishna and stopped her own efforts. At that moment Krishna intervened and saved her. But, whom could Adithya surrender to, when he did not believe in a God? He was neither a Hindu nor was he a Buddhist.

The wait seemed to be forever. But the knife did not come down. A familiar voice came from somewhere. "Stop, O' prince!" That voice halted the sword that was about to descend on his neck, and thereby stopped his death.

A few seconds passed in silence. As Adithya who had waited for the permanent peace called death, stood unmoved, and Shanbaga Perumal slowly lowered his sword and sheathed it, the attention of all of them turned towards the direction of that voice.

There stood Satthama Govida, his face devoid of any feeling.

"Respected master, he is a foreign spy," said Perumal.

"O' prince! On our way here, he saved our lives from the pirates. I had then promised him that at the right moment I would recompense that deed. If he had not done anything then, we would all have been captured by the pirates and faced a torturous death. Hence, please help me to keep my word" said Govida.

"O' Master! Shall we then allow him to board a ship, return to his country and help our enemies?" asked Perumal sarcastically. "No, my prince! Get him onto a boat and put him out to sea. Give him the whole night to leave our country. If he manages to go out of eyeshot by then let him survive. On the contrary, if he is found on our soil tomorrow morning again, you may do what you please with him" said Govida.

Even in the most adverse situation in life, if there is the faintest chance of escape, any man will try to make the best of it. With death round the corner, and in a mood to surrender, Adithya, when given a chance to survive, regained his vitality and courage in an instant. Yes. Within those few seconds, he transformed himself. He expressed his gratitude to Satthama Govida, and was taken by his captors to the beach and put in a small boat. He was untied and left, a free man. A free man cast at sea to make his own future.

Ezhuth Aani

In accordance with Satthama Govida's demand, he was given two oars and drinking water. He told the youth, "Young man, I have fulfilled my promise. Your life is now in your hands. Go away somewhere before dawn. If you are captured by these men again, nobody can save you."

Chapter 7

Left to himself, Adithya gauged his situation. On the south was an island called Mannar, and beyond it, sand dunes and limestone shoals in an intermittent formation called the Sethu Bridge, which extended all the way up to Rameshwaram in India. If one sailed westwards one could reach India. But he doubted himself if it were possible for a lone man to row a boat and reach India before dawn. He knew only too well, that if he were to be in distress in the middle of the sea, the Sinhala navy could identify him easily, and there was nowhere for him to hide on the seas.

At the same time, he knew that if he went north he could reach the Jaffna Kingdom which was under the control of the Tamils, and once there, he had a greater chance of escaping from the clutches of Shanbaga Perumal and leaving Lanka. Hence, he began rowing northwards. He decided to get to the middle of the sea, and once beyond the view of the navy on the shore, to row the boat northwards. With the help of the North Star, he rowed north. As he rowed continuously north for several hours, his shoulders and hands began to lose their energy. The pain incurred earlier in his back started to trouble him again. On the other hand, he was very thirsty and drained.

With the drinking water in the boat exhausted, hunger, fatigue and dehydration took their toll on him. His hands became totally powerless and he felt giddy. Physically weak, he now began to lose his senses. But he strived to keep the boat moving.

Whether to relish over his struggle or otherwise, the sun slowly began to peep from the sky. Reddening the eastern sky, the sun heralded his arrival.

On a cloudless sky, observing the stars, Adithya had been calculating his direction; but with the arrival of the sun, the stars disappeared, and he rowed the boat keeping in mind the fact that the sun rose in the east. But with his mind in turmoil, he suddenly doubted if the sun rose in the east or west. The question also arose as to whether it was sunrise or sunset.

In mid-sea, with no sign of land, Adithya lost control of the boat completely. At this time, caught in a huge wave, the boat began to drift and be carried away.

For the second time in the same night, he was caught in the grip of forces beyond his control and began to surrender to his destiny. Yes! He let go of the oars and slid down into the bottom of the boat. He did not even have the ability to understand clearly that death was inevitable. Soon, Adithya fainted.

How much time passed, he did not know. But, when he opened his eyes, the sun had begun to set. Recollecting that he was on the seas, he began to survey his surroundings. He was not on water anymore but on dry land. Yes. The sea which had rocked and lullabied him into his faintish slumber could be heard roaring in the distance. But he was on stable land. Yes. He was laid on a hard rock. Beside him sat a man, observing him worriedly. A middle-aged man, he was tall and majestic. "Brother, are you Tamil or Sinhala?" he asked.

As he could understand Tamil to a certain extent (due to his mother) he could converse with that man. He was hesitant to narrate his entire story openly to a complete stranger. He told the latter that he was a foreign merchant, and that he was ship wrecked. Though the stranger knew that he was lying, having seen him floating in his boat, he did not compel him to tell the truth. He decided that his approach would be to first nurse him back to health, obtain his trust, and then gather the information about him. The stranger was in a position to tell the truth. Yes! Truth is a noble concept. It is an empowering force, capable of freeing us and help us gain independence and self-respect. But, in reality not everyone is in a position to utter the truth at all times. Only those who are in positions of strength have the courage to tell the truth. This further increases their self-respect and self-confidence and makes them feel good. But, when those who are on thin ground in life, speak the truth ignorant of its consequences, they get entrapped into problems and worsen their situation. Yes truth is the property of the strong and the powerful.

Adithya was in a very weak position. How could he, who was at the mercy of a stranger, speaking a different language, in a foreign land, part with all the information about himself? The stranger, on the other hand, was on his native soil, and on his own back yard, with nothing to fear. Hence, he had no hesitation in speaking about himself.

The stranger said that Adithya was on the shore of an island called Neduntheevu (Delft), that his boat had been wrecked on the sharp rocks, that he had seen him helpless, and that after strenuous effort he had lifted him, placed him on a rock and taken care of him.

"You are in a Tamil area. For the time being, we have escaped from the dominance of Shanbaga Perumal and Parakrama Bahu, and are functioning as a separate kingdom. But, we don't know how long our freedom will last" said the stranger.

"I do not know much about your local politics. Please explain" said Adithya and drank the water which the stranger gave him. As his dehydrated condition began to improve gradually his feeble hands regained their vigour and strength. He then asked, "How did you find me? Why did you save me?"

Peering at him sharply, the stranger said, "We are expecting an attack from King Parakrama Bahu any time. Our navy is stationed in various islands. Apart from that, many teams are being sent in rotation on reconnaissance missions beyond our front lines.

Ezhuth Aani

We saw your boat in advance. But we waited to see what would happen. By then, your boat had run aground. As it smashed against a rock, water began to enter it. I rushed and saved you."

Only then did Adithya understand that the stranger did not function as a single entity; that there was a group behind him; however, he was not a leader who would send the others to the front and hide behind; on the contrary, he was a leader who led from the front.

"Where is the rest of your party?" he asked; the stranger replied, "They'll come when necessary. Right now their presence is not needed; I've not called them."

When asked, "Who are you?" the latter replied, "I am King Gunaveera Singai Ariyan's servant. My name is Kaalingan." He added, "I am not bound to the traditional army. My armed unit is called the Special Forces. We are under the direct control of the king himself. We report to him only. Our regiment functions just like the rapid deployment forces of the Pandya Kingdom.

"I know that you are not a merchant. Will you tell me the truth at least now?" asked Kaalingan very casually, with a bland expression on his face. Saying that until he was able to get up and walk, he would not leave him alone, Kaalingan told the youth, "I know that what you said was not true. I shall wait patiently till you tell me details about yourself voluntarily."

Whether it was due to the extraordinary trust in the stranger or otherwise, Adithya narrated his entire story to him without any reservations. He too listened to him patiently. Then the stranger asked, "Are you sure that King Parakrama Bahu will help you?" The youth said, "I have faith in the king. But the prince is of the warring type. He does not like me. So, whoever has the upper hand will decide what would happen."

Adithya had told the stranger everything except the fact about the emerald Buddha. That was because he had promised Vajragnani that he would keep it a secret. Adithya thought to himself, 'Truth does not consist only of black and white colours. There are different hues and different shades'. His mother had told him many stories from the Mahabharata. One of the frequently narrated stories was that of Aswatthaama. Aswatthaama was the name of Drona's beloved son. Krishna named an elephant Aswatthaama, killed it, and proclaimed that Aswatthaama was dead. The news spread to Drona who was in another sector of the battle. Overcome by grief, Drona could not fight effectively and was eliminated. Krishna performed an act that was unethical though technically he told the truth.

As hours passed, Adithya was able to walk. Having lain on a hard surface in the same position, his back and the lower part of his feet had become numb and were painful. The stranger took him to their clandestine camp. As he limped slowly, the former also walked patiently with him. Crossing the beach that had sharp stones and rocks, and open land, they entered a dense palmyrah grove. When he stepped on the small stones and thorny fronds of palmyrah on the path, he could not bear the pain in his feet. The darkness of the night combined with the density of the trees, had steeped the whole place in total darkness. Because he was familiar with the paths, Kaalingan took the youth along footpaths with less stones and thorns.

After walking a short distance, a small hut with thatched roof could be seen in a clearing. As a lamp had been lit inside, the small rays of light emanating from it lent an aura to the hut.
As he neared the hut he uttered a password, and those inside opened the door. There were two companions inside. As they had already known about Adithya's arrival, they had prepared food for him, herbs for his ailment, and dressing for his wounds.

"You eat and rest. We'll talk in detail tomorrow morning" said Kaalingan.

The moment his body hit the floor, the sleep possessed him completely. That day's incidents combined with the effects of their medicines, laid him down altogether. When he opened his eyes, it was past noon the next day. Kaalingan had gone off somewhere. Only one associate of his was in the hut. He was reluctant to talk. He behaved not like a friend but like a guard. But he ensured all Adithya's needs were met.

Kaalingan who came again that evening, said "Adithya! Get ready. If we go to Nallur it'll be easy to make arrangements for your travel."

Neduntheevu is the largest and furthest of the islands forming a ring south west of the Jaffna peninsula. If the main island of Lanka is the body, Jaffna peninsula projects out like a head, joined to the mainland by a narrow isthmus of land, which is like a neck. There are many smaller islands and islets that surround the "head" like a necklace or a tiara depending on one's imagination. If one were to cross the ocean between these islands at once, one could reach the Jaffna Kingdom. But, in many places this ocean had big whirlpools and swift currents, as well as sand dunes.

If one were to leap from island to island, one needed boats in every place and horses to cross the islands. Opposite to Neduntheevu on the east there was a promontory from the mainland called Irangkondu Mundhal, jutting into the sea. If the wind and current were favourable, one could cross this sea stretch in one night. But, on the way was an island called Paalaitheevu. Near this island there were sharp rocky outcrops. In the sea, too there were big currents usually. Due to this, many shipwrecks took place near Paalaitheevu. If one crossed this danger one could reach the point called Irangkondu Mundhal. Here, there was a small camp of the

Jaffna army. Beyond that, if one travelled a few miles, settlements like Veeravil and Pallavaraayan Kattu could be reached.

Kaalingan made arrangements for their journey. He had a small sailing boat with him. He collected drinking water. On a sea voyage, if any mishap were to occur, and one had to spend many days struggling on the seas, the first need would be drinking water. Even if there is water everywhere salt water cannot be used for drinking. Later, taking into account the direction of the wind and the currents in the sea, and waiting for a favorable time, he raised anchor.

It was a moderate sized boat. Not more than four people could travel in it. The sail attached to the mast in the centre, could be adjusted according to the direction of the wind, to a certain extent. Apart from this, there were oars and a rudder. They had to coordinate the rowing and the rudder position as well as the sails to travel in the direction of the destination.

The two of them rowed the boat towards their destination, with the moonlight and the stars for guidance. After many hours' travel they spotted land far away. Kaalingan said, "That is Paalaitheevu. Adithavarma, if we are not careful here, the boat will be carried away by the rip and will dash against the rocks."

No sooner had he said this, than a strong wind began to blow. The boat too started moving towards Paalaitheevu. As he had expected this, Kaalingan said, "Help to lower the sail; quick." Immediately, both of them lowered the sail, and the impact of the wind on the boat began to decrease. Very skillfully, making quick orders regarding the oars and the rudder Kaalingan steered the boat away from Paalaitheevu. With Adithya's able help Kaalingan ensured that they were on the right path.

Having crossed the danger of Paalaitheevu, Kaalingan was more relaxed. The caution, tension and agitation which he had shown till then left him, and he began to talk calmly.   He said, "Adithavarma! Just as your country is facing danger, ours too is facing on the threshold of war." The youth asked: "I don't understand your country's politics. Please explain in detail." He added, "Is it racial? Is it based on language? Or is it based on religion?"

To that he replied, "No, no. This is a fight for our land. For a long time we have been living in this area. Our desire is to live as we wish on our land. This is the land of our ancestors. We do not like people from other places trying to rule us and changing our lifestyle. All of us have come from India at various stages. Those who settled in the southern parts while maintaining their ties with India, evolved the Sinhala language for themselves at the same time, and developed it. There are many Sanskrit and Tamil words that have been assimilated into Sinhala. As for us, we preserved the Tamil language and culture. Though there were regional differences, we retained the Tamil identity.

"In spite of this difference Tamil has been given the pride of place in the Sinhala royal court for centuries. Several Tamil literary compositions have been staged in the presence of the Sinhala kings in their royal court. Spoken and written Tamil plays an important role in the Sinhala royal court. Therefore, this is not a language issue.

"This is not a racial issue either. Many Sinhala kings have married ladies from the Pandya kingdom. More than half the blood running in Sinhala kings is Tamil. Similarly, several soldiers and aristocrats who had migrated from India have integrated themselves with the Sinhala society. Nobody considers them as of a different race. In the army that is preparing for a war on the Tamil kingdom, there are many Tamils.

"This is neither a war between religions. I am a Buddhist. Several Tamils have been Buddhists, and continue to be so. Similarly, after Polonnaruwa period many Hindu gods have entered the Sinhala people's worship in various forms. This may be a manifestation of Mahayana Buddhism, or the result of the close marital and political ties which the Sinhala kings had with the Pandyan Kingdom. Except for a few fanatic Theravada Buddhists, nobody worries much about religion. Many of the Sinhala kings have endowed grants and concessions to Hindu temples.

"This is a land issue. Because of our love for our soil, we are taking great pains to safeguard our freedom. Just as Cambodia is fighting for its independence, we are also fighting for ours. We are fighting for sovereignty over our land. We are fighting for autonomy."

As he was explaining like this, strong winds and rain lashed the boat and proved their might. However strong Man may be, he is weak and powerless before Nature. Luckily, the wind and the rain stopped after some time. Later, they were lucky to have tailwind and their journey proceeded briskly again. Both of them had become wet due to the spray of the salt water. In the rain that followed they became fully drenched. How could one sail in the sea without getting wet. They continued with their work, leaving their dampness to dry in the heat of their own bodies. The rain water helped to reduce that stickiness of the salt.

Eventually they reached the mainland. There was a camp of the Jaffna army there. When they reached that place the sun was at its zenith; it was noon time. The sentries who knew Kaalingan took them inside the camp. In the camp consisting of several huts, the soldiers were carrying out their respective tasks meticulously. Everything was being done in a disciplined manner. After the two of them had eaten and rested, Kaalingan received two horses from the camp captain. Mounting the horses, they undertook the next stage of their journey.

Ezhuth Aani

The Jaffna peninsula protruded like a head from the top of the island of Lanka. The neck supporting this head, however, was a very narrow isthmus and was surrounded by the sea on both sides. Like a maiden bending her head in shyness, Jaffna appeared to bend and touch the chest in many places. Because of this, in several places the sea between the peninsula and the mainland was very narrow.

This land had a unique nature of its own. On one side were the shrub bush and palmyrah groves; the seaside, on the other hand, consisted of black sand and mud. There were plants that thrived in salt water and there were plants with unique air roots that jutted out from the water like small spikes. There were plenty of inlets and bays, with the shoreline being very irregular. Those unfamiliar with the landscape could lose their way easily. Quicksand can be found at unexpected places. This soil had an exclusive aroma to it. Only those who have experienced it will understand the scent of the wind, which transforms the salty sea water into a spray with a unique fragrance and sprinkles it over the entire area.

As they mounted their horses and continued their journey, Kaalingan asked, "Adithavarma! You have been to the southern parts of Lanka. You have seen the landscape there. Now you are seeing our soil. Do you understand how unique our land is? What is wrong in our ruling our own land? We will not allow others to encroach upon our land." When he said this, his face lit up with his love for his soil. Call this patriotism, call this exclusivism but this certainly is how the people of this land feel about themselves, thought Adithya.

Adithya then asked: "I feel that an outside force may be watching the two of you clashing in this island! If both of you are united it'll be difficult to defeat you. But if you fight among yourselves foreign forces may enslave you both!"

Steeped in the pride of his land, Kaalingan did not much relish the reality of the young man's point. Adithya's matter-of-fact statement brought Kaalingan from the lofty skies down to earth. The reality is that if the people who inhabit a land cannot solve their own problems amicably it will pave the way for others to exploit and rule the divided land.

Both of them proceeded towards Nallur in the Jaffna peninsula. In many places, they had to walk through waist-deep water. In many others, mud and thorny bushes made their travel difficult. What appeared like a sea was, in many places shallow and as there were sand dunes here and there, they could cross over without a boat. At the same time, some places were quite deep. As Kaalingan was very familiar with the area, he knew where he could plant his feet safely. The Jaffna seascape can be cited as an excellent example to prove the verity of the adage 'Look before you leap'.

As they travelled, Kaalingan narrated to Adithya the history of the Tamils. From ancient times, migrants from India governed their daily lives themselves. The Sinhala kings of Anuradhapura did not disturb them much. In the Vanni belt between Jaffna and the Sinhala areas, there were many autonomous Vanni settlements. The Vanni leaders lived there without accepting Sinhala hegemony.

During this period, Maagan of Kalinga and the Javanese Prince Chandrabhanu established a separate kingdom in the north, with the help of the Tamil kings of India. The island of Lanka was overrun first by the Cholas and then by the Pandyas. Finally, Aryachakravarti, one of the Pandyan generals, declared the Jaffna Kingdom as a separate unit and enthroned his dynasty.

In India, the Tamil kingdoms declined gradually, and Jaffna flourished as the only Tamil kingdom at that time. The Sinhala kings, who had slowly moved their capital southwards due to the successive attacks of the Tamil kings of South India, attempted to bring the whole country under their control when the power of the

Ezhuth Aani

Tamils waned in India. It was at this time that the Vijayanagara Empire took shape in crntral India as the successor of the Chera, Chola, Pandya, Pallava and Chalukya kingdoms, stalling the Islamic expansion and safeguarding the Hindus' traditions.

Kaalingan said, "We need the Vijayanagara Empire's help. The king has ordered me to go there for that." Adithya said, "The next stage of my journey is to visit Vijayanagara. My mother is a Vijayanagara princess. She went to Cambodia after she married my father. I have spent many years of my childhood there."

Kaalingan had not helped Adithya, expecting something in return. But now, both their goals seemed to be converging! This is what happens in life at times. When help is rendered spontaneously without any ulterior motive, it brings unexpected benefits.

After a few days' travel, they finally reached Nallur, the capital of the Jaffna Kingdom. On the way, though the people's settlements were sparse initially, as they neared the Jaffna peninsula, the land was densely populated. Kaalingan had some acquaintances wherever they went. Not only the military camps but even the ordinary civilians were quite familiar with him and willing to help arrange for their food and accommodation.

The Jaffna peninsula was a prosperous, fertile land. Fields of red soil could be seen everywhere, and also wells for irrigation. To draw water from the wells, sweeps and coir ropes with buckets were installed. In some places, bulls were used to draw wheels with a series of buckets. The buckets would go up and down, drawing the water and supplying it to the fields.

"You have the water problem only now. We have had it right from ancient days. There is no river in the Jaffna peninsula. Under normal circumstances, people should have avoided a place without a river and settled down elsewhere. But, we have used the ground water and transformed this land into a fertile and rich country" said Kaalingan. Adithya too, observed the various methods of rigging wells and arrangements to draw ground water, very carefully.

Finally, they reached the capital city of Nallur. It was situated on the banks of Lake Yamunaari, which was surrounded by green fields. The big streets made of clay and paved stones were lined with trees and flowering plants. From the centre of the city, the roads ran radially in eight directions, symmetrically. Mounted and armed soldiers who roamed the area reminded the people that war was not far away.

In a place called Muthirai Sandhai was the king's huge palace. Around it were many settlements. Here, members of the royal family, the ministers, military officers and the Hindu Brahmins lived. A solid wall was built around this settlement. In the middle of the city was the Kandasamy temple, with its tall towers; an excellent symbol of Dravidian architecture. Apart from this, there were big separate temples for Siva, Ganesh and Kali.

On reaching Nallur, Kaalingan went to the palace, presented his credentials, and left for his lodge in a place called Kalviyankaadu, along with Adithya. In Kalviyankaadu, situated at some distance north of Nallur, there was a Special Forces camp. When they went there, Adithya understood that Kaalingan was no ordinary man. From the manner in which he was treated by the others, it was clear that he was a highly respected leader in the hierarchy. Some leaders govern from the top. But, Kaalingan maintained direct contact even with the lower cadres of soldiers. Instead of staying in the capital all the time, he travelled to every nook and corner of the country frequently, and supervised the security arrangements.

The next day, they received the invitation from the king. As Kaalingan was taking Adithya with him, he had requested special permission from the king to grant audience to both. The moment they crossed the ramparts of the fort and entered the palace, Adithya felt as if he had stepped into a whole new world. Outside, efforts and arrangements were being made for the impending war everywhere. Regular patrolling by the mounted soldiers, and parades by the infantry, indicated the readiness of the army in the city outside. But within the palace there were no traces of war preparations at all. Wherever one turned, there was music and dance; in every room some art was being taught rehearsed or premiered. The two of them crossed all these and reached the inner sanctum. Here again, another environment awaited them.

Several scholars were seated peacefully, steeped in academic endeavour, with their palm-leaf manuscripts and quills, making copies of ancient literary works and creating new ones. If one went beyond them, one could see Tamil pundits engaged in debates. Adithya thought that in ennobling themselves through education, these people were unsurpassed. At the same time, mere academic learning was of no practical use. However learned they may be, unless they were able to defend themselves in a war, they could not hope to retain the benefits of their education.

King Gunaveera Singai Ariyan met them in a separate chamber. Seated on a large throne, the king received Kaalingan and acknowledged his greeting. He then asked both of them to take their seats. As soon as they sat on a small couch opposite the king, Kaalingan said, "O' king of kings! This is Adithavarma; one of the princes of Cambodia."

Smiling at him, the King said, "Welcome to our land." Then, looking at him keenly, he asked "What brings you here?" Adithya too looked at the king. But, unable to bear the intensity of the latter's gaze he avoided eye contact and shifted his gaze to the king's face and body. Short and broad, the king was stout and muscular but without an ounce of excess fat. His hands were like the boughs of a big tree. The scars on his shoulders and chest bore witness to his martial history. His large moustache and a huge scar near it appeared to be symbols of his valour. It was obvious that he was a veteran of many battles. One look at him and Adithya realised that it was not easy to defeat him in a war. This was the puissant symbol of freedom.

Before Adithya could answer the question, Kaalingan replied. "O' king! He came to Lanka to ask for military aid. But, he became a victim of the wrath of Shanbaga Perumal, our enemy, and is now trying desperately to leave the country. His mother is one of the princesses of Vijayanagara. He wishes to go to India, and seek the assistance of Emperor Devaraya. If you permit me, I too can go with him, explain the danger that we are facing, and ask for help."

"Kaalinga! Have I ever refused you anything? I have no objection to your going with him." He then addressed Adithya: "In our childhood, Kaalingan and I were very close friends, and went around freely. But, after I entered the golden cage called the royal throne, Kaalingan has served as my eyes, ears, hands and legs in the outside world."

Later, after a few formalities, the king's order was inscribed on a palm-leaf and sealed. In the missive addressed to the officer in the port city of Parutthithurai, it was ordered that he should provide the two of them with all facilities and arrangements for their travel. In addition, a letter was also written to the Emperor of Vijayanagara.

The next day, they travelled to a town called Vallipuram near Parutthithurai. In the middle of a vast expanse of white sand and sea, was a Hindu temple. It was called the Vallipurathazhwar temple. Though it was a temple for Vishnu, a big Buddha statue had also been consecrated here. It was another proof of the unity of the Hindu and Buddhist people of ancient times. From Vallipuram, they took a small boat to reach Parutthithurai. In accordance with the king's orders, the boatmen ran a free service between these two coastal towns for the benefit of pilgrims.

Ezhuth Aani

Parutthithurai port city was an important centre where large ships anchored. This port situated right at the top of the island of Lanka, served as a transit point between the eastern countries like China and Siam, and many of the ports on the east coast of the Indian sub-continent. Sailors and traders from many countries would break journey and rest here. Moreover, this port also served as a warehouse from where commercial goods were distributed to the northern cities of Lanka. The shore was beautified not only by palmyrah but also by coconut trees, and presented an idyllic sight during sunrise and sunset.

During their sea voyage, both of them exchanged their personal details. Kaalingan was born and brought up in the coastal region. He explained the Jaffna society's caste system. Farming and land owning class were called Vellalas. They comprised the majority. Aryachakravarti was believed to have descended from a Brahmin family belonging to Ramanathapuram in Pandyan kingdom. However, there was a belief that they too were Vellalas. Whatever the case may be, unlike India it was the Vellalas and not the Brahmins who dominated in Jaffna. Of these some were landowners, while the majority consisted of lease holders who cultivated it. In all, it was the Vellalas who controlled most of the land. Those who lived in the coastal areas were called the Karaiyars. They controlled the maritime wealth. The rest of the society was relegated to menial tasks and were subdivided by the traditional family occupations. However hard those people toiled, they could never become landowners. The Vellalas held most of the lands, and the prevalent Desavalamai law made it difficult for land to be sold to outsiders or to other castes.

Adithya was surprised to hear this. In Cambodia too, class distinctions did exist. Members of the royal family and the landowners were born into authority. However, in Jaffna society every man was branded with a 'caste' at birth and one man was enslaved and exploited by another in the name of that caste.

Adithya said: "Perhaps it was because we embraced Buddhism that this caste system did not take root in Cambodia." To that Kaalingan replied: "There is no connection between religion and caste. I am a Buddhist. Similarly, most of the people in southern Lanka are Buddhists. Nevertheless, the caste system is quite prevalent there. Gautama Buddha rebelled against the Brahmin caste scheme called Varnashrama Dharma which placed the Brahmin caste at the apex of society. He preached that caste was not determined by one's birth, but by one's actions. But, the Buddhist Sinhala people too have allowed the cancer of caste to infiltrate into their society.

"Man adopts various ruses to rule over others. One of them is 'caste'. Using that curse, men of one section enslave another section of the society."

Chapter 8

The two of them disembarked at the port city of Machilipatnam on the east coast of India, and travelled towards Vijayanagara. They procured two horses in Machilipatnam. Kaalingan learnt details of the rise of Vijayanagara from Adithya.

The Vijayanagara Empire safeguarded South India from the Muslim invasions and established itself as a bulwark of Hindus in the centre of India. It was a time when the Hindu Kingdoms of the Pallavas, Cholas and the Chalukyas had fallen and the Hoysala Yadhava, Kakatiya and Pandya Kingdoms had been destroyed by wave after wave of Muslim invasions. The great Muslim kings like Alaudin Khilji and Mohammed-bin-Thuglaq had repeatedly plundered South India. It was at this time that the Vijayanagara Empire was established by Harihara and Pukka. It was built on the banks of the Tungabhadra River, in accordance with the instructions of Pukka's guru Vidyaranya. Madhava Vidyaranya, who belonged to the Sringeri mutt, followed the Hindu doctrine of Advaita or non-dualism.

This Empire brought under one umbrella an integrated South India. Defeating the Muslim sultans ruling here and there, and with the support of the various sections of society, and diplomatic persuasion, it halted the Muslim onslaught at Central India. "Islam, which in countries like Java spread through commerce and peaceful propaganda, was imposed in India at knife point. Those who refused to convert to Islam were killed mercilessly. Nevertheless, there are many beneficial aspects in Islam. The caste distinctions, which are determined at birth in Hinduism, are not found among the Muslims. There is universal brotherhood in the religion. For these reasons it does have mass appeal." said Kaalingan.

Adithya then said: "In Cambodia, Hinduism, Mahayana Buddhism and Theravada Buddhism have been in vogue alternately. Whichever religion the King followed, the people too followed. But, no large-scale conflicts or violence have taken place in the name of religion. The western religions on the other hand say infidels may be killed. Where is the humanitarianism that is supposed to be preached by these religions?"

Kaalingan replied, "We cannot say that our religions have totally abandoned violence. History records that the Tamil Nayanmars, who advocated the Bhakti path, and brought about a renaissance of Hinduism in South India, had the Jain monks impaled. Similarly, when Adi Sankara led his renaissance movement, innumerable Buddhists were either killed or forcibly converted. In the same way, when the King Maha Parakrama Bahu enthroned Theravada Buddhism as the royal religion, the monks who belonged to the Abhayagiri Vihara and who followed Mahayana Buddhism, were defrocked and expelled from the Buddha Sanga. Thus, without exception all religions have been the curse of mankind at some point or other."

Later, they focused on their mission. Kaalingan again said, "Our problem has nothing to do with race, religion or language! It is about land! Whoever is willing to help us, we are ready to accept it gratefully, irrespective of the race, religion or language of the benefactor!"

Be careful what you wish for, thought Adithya. To bring foreign forces in to what was essentially a conflict between brothers could create more problems than could be imagined, he thought. He remained silent.

The path they took on their journey was rugged - through forests and mountains. As the horses trotted on uneven surface, both of them had begun to have backache after hours of riding. As it was evening time, when they saw a Kali temple in the forest, they decided to spend the night there.

Ezhuth Aani

It was a dilapidated temple. The water in the tank near the temple had dried up and become a muddy pool. The temple had had the outer door removed. They understood the reason only when they crossed the outer pavilion and reached the inner sanctum. All the idols in the temple had been disfigured or removed. Those who had engaged in this vandalism had spared the lofty tower, perhaps because it was too difficult to scale. Yes. It was the result of the successive Muslim attacks. The invaders, who were iconoclastic, had indulged in destruction of idols wherever they went.

For these two who were tired, it was merely a transit point. So, they did not worry too much about the idols that were not there. They tied their horses to the trees outside the temple, and cut the tall grass nearby as fodder for the horses. The little water in the dried up tank was like nectar to them and their horses. Going up to the sanctum sanctorum, they closed the inner door and slept soundly.

The moment their heads touched the ground, sleep embraced them. How long they slept, they didn't know. But, they woke up late - whether due to the sun's rays peeping through the gaps in the tiles of the high roof or whether there was a noise that woke them, they did not know. The first to get up, Adithya tried to open the door, and only then realised the stupidity of what they had done. Yes. Both sleeping in the same place was the first blunder. Bolting the door from inside was the second. Someone had locked the door from outside. However much they tried, it just would not move. The heavy temple doors are not easy to break.

Adithya removed his clothes. If they could somehow reach the high roof, they could remove a few tiles and go out; this was his plan. Their dress could be used as a rope. But, how would they attach the rope to a solid rafter or frame in the roof at that height? He realised that his plan wouldn't work.

Both of them sat on the floor and wondered what to do. As time passed, the light shining through the tiles increased, making the visibility better. Adithya said, "I don't pray. But, now I request Kali, to show the way to take us out from here." Suddenly, Kaalingan shouted, "Look there!" As the whole chamber had been filled with light, only then did their eyes fall upon a trident in a corner. Those who had destroyed the idols had left the trident behind. Trident is the weapon of Goddess Kali.

The points of the long, heavy trident were very sharp. From the length of the trident, which was equal to a man's height, it was possible to surmise how tall the Kali idol must have been. Both of them tied their clothes so that it was like a rope long enough to reach the roof. Then, they bound one end of the rope to the point of the trident. Kaalingan said, "We'll get only one chance. Who's going to throw the trident, you or I?" For Adithya who was accustomed to throwing knives unerringly, this did not appear to be a big challenge. But the cost of failure weighed upon his mind. He hurriedly set aside the negative thoughts. The trident should be thrown vertically upwards so that it went through the roof. Then, by pulling the other end of the cloth-rope, the trident should be maneuvered to get caught horizontally in the truss frame of the roof. This would cause the cloth rope to be anchored to the roof. Later, they could climb up the rope. If the trident gave way or the cloth ripped they would be doomed!

Although he was nervous, Adithya got to work, without showing any sign of his fear. The first part of the plan was executed perfectly. Only when he began climbing the cloth-rope, he realised how dangerous his task was! Just as he reached the roof the cloth suddenly began to tear. He knew he would soon fall down. Luckily, he did not lose his presence of mind. In one leap he caught hold of the frame of the roof with his right hand, even as the cloth tore fully and hung in his left hand.   Throwing off the torn cloth he caught the beam with both his hands, and removing a few tiles looked at the world outside. He realised that Kaalingan could not use the same route that he did as they had lost the rope.

Peering down, he asked the latter to remain quiet, and clutching the branch of a tree nearby, he climbed down on to the ground. Entering the temple, he looked around cautiously to see if the enemy was hiding before going in.   The   doors   of   the sanctum sanctorum were closed and bolted, but not locked. He understood that they had been robbed by petty thieves. As he entered, Kaalingan asked, "Where are the horses?"

Yes. They realised that the motive of the thieves was to steal their horses and nothing more. Even so, the reality hit them. In this vast forest where could they go on foot? They knew that their plight was miserable. Ruing the fact that they did not take adequate precautions on the previous night both of them sat down, not knowing what to do next. But, self-pity is a terrible feeling. It saps the energy from the soul. They could not allow this feeling to get the better of them. They were trained soldiers not ordinary men, and leaders at that.

Wondering how to travel in a forest without horses, they began to walk in the direction they had been travelling. Kaalingan said, "Since there is a temple, there must be people and houses nearby. Let's hope for the best. Some clue will appear soon."

After they walked for some time, they could see at a distance the dome shaped top of a mosque. On seeing it, Kaalingan said, "This looks like a Muslim village." Adithya asked, "Are they people who have changed their religion at knife point?" Kaalingan replied, "Now I understand. What happened to the Kali temple has happened to this village also!"

"I have heard that those who convert to a religion become more fanatic than those who were born in that religion."

"Yes. These people might treat us with hatred. But, we have no other alternative except to seek their help. Some years back they too were Hindus, weren't they? How can they hate their past?" Kaalingan said.

Only when they reached the outskirts of the village did they realise the attire they were in. They had had to leave their shredded clothes in the temple. If they entered the village clad just in their loin cloths, they would be beaten up! Kaalingan then said, "You remain hidden here. As I am older, the chances of their suspecting me are less."

There was a small rivulet close by. Kaalingan got into it, and waded in the water until the rivulet reached the middle of the village. Luckily, the first to cross his path was a men's bathing ghat. Many men were bathing in various states of undress. Kaalingan approached them and agitatedly began searching for something on the banks of the stream. Then, one of the men there asked him in Kannada, "What happened? Who are you?"

Kannada and Tamil are somewhat similar. Many words are common to both the languages. Hence, the two men were able to communicate with each other with some difficulty. Kaalingan said that he was a traveler, and that when he was bathing somebody had stolen his clothes which he had left on the bank.

When that man explained all this to the other villagers, they surrounded him. Most of them looked upon him sympathetically, while one man alone asked, "Are you a Hindu or a Muslim?" Even before he could reply, his loin-cloth was removed and they learnt that he had not undergone circumcision. "He is a Hindu thief! Of late, our horses and cattle have been missing. If we interrogate him, he'll come out with the truth" said the fanatic and started beating him.

Ezhuth Aani

Then, an elderly man stepped forward. "Stop! Even if he is a Hindu, it has not been proven that he is the culprit! Have you forgotten that we were also Hindus a few years back?" The speaker must have been the village Elder. His words commanded respect. On his orders, Kaalingan was offered food and clothes, and then interrogated.

He confessed that they belonged to another country, and that they had lost their horses on their way to Vijayanagara for trading purposes. Taking him along, the villagers reached the place where Adithya was waiting. Hosting them affectionately, they requested the two of them to convert to Islam. "We were also Hindus. Only after converting to Islam, we have realised what a noble religion Islam is. Branding us as lower castes, Hinduism had relegated us to an inferior existence. Now, we live as equal men with self-respect" they said.

They were given two days' time to convert. "If you refuse to follow our path, it'll be difficult for you to escape alive. However, we shall not compel you" said the Elder. For the next two days, they were confined in a house in a corner of that village. They were looked after well. They were not disturbed in any way whatsoever by the villagers.

When the deadline was over, they were taken to the centre of the village. The village council had gathered there. The committee of judges which enquired them announced that they were accused of theft. Then, the list of things missing from the village was drawn up and read aloud.

They were asked only two questions. First, 'do you admit your guilt?' Second, 'Will you accept Islam?' To both, their answer was "No."

Kaalingan asked the youth, "Adithavarma! Shall we pretend to accept their religion?"

To that, Adithya replied, "Religion is a personal matter. Who are these people to convert me?" They then fell silent. When the inquiry was over, they were sentenced to death. They were taken back to the house where they had stayed, and were confined.

Kaalingan asked, "Aren't you scared of death, Adithya?"

Adithya said, "I am a warrior. I've never been afraid of death. Since the day I volunteered to fight for my country, every day of my life is a borrowed day. Today, tomorrow, or any day, I'm prepared to die. But, instead dying like a coward it is better to fight and fall."

Death having been made certain, every subsequent day seemed a prolongation of the throes of death. Some more days passed in this manner. It would have been far better to be put to death in an instant rather than wait in indefinite limbo. Their guards, however, refused to talk.

One day there was a sudden commotion in the village! Everyone ran helter-skelter searching for places to hide; there was confusion all round. The men guarding their house also ran away. Somebody was banging on the door. As they opened the door, some soldiers rushed in. They pushed the two of them on to the ground and stomped on them. They then tied their hands behind and dragged them along.

In the middle of the village, all the men were made to stand in a row with their hands tied behind their backs. Far away, the wails of the women could be heard. Adithya understood that they were being molested. The village was under attack! The mosque in the centre of the village had been set on fire. Those who opposed the marauders were killed instantaneously. Those who surrendered were bound. Mounted soldiers could be seen everywhere.

Swords in their hands, they tried to intimidate and threaten the villagers who cowered in fear. On one hand, the women's screams; on the other, the men's pleas; the sounds of sorrow and grief could be heard everywhere. The noise of the logs cracking as they burned was like a rhythmic beat for this lament. This was man's cruelty to fellow man at its worst!

Then, suddenly the soldiers stopped their destructive acts. They sheathed their swords and stood in a formation. All of them turned their attention towards one direction. Yes. A well-built youth was riding on a horse towards them. He must be their leader! The frontline soldiers who met the leader were explaining what happened, to him.

This was a Hindu army. It was obvious from their garb and mannerisms. They were trying to avenge the atrocities perpetrated on the Hindus, in the same manner.

Suddenly, Adithya shouted "Sangama!" Hearing his voice the newcomer turned in his direction, and after peering at him for a second, shouted "Adithya!" Jumping down from his horse, he ordered Adithya to be freed. He then hugged him warmly. Their eyes moistened.

"After how many years Adithya! That too in a totally unexpected manner like this!" said Sangama. "In an unexpected place, in an unexpected situation!" said Adithya. "What are you doing here?" asked Sangama. "I can ask you the same question" said Adithya.

"Okay. I shall go first" Sangama said.

"I am now an officer of the army of Emperor Devaraya II. It is a few weeks since we brought this area under our control. There are pockets of resistance here and there. Many villages that have been converted are working against us. Our current target is to neutralize them." said Sangama.

"I shall tell you my story in detail later. But I want to ask you one thing. Do you think that by destroying these villages you can neutralize them?" asked Adithya.

"Can you suppress violence by violence? These people may have been Hindus earlier. But now, they are Muslims. By punishing them for their beliefs, can you transform them to be loyal to the Emperor?"

"The right to rule is not only a divine gift to the royals. It comes with a big responsibility. It is the king's duty to treat all his subjects equally. It is the duty of the king's army to protect all the citizens irrespective of who they are. Your conduct is like the watchman thieving the goods entrusted" said Adithya. He added, "Have you forgotten what our guru Madhura taught you?" The Jain monk Madhura was their guru. The most important tenet of Jainism is Ahimsa or non-violence. Truth and Ahimsa are the most important of the five vows that govern the lives of the Jains.

Their guru Madhura had also taught them his religious beliefs. When Adithya pointed this out to him, Sangama realised his folly. He ordered his soldiers to release the villagers and not to trouble the women. Later, he took Kaalingan and Adithya along with him. Their platoon moved towards Vijayanagara speedily.

As they approached the capital, the number of security checks increased. But, because of Sangama Raya's high rank, they were able to reach the capital without much delay. What attracted Adithya on the way were the war elephants. He remembered seeing many elephants in his childhood. From his childhood, he had been taught elephant riding as part of the war games. Now the Vijayanagara forces had elephants many times greater in number than those he had seen in the Angkor Empire in Cambodia. Making use of their elevated position on elephant backs, many soldiers were ready to launch an attack on the enemies. Behind every infantry unit these soldiers on elephants stood in formation. In their hands they held not only spears and bows, but another object. Was it the new weapon mentioned by Vajragnani? It was a long tube with a handle, and a trigger to operate it. Although he had heard that King Parakrama Bahu had these weapons, this was the first time he was seeing them. He had seen fire arms carried by carriages, but never seen personal firearms like this.

Another wonder awaited Adithya, who was already in awe of the growth in Vijayanagara Empire's vast arsenal of weaponry and military strength. In some places at the rear of the armed formations were cannons on wheeled carriages. The methods of war had changed completely. Those having new technology and weapons had a huge advantage over traditional powers who failed to adapt. These cannons were much more modern than the ones Adithya had seen earlier in his childhood.

When these weapons were introduced to the Indian sub-continent, the Islamic armies which possessed them were able to establish their supremacy very quickly. But the Vijayanagara emperors embraced these innovations and succeeded in modernizing their armies. With the slogan 'Protectors of Hinduism', unifying people despite racial and linguistic differences, they had paved the way for a strong empire to be built; however, being pragmatic they had also recruited Muslim soldiers and engineers in their army. While the other Indian kings buried their heads in the sands of time and were destroyed, the Vijayanagara emperors adapted themselves to the changing environment and survived.

Vijayanagara possessed several layers of security and ramparts, and appeared to be a well-fortified citadel. Sangama accommodated Kaalingan and Adithya in his barracks and went to meet his uncle, the emperor. Sangama's mother was the emperor's cousin. Although closely related, the emperor had ordered that he should join the army as an ordinary soldier and rise in rank through his skill. At other times, he was given the chance to meet the emperor as a nephew.

On Sangama's request, time was allotted to Adithya and Kaalingan to meet the emperor. But he only agreed to meet them separately. That afternoon it was Adithya's opportunity to pitch his case. His mind was in a state of confusion. On one hand, he had sought and obtained a promise for military aid from King Parakrama Bahu. At the same time, Kaalingan was going to ask the emperor to help the Jaffna Kingdom against Parakrama Bahu. Now, he was going to ask the emperor too to help Cambodia. In other words, he (Adithya) was seeking the help of two enemies. Was this fair? Should he confess this to the King? Should he stop Kaalingan from meeting the king? That is, if he could ensure the victory of Parakrama Bahu the chances of him helping Cambodia would be better.

With such various thoughts Adithya entered the King's chamber; the latter welcomed and hugged him. "Adithavarma! I haven't seen you since childhood. You have grown tall like your father! I have heard about your exploits from travelers and merchants who come here. What do you want? Is your mother keeping well?" The emperor spoke very fast. Normally, he would listen carefully to others, and then answer in measured words; but in his excitement at seeing Adithya, he was expansive. Even before the youth could reply, he said, "You are welcome to stay here. If you so desire, I shall have you married to one of the royal maidens and give you a high position."

Adithya said, "Your Highness! You must forgive me. As far as I am concerned, Cambodia is my country. I shall be happy to lay down my life in the service to my country."

Ezhuth Aani

"Aha! I appreciate your patriotism." Saying this, the emperor looked at him intently. "Did you seek Parakrama Bahu's help?" "Yes" nodded Adithya. "Doesn't your companion know that you have been assured of help by Parakrama Bahu? He has come seeking my aid against Parakrama Bahu" said the emperor, laughing heartily.

Adithya stood with his head bowed down, as if he had committed a serious mistake. But the King said, "Adithya! Don't be confused. There is no need for any doubts in this. Your loyalty should be only to your country. Friends and enemies may come and go. You should not have permanent friends or enemies. You should only have permanent goals. In working for your country, you should willingly accept anybody's help. In the same manner, your friend will also display his loyalty to his country. You should be very clear in this. In your service to your country, you can lie and even deceive. There's nothing wrong in that."

The emperor continued: "Adithya! Don't worry. I am expanding my navy under the leadership of Lakkanna. I shall certainly send you the necessary help at the right moment. At the same time, we have many advantages in sustaining the Jaffna Kingdom as an independent unit. Hence, I'll arrange to help Kaalingan also."

The emperor then spoke about Adithya's mother and other matters. Finally, he asked, "Do you need anything else?" Adithya then asked, "Your Highness, will you send me to Babylonia?"

"Why do you want to go there" asked the emperor. "It is said that in Babylonia there are scientists who know how to harness the power of lightening, by means of chemical reactions. I want to find out if that power can be used for our agricultural needs" Adithya said.

"It is not very difficult to send you there. But, wherever there is scientific progress, we come to know about it first. My opinion is that your going there is not likely to be very beneficial." The emperor sent him to meet his ministers. The minister in charge of foreign trade made all arrangements for his travel. A place was reserved for him in a ship that was to leave for the Arab countries in the next few days. At the same time, Kaalingan too obtained an assurance of help from the Emperor and prepared to return to Jaffna.

The day dawned when both were to depart. Adithya and Kaalingan hugged each other warmly. "My friend! Hailing from different places, we travelled together for some time in the journey of life, due to the play of destiny. Now our paths are going to diverge. Each has our own duties. Nevertheless, I shall remember the days we spent together, as very happy ones." As he said this Kaalingan's voice quivered.

Adithya too said, "My friend! If by any chance we happen to meet again, I shall certainly recompense you. You have saved my life." They then went their separate ways.

Chapter 9

Once again, a sea voyage! Seeing the ocean blue, his eyes became tired. With the spray of the sea water and the sticky sweat of the body, he spent several days within the confines of the wooden ship. The longing to return home began to possess him. He wondered, "How many more days will I travel like this? When will I return to my country?"

The majority of the people in the ship did some work or the other. They engaged themselves in doing the work allotted to them. Only a few including Adithya were merely passengers without any assigned task.

He stood on the upper deck and was watching the sea. Suddenly a drop of blood fell on his upper garment. When he tried to find out where it came from, he understood. His lips had cracked and his gums too had eroded. Sores had begun to appear on his hands and legs also.

Realizing that he was suffering from some disease, Adithya was at a loss not knowing what to do. So far, he had always trusted his ability to overcome any difficulty and hence, been quite confident of himself. He had never thought that he could be afflicted by disease. Shaken to the core, he was startled by a voice saying, "God loves you." Almost in a faint, and feeling dizzy, he looked in the direction of the voice. There stood a man in a white dress, the very embodiment of serenity. His body was flawlessly fair. With blue eyes, and golden hair, Adithya had never before seen a man of that appearance. He was further amazed when he heard the man speaking in Kannada.

"Who are you?" he asked. "My name is Francois. I am a religious leader. Unlike your eastern religious heads, we don't immerse into ourselves. We go out into the society and spread the good news of the Lord!"

Saying thus, he asked the youth, "Have you been out at sea for a long time?" When Adithya nodded in assent, the latter said, "What I thought is right."

"What did you think" asked Adithya. "You   lack   fruit nutrients. Those who undertake long voyages on the seas eat only dried meat and grains. The nutrients found in fresh vegetables and fruits are lacking in their food. That is why they suffer from such skin and oral problems."

Saying so, he offered the youth some of the dry fruits which he had with him. After eating them for a few days, his health improved slowly. During these days the stranger became very friendly with Adithya. He questioned the youth and learnt a lot about Cambodia. He said that he was eager to come to Cambodia and render service, and hoped it would be possible, God willing.

Adithya said, "I respect your faith. But as far as I am concerned, our destiny lies in our hands. If our intention, thought and deed are all right, we can attain Nirvana or Salvation."

To this, Francois replied "My friend! No matter how much good you do, unless you acknowledge the Son of God you cannot go to Heaven." After that he did not talk much about religion to the youth. But he asked eagerly about the political situations in India, Lanka, and Cambodia. He said he had stayed in India for a few years, and that he would go to his country and return with the others to continue his service.

Adithya told him about the purpose of his voyage. He said that he was searching for the instrument that turned lightning into energy which he had heard was in Baghdad in Babylonia, and that he was trying to know about the machinery for pumping water and one way valve technology. Francois assured him that he would help him to the best of his ability.

Both of them disembarked at the Port Hormuz. Francois was to travel by land to Spain, his motherland. As his associates' church was in Baghdad on the way, he decided to go there first. He told Adithya that he would use his connections in Baghdad to arrange for him to acquire whatever knowledge he needed.

It was a tortuous journey to go from Hormuz to Baghdad. First, they went by ship from Hormuz, which was in one corner of the Arabian Gulf, to Basra which was in another corner. Then, they took a small sailing boat from Basra and travelling along the River Tigris, they reached Baghdad city.

On the way, Adithya saw scenes which he had never before seen in his life: deserts on both sides with miles and miles of sand and more sand, interspersed with cities having many mosques. The unique climatic change - of unbearable heat during the day, and cold that could freeze one to the bone during the night - had begun to take its toll on his health. He had fever, and spent three whole days sleeping. Francois tended to him patiently till he recovered.

Finally they reached Baghdad. With teeming markets and mosques, the city appeared over crowded. The streets were full of people. Some placed their loads on camel backs and walked alongside. Adithya was seeing camels for the first time. Baghdad was surrounded by two ramparts. They were very wide and high. In the centre of the city was the Caliph's palace. Its architecture was entirely different from that of Cambodia. The Islamic buildings with high columns and dome-shaped roofs were very beautiful. The mosques had minarets in all four corners. The roofs and the marble floors were decorated with intricate designs.

Tents were put up on both sides of the narrow streets and trade was brisk. On one side were gems and ivory; on the other, perfumes and grains; on yet another, were Chinese silks and clothes embroidered with zari work – the traders were having a field day.

Francois's associates stayed in a house which was in a corner of a secluded street lined with trees on both sides. The house was not easily visible to outsiders. Francois went there, and on introducing himself in the Armenian language, he was admitted. The two men who received and hosted him wore Arabic dresses, but the crosses that hung on their chests identified them as Christians. Francois said, "Christians had been living here since ancient times. But, King Timur killed several hundred thousand Christians. But even the great Timur too, has passed into the dust of time. All man made empires will crumble. The day is not far off, when our religion will spread all over the world and rule the world. However, for the time being, we have to live in fear and hiding." There were about twenty Christians staying there. They would spend the daytime in prayer and meditation; at night, they would walk the streets proselytizing with their Bible, and engage the population in religious discussion.

Francois introduced Adithya to them. "He is a prince of the eastern country of Cambodia. Through him, we can take our religion to Cambodia. But, right now we must help him with what he wants." As soon as he said this, the others asked eagerly, "Has he accepted Jesus Christ?"

"Not yet. But, the Lord will convert him step by step" said Francois. He then asked if any of them knew about the lightning tool mentioned by Adithya. As none of them knew about it, he told them that the next time they went to the city for preaching, they should make enquiries all round.

Baghdad was a sleepless city. Throughout the night, trade flourished with the help of torches. Francois's friends enquired from all the people they met during their missionary work, about the new

Ezhuth Aani

invention. One early morning one of them came rushing excitedly. Yes. He had come with news about their quarry.

The loud calls for prayers were being made from the minarets. It was pre-dawn. Francois's friend took Adithya along. He took him to a dilapidated building. Once upon a time, for several centuries, it had stood majestically as the world's first university, Bayt Al Hikma. Well not exactly the first University if the great Indian Universities of Takshila and Nalanda were taken into account. During the Mongolian invasion Baghdad was ransacked and the university destroyed. Now, it had become the sanctuary for a few lonely scholars. It was there, that they met the scientist called Abu-Bakr. He was the one who invented the battery and the electric light bulb. Only after patiently talking to him for a long time and winning his confidence, did they get shown his creations. That gadget shone like lightning, tearing the darkness of the night.

When he saw this, Francois's friend was stunned. Returning to their hideout in silence, he described what he had seen to Francois.   As they listened to his description, the others' faces turned pale as though they had seen a ghost.

Finally, it was Francois who spoke. "My friend! These magical tricks are the work of Satan! If we support them, it'll be a challenge to the authority of the Church. Hence, it should be stopped from getting out to the people."

Adithya objected to this. But, in one voice all the others said that it was black magic inspired by Satan. Collectively, they decided that the instrument must be destroyed somehow. "My friend! Ask me for anything; I'll help you to acquire it. But don't ask me for this" said Francois. The next day the others went out leaving Adithya behind. They refused to divulge what they did. But Adithya learnt later that the scientist called Abu-Bakr was found dead in his laboratory. None knew whether he had committed suicide or he was murdered.

After that incident, Francois went out of his way to help Adithya.   Valves for pipes, and models of machines for drawing water were being invented at that time. The western countries were on the cusp of a renaissance. Mongolian invasions served to decrease the power of the well-developed Islamic countries; in the same manner, they also served as the stimuli to bring about great changes in the western countries that had been held back by the Church after the fall of the Roman empires.

The Mongolian invasions were also responsible for spreading Chinese inventions throughout the world and developing them further.   With the help of Francois's friends, Adithya gathered the blueprints of these machines and other relevant details. Similarly, he learnt about how modern weapons could be produced. Several months had passed in this way. Adithya had accomplished almost everything he set out to do when he left his motherland.

One day their hideout was raided. The Caliph's officials investigating the murder of the scientist Abu-Bakr had identified this as the work of Christian fundamentalists and had zoomed in on their hideout. At midnight many of them had gone out on their missionary work. Francois dragged Adithya and ran through the grove for a long distance. Walking and running alternately, they went along narrow single tracks and reached another hideout.

Francois said, "Before sunrise all of us must leave this place. Those who besieged that house will lie in ambush and catch the others when they return early in the morning. They will torture them and find out about this place too."

He ordered those staying in that second house to disperse without leaving any trace; after a month, for one or two people to come back to assess the level of surveillance before they return. Both of them left Baghdad dressed as Arabian traders.

Adithya said, "Francois, you have saved me many times. I do not know how to thank you." Francois replied, "My friend! The Lord has a plan for every one of us. My desire is that in the war against Satan, you should contribute your might and save your countrymen from Hell. But I shall not compel you."

Adithya said, "My immediate duty is to return to my land and save it from destruction. Everything else can be attended to later."

"Our Lord is very patient. He will accept you when you are ready."

"May I ask you something?" asked Adithya. "By all means" said Francois.

"It was your men who killed Abu-Bakr, is it not?" asked Adithya.

"I shall neither admit to what you say, nor refute it" said Francois.   He then added: "We are engaged in a sacred war. We are fighting with Satan's forces. Many of the predictions mentioned in the Bible are proving to be true. The book of Daniel and the book of Revelations describe these. The world is going to end soon. It is our duty to save the people from this destruction. The Holy land of Palestine is in the enemies' hands; the Holy city of Jerusalem is in the hands of the enemies. Several Crusades have taken place. But the eastern paths are all in the hands of the Muslims. It is they who control the trade routes to India and China."

"In this war, we are not concerned with individual lives. People like Abu-Bakr are Satan's agents. By means of the gimmicks that they perform in the name of science, they are confusing the people and undermining the authority of the Church. The grip that the Church had over society for the past thousand years has now begun to loosen.

Ezhuth Aani

"But the day is not far off, when our sailors will control the oceans. The technology of ship-building is developing very fast in our countries. Our seamen are going in all directions to find out the sea routes to India and the other eastern countries. Modern weapons are being produced in our countries.

"In one or two generations, we shall rule the seas. Only he who rules the seas can rule the world. After we have found the sea routes, we shall move from the east and the west, and capture this land again. We will rule it, I swear."

Overcome with emotion, he could not continue. Both of them travelled through the desert and reached the port city of Beirut on the east coast of the Mediterranean Sea. From there, Francois went by sea to his country. As per his arrangement, Adithya went by ship to a port called Said. From there, he journeyed by land to the port city of Suez. From Suez he travelled to Kozhikode by sea.

He had begun to yearn to be back in his motherland. It was almost two years since he left his land. He took the land route to India's east coast and journeyed to Malacca. From there, again a sea voyage and then along Mekong River inland; finally he approached Angkor.

How many days! How many experiences! How many times on the edge of life and death! After all these days, will anyone remember him? Will his strategies yield fruit? Will the technology he learnt be implemented? How many questions! How many doubts! How many guesses! With fear on one side, and expectation on the other, Adithya set foot on his native soil.

PART – IV

Chapter 1

All along the River there was increased movement of boats and greater security than before. Though the River Mekong was drier, there was enough water for boats to ply. Boats continued to transport people to Pnom Penh frequently. At the same time, the Cambodian military patrols and checkpoints were also more stringent. The Tonle Sap Lake had shrunk, but there was still sufficient water left to enable navigation in many parts.

One of the soldiers recognized Adithavarma and greeted him; after that he was treated with great respect. As rumors had spread that he had died, they were delighted to see him back. His long absence had been taken as an indication of his demise. In due course he reached Angkor and went to his mother's palace. But disappointment awaited him there. Yes. His mother was one of those people who had evacuated to Pnom Penh. Her palace was empty. A couple of servants stayed there as care takers.

Suddenly a loud neigh filled the air! Then, the hoof sounds of a horse trotting! Ha! A horse was running fast towards him. Only when the majestic, tall, brown mare came closer did he realise that it was his Vibhanji. With her bridle removed, she had been going around the house grazing like a wild horse. She had been left to her own devices. His servants fed her regularly when she was with him. When he left she was a very haughty horse that would not accept anyone else as her master, except perhaps just Mandagini! A proud horse indeed! But today, an orphaned horse!

He hugged Vibhanji lovingly. Stroking her for a long time, he kissed her. Having waited for his return, Vibhanji too regained her former vitality and appeared rejuvenated as if she had had a new birth. Adithya bathed and bridled her and transformed her back into his old Vibhanji. "I had entrusted you to the care of a mistress.

Where is she? How can she leave you unattended like this?" asked Adithya. As though she understood, Vibhanji shook her head, and then appeared distressed.

"Where is she?" he asked again, and leaped on to Vibhanji's back. His next stop was the king's court. Having bathed and rested, Adithya went to the royal palace. The security in the palace was high. Adithya felt that everyone was in a state of readiness for war.

"Welcome Princeling! The hope that you would return had decreased gradually in my mind" said the king. He then took the youth to a separate inner room.

For the next few hours, Adithya described his travels, the trials he met therein, and his achievements. He narrated how he obtained assurances of help from Parakrama Bahu and the Vijayanagara Emperor. He explained how Parakrama Bahu offered only weapons, while the Emperor Devaraya was willing to send his armies. Later he described the new technology that he had learnt from the Arab and Islamic countries.

The king looked worried. The doubt had entered his mind as to whether the Khmer dynasty, which had ruled for six hundred years, would be able to continue to do so. He said that he was expecting a great political change in China. If his friends succeeded, conditions would be favorable to him. Otherwise, his future would become questionable.

The king then asked Adithya to remain in his palace for longer. "Adithya! You take rest. I have to discuss certain important matters with you" he said.

How many changes in two years! Many of the nobles, wishing to avoid the danger from the north, had migrated south towards Pnom Penh. Among the ordinary citizens, those who could afford had migrated. The others stayed back, letting events take their own course.

In these two years how many changes in Adithya too! Greater composure and patience than before testified to his maturity. Similarly, for the first time in his life, he realised that there were people who held worldviews different to his; each one thinks that his own belief system is the best; however, if one accepts the fact that there are people who think differently, and works out a way to live and let live, there would be no conflicts among mankind. The world would become a veritable heaven. He reflected that those who built fences of nationalism, religious fanaticism and racism around themselves did in fact have a tunneled vision and led a miserable life.

In the evening the king summoned Adithya again. This time the chief minister and the other ministers were also present. "Adithavarma! Since I do not have a direct male heir, it was expected that I would declare one of the princes of my own lineage as the titular prince. Though there are many princes who are eligible to claim their right to the throne, it is you whom the people call Princeling very affectionately."

Saying this, the king remained silent for some time. Adithya too waited eagerly looking at the King for his next move. A slight expectation raised its head in a corner of his mind, that perhaps the king might pronounce him as the Crown Prince. He had never nursed the desire to become the king. He had dedicated himself to the service of the country and participated in the wars without any expectations. He had never longed for any returns. But, if the King were to propose his name, he was prepared now to accept it.

"Adithavarma! This is a very dangerous period in the history of our country. War clouds have gathered over us. Skirmishes have already begun in the northern borders of our country. Many of our enemies have got together and forged a dangerous alliance.

"A large scale war may break out any time. Nobody knows who will die and who will prevail in the war. There is no guarantee for my life. Tomorrow if I were to die the nation will be like a headless torso and things will come to a standstill."

As the King continued to speak, Adithya was almost sure that he would be named the successor. "At such times, second level, why, even third level leadership should be very obvious. The chain of command should be crystal clear. If the commander in chief dies or is impaired, not only the soldiers but even the people and the palace employees should be informed in advance as to whose orders they should follow. Otherwise, there will be chaos in the country, and this will be advantageous to the enemy." The king paused. Adithya began planning what he should do when the king declares him as his heir. He debated in his mind whether he should kneel down or bow his head and pay obeisance with folded hands. But his inner mind warned him: "Adithya, don't be greedy. In recent times, whatever you desired has not come to fruition. Why should you be appointed? You know your weaknesses. Surely there are better people around! Why do you desire something you don't deserve?"

Although Adithya had disciplined his mind well, his heart raced in anticipation in spite of him. 'Jayavarman II, Suryavarman, Jayavarman VII - followed by Adithavarma? How will history record my name?' Such thoughts fleeted across his mind. At the same time, he recollected Lord Buddha's teaching too: 'Desire is the root cause of all unhappiness. Desire will always lead to sorrow.'

With such varied thoughts, Adithya waited patiently, eager to hear what the king would say. "After you left, there was no news about you for a long time. There were rumors of your death. Even your mother did not like to remain here, and went away to Pnom Penh."

Ezhuth Aani

Adithya wondered, 'Why this change of track?' He knew the direction of the discussion was not so favourable now.

"Adithavarma! We waited for you. At the same time, I was under compulsion to announce my heir. As the situation in the land deteriorated, the pressure on me also mounted. We had to keep the morale of the people high. There was a practical need too, to make a determination fast, as the war approached. In the interest of the country I had to set aside my personal sentiments and take some bitter decisions"

Adithya now understood clearly that his momentary desire had been snuffed out. Right from childhood, though he was loved and respected by many, he had never functioned with the aim of becoming the king. He had not nurtured any designs on the throne. He had performed his duty towards his country with dedication, but had not expected any rewards or positions in return. On several battlefields he had staked his life and led the armies, but never with the aim of gaining popularity or obtaining other benefits. Hence, he did not take this disappointment to heart. But the questions arose in his mind: 'Who is the chosen one? Whose service to the nation is more important than mine?'

"Whom have you chosen then?" he asked. By asking this question, Adithya had relieved the king of the predicament of how to announce his decision. For the king was still continuing his lengthy preamble not knowing how to get to the point. He was offered the opportunity to go straight to crux of the matter.

"I'm sure you know my uncle's grandson, Mahendravarman! He went to China in his childhood, and grew up there. His father was our ambassador there. He has now returned and is responsible for our war preparations.

"By declaring Mahendra as my heir, the country has received many benefits. I shall explain to you the details later" said the king, adding "But..."

Adithya did not show any agitation in his face. To the courtiers who stared at him expecting to gauge his thoughts, he appeared to be stone faced and emotionless. If they anticipated that he would reveal his innermost feelings, they were in for a disappointment.

"But what, your majesty?" asked Adithya in a flat tone and with a poker face.

"I appoint you as the commander of my navy. Our supply and escape routes depend on protecting the access to Tonle Sap Lake and the River Mekong. We need to control the route to Pnom Penh. If at any time we have to evacuate from Angkor, these waterways will be the best route of transport. Furthermore foreign aid via sea route can arrive in Angkor only if we keep these paths secured. It is vital that we protect them. Moreover, using the technology that you have learnt from the other countries, you can draw up plans for bringing water from the Mekong River to Angkor, and implement them. I shall invest you with all the authority and resources to carry out this work." With these words, the king signaled that the meeting was over and went away.

The other ministers and the chief minister greeted and complimented Adithya on his appointment. Adithya smiled to himself. They were congratulating him on his hollow victory. But he was determined not to let personal disappointments come in the way of national duty.

Later, on reaching home there was turmoil in Adithya's mind. When he thought how Mahendravarman - one younger to himself, inferior in courageous feats, one who had been enjoying a carefree life in a far-off land reputed for beauties when Adithya had

Ezhuth Aani

willingly accepted the scars and wounds inflicted on the battlefield - could become the crown prince having the power to issue orders to him, anger and jealousy consumed him. At the same time, he also felt that the king would have done what was good for the country at that time. Well Adithya was not in the right place at the right time.

No matter what, Adithya who had taken an oath of allegiance to the king and his people was not going to allow his personal likes and dislikes interfere with his work. There was a lot to be done.

Desire is like a disease. Once it takes hold in the mind, positive traits such as honesty and sense of fair play will disappear. Balanced objective thinking will become impossible. Hence, Adithya packed off such feelings and focused on the tasks ahead.

What he needed first was peace. Where could he go in search of peace? If he were to carry out the responsibilities entrusted to him by the king, where could he begin, and where could he end? He needed a serene place to sit and collect his thoughts. Mandagini's memory also haunted him now and then. When he thought where she was, what she was doing, and how she was, he felt a painful joy in his heart. If he could find her somehow his life's problems would be halved, he thought.

When a human being freely shares his or her innermost thoughts without having to weigh the consequences with another human being, the mind becomes lighter. This is friendship. When this happens with romantic feelings, it becomes love. Love is a union: first mental and then, physical, Adithya thought.

In his life, Mandagini was the first woman who had possessed him fully, body and soul. All these days, when he was travelling in other countries, he had relegated her memory to the back of his mind. But now that he was back in his motherland, his old memories came flooding back.

On one side, a pain in the heart; on the other, a churning in the stomach. When he thought 'Would she have found another lover?' he felt a pang of jealousy. When he thought 'Oh no! She'll always be mine' he felt calm. Adithya was subjected to a multitude of feelings in an instant.

He could not sleep. At the same time, he was not awake enough to concentrate on anything. Tossing and turning on the bed, he could not relax. When the sun was about to set, he mounted Vibhanji and went to the slopes of the Kulen Mountains. Wasn't it the sacred place where Jayavarman II proclaimed the Angkor Empire? Adithya went there hoping that he would find peace of mind at least there. And it was there that he first kissed Mandagini.

With his old memories occupying his mind, he reached the banks of the river. It could now be called a rivulet rather than a river. The Shiva lingas that had been immersed in the river water at one time were now almost fully above the water level. The water flowed only in a few places in the middle of the river; the rest was covered with mud and slush. The grass on the banks too, had withered.

Dismounting from Vibhanji, Adithya climbed on to a rock on the edge of the River bank. Vibhanji too, began sniffing the dry grass nearby. How much time passed he did not know. Suddenly, Vibhanji neighed loudly, and crossing over the Siva lingas in the river, she reached the other bank.

With a start, Adithya returned from his reverie to the earth. Drawing his sword, he stood up and looked in the direction where Vibhanji had gone.

There... Vibhanji was being hugged and caressed by ...Yes. Mandagini herself!

Ezhuth Aani

"Mandagini" he shouted loudly and crossed the river. It would be more appropriate to say that he flew across.

Without responding to his question she was fondling Vibhanji and talking to it. She refused to face him and avoided eye contact.

"Ask her why she left you like an orphan in my house, if she really loved you so much," said Adithya.

"Tell him that it is but proper that I return what does not belong to me" said Mandagini.

"Tell her that handing over to the owner is one thing; leaving you like an orphan in his house is another" said Adithya.

After a short silence Mandagini said, "I handed her over to the owner's mother. How would I know that she would leave her and go?"

Now, instead of talking to Vibhanji, they began addressing each other directly. Though she could not understand what they were saying, Vibhanji must have been very happy to see two souls whom she loved, who in turn loved her, and whom she had carried so lovingly, talking to each other.

"When did Vibhanji go to my mother?" asked Adithya.

"Three months ago ... Only then I realised that she did not belong to me."

"Why this sudden enlightenment?" asked Adithya.

She did not reply to that. However much he tried to look at her, she avoided eye to eye contact, and looked at the ground and then at some object far away.

"Are you angry with me?" asked Princeling.

"Who am I to be angry?" said Mandagini.

"Stop acting! Tell me directly what you want to say! Women are always like this! They'll think one thing and say another! If you are angry make me understand why! If you keep talking captiously like this you'll not get a solution to your problem! I have been on the verge of death in so many places. I've never been agitated or scared then. However, now when I talk to you an unknown fear seizes me. Tell me directly what you want to say" said Adithya.

For the first time Mandagini looked in his direction. As soon as she saw him she noticed that he had lost weight. When she thought how he must have struggled during the past two years and how many harrowing experiences he must have gone through, she felt sympathy for him on one hand, and sorrow on the other.

Try as she may to suppress them, her feelings began to overcome her. How could she forget their relationship? There was turmoil in her mind also. When rumors were afloat that he had died, she did not believe them. At the same time she couldn't remain unaffected. As the days passed, she too began to think that he would not return. In that respect, his return made her very happy. But his having come at this time was quite awkward for her.

"Mandagini, why are you silent?" His voice broke her line of thought. But she didn't say anything.

"Why don't you say something, The girl?" he asked holding her hand.

Ezhuth Aani

"Stop Adithavarma!" said Mandagini, as she shook her hand free from his hold.

"Why this pretense? Have you forgotten what it was like?" he said, as he hugged her tight.

Whack! A powerful slap landed on his left cheek. Angrily he tried to hold her tighter. But her words "Don't touch me! I'm another man's wife" froze him.

His tight grip slackened. His hands and legs went lifeless. "What are you saying, Mandagini?" he asked slowly in a feeble voice.

"Yes. I have married another man" said Mandagini, and began sobbing inconsolably. Her breasts moved up and down with her sobs. Though he noticed their beauty he did not stare or try to touch. They were now out of bounds for him!

It took Adithya some time to absorb the situation. He then asked, "Whom have you married?"

"Mahendravarman!" The moment she uttered the name, he realised that for the second time in a single day, he had lost to Mahendra.

Very, very hesitantly he asked, "You ...how..."

She answered, "Adithavarma! Ask my father under what circumstances and what pressure this took place." She then said, "In such conditions it is not proper for us to meet in isolation. Please leave this place."

Reluctantly, he mounted Vibhanji and returned to his track. Her voice trailed behind him. "Adithavarma!" "What's it?" he asked; she replied, "Understand just one thing. Until I got married, I kept

Vibhanji with me and took good care of her. Only after that I handed her over to your mother. I didn't know that she would leave Vibhanji and go to Pnom Penh."

She added, "Come tomorrow to my father's ashram. He will tell you everything in detail."

As he turned she asked "Is it hurting?" with concern, about the slap.

"The hurt is not on the cheek; it is in the heart" he said, and without turning, he left for Angkor again. Had he turned, he would have known that she was sobbing her heart out. Yes; destiny had parted them in spite of themselves. Caught in the grip of circumstances they were like leaves caught in a storm.

His plight on the other hand, was miserable. He had never imagined that as soon as he returned home, he would meet with shock after shock like this. His world had changed. He was miserable. He wanted to disappear from the face of earth.

Returning home, he went to bed without eating, and woke up the next day when the sun's heat became unbearable. His inner mind ordered him, 'Adithavarma! Focus on your duty; don't think of anything else.'

Chapter 2

From the top of the hill, Mahendravarman surveyed the plains all around. This place called Preah Vihear was a temple constructed during the times of Suryavarmans I and II. This temple situated in the Dangrek mountain range, was on the borders with the lands under the control of the armies of Ayutthaya, Annam and Champa, which were united under the leadership of Ayutthaya. Jayavarman VII had ruled over large areas of lands beyond this mountain range; but now the borders had shrunk. However, in the large-scale war that took place two days back, the armies led by Mahendravarman had routed those of Ayutthaya.

In that battle, for the first time, Mahendra had used the new weapons which he had made from the knowledge gained in China. Unable to bear the volley of shells which Mahendra's armies rained from atop of the mountain, the enemy scattered, and the Cambodian cavalry penetrated their ranks and attacked them with lightning speed. Due to this debacle the Ayutthaya army retreated several miles.

Mahendra pulled back his armies to their original positions. This was a defensive battle. He did not have the man-power to capture and control large areas of land at present. His current strategy was to intrude and attack, and then withdraw to the original position. His calculation was that if he overstretched himself, he would be lured into the enemy's trap and be defeated eventually. He did not have enough men to hold the captured territory. When there was a scarcity of food in the land, expanding the army was a difficult task. If trained men were not fed or were not paid properly, a rebellion would break out.

This state of affairs might change in a few months. Mahendra and Boloma had implemented the wind powered irrigation schemes which they had studied, and were waiting for the next harvest. If food scarcity in the land was eased, the army could be expanded. After that, the defensive army could transform itself into an offensive force.

Yes. It is not the military strategies alone that determine the consequences of a war. The economic conditions, steady supply of arms and man-power, and leadership are also major factors. If self-defence is an army's sole objective, it would lose its vitality. The morale and potency of the soldiers would be depleted soon. In many wars, it's the aggressor who wins eventually. But, only if he secures his supply and escape routes as he marches forward, will he be able to cut his losses and retreat should there be unexpected setbacks.

During Mahendravarman's time, the Khmer Empire was on its knees struggling to survive; struggling even to breathe. An expansion of the Empire was beyond his contemplation. Mahendra did not have that urge for dominance which the Suryavarmans and Jayavarmans had. One who merely aims at survival does not achieve major victories. At the same time, one who dares to move forward trusting his instincts is more likely to succeed.

The leader of the contingent standing next to Mahendra said, "As long as we have the sophisticated weapons The Prince acquired from China, our enemies cannot match us."

To this Mahendra replied, "Shanthivarma, only as long as our supply lines are uninterrupted will our weapons reach us. It is easy for us to attack our enemy from this elevated fortification. But, it is essential that the weapons and other necessities reach our armies continuously. As we are on top of the hill it is difficult to heave them up. If the enemy surrounds us, we will not be able to move from here. Every strength has a corresponding weakness."

Saying thus, he ordered spies to be sent behind enemy lines. It was easy to detect large troop movement in the plains far away.

Ezhuth Aani

But it was possible for the enemy to move stealthily in small groups under the cover of the vegetation in darkness. For this reason both adversaries had been sending their own reconnaissance parties inside each other's spheres of dominance.

The Preah Vihear fortified temple was about 130 miles from Angkor. Stationing the cannons here was testimony to Mahendra's military acumen. The steep hills provided a great advantage to the forces with gun positions there. This was their first victory and was a major turnaround in the fortunes. Earlier skirmishes had all resulted in the Angkor armies retreating in the face of enemy assaults; this was the first time they were able to fight and turn back the enemy. Mahendra said, "We must decide our battleground. We will not allow the enemy to decide when and where to fight our battles."

Mahendravarman's contribution to this first victory was enormous. Within a year of their return from China, several important improvements had been achieved due to the organisational skills and hard work of Mahendra and Boloma. From the military point of view, preparations for war were going on very fast. The army had been modernized within a very short period.

A new tax was imposed on the people, and the money collected was entirely utilized for technological progress. The king had placed the treasury at the disposal of Mahendra. Sulphur was dug up from the banks of the volcanic lake called Yeak Laom, situated nearly 200miles east of the Preah Vihear temple, where Mahendra had set up his line of defense. Saltpeter for the explosives was obtained from the Battambang mountain caves.

Their arms factory was situated in Preah Vihear City, which was fifty miles south of the fortified temple. Large numbers of shells and cannons were manufactured there. Initially there were frequent fire accidents and human casualties. But in course of time they refined their manufacturing methods, and accidents became rare.

The weapons are only as effective as the skills of those wielding them. It was not enough to have the weapons alone. Cannon war was totally new to the Angkor army. The troops had to be trained in the modern methods. Shells do not travel in a straight line like arrows. They take a parabolic flight path towards their target. Hence, they have to be fired in a trajectory that takes the travel distance, direction and velocity of the wind etc. into consideration. If not fired skillfully they would only provide a fireworks display and travel harmlessly to fall beyond enemy lines. Special training is necessary for all this. Boloma trained a few handpicked soldiers as the core group. Later these highly trained personnel were able to disseminate the training to other units of soldiers. Thus, several cannon batteries were formed.

Initially, sulphur was obtained from the Yeak Laom; however, Mahendra soon discovered that this supply route was very long and tenuous, and defending it would unnecessarily tie down a disproportionate number of troops along it. Subsequently, a group of people led by Boloma scoured the entire country and discovered the Kampong hot spring southwest of the Battambang caves. As this was west of the Tonle Sap Lake and the river, and closer to Pnom Penh, it was naturally protected from the enemies.

Their factory was shifted to a place called Pursat, which was between the Battambang caves and the Kampong hot spring. By means of this, the uninterrupted manufacture and supply of shells was ensured. Mahendra's defense arrays were formed using natural barriers such as lakes, rivers, and mountains.

The Mekong River flows about 180 miles east of Angkor city. In Strung Treng another river called Seekong joins the Mekong River. For several miles on both sides of this city, on the western bank of the Mekong River, many tall windmills had been built. By means of these windmills water was drawn from the river and was channeled to the fields stretching very far and beyond. Rice was cultivated in this vast expanse, using the newly established irrigation system. It was expected that with this harvest there would be surplus grain in the country. Huge granaries were being constructed in many places to store the grains.

Similarly, south of Angkor city in a place called Pnom Krom, on the north-eastern bank of Tonle Sap Lake, a series of windmills were built, and wind power was used to fill a large tank called West Baray, west of Angkor city, with water from Tonle Sap. From West Baray a canal network had already been built to irrigate the fields. Fields west of Angkor city were made cultivable by this. But the area east of the city remained parched and arid.

Mahendra had effected several revolutionary changes on his return to his homeland. The king too placed his complete faith in Mahendra. As days passed, the king placed all his resources at Mahendra's disposal. It was then that the king declared Mahendra as his heir.

"On the east, Champa and Annam have come together. Our eastern front is facing a greater threat than the other sectors," said Mahendra.

"I am waiting for information from our friends. If the Chinese armies stationed in Annam come to our aid, not only our eastern but our northern borders too will be secure. If the Chinese can attack from behind the armies retreating to escape from our fire, we can annihilate them in a pincer movement." said Mahendra. He added, "Nevertheless, we must be prepared to stand on our own feet should our friends not be able to come to our aid. We need to build up our own strength."

When news of the first victory reached Angkor city, the people were jubilant. Half the battle is won in the mind. If we believe firmly that we will win, it is easier to achieve victory. People should believe that the king will win. If the people lose their faith in the king, they will try to leave the country. If the population deserts a country, the military too will become depleted. The man-power, food and other necessities of the army are all sustained by the people. Faith is a vital element. Faith of the people and credibility of the entrepreneur are very important for any enterprise. Whether it is a commercial establishment or a bank, if people lose their belief in the sustainability of the venture, they will only try to desert it like rats from a sinking ship. The snowball effect will result in an exodus and failure of the mission. Initially, failures may be able to be glossed over by individual charisma and dynamism of the leaders. However if tangible results are not shown to establish credibility, the venture will fail.

As far as the ordinary people are concerned, their lives will go on no matter who rules. They do not have the need for empire building or dominating other countries. All that they aspire for is to lead a normal life. Under such circumstances, it is very important to indoctrinate the people and keep them buoyant and motivated. Victory celebrations serve the purpose of creating an aura of invincibility and help build trust in the ruler.

The king arranged for a victory celebration in honour of Mahendra. The whole of Angkor wore a festive look. The people, who had been accustomed to hearing only depressing news of defeat, drought and starvation, were delighted to have this opportunity to forget their mundane life momentarily and indulge in festivities.

Mahendra handed over the border command to Shanthivarman, and returned to Angkor City. Although he was not particularly keen to celebrate minor victories, he knew only too well the necessity of keeping the people in a state of perpetual jubilation.

Ezhuth Aani

If the people who had left Angkor returned, the army could be expanded, and it would be possible to augment the defences. Wars can be helpful for a struggling nation's economy also. In addition to the increased economic activity and employment opportunities created by the war, when the momentum shifts the Cambodian army could advance and plunder the enemy's resources. History has recorded many instances where an army on the verge of defeat had become the aggressor when the tide turned. For all this the people should be kept on a war footing and need to be fed good news from the front continuously.

Chapter 3

Angkor Thom or Big City was built by Jayavarman VII, a little south-east of Yasodharapura. Since then, this had been the capital.

A huge wall had been built around the city which spanned four square miles. There was a moat around the wall. Some distance from the moat adjoining the eastern wall of the city, flowed the Siem Reap River. Of late, both the river and the moat had dried up.

In the middle of the city was a temple called Bayon. This temple which contained symbols of Mahayana Buddhism, had towers with 216 faces. The towers were in the form of human faces. The face was that of the Bodhisattva, Avalokateswara. Many buildings had been constructed on the east-west axis facing the eastern gateway. From the outer perimeter streets ran towards Bayon. Inside the temple there were two raised pavilions. The statues of Bodhisattva could be seen everywhere.

In the outer pavilion, sculptures depicting the exploits of the Cambodian kings and the everyday life of the people were carved. In the inner pavilion, divine forms such as those of gods and Bodhisattvas were carved. Innermost was an elevated terrace-like platform. On this were towers in the form of human faces. On all four sides of each tower were carvings of human faces.
About fifty towers were built on which more than two hundred faces were carved.

In the Bayon temple, special poojas and worship were performed to celebrate Mahendravarman's victory. Everywhere people moved about enthusiastically. The whole place was agog with optimistic expectations. The wall surrounding Angkor Thom city was more than eight yards in height. Here there were outer gateways in the east, west, north and south. A victory arch had been built five

Ezhuth Aani

hundred yards away from the eastern gateway. Mahendravarman was brought in procession through the victory arch. Streets had been laid from all the outer gateways towards the Bayon temple. These were lined with the forms of various gods. People thronged these streets with joyous abandon. Today was a day to forget all their worries. The realities could be dealt with tomorrow.

Inside the city various palaces and temples had been constructed. Canals had been dug in many places in the city, but they were mostly dry now. It was only during such festive times that the ordinary people could move about freely in the centre of the city.

The Hindu temple called Angkor Wat, built by the Emperor Suryavarman II, was two miles south-east of Angkor Thom, the present capital. This was originally a Vishnu temple. It was known as Varavishnu Loka among the people. But it was gradually transformed into a Buddhist temple later. Unlike Bayon, Angkor Wat temple was built in the Hindu tradition, in the shape of Mount Meru.

There were three concentric rectangular galleries, one atop the other, which tapered as it rose from the ground. At the top were five towers representing the peaks of Mount Meru. It was surrounded by a moat which represented the ocean, though it was dry. This complex too was surrounded by a five foot high wall. The area enclosed by the wall was five hundred acres.

Each of the three galleries was higher than the one below it. All along the galleries there were pillared halls. There were steep steps leading to the galleries. At the top, above the sanctum sanctorum in the centre was a lofty tower. Around this on all four sides smaller towers were constructed. Religious artefacts of Hinduism and Buddhism were found widely scattered everywhere. While the central sandstone building dominated the landscape, smaller wooden government buildings as well as palaces were to be found everywhere. Adithya's palace was also in the Angkor Wat complex. Palm trees and parks dotted the place. The palm trees could survive the drought, but the flowering plants had wilted.

The Victory day celebrations gave the people easy access to all the main areas of the twin cities. On normal days people could come to these areas only on official work. The settlements of people were found surrounding these two temple towns. These habitats stretched in all directions for several miles; in particular, in the north east they could be seen till Mahendra Parvatha. The population density progressively decreased towards the periphery. Rice fields could be seen everywhere. On the west these were irrigated to a certain extent and appeared fertile, while those on the east were drought-ridden.

On the east and west of Angkor city there were two huge reservoirs. These, called East and West Baray respectively, were used to collect the rain water, and the water diverted from the Siem Reap River. Water thus collected was used to irrigate the lands with the help of canals that ran from these reservoirs. They were enormous constructions that could contain vast amounts of water. Due to the drought the East Baray was dry; but by means of Mahendra's latest irrigation methods water had been drawn from the Tonle Sap Lake on the southwest side, and the West Baray was full to the brim. The fields on the west were fertile.

Nearly one million people had been living in the greater Angkor area; but since many had moved out, there were only 800000 people living there now. Supplying food and drinking water to these people was a very difficult task. Because of Mahendra's innovative strategies, these needs were able to be fulfilled to a certain extent now. It was expected that with the next harvest, there would be surplus grain in the country.

It was in these circumstances that Mahendra's first victory was being celebrated. The people were enthusiastic in the expectation that all their difficulties had ended, and that better times lay ahead. The festivities which began in the morning went on till midnight. Torches were lit and the whole area was bathed in bright light.

In the middle of each Baray on a small island, temples called Mebon had been built. The light from these temples and the light from the city combined to colour the water with a golden hue. People wondered whether the gods had poured molten gold into the water.

As if this was not enough, there was a fireworks display using the new Chinese technology, sending the people into rapturous applause. The people spent the whole day and night in cheer and jollity, firmly believing that their victory was imminent.

Mahendravarman, who had returned from the battlefield, and his wife Mandagini were welcomed through the victory arch by the king. After worshipping at the Bayon temple, the king took them to a raised dais erected in front of the temple, and introduced them to the people. The cheers of the crowd resounded to the skies. The royal couple was the cynosure of all eyes. Having such a glamourous young couple at the helm helped to unify the people and lift the mood.

When the king said, "The time has come for the crouching tiger to leap. We shall go beyond the heights reached by kings Jayavarman II, Suryavarman II, and Jayavarman VII, reclaim our lands, and go back to our former golden era." His speech was repeated by the speakers stationed at satellite meetings all over the city and outside. Though many of the people who thronged the streets could not enter the city, it was possible for them to hear the speeches.

When Mahendra spoke, he said "There's still plenty of work to be done. First, we should ensure our safety before advancing." But, when people are flush with a war victory, who is in the mood to listen to such sane counsel? The attitude of the crowd was that the war had already been won. The celebration was grand. The festivities continued the next day too. The emotional speakers urged the people not to leave Angkor, and to request those who had already left, to return.

A guard of honour took place the next day. In addition to the elephant regiment, cavalry and infantry, the newly formed cannon division also took part in the parade. The cannons were placed on carriages drawn by horses. Besides, hundreds of soldiers marched, carrying smaller fire arms on their shoulders. This guard of honour was received by the king and Mahendra, standing on the steps of the Bayon temple.

In addition, there was a naval display in Tonle Sap Lake. The people were able to see the flotilla from the shore at Pnom Krom. Adithya, who was responsible for the navy, was not present there. He was not in favour of such entertainment. It was a waste of precious funds and ammunition. Along with his assistants, he was immersed in his work - an attempt to pump up ground water from the east bank of the East Baray. Using the new methods he had learnt, he was trying to produce tube wells, pipes, valves and so on.

In the midst of the festivities, a messenger arrived looking for Mahendra, who immediately left from the scene.

Chapter 4

To forget his personal disappointments, Adithavarma had immersed himself in fulfilling the responsibilities given to him. Cambodia already had a navy in the Tonle Sap Lake. But, most of the ships were anchored in areas around Angkor city. Since the day he assumed office, he had arranged for ships to patrol the west bank of the lake. Apart from this, he had stationed his ships in Mekong River, which ran several miles south east of the city.

For all this, they needed to build more ships. With the funds and authority given to him by the King, he appointed thousands of workers. Hundreds of trees on the west bank of Tonle Sap were cut down. The work of ship building went on in full swing.

There were not enough weapons to be fitted on the ships. Hence, he had to wait until King Parakrama Bahu sent his promised cache of arms. But, to transport the weapons from the ocean port to Angkor, naval units were stationed at the estuaries of the Mekong River and in Pnom Penh. As the arms factories set up under orders from Mahendravarman had as their first priority the production of arms for the army, the needs of the navy had to wait.

More than all this, the project closest to Adithya's heart was the harnessing of the ground water resources for irrigation. He had seen how, in the Jaffna peninsula which had no river at all, the underground water was used extensively. He combined this with the technical know how he learnt in Baghdad.

Adithya's method involved cutting a tree, removing the core, turning it into a tube, and sinking it into the ground till it reached the water table, and then sucking up the water to the ground level. To carry out this process, two things were necessary: first, a piston that moved up and down, and drew the water up with it; second, an engine to move the piston. The piston would be such that it would fit snug to the wooden well; when it went down it would draw the water into tube well; and brought the water column up with it when it came up. It had flaps around the circumference that acted as a one way valve. The water thus pumped up could be channeled into pipelines. The water drawn by this piston was raised high above the ground, and then taken by pipes to the East Baray reservoir by pressure gradient. This water-pump was initially operated by men or animals. After the pilot project proved this scheme to be feasible, Adithya utilised the windmill technology introduced by Mahendravarman to power his apparatus.

Day and night Adithya laboured tirelessly, to implement his new irrigation system. Hundreds of wooden tube wells were sunk, and the East Baray reservoir had begun to fill up. From here, distribution canals already in place supplied the fields. Adithya was able to forget his personal sorrows by distracting himself with his work. Adithya disseminated his technical knowhow to anyone who was interested. Private entrepreneurs were allowed to dig tube wells for private citizens. Yes. Under the ground there was a sea of water. This would not dry up even if Tonle Sap Lake dried up.

Many months had passed since Adithya returned home. At that time, although news about the conflicts in the northern battlefields reached him sporadically, he did not much care about it and focused his energies on carrying out the duties allotted to him to perfection.

He also heard the news about Mahendravarman suddenly leaving the victory celebrations. It was rumored that the Preah Vihear bastion had been besieged unexpectedly, and that many including Shanthivarman had been trapped there. It was said that Mahendra had rushed there to break the siege and relieve his troops.

It was known that Mahendravarman expected the Chinese army stationed in Annam to attack Champa from there. However this was contingent upon a regime change in China which was thought to be imminent. It was also said that the emperor-in-waiting of China was Mahendra's friend and relative too.

One fine day, Adithya was engrossed in his work early in the morning, instructing the workers. Whenever he was in Angkor he spent most of his time near East Baray. At other times, he would go to the western and southern parts of the country, to supervise the navy's war preparations and the ship building activities.

A leader should not take all the work upon himself. He should employ others, train them and delegate the responsibilities to them. Adithya skillfully managed his subordinates and was able to get the multiple tasks assigned to him done simultaneously at various parts of the country.

The morning sun was reddening the waters of East Baray. The workers too were engaged in their work enthusiastically. As they anticipated victory in the war, their eagerness had increased manifold. Faith is an important necessity in life. Whatever the suffering or the setback, as long as there is faith, and belief that a better future can be achieved, one can bear it well. If we have the hope that someday our sorrows will end we can handle any adverse situation easily. Moreover, when the workers saw the results of their endeavours and how utilising underground water was a realistic proposition they worked with greater conviction. Adithya over saw the work seated on Vibhanji. After losing Mandagini, Vibhanji was his only companion.

He could see someone riding a horse coming towards him in the distance. Though the form appeared to be that of Vajragnani, he could not see properly in the glare of the sunlight. Only when the horse was close did he realise that it was indeed Vajragnani. After he knew he had lost Mandagini, he had avoided meeting Vajragnani. Though she had said, 'Ask my father', he did not follow through.

As soon as the rider came near, Adithya jumped down from his horse and paid his obeisance. "My respects to you, Sire" he said. Vajragnani too jumped down, "Mandagini told me about your arrival."

"Aditha! All of us thought that you had died. I had sent you on such a dangerous mission." His face showed genuine concern. However much he had practised controlling his mind, he could not hide the fact that he truly had great respect and love for Adithya.

"Why didn't you come to me on your return?" he asked. His voice indicated his disappointment and hurt.

"I was engrossed in my work, Master" he said, looking at the ground. He knew that the lame excuse which he offered would not be believed by his master.

"Even if you had tried, it would have been difficult. I had gone to meet the Buddhist monks in Ayutthaya and Champa. There, I heard about the dangerous situation you got yourself into in Lanka."

"O' Master! On whose side are you? Both parties seem to be friendly with you" said Adithya. "Adithavarma! I am on the side of mankind. The cultural treasures found in Angkor do not belong to Cambodia, or Ayutthaya, or even to Champa. They belong to the entire humanity. Saving them from destruction is my first and foremost duty. The rest is secondary.

"Listen, Adithavarma! In all the efforts pertaining to the preservation of the Cambodian Empire from destruction, I shall help to the best of my ability. But, if by any chance you are unable to change the cruel reality of destiny, and your efforts meet with failure, I have to have a contingency plan in place to preserve these treasures." said Gnani.

Ezhuth Aani

"What is that plan, Master?" asked Adithya.

"I am not going to talk about it now. As far as you are concerned, prudence demands that you continue to involve yourself wholly in the work that you have been carrying out successfully. You should never entertain the thought that your labour is futile" said Gnani.

He added: "Adithavarma, forgive me. I was under compulsion to take certain decisions in the interest of the country, setting aside personal likes and dislikes."

"What pleasure did you derive from separating Mandagini and me?" asked Adithya, in a feeble voice.

"Pleasure? Oh no. That must have been the saddest decision I ever took in my life" said Gnani, emotionally charged. Adithya had never seen him like this before.

"Adithavarma! Understand me. Personal likes and dislikes should not come in the way of the nation's service. Will you give me an opportunity to explain everything in detail?" said Gnani.

"Who am I to give or deny the master an opportunity to say what he wants? You may say what you want to say" said Adithya, in frustration.

"Aditha! Mandagini is not my daughter" said Gnani.

"I guessed it long ago. How can a Buddhist monk like you have a family? I know that she is your adopted daughter" said Adithya. "Do you know who her father is?" asked Gnani. "No" said Adithya.

"He is the former Emperor of China. His own uncle usurped the throne and became the emperor. He burnt the palace and killed the emperor's family" said Gnani.

"What about Mandagini?" asked Adithya.

"The emperor alone escaped, and went into hiding. Living incognito he came to Cambodia and stayed here for some years" said Gnani. "Mandagini's mother was a Cambodian princess. She died during childbirth" added Gnani.

"Mandagini came into my custody as a motherless child, who could not openly claim her father. I brought her up as a peerless, skillful lady. I taught her almost every art and science I knew." When he said this, his face shone with pride.

"I know that only too well" said Adithya. "She is the only lady who can equal me in fencing." He added: "I doubt if there is a man alive who is equal to me in warfare. But she is. Not only in valour but in sharpness of intellect too, I have never seen a lady like her."

"Aditha, I know that the attraction between the two of you is like an iron and a magnet. Nevertheless, when you did not return we thought you were dead. Aditha! It was at that time that Mahendravarman, who was in contact with my childhood friend, came with a missive from him."

"Does Mahendra know him?" asked Adithya.

"They met by chance. If Fate crosses our lives, none can stop its play" said Gnani.

"Listen Aditha! He had asked me to declare openly that she was his daughter...Moreover..."

"Moreover what?" asked Adithya. His heart beat increased.

Ezhuth Aani

"Moreover, he said that if Mahendra was declared as the crown Prince and was married to Mandagini, official ties could be established between China and Cambodia; subsequently, he could order the Chinese armies stationed in Annam to move in support of us. But ..."

Adithya waited eagerly to hear what he was going to say. "But, first he must come to power! His rebel armies were ready to march on Beijing. The eastern part of China had come under their control. But, at that time he did not have governing authority.

"In that situation, we did not have any other alternative. Our only option was to accept his conditions and wait for his victory. As we did not get any information about you, we concluded that you must have died. Hence, we decided to get Mandagini married to Mahendra" said Gnani, and unable to look directly at Adithya's eyes, looked at the ground.

"Did she agree to it?" asked Adithya.

"It took us several months to get her to consent. My heart aches even now, when I recollect how agonized she was. But, I took the decision not as a father, but as a patriot. I had to control my own feelings, steel my heart and decide. But now, she's another man's wife. All of us have to accept this reality and move on. My request to you is that both you and Mahendra should work together with the same objective for the good of Cambodia" said Gnani.

"My master, have I ever slackened in serving my nation? Do you suspect my patriotism?" Adithya asked in a pained voice.

"I have not underestimated your patriotism at all. But I just wish to tell you that I do understand the magnitude of your loss. I want you to know that" said Gnani.

Later, Adithya described to him his experiences in Lanka, and the assurance given by King Parakrama Bahu. "The ship carrying arms has not arrived as promised by King Parakrama Bahu. If it does, we can strengthen our navy and consolidate our control over the west bank of the Tonle Sap Lake. In addition, if we can dominate the Mekong River also, it will form a natural barrier to stave off any attacks from the east. Moreover, if Pnom Penh area is to be strengthened as the rear base of Cambodia, the waterways from the sea to that city have to be safeguarded." Adithya explained to Gnani his strategy.

"However important war preparedness may be, it is far more important to revamp the irrigational infrastructure. Though the Mekong River, originating from the snow-clad Himalayas has not dried up, the Siem Reap and other Rivers originating from Kulen hill have dried up to a large extent. The Tonle Sap Lake is also shrinking. If the monsoon fails next year too, the situation will become critical. Mahendra's windmill project is good. However, tapping the ground water is the only permanent solution to our water problem" said Adithya, who explained the new methods which he had learnt to Gnani.

"Aditha! Your service to this country is invaluable. May it continue as always" said Gnani, and took leave of him.

Chapter 5

Ever since he left hurriedly in the middle of the victory celebrations, Mahendravarman had no rest, with crisis after crisis requiring his urgent attention. First, several days were spent in the attempt to rescue Shanthivarman, who had been besieged in the Preah Vihear hill temple fort. As the Chinese armies did not come to their aid from the north east as anticipated, the Cambodian forces were left to fend for themselves.

Because of the siege, it was not possible to supply food or arms to those who were trapped atop the hill. In this situation, one could not say how long they would be able to withstand the adversity. The Champa armies had surrounded the southern part of the hill also which meant all supply and escape routes were cut off. Under such circumstances there was no option but to send a retrieval force of highly trained commandos who would penetrate the enemy lines and evacuate those trapped on top of the hill fortress. This meant this naturally fortified bastion had to be abandoned bringing the frontier ever more closer to Angkor. Furthermore the heavy weapons too had to be left behind, augmenting the enemy's arsenal.

Recovering from this setback, Mahendra supervised the restructured frontlines of the army. After ensuring that the defence lines were strong, he rushed to secure the safety of his ordnance factories and supply routes in the west.

It was then that the news arrived. The former emperor had sent word that the Chinese rebel armies had been routed outside Beijing, and therefore, Mahendra was not to expect Chinese aid thereafter. This disappointment induced Mahendra to work even harder. If one were self-reliant why should one depend on others? What he needed was more arms and safe supply routes. The importance of the western frontier became obvious to him. If the Ayutthaya forces moved from the west they could threaten the very existence of the cannon brigade.

Saltpeter was collected from the Battambang caves in Mount Sampieu. Every evening and morning millions of bats would leave and return to these caves respectively; nowhere else in the world could such a sight be seen. When these bats flew together they created the impression of a dark cloud extending for several miles, eclipsing the sun himself. On a clear blue sky, this 'flying' cloud was a strange novelty to people who had not seen it before.

The Cambodian soldiers collected saltpeter from these caves. It is the bats' waste that solidifies in course of time into salt. The waste deposited every day for thousands of years had solidified (with its water content having evaporated) into white salt. It had accumulated on the walls and floor of the caves. The soldiers engaged in mining work, had to carry out their task during the night when the bats were away. They had to wear clothes that covered their whole bodies to protect themselves from attacks by the bats.

The saltpeter that was dug up with shovels was collected in jute bags, bundled into horse-drawn carts and taken to Pursat. Every convoy of carts was escorted by mounted soldiers in front and in the rear, for protection. At least two convoys were sent every week. Due to lack of rains, the necessity to prevent the saltpeter from getting wet did not arise. Nevertheless, in anticipation of rain affecting the shipments, sheets made of Chinese silk were also taken in the carts. Heavy military presence could be seen on all the roads leading to Pursat. Mahendra had taken elaborate precautionary measures to ensure that the enemy spies or their fifth column did not ambush the convoys and obstruct this supply route.

But on the western side of the Mount Sampieu, the defence was not adequate. Although the Ayutthaya and Champa armies were stationed mostly on the northern borders of Cambodia, if they were to suddenly turn to the west, the Cambodian defences would be exposed. It was necessary for Mahendra to be able to meet the challenge if and when it occurred. He had deployed small groups of mounted soldiers to roam the hills on the western border. In addition, he had placed cannons at regular intervals on the hilltops facing west. Moreover, soldiers armed with shoulder fired arms on elephant backs were kept in readiness, to move towards hotspots.

As soon as he had ensured the defence measures on the western border, Mahendra travelled to Pursat. His ordnance factory was located there. Not only cannons and shells, but also swords, spears, arrows and many other weapons were produced here. Factories were set up in systematically planned manner. Not only the raw metal, but also the unusable utensils from households, were melted and made into weapons. Several collection centres were established in various parts of the country to collect these old utensils, and these were sent as consignments to Pursat.

The metal ware received from the populace were sorted and recycled at the factory. New weapons were produced every day. They included pipes for shells, and arrows to fling the small arms. Pursat city was well protected by two natural barriers: on one side, the Cardamom Mountain range on Cambodia's west; and on the other, the Pursat River flowing into Tonle Sap Lake. Coconut trees and rice fields lined both sides of the road leading from Mount Sampieu to Pursat city. The crops in these fields had wilted, indicating the drought in the land. The River Pursat which ran along Pursat city had also dried up and was now merely a stream.

Pursat could not be approached easily by enemies. It was surrounded for several miles by forest, and on the west there were mountains and beyond them the sea. Sulphur from the south and saltpeter from the north were brought in, and arms production went on in full swing.

As he neared the factory, Mahendravarman was happy to note the increase in the security measures. This factory was located in a clearing in a place several miles away from the city. Access was only through the forest paths. Many rings of defence had been built around the factory.

The work of refining saltpeter went on on one side; and on the other, that of processing sulphur. On yet another mixing both and making explosives. The production was going on in earnest.

Outside the work shop, there were warehouses. Tall wooden structures had been built to store the raw materials brought from both directions of the country regularly in convoys of vehicles. On another side, the gunpowder produced in the factory was packed into bags and stacked neatly. These bags were loaded into carts and taken to another workshop in Pursat. It was here that the shells were prepared. The gunpowder was stuffed into metallic balls and cylinders and sent to the war-front in lots.

When Mahendravarman reached Pursat, the soldiers who received him presented him a guard of honour, and took him to an office in the middle of the industrial complex. As soon as he entered the office Boloma welcomed him. "My friend, welcome! We are meeting after several months! I have carried out all your orders. We are producing more than a hundred shells and also other types of weapons every day. We have a stock pile of firearms enough to last many months on the battlefield" he said. He addressed Mahendra only as 'friend' and in the singular without the honorific. After Mahendra became the Crown Prince, Boloma did not give him nor did Mahendra expect greater respect like the others gave. Nevertheless, Mahendra knew that his friend loved and respected him.

After that, Boloma explained to the Mahendra his administrative procedures. Every shell and cannon ball was marked with a number and catalogued so that it could be identified. Details, such as where every batch of shells and cannon balls was sent and how many were sent, were recorded diligently.

"My friend! I learnt from the Chinese the need to document everything. Otherwise, we'll never know the state of our stocks or their safety. If we do not have a proper documentation in place, it will be easy for our enemies to steal or sabotage our arms" said Boloma.

"My friend! I would have lived and died a slave; but you entrusted me with great responsibilities and helped to bring out my latent skills. I am indebted to you forever. Even if I were to die tomorrow, I'll die with the happy thought that I have achieved something in life. Had I continued as a slave, I would have died as an anonymous orphan; nobody would have known that I lived and died. You have given me an identity! Thank you, my friend" he said, embracing him.

Later, Mahendra supervised the defence measures, and returned to Angkor city. Satisfaction was writ large on his face. He was once again confident that Angkorean forces would prevail in this battle. If they could survive the drought for some more time, everything would be alright, he thought.

Chapter 6

Boloma was engrossed in his work as usual. He recalled the changes that had taken place in his life, since the day he escaped from China with Mahendra. He had stayed in the arms factory in China for many days, and learnt the necessary scientific and infrastructural knowhow. When they returned to Cambodia, he was introduced to the king by Mahendra, and appointed as the officer in charge of arms manufacture. Though initially, he had language problem, in course of time he was able to communicate with the Cambodian soldiers fluently. The soldiers, who were skeptical about obeying Boloma who looked different from them, came to love him deeply after seeing his knowledge, administrative capacity and loyalty. As one who had earned Mahendra's trust, they accepted him as one of them. Working hard under his leadership, they transformed Pursat into a centre for arms' manufacture.

Though the transport of sulphur was a problem in the beginning, this eased when they began procuring it from the hot springs of Kampong. Pursat was set up as a centre after Preah Vihear was deemed untenable as the mains ordnance depot. In addition, as it happened to be protected by natural barriers from the enemies, Mahendra and Boloma opted to relocate the factory to Pursat.

The whole area was heavily fortified. Within the complex, rows of houses were built for the workers in Pursat city. Apart from these, many camps were set up for the defence personnel. Moreover, lodges were also built for the temporary stay of those who brought the raw materials, transport workers who took the arms for distribution, and the soldiers who were in charge of protecting the convoys.

Although he had only been a slave in China, Boloma had observed keenly the administrative practices prevalent there.

Ezhuth Aani

Boloma knew that in places like these, where there were only men, women were necessary to satisfy their sexual needs. Otherwise, it would be difficult to maintain law and order.

The higher officers were allowed to bring their wives, but this concession was not given to the workers. They were allowed to go to their villages once in six months. To take care of their needs at other times, courtesans were accommodated in a particular street. It is not easy to manage the workers, those in transit, and those going on leave. Scribes were appointed to record on paper imported from China, the activities of all these people.

Boloma also arranged for the weapons to be listed, and to record where they were being dispatched. Although missiles and shells were identified individually, the other weapons were weighed and sent as packages. That is, the weight of a thousand swords, that of arrows, and that of spears was first calculated separately, and then they were packed in bundles by weight and registered.

By means of such streamlining, Boloma was able to know precisely how many weapons were there at any point in time in any corner of the country, and how much more was needed and where. Weapons are instruments of destruction. If they are to be used for our defence, we must control them. Otherwise, our own weapons will cause our destruction; this was Boloma's rationale for the extensive documentation practices.

Boloma's administrative skill was new to Cambodia. The people of Cambodia, who had achieved many things under the charismatic leadership of individual greats, had not been introduced to such smooth administrative machinery. Mahendra wondered whether it was because of lack of a well-oiled civil service that large irrigation canals had been allowed to be silted in Cambodia. Acknowledging Boloma's skills, Mahendra gave him more responsibilities. As the social recognition and status bestowed on him in Cambodia were way beyond his wildest imagination as a slave, Boloma went about his tasks with greater enthusiasm. Seeing his untiring work and vitality, the Cambodians gave him a lot of respect.

Every day, Boloma set to work thinking what could be his next innovation. On the assumption that yesterday's experiences are the basis for tomorrow's progress, Boloma sought to improve every day on the previous day.

Seated on his horse, Boloma was watching the setting sun, and reflecting on the day's proceedings. The sky nymph's face had become blood red as she seemed to mourn her lover's parting. But there were no tears. Yes. It was many months since they had seen rain. There was not a single cloud in the sky.

Just then, his attention was drawn to something far away. What was it on the horizon? A cloud? No, not at all. Doesn't it look like smoke? As he stared, wondering what it was, the waft of smoke in the air shocked him.

Yes! It was a bush fire! As a child in Mongolia, he had seen tongues of fire travelling at lightning speed and consuming all in their wake, when the prairies caught fire. As there had been no rain for several months, there were dry leaves and grass everywhere on the ground. The trees were also leafless and dried out. He knew that if these caught fire, it would not be possible to extinguish it. The fire will have to burn itself out naturally.

As he was thinking and debating how far the fire was, a black dot appeared to come towards him. Though initially it looked like a dot, he soon understood that it was a flake of ash floating in the wind. He knew also that immediate action was necessary.

He sent his mounted soldiers in all four directions to collect information. He knew that a jungle fire will move in the direction of the wind very fast. It was difficult to out run it. His experience told him that the only way to escape was to stay underground till the fire passes.

Calling all the people together, Boloma told them, "Friends! We have a bush fire in our vicinity. No one can out run a fire like this. We don't know which direction it will travel yet. But if we don't prepare ourselves now, all our labour of the past will be gone. To save our arms, ammunition and cut our losses, the only way is to hide them underground. If we are under the ground, the fire will pass over our heads."

After this, throughout the night they engaged themselves in digging large trenches. Choosing an open space, they dug two large trenches; one for themselves, and the other for their arms. The arms and ammunition were buried underground and covered with a thick layer of soil. The trench for the people was smaller and had a small entrance at the ground level and a large area under the ground. It was decided that after the arms and ammunition were buried, only a few essential personnel would remain and the rest would evacuate to safer ground far away. It was a race against time. All hands on board were utilised, under Boloma's skillful leadership.

While they were engaged in digging, the soldiers who had gone on reconnaissance returned. The fire was raging many miles away on the south west. It was clear that though the fire was spreading away from them, if the wind changed course it would come towards them.

As they worked throughout the night, the pits were nearly ready by dawn. The arms and raw materials were then transferred into the pits. The fire had driven away the cold of the night and made the place uncomfortably hot. Moreover, in the darkness of the night the raging fire could be seen in the distance. Boloma knew that though they might escape that day, the danger from the fire would continue for many more days. Hence, the entire factory was dismantled. All things that could be kept underground had been removed. But, Boloma's face still did not indicate satisfaction. Something was bothering him.

The fire on the mountain was spreading towards the top. But he knew that any moment it might change direction, and spread to the other side across the valley. After they had stored first the weapons and then the ammunition, Boloma asked all of them except a chosen few to leave the scene. He decided that the majority should leave with whatever they could take with them, and the rest of the arms should be stored underground. Later, in the other trench a few important men would stay behind. The trees around the trenches were cut down, and a fire break was set up to prevent the fire from approaching.

No one can predict in which direction a bush fire will travel. It is the direction of the wind that mostly determines which way the fire will move. If it begins at the foot of a hill, it will normally move upwards. But, it could suddenly leapfrog on to the trees on the other side of the valley. In addition, the logs from the burning trees as well as the embers may explode, fall far away, and start satellite fires.

As expected by Boloma, the fire that raged here and there finally began to approach them after a few days. Moving quite fast, it finally reached them. A fire will not go out easily. Only after it has destroyed everything in its path, will it subside. In a place where there was no water, there was no way of fighting a fire of this magnitude. Unless Nature takes pity and sends down rain, it is nigh impossible for man to extinguish such fires.

It was certain that their factory and all the other buildings would be engulfed by the fire. This was inevitable. In life sometimes we need to rebuild from scratch. But Boloma was determined to make the rebuilding process easier.

Ezhuth Aani

Just before the fire could reach them, Boloma was engaged in removing the records from his office. In a few moments the fire would reach them. He was working fast. All he needed to do was to remove the last ledger of records. Then he could run back to the safety of his bunker. Rebuilding would be much easier if the documentation could be saved in its entirety. Boloma was obsessed with perfection and could not accept any gaps in the documentation and audit. But the fire was approaching fast.

The demon called fire which had raged here and there was finally moving towards them. Ah! He had removed the paperwork which he went to take. Now he only had to run to the safety of the bunker. His men were urging him to return fast. The fire is still a little distance away. He had only to run a few hundred yards. He ran fast! But the heat was closing in on him. Boloma ran for life. Finally, he reached the heap of soil which they had removed from the trench. The heat had suddenly become unbearable! His clothes had caught fire! Boloma removed his clothes and rolled on the ground. The heat was all over him! Pain! Yes his whole body was in agonising pain. His eyes burnt. Then he couldn't see anything. And he blacked out.

When he opened his eyes, he sensed that he was lying on a mat placed on the ground in a tent. More than half his body had suffered burns, and a herbal paste had been applied. He could not bear his thirst. Many around were watching him anxiously. Slowly, he began to recognize them. Mahendravarman, his wife Mandagini, and a man who looked like a doctor... They were talking something. Then everything went blank. Many moments passed, with Boloma becoming lucid and unconscious alternatively.

"I don't think he will survive. He is highly dehydrated. Even if we treat that, he'll have fever and shivering, and die in a few days; that is all I can say. In my experience, people with such a high degree of burns will certainly die" said the physician.

When he said that, Mahendra bemoaned. "My friend! We came together by chance. Your service to our country has been invaluable. If we prevail, your name will be inscribed in golden letters in our history." Boloma spoke something - incoherently and deliriously. Finally, he fell silent. Even Mandagini, who had not shown any emotion all this while, shed tears.

Mahendra was firm in his policy that the arms manufacture begun by Boloma would not be stopped. He was determined that these setbacks would not halt their struggle for survival under any circumstances.

Because of Boloma's final actions, they did not find it difficult to reconstruct their factory again, and to recover the arms already buried. Due to Boloma's careful preparation the rebuilding process was not as hard as it was on the first time. Like a phoenix the factory rose again, in a short while.

It was incredible that Boloma, who had taken such meticulous care, should have met his death trying to save a bundle of paper! It was doubtful, whether even a monster guarding a hidden treasure would risk its life trying to save the list of his treasures! In times of danger, even great minds fall prey to disastrous ideas and commit major mistakes!

Ezhuth Aani

Chapter 7

After Boloma's death, Mahendra personally supervised the task of recovery and rebuilding. At the same time, the enemy, having learnt about their losses through spies, massed his forces on the western border and redoubled preparations for a massive onslaught.

In the northwest, the Sampieu mountain range was very picturesque. This region, full of hills and caves, was very vital for Cambodia's defence. If this area were to fall into the hands of the enemies, the Cambodians would not be able to obtain the saltpeter for their explosives; also, the enemies would easily be able to access the western bank of the Tonle Sap Lake. Mahendra's priority was to halt the enemy on the western border. He too piled up his forces there.

The destruction of their explosives factory in the forest fire and the death of Boloma were big blows to Mahendra. But there was no time to stop and think or to grieve. Although the bush fire appeared to be a bad omen, Mahendra tried to convince himself that it was nothing but a natural occurrence.

Boloma's death affected Mahendra profoundly. Together they had overcome ever so many hurdles and dangers. How many times had Boloma saved Mahendra and vice versa! In how many arenas had they stood shoulder to shoulder! Though Boloma's death plunged him in sorrow, he feared that it might affect the soldiers' morale if he displayed his feelings. He kept his emotions to himself.

Because of the loss of his arms factory his war preparations were pushed back by about six months. This necessitated working harder than ever before. Though Mahendra strengthened his gun positions on the hills, he allowed his soldiers in small bands to roam and dominate the valleys. He was determined that after the Preah Vihear debacle, he would not let the enemies besiege their defence lines again. His soldiers were able to watch from their bases on the hilltops the enemy troops grow in numbers at the border. He could not do much about this build up.

As both the sides kept strengthening their forces, a temporary stalemate prevailed. It appeared that both sides were reluctant to start the fighting. Some weeks passed with a lull in fighting. Both sides refused to blink. One night, a small raid party led by Shanthivarman was sent under the cover of the night, through the woods, behind the enemy lines. They waited for Mahendra's signal. As soon as Mahendra signaled from the hilltop with torches, Shanthivarman's commandos started the surprise attack from behind. Even as the Ayutthaya armies were confused thinking they had been surrounded and their supply lines had been cut off, the cannons on the hilltop began to rain down a volley of shells. The Ayutthaya armies which had been scattered by this stealth attack were again attacked in a second wave by the Cambodian forces positioned on the plains.

The magnitude of this defeat, which took place in darkness, was seen only after it dawned the following morning. Many of the Ayutthaya soldiers were lying dead. Some others ran in disarray into the forest. A major part of the army retreated several miles back into Ayutthaya. The next few days were spent by the Cambodian soldiers conducting mopping up operations, neutralising the Ayutthaya soldiers who had hidden in the forest. The Ayutthaya soldiers who surrendered and those who were arrested were sent to Cambodia to work as slaves.

On the whole, this was a major victory. It was indeed a great victory that could potentially change the course of the war. Unlike the Preah Vihear victory, the enemy forces did not just retreat a little with their command structure intact. The Ayutthaya army had lost its chain of command in the region completely, and scattered in total defeat. Was this a turning point in the history of this war? That was how the ordinary Cambodians wondered.

After this major victory in the northwest front, the Cambodian troop morale was high. They freed themselves from the siege mentality, and began breathe free. We shall win the war. The thought that they would restore Angkor city to its former fame and glory began to take credence.

Mandagini's mental state was more complicated. She had been pressurized by the elders into marriage with Mahendra for two reasons: that her lover had died, and that Chinese aid was necessary. But, both had been false. Adithya had returned alive, was living in close proximity to her and causing her mental anguish. Similarly, the Chinese rebel forces who were supposed to have come to their aid had been defeated and annihilated. And when she knew that the rebel leader was her father, his defeat too affected her. On the other hand, her duty to her husband had to be performed. Not only the social norms, but also Mahendra's appearance, personality and sharp intellect commanded her respect for him. Perhaps if she had not met Adithya, she may have loved Mahendra whole heartedly. However, as his wife she had the duty of participating in his official activities and playing her role to keep the people in high spirits. Her mind that had been torn between two dilemmas was gradually beginning to accept the current reality. She was the Crown Princess! Her subjects were struggling for their survival. Under her husband's leadership their struggle was moving towards victory. People love to celebrate their heroes. And when they felicitate the hero, they expect the wife also to be present beside him. For the benefit of their happiness, she was under compulsion to perform this duty properly. Step by step, she accepted the position of being Mahendra's wife, body and soul. Of late, she was slowly ridding her mind of the memory of Adithya.

Adithya too engrossed himself in his duties, as far as possible - increasing the naval resources in the Tonle Sap Lake and the Mekong River; and implementing the schemes for exploiting ground water for irrigation. Half of the time he was away from Angkor. When he was in town he spent his time carrying out his duties from dawn till midnight. Whenever Mandagini's face appeared in his mind, a familiar pain panged his heart. When he thought of his inability to change his circumstances, he became angry with himself. But, what could he do under the existing conditions? He did not wish to create any other problem in her life. If he loved her truly, he should consider her happiness to be more important than his personal welfare, is it not? Thus, unable to neither accept his situation nor change it, and accepting the fact that he was a pawn in the hands of Fate, he involved himself even more dedicatedly in his work. Occasionally he thought that he should achieve something better than Mahendra and show Mandagini what she had lost; this made him work harder. He did not fail to realise the truth that the fate of the country rested on Mahendra's success. More than the thought that Mahendra should fail, the thought that he (Adithya) should achieve more, and that he should serve his country better, was predominant in his mind. This was a healthy competition, not jealousy. But, he understood clearly that the prize he could have potentially won in the competition, had left him forever.

Unable to change their destiny, both the lovers went about their duties enduring their mental agony. Of the two, Mandagini's condition was worse. As Mahendra's victories and fame mounted, she was compelled to accompany him to several functions. People wanted to see the celebrity couple. There was a time when the king and the queen graced the stage together; now, people expected the prince and the princess to appear together. Didn't they represent the future of the country? Weren't they the country's hope? If the people did not have faith in a bright future, rebellion would break out in the land. Mahendra had to go beyond his military duties and participate in such celebrations to cheer up the crowds. Mandagini was forced to help her husband in his task. Whatever her inner thoughts were, she had to appear to be happy. In course of time, she became used to her new life.

As the days passed, the thought 'Victory is certain' began to dominate in people's minds. People will always bet only if they thought their horse would win. They began to support Mahendra's authority and influence wholeheartedly. The first small victory and the subsequent defeat of greater magnitude left the people's minds; only the latest victory remained in their thoughts. The fact was that the enemy had been shattered and driven to a state of disarray from which he could not recover quickly. Thus, life started to return to normalcy. People felt that the war clouds had blown over. In the north-west front the enemy had been beaten back, and in the north-east a stalemate had been established. A solution had also been found for the water problem.

As life returned to normalcy, people began to forget about the war. Even Mandagini started enjoying the thought that the war had ended. The work given to the Princess during peace times is quite different from that given during the war. Every day some task was given to her, such as performing worship in the temples, giving alms to the Buddhist monks, and supervising the work of the sculptors and builders. Though privileges were aplenty for the royal family, duties too were obligatory.

One day, as they were returning from the Bayon temple after offering worship, there was a sudden flash in the sky. She could not believe her eyes. Even as she thought that something had gone wrong with her eye, there was another streak. This time the sound of thunder too accompanied it. The wind began to whistle and whirl around. Black clouds filled the afternoon sky and the world darkened. The rain came in torrents. The people were very happy, thinking that their prayers had been answered.

Like the peacock rejoicing over the advent of rain, the people forgot their sorrows and enjoyed themselves. It rained heavily for several hours and the land that had been parched became slushy, the dry river turned into a stream; the heavenly mother, fed Earth who had been thirsty all this while, with the nectar called water. The fields shone with new vigour. The droplets of rain on the leaves twinkled like diamonds. Gradually, the East and West Baray reservoirs began to fill to the brim. Then the wind, tired of blowing, took a break. Fireworks of lightning and thunder subsided, and the Sun stuck its head out and peeped slowly. The clouds dispersed and moving some distance away began to display their power elsewhere.

The birds which had run for shelter signaled their return by cackling and chirping. Irrespective of the differences in their colour and language, parrots, pigeons, mynahs, crows, and koels - each with its own distinctive identity - sat side by side on the same branch and peacefully coexisted. Perhaps it was a blessing that they did not possess man's reasoning power. Rationalist Man divides one man from another using any excuse possible, and divides and destroys himself.

As soon as it rained, bells were rung in temples and viharas. Festivals in honour of Lord Indra were organized hurriedly. Indra was the god of rain. To express the people's gratitude to Indra, special worship was offered in the Angkor Wat temple.

In sum, the people rejoiced as never before. They swam in all the waterways that were fast filling up, enjoying themselves. The heavens had taken pity on them. The people thought that thereafter all their sorrows would end.

In the festivals for Lord Indra, music and dance were premiered. Though Mahendra and Mandagini participated in these festivities, in a few days Mahendravarman had to leave for the north-west border again. He did not want to relax the vigil and give the enemy a chance to launch a surprise attack. Mandagini performed her duties – both physical and ceremonial - and saw him off.

Later, to encourage the people she had to take part in many functions alone. The king and the queen also went to several places and participated in the festivities together.

The life of a princess was new to Mandagini. Accustomed as she was to roaming around like a free bird in her father's hermitage and the surrounding forest areas, she did not like this pompous but disciplined life style. This was a gilded prison. Nevertheless, considering the need for performing her duties to the society, Mandagini played along in silence.

After a few days passed in jubilation, it started raining again. This time the wind was not very strong. The lightning and thunder too were not severe. But the clouds were very dark and loomed large over the skies. They did not move. But, hiding the sunlight, they dumped the water that they carried in an unmitigated deluge. There was no indication of a respite in the rain.

The people confined themselves to their houses. The rain did not show any signs of stopping. The West and East Baray broke their embankments. The parched fields that had longed for water now looked like a vast expanse of water.

As it rained incessantly, water began to inundate houses in the low-lying areas. Unable to remain in their houses, many of the people moved towards higher ground near the Kulen Hills. They took with them whatever they could carry. Unable to move out, many others got on to the roofs of their own houses. The whole of Angkor region looked like an ocean, with the rooftops as small islands.

The people who celebrated Lord Indra with gratitude for the rain, now prayed to him to stop the rain. Too much of anything is bad, they say; too much rain is worse than a drought, the people thought.

While the common people were suffering like this, a few were working overtime to carry out their duties. They were Adithya's naval units. As soon as he sensed the danger of a flood, Adithya began relief work fast. He had already stationed his war ships in the Tonle Sap Lake and the Mekong River. Many boats were kept around each mother ship. He sent his soldiers in these boats, with instructions to help and retrieve the people stranded on rooftops and tree tops, and to provide them food and accommodation. Tonle Sap Lake had increased its dimensions manifold now.

Chapter 8

Mandagini too, carried out her duties day and night. For those refugees who had to evacuate from their homes, she made arrangements for temporary food and shelter, and for those who were trapped in their houses and unable to move out, food packets were distributed. These food parcels were wrapped in banana or palm leaves. Scarcity of drinking water assumed monstrous proportions. Though there was water everywhere, the people were advised not to drink it due to contamination by human and animal waste. Human corpses and animal carcasses could be seen floating in the flood waters. It was announced by Vajragnani that there was risk of an epidemic, and hence, people were advised to boil the water before drinking it. But, in such an emergency, where could they boil the water, cool it and drink it? So, they drank any water that was available.

It was at this time, that a messenger arrived from the northwest border. The rain had subsided somewhat in the Angkor region. But, the messenger said that it was still raining in the Battambang caves area, and as there were landslides in many places they had not been able to communicate with Prince Mahendravarman. Taking advantage of the situation the enemies had started attacking again. It was a miracle that the messenger was able to pass through enemy lines, landslides and other barriers to reach Angkor.

Mandagini was devastated on hearing this news. Firstly her husband had to be evacuated to safety. Then the country's defences had to be rearranged after the floods. She knew that the only person who could handle this crisis was Adithya. But, how could she seek his help? The last time she met him, she had slapped him. How could she now have the gumption to ask him to save her husband's life?

When she found him, he was engaged in an attempt to save his tube wells from destruction from the floods. The East Baray had breached its embankments and flooded the surrounding areas. The wells were in danger of being silted due to excess water and sludge.

Ever since he returned to Cambodia, Adithya had not had a haircut; nor had he shaved himself. There were various reasons for this: his workload on one side, and the loss of Mandagini on the other. She too noticed the changes in his appearance. She understood that he was still grieving for her. What about her? She too could not remove him from her thoughts completely. When she met Adithya the old memories came flooding back. Nevertheless, considering her social and moral obligations, she controlled her emotions.

"Adithavarma seems to be engrossed in his work" Mandagini said.

Raising his head just then, Adithya asked "What is the reason for the princess to come in search of this slave?" He still remembered the pain of her slap. "Adithavarma, a great natural disaster has befallen on the north-west border of the country. The enemy has taken advantage of this situation and advanced into our land" said Mandagini.

"Here too Nature has taken its toll. I am engaged in saving the people from that" said Adithya. "The incidents taking place there are more important than what is happening here. The Prince has been besieged!" said Mandagini.

"What are you saying Mandagini?" asked Adithya. He never contemplated that such an eventuality could occur. Mandagini recounted the message from the frontline. "But, my duty is here. My first priority is to salvage the infrastructural facilities here from total destruction, and to help the people affected by the floods. Moreover, I am not the Commander in Chief. When there are many men like

Shanthivarman capable of leading the army, why have you sought me, princess?" asked Adithya.

Happy as she was when he called her 'Mandagini', she was angry when he called her 'princess'. Moreover, she felt that he was unconcerned about her husband's safety. "Adithavarma! Do you think you can kill my husband and make me yours? What depravity is this? Shame on you! As the princess I order you. Rescue my husband who has been besieged on the northwest border. All the facilities necessary for this will be made available to you" she said.

"Mandagini! Stop your accusation! 'Tis true that I loved you once. Now I know that it was not love but lust. That very day when you slapped me, I removed you from my mind. Don't lay such atrocious blame on me" he said. His face revealed the fact that he had lied when he said he had forgotten her. But as she was looking elsewhere and not at his face, his words pierced her heart, like a spear.

Adithya added: "You know very well that when it comes to my national duty, I don't give room for personal considerations. How could you think so low of me?" His voice indicated great pain. He continued: "There is inundation by floods everywhere, and the land routes have been obstructed by earth slips. But, as the Tonle Sap Lake has not been affected much, we can reach the western border by boat, especially as the lake has greatly increased in size with the rains. Where large ships cannot sail, small boats can go. I shall take fifty of our best soldiers there. I shall save Mahendravarman even at the cost of my life." "Thank you, Adithavarma" said Mandagini. As she left, Adithya called out "O' princess!" She looked at him as if to say 'What?'

"I wish to tell you one thing. This is a duty which I am doing for my country, not a personal favour for you" said Adithya. Though she knew from his voice that he was lying, Mandagini pretended she did not notice it.

"Adithavarma, your beard will be an obstacle to you in performing your duty. So, please shave it off" said Mandagini.

He understood that she did not approve of his current appearance. But, her pride would not allow her to say it directly. He also understood that she still had some concern for him. The fact that Mandagini was interested in his welfare was a greater fillip to him than thousands of stimulants.

"I'll do my best" said Adithya, as he left.

Chapter 9

The Tonle Sap Lake was many times larger now and looked like a sea with huge waves. But, steering a ship without colliding with the submerged trees and buildings was the sailors' challenge. Large ships would be taken up to places known to be deep enough, and then the soldiers would go in boats. With the ships carrying cannons promised by Parakrama Bahu not having arrived yet, and with the bushfire setback to the ordnance factory, Adithya's navy had only a few gunboats. He stationed them in the west as far as they could go.

At midnight, the soldiers rowed the boats. At the rate of ten men to a boat, five boats carrying fifty men rushed westwards in the darkness of the night. While the land routes had been blocked by landslides, the waterways were easier to navigate. Securing the boats on the banks of the lake, the men went walking towards Battambang.

Mahendravarman and his platoon had been besieged on Mount Sampieu. The Ayutthaya soldiers had encircled the hill and were encamped there. Every time the enemy at the foot of the hill tried to advance up, he was pushed back by the volley of shell fire and rocks rolled down from above. But, how long could this last? Due to the scarcity of arms, food and drinking water, the trapped Cambodian soldiers engaged only in defensive warfare.

The commandos under Adithya's leadership divided into two groups. In the darkness of the night, on muddy soil, they moved as quietly as they could. Moving north and south of Mount Sampieu, they waited for Adithya's signal. While the enemy armies were asleep in their tents, the Cambodians stationed themselves as close to them as possible. Then, at Adithya's signal of a burning arrow, the ships in the lake began to rain down shells. Not having expected an attack from the lake, the Ayutthaya soldiers were confused and began to scatter north and south. At that time, Adithya's ground soldiers began their attack.

As the horses of the Ayutthaya soldiers got stuck in the mud and wet sands wherever they set foot, the army's usual contingency plans were in disarray. The Cambodian soldiers trapped atop the mountain, descended at this time attacking the enemy simultaneously. The besieged soldiers on the hill had been waiting for an opportunity for one final assault to break through. Taking advantage of the enemy's confusion, Adithya's soldiers also intensified their attack.

The Ayutthaya armies which had not expected such attacks from all sides abandoned their siege and retreated several miles west towards their own country. Their detailed knowledge of the mountain paths was an added advantage to the Cambodian soldiers. The leader of the force that came down the hill was Shanthivarman. Adithya asked him, "Where is the prince?"

"The prince is not well. He is safe in a mountain cave" said Shanthivarman.

Adithya said, "We don't have much time. When it dawns, the enemy will realise that our numbers are small. He will then regroup and move forward again. We cannot retain this area right now. Let's take the prince and go back to our ships."

His soldiers took Adithya to the cave where Mahendra was.

Mahendra was not someone who would hide himself in a cave when a war was going on. Everyone knew this very well. All these days he had toiled at the helm for the defence of Cambodia; if he were to stay back sending the others to the battlefront, there must be a valid reason.

As soon as he saw Mahendra, Adithya understood that he was very ill. This is not a simple condition like fever, diarrhoea or lack of nutrition. His face was blanched. His hands and legs had darkened. There were many lumps on his groin and in his armpits. He had difficulty in breathing too.

Mahendra said, "Adithavarma, I don't believe that I'll survive. I think I have caught the Bubonic plague. You may also get infected. So, leave me here and get back to safety."

When it rained, the problems of those trapped on the hill multiplied. With their ammunition getting wet, many of the weapons became unusable. Also, a major part of their dry rations became damp and began to decay. In the meantime, as their habitats were flooded the rats came out in numbers towards their tents in search of food. It was under these circumstances that many of the soldiers began to fall ill.

"Mahendravarma! I have given my word to your wife that I would hand you over to her alive. I will keep my word even at the cost of my own life. If the plague is the prize for the discharge of my duties, so be it. You needn't worry about anything. It's my responsibility to take you safely to your wife" said Adithya.

They then tied a cloth to two poles and prepared a stretcher. They laid Mahendra on it and taking all their men, they hurriedly left towards their boats again.

When the sun arose the world could see the destruction wrought by the horrible battle. Adithya's small unit had killed or maimed hundreds of Ayutthaya soldiers. The corpses of the dead and, the groans of those on the verge of death made the whole scene very ghastly. Many of the tents of the Ayutthaya soldiers had been burnt and were smouldering. Under normal circumstances, war ethics demand that the dead be buried and the wounded be attended to. But, in this emergency, they had no time for all that. They removed the Cambodian soldiers who had died and sent them to a watery grave in the Tonle Sap Lake. They carried their own wounded and rushed to their ships. They had to make several trips to the ships on their boats.

Mahendra was laid in a chamber in the Angkor Thom palace. Though he was lying on a soft mattress, his whole body ached unbearably. Whichever side he turned, the relief that he obtained was only momentary. So, he kept tossing and turning in bed. Now, the tips of his fingers and toes had become black. His face had lost its radiance. The state of his body kept changing, with intermittent fever, seizures, and profuse sweating. He slept on and off. When he was conscious, he often murmured something incoherently. At other times he spoke normally.

Mandagini sat beside him, anxiety and worry written all over her face. She knew that he was not going to survive. She was grateful to Adithya for bringing Mahendra back risking his own life. She was very angry with him at another level. She was angry that he had driven her to such a pass and placed her in a quandary by returning from his overseas sojourn too late. Now she was going to be widowed.

Despite her mixed emotions, she did not fail to notice that he had shaved himself. The thought that he still valued her opinion, gave her satisfaction and a kind of pride. She chided herself for entertaining such thoughts when her husband was on his death-bed.

Adithya was standing in another corner. He could not desist from looking at her beautiful face. At this critical juncture, though he had his own problems and responsibilities, he could not help thinking that at least under the pretext of Mahendra's illness, he had an opportunity to be in the same room as Mandagini, and keep looking at her. Though he kept telling himself that this was wrong, he could not refrain from thinking of her in spite of himself.

Ezhuth Aani

Apart from them, Vajragnani too was in the chamber, seated on one side. During his meditation he had learnt that the belief that this epidemic was directly contagious was wrong. He did not prevent the others from being with Mahendra. Whatever their thoughts, all of them were reluctant to break the silence. Waking up suddenly, Mahendra summoned Mandagini to his side.

"Mandagini! If Adithya had not come there, I would have died without seeing you. Even before he could come, I was afflicted with the disease. Not only myself, but some of our soldiers too, have been affected. Trapped as we were with scarcity of food, water and weapons, this illness was the last straw. Had the enemy begun the final assault on the hill about a couple of days earlier, we would not have been able to survive the attack.

"He not only saved us, but even after knowing that I was affected by the plague, unhesitatingly he carried me here. He has kept his word to the letter and the spirit." Having said this, Mahendra fainted again. Mandagini looked at Adithya with a mixture of gratitude, respect and pride.

Chapter 10

After Mahendra's death, the Cambodians did not have time to mourn his loss. The Ayutthaya forces from the west and the Champa armies from the east had begun to move towards Angkor. A new frontline was demarcated on the west bank of the Tonle Sap Lake. On the east, the Champa armies were stopped beyond the River Mekong. For the time being the Khmer navy still dominated the lake and the river.

Adithya had taken charge as the commander of the army. But he refused to accept any official ranks or titles. As the princess, Mandagini supervised the forces defending the Angkor Thom City and its surrounding areas.

The flood had receded. The rain that had appeared suddenly had also ceased, and the sky was cloudless again. The temperatures were rising once more. The parched earth, which had been thirsty for several months, absorbed as much water as it could. The dampness of the soil had begun to dwindle gradually. The East and West Barays, which had overflowed, were still full. Water flowed in the rivers too.

However, the impact and destruction of the storm and the flood continued. The irrigation schemes implemented with great care and hard work by Mahendra and Adithya had all but vanished. The windmills had fallen and the tube wells, silted. It would take at least one year to re-establish them. But, they did not have one year to spare. With the war at Angkor's doorstep, it was mandatory for all able-bodied men to go to the front. The destruction wrought by the flood could be seen all over the fields. The crops submerged in the waters had decayed. The fields in the upper regions had survived the ravages of the flood. But the yield could be harvested only after another month. Even then, it was expected to be meagre.

Ezhuth Aani

Many of the granaries had been submerged in the flood. The damp grain had become rancid. In the meanwhile, the rat menace had also increased. It seemed as though millions of rats had suddenly invaded the land.

The armoury too was depleted. The damp explosives were unfit for use. Many of the cannons which they depended on were now inoperable. People were panic-stricken. Fear is more damaging than famine or disease. If people are convinced that they are on the verge of a defeat, it would be very difficult to motivate and prepare them for war.

The overseas help that they expected had not arrived yet. How could Cambodians escape from this great impasse, when they were thus isolated? All efforts on multiple fronts had failed due to factors beyond their control. How do they bring back the golden period of Jayavarman VII? Engrossed in such various thoughts, Adithya reached the ministers' council.

Yes! Considering the emergency, the Cambodian king had called for a meeting of all the ministers, some of the prominent merchants and a few of the ordinary citizens. The meeting was held in a private chamber of the main palace in Angkor Thom. Everyone who entered took an oath that he would be faithful to the king forever and an oath of secrecy that they would not, under any circumstance, divulge the subject of the talks taking place there. Vajragnani alone was exempted from the oath-taking. Why should he be bound by the ruler of a country? On the contrary, it is the king who has to submit in the presence of a monk!

The meeting began. The king presided. Beside him sat Gnani. On one side of them sat Mandagini, and on the other, Adithya. The rest sat in rows according to their status.

"The kingdom built 600 years ago by Emperor Jayavarman II, is on the verge of collapse now. Anticipating this danger several years ago we had sought to take several alternate measures. I sent some of our most capable men to foreign countries seeking their help. We did not ask for just arms and men. We sought the latest irrigational technology and the chemical engineering knowledge required to produce weapons, and succeeded in acquiring them. Our highly capable princes returned home and introduced many progressive schemes. But, we have not been able to conquer Mother Nature!

"First, the Mother produced severe drought and famine. When we implemented new irrigation methods, she unleashed a storm and flood with great fury and destroyed them. Similarly, she inundated the fields and submerged the ready-to-harvest rice crops. We prepared arms. But, she sent a bush fire and burnt our factory down. We lost our weapons expert too. We rebuilt the entire factory. But she wetted our explosives in the rain and rendered them useless. As if all this were not enough, she struck us with an epidemic and killed the prince, the object of our love and respect." When the King said this, his voice quivered. Mandagini too, wiped her tears.

"Did we lose only the prince? We also lost Boloma, who set up our arms factory and maintained it so well. At this time, when our enemies have joined hands, our friends have failed us. The rebel faction we banked on has lost in the Chinese civil war. We thought that the Chinese armies stationed in Annam would help us. But, they are now helping Champa. Information has it, that the warship carrying cannons sent by the Lankan King Parakrama Bahu was caught in a storm and sank. We expected the Vijayanagara Empire to help us. But, it appears that their priority is to help the Tamil Kingdom in Lanka first.

"Messengers from the western countries visited us. But, they were interested only in spreading their religion. Moreover, they cannot help us as the land routes are all in the hands of the Muslims.

Ezhuth Aani

Until they find sea routes they will not play a role in this region. Wherever we turn we are faced with disappointment. We have come to a stage where we are trapped in a cobweb laid by cruel Fate, and are about to be annihilated. Builders of an empire, we have now been driven to our knees by our neighbouring countries.

"We have only two options; both unsavoury. First, to fight and be destroyed. Though we will retain our self-respect, neither we nor our descendants will be here to proclaim it. The other is to surrender; and to live as slaves. To tolerate the enemies taking our women in front of our own eyes; to pack up our pride and submit to foreigners."

When he said this, his anguish was obvious on the king's face.

At this juncture Adithya intervened. "King of kings! The tiger will never eat grass, however hungry it may be. Our Cambodian Empire, having a land area larger than some of the great Empires of India, and a history longer than any of theirs, shall never surrender. We shall never remain mute spectators if strangers try to lay hands on our ladies." When he said this, his eyes met Mandagini's for a second.

"O' King of Kings! Right from birth we've been trained in the art of war. It's a sport for us. In war, we win or we die. There is no room for any doubt in this," shouted Adithya, in a frenzy.

There was a knock on the door. A messenger asked for permission to tell the King something urgent. After speaking to him, the king said "It appears that the Champa armies are breaking through our positions in the east and progressing. They have come up to Stung Treng city." Adithya then said, "I have fortified Stung Treng and the rivers close to it. I've anchored our warships in Mekong River. It will take many weeks to break our defence formations. But, I will have to go there immediately and supervise our armies."

Vajragnani, who had remained silent all this while, now spoke. "Adithya! Anger blunts one's ability to think. You should weigh the pros and cons of a matter before coming to a decision. Listen to me patiently."

He continued: "O' King! In addition to the two ways you mentioned, there is a third way. Permit me to tell you."

"My Master, why do you need my permission? You may state your opinion any time."

"O' King, listen! I had foreseen that such a situation would arise someday. I had spoken about this to some of my friends. Many of the Buddhist monks in Ayutthaya are known to me. Moreover, many of the princes of Ayutthaya and Champa are my students. The commander of the Ayutthaya armies is Prince Raamaadhipathi. He is my student and a devout Buddhist. Very just. His guru, Satthama Govida is an acquaintance of mine. At the same time, the chief of the Champa armies, Maayijan, though also my student, is a cruel man. If we were to fall into his hands, not only will Angkor be annihilated totally, but our women will become sex slaves and the men will be murdered.

"But I have a plan" said Gnani.

"What is it?" asked the king. The others were hanging on every word that Gnani was about to utter.

"As soon as I sensed the possibility of such a situation arising, I approached Raamaadhipathi through some of my friends. I chalked out a peace plan. After heated dialogues there was agreement on some of the points. But only if the king ratifies it will the treaty come into force."

Ezhuth Aani

"What is the agreement?" asked Shanthivarman.

"Shanthivarma! Listen patiently" said Gnani, and continued.

"First, the Angkor region must be handed over to the Ayutthaya armies." The moment he said this, Adithya sprang to his feet shouting, "Stop, my Master."

"Sit down, Adithavarma" ordered the king. He then gestured to Gnani to continue.

"Even if we hand over the Angkor region, they will not enter the cities. This whole area will be converted into a Buddhist monastery. The Buddhist monks will be the caretakers of these art treasures and prevent them from destruction. Being denizens of the forests, these monks together with the surrounding forests will ensure that the cultural treasures are screened away from the eyes of the outside world, and preserved for posterity. Man will find them one day, and the area will be restored to its previous glory for the entire mankind to enjoy.

"The Ayutthaya soldiers will protect this region from falling into the hands of the Champa armies. Moreover, they will give us time to evacuate to areas around Pnom Penh, by land and by water. If the ordinary citizens and women move out first, the soldiers can retreat in stages. But..." said Gnani and paused. "But what?" asked the king.

"But, all our military might must be used to obstruct the Champa armies that are moving from the east. If they reach here first, they are sure to demolish these temples!" said Gnani.

"What is Ayutthaya's gain in this?" asked the king.

"This is where my personal loss is going to help us" said Gnani.

"What is that loss?" asked one of the ministers.

"The Emerald Buddha" said Gnani.

"The Emerald Buddha is with you?" screamed Shanthivarman in surprise.

"Yes. Yes. The Emerald Buddha himself" said Gnani.

"First, I sent word that I would give Parakrama Bahu the Buddha, if he helped us with arms. But, his aid has not arrived. Hence, I'm not obliged to keep my word to him" said Gnani, looking at Adithya.

"O Master! I do not know on which side you are moving your pawns. On whose side are you really?" asked Adithya.

Mandagini, who had been silent all this while said, "Adithavarma, You are not qualified enough to doubt my father's integrity! Please shut your mouth." Her voice sounded greatly distressed.

"It doesn't matter. Let him speak, Mandagini" said Gnani. He added, "I am on the side of the human race. I'm for the entire mankind."

"Master, pardon me. But I don't understand why we should surrender like cowards. Was it for this that Mahendravarman, Boloma and I toiled all these years?" asked Adithya. "Adithya, listen. Man's endeavour is necessary. If man does not attempt anything, he cannot achieve anything. But, there is no guarantee that all our efforts should end in victory. Our maturity lies in acknowledging our limitations when conditions turn adverse. Your labour and hard work are very praiseworthy. But it is foolish to be adamant and continue on the same track when our plans fail." said Gnani. He added, "O' King! It is your duty to protect the people. They have reposed their faith in you. This faith is not your birthright or personal asset. It is a sacred responsibility that has been entrusted to you.

"Is it fair on your part, not to accommodate yourself to changing conditions and accept the ground realities, and let yourself and your citizens be destroyed? Is it not your duty to protect the treasures wrought and gifted to the world by great emperors like Jayavarman and Suryavarman? Is it not your duty to ensure that the Khmer tradition, culture and lifestyle which have existed for 600 years, continue even after you?

"O' King! This setback is not permanent! Someday these treasures will be available to your descendants once again. History will depend on your decision. You can go down in history as the king who saved his people and preserved their culture, or the foolish king who walked into destruction with his eyes open. I request you humbly that you should do your moral duty and choose wisely. There's nothing more to be said." Gnani sat down with these words.

The meeting ended. The king agreed to his plan. It was decided that: in a couple of days the royal family, women and children should move by land or water to the surrounds of Pnom Penh; that a group of Buddhist monks under the leadership of Vajragnani should be stationed in Angkor Thom and Angkor Wat; and that the armies led by Adithya should halt the Champa advance in the east on the banks of the Mekong River, to give time for the mass migration. On the west, the Ayutthaya forces positioned beyond the Tonle Sap Lake, had given an assurance that they would not attack and that they would observe a ceasefire.

Finally, Mandagini took leave of Vajragnani. "Father! Ever since I can remember, you have been my father and mother. The education you provided me with is unique and not easily available to any other lady at this point of time. Not only warfare, but meditation and mental discipline too. It was due to the training you imparted that I have been able to endure the sorrows in my life. How will I live without you?" she cried.

"Mandagini! I did what was my duty. It is my good fortune that I had the opportunity to bring up a delightful treasure like you. My mind which had attained equanimity devoid of likes and dislikes, experienced a father's love, respect, and fondness by your arrival. You enriched my existence. Nevertheless, nothing is permanent in life. This is Nature's law. You will acquire a new life and new responsibilities. There are many duties that you have to fulfill for Cambodia. If you cling on to the past, only sorrows will remain. Farewell, my child! May you succeed in the execution of your duties! If possible, I shall come and see you in times of peace" said Vajragnani and left. Only Adithya and Mandagini were in the chamber. They were standing in front of a statue of Vishnu with eight hands.

"Adithavarma, why can't you move to Pnom Penh with the king?" asked Mandagini.

"The princess should know that a soldier will never run away from a battle in fear" said Adithya. He added, "Moreover, if Master's plan is to succeed, the Champa armies have to be delayed east of River Mekong for as long as possible. The king knows that no other man can do this as well as I can. In addition, if it is known that I myself retreated, our soldiers' discipline will disintegrate. In such a situation, your father's plan will be shattered!"

"Will you save yourself?" asked Mandagini.

"O' princess! You know that in a war there is no guarantee for anything. But, if I can make the enemy retreat without incurring much damage to our army, I shall do that. To accomplish this, a small army unit has to remain in the warfront, and keep the enemy at bay. This unit will mostly be destroyed. That is, this is a suicide force. I will lead it myself" he said proudly.

Mandagini sobbed quietly.

"Can a princess cry? How many duties await you?" Adithya asked.

"Stop calling me princess. Call me just Mandagini" she said.

"Don't cry, Mandagini. Each one of us has his or her duty in life. In the conduct of this, there is no room for personal feelings" Adithya said. He added, "In this life we have not been lucky. At least in the next, I hope we are together."

"May I ask you something?" said Mandagini.

"By all means" said Adithya.

"I wish to see one last time the land where I grew up and played as a child. Will you take me?" asked Mandagini.

"Certainly" said Adithya.

He, on the edge of death; she, in the pangs of separation; must life end thus? Separated from her father, her husband dead, leaving her motherland, unable to see her ex-lover ... the very thought of all this made her extremely miserable. An ache in her heart, a longing in her mind. Life brings with it innumerable joys and sorrows. The state of not being able to see her loved ones, and her beloved soil, ever again produced in her mind, a total numbness.

A journey is one thing. It is temporary separation. But, leaving one's land forever is a totally different proposition. Only those who have experienced it will understand the feeling.

Ezhuth Aani

Chapter 11

With a heavy heart and moist eyes, Mandagini asked him to come with her to the East Mebon temple. The East Baray Lake was about five miles east of Angkor Thom. This reservoir extended for several miles eastwards. The temple was situated on an artificial island in the middle of the lake. It was built during Rajendravarman's time. The two of them went along the street adjoining the south bank of East Baray. Adithya was riding his Vibhanji and Mandagini was riding another horse. The waters of the lake shone, reflecting the golden red of the setting sun in the west. First, they went to the temple called Preah Rup on the southern bund of the lake. Made of red bricks, this temple glittered in red hue in the light of the evening sun. There were towers in all four corners. In the middle was a large tower. The main entrance was on the east. There were figures of elephants and lions in many places. Built at different levels, this temple with its elevated sanctum sanctorum in the middle and the tower on top looked like a hill. Yes. Many Angkor temples were modeled on Mount Meru.

The temple was deserted. The King had proclaimed that the people should move out of Angkor within two days. The people were intent on taking their possessions and moving towards Pnom Penh by any available means. Those who could afford it hired one of the boats that operated in the Tonle Sap Lake. Those who owned carts or carriages loaded their possessions in them. The rest migrated on foot. The owners of animals like sheep, cattle, horses and mules, tried to take them with them often loading their belongings on their backs. The attention of the people was mostly on the Tonle Sap Lake on the southwest of Angkor, and its surroundings. Those areas wore a festive look with the influx of so many people. Men who moved out with their families focused on the safety of their families. Men who were alone earned money by driving the vehicles of the rich or by carrying palanquins. The disabled and the aged were helped by the soldiers.

While the western part was crowded, the eastern side was desolate. Except for some guards, there was absolutely nobody there. In the temple too, neither the priest nor the monks could be seen. A group of monks under the leadership of Vajragnani had begun to take charge of the main buildings of Angkor Wat and Angkor Thom. They were yet to come to the smaller temples.

Mandagini asked, "This place which had been occupied by so many people all these days, will soon become deserted like this. Is this how life always ends?"

Adithya replied: "Mandagini! Life is a cycle; a wheel; what is alive today will die tomorrow, and regenerate the next day; that is Nature's law. The monks under Master's leadership will come here only for meditation and other such activities; they will not protect this place from being engulfed by the forest. They are denizens of the woods. If there is no human presence, the forest will gradually overrun this place. But, someday once again, it will be discovered and restored and be known to the world. It is an art treasure, a unique construction and a wonderful creation. Surely it will rise again. When and how it will happen, I don't know."

Leaving their horses by the shore, they went to the beach near the Preah Rup temple. All the smaller boats having been taken by the displaced people, only a large boat remained. It had not been taken because it was too big to be transported by land to the Tonle Sap Lake.

Both of them rowed the boat towards the East Mebon Island. They sat on the steps of the temple in the middle of the island, looking at the water silently. "Adithya, when I was a child, I used to come here often with my father. How many times have I swum in East Baray Lake?" said Mandagini.

Ezhuth Aani

"Do you swim well?" asked Adithya. "Yes! My father used to call me 'fish'" said Mandagini. She added, "I will not be able to swim in this lake anymore!" Tears ran down her cheeks.

"Don't worry, Mandagini. You have crossed one stage in your life and are about to enter the next. All will be well" he said, and held her hand reassuringly. Then, realizing that she was not his, he tried to extricate his hand. Implying that 'it is alright' she tightened her grip on his hand. Intertwining their fingers, they sat silently. How long they sat immersed in thoughts, they did not know. With the sun having set, darkness had begun to engulf that area. Both of them sat there, unable and unwilling to terminate their company. Though their hearts wished to take things further, their reason said that it was wrong. They remained as they were. The memories of old times welled up in their minds.

As they sat oblivious of the world, the sudden sound of something moving in the water startled them and they got up. Unsheathing their swords, they rushed to the place where they had tied their boat. Only then did they realise that, as they were gallivanting in their dream world, somebody had taken away their boat. It was clear that it was too far away for them to recover it.

"My fish! Destiny has it that you should swim here one last time! Come on; let's see your skills!" said Adithya.

It is not easy to swim with two knives at your waist and a sword in your hand. Is that a challenge for a mermaid? She tightened her dress and leaping into the lake, began swimming towards Preah Rup. He followed her. Both crossed the lake quickly, and reached the opposite shore. There, the next shock awaited them! Yes. Their horses had vanished!

328

As soon as they reached the temple, Adithya realised that they were surrounded by enemies; with lightning speed, he dragged Mandagini into the neighbouring reeds and crouched. With the sun having set fully, in the dim light of the full moon, with water droplets running down her chest and her wet curls clinging to her body, Mandagini glistened like a beautiful goddess. Even in this hour of danger, he could not help relishing her beauty. Understanding the situation, Mandagini too crouched, alert.

They heard two people talking. "They got on to the bank here. They must surely be hiding in the grass" said one of them.

In that area, where the grass and dense bushes had grown to the height of a man's shoulder, a few tall palmyrah trees stood like misfits.

With her sword tucked at her waist and two small knives in both her hands, Mandagini stood ready. Since a man spoke, there must be another. But, what was the guarantee that there were only two of them? Adithya signaled to her to be patient.

Nearby, the soft sound of the waves breaking on the banks of the lake could be heard. All around, the buzz of the cicadas filled the air. No other sound. An eerie silence prevailed, where one was afraid to take a breath, fearing that the enemy may hear it. It was a game of chess. Whoever lost his patience and made the first move would betray his position.

With both parties waiting silently, suddenly there was a thud. Yes. From atop a tree a dead body had fallen. Adithya turned and looked at Mandagini. She stood with a knife in her hand, as if nothing had happened. Weren't there two knives in her hands? Adithya realised that he was in the company of an extra ordinary woman, more alert than he. He had mistaken the rustle of the palmyrah fronds to be due to the wind. She had recognized it to be a

Ezhuth Aani

man's movement and had killed him nonchalantly. He was proud of her. At the same time, he felt proud of himself too, for having won her love once upon a time.

When one of their companions fell, the others came running there with their swords drawn. There were about fifteen of them. They were like hounds who knew that their prey was close by. Gathering in a place, they formed a ring and looked around.

Mandagini wrested a knife from Adithya's waist. He too stood ready, with a sword in one hand and a small knife in the other. Both communicated with each other with their eyes.

Suddenly, three of the men in the ring on their side, screamed and fell with knives stuck in their chests. At the same time, with their swords drawn, Adithya and Mandagini entered the gap created by the fallen men and broke through their circle. Due to the speed and impetus of the sudden attack many of the enemies fell within the first few minutes. With their ring formation in disarray, the others were confused and scared. While those who resisted fell, the rest ran for life. Adithya managed to catch one of them by his throat. At knife point, he asked the man, "Tell me the truth! Who are you?"

"We are soldiers of the Champa army. We have been sent to penetrate into Cambodia and carry out sabotage and espionage." He said that they were going around in the land of their enemies in groups of fifteen, and that some of their spies had even mingled with the evacuating population.

Moreover, he said that one of his companions had taken away one of their horses, while the other horse kicked the man who tried to mount it, and escaped.

Adithya dispatched the man to heaven and washed the swords and knives which they had used in the lake. Mandagini could not help admiring his body as he washed the knives, bending over the bank of the lake in the moonlight. She lost herself again in nostalgia.

At that time, a horse came neighing and stood near him. Yes! It was Vibhanji. Seeing her master and mistress together again, she jumped for joy. Her brown-colored face had a new lustre.

Mandagini hugged Vibhanji. Adithya who returned from the lake saw the two of them in an embrace, and lost himself in old memories. This union was happening after several years. The seriousness of the loss of Mandagini's horse was obvious to both of them.

Saying "If we delay any longer here, their companions may return," Adithya mounted Vibhanji. Mandagini sat in front of him. "Where do you want to go now, Mandagini?" asked Adithya.

"Where the Angkorean dynasty began" said Mandagini.

Yes. Jayavarman II had laid the foundation for his empire on Kulen hills. Now, after several centuries, that empire was about to dissolve into a void. On their way, Adithya gave the guards in Angkor Thom, a letter carrying his seal. In it he had ordered the strengthening of the defence of the surroundings of East Baray.

The guards watched in amazement, Adithya and the princess riding on the same horse. If Mandagini wanted, she could have obtained another horse from the guards. But, she was eager to ride together, close to him. They may never meet again. This may be their last time together. Both did not wish to end their closeness.

They rode towards Kulen Hills. In accordance with the Cambodian tradition, she did not wear an upper garment. The usual garlands made of flowers and leaves which she wore, had been lost during her swimming and fighting. Her wet dress had begun to dry with her own body heat. But it stuck to her showing her form well. As Vibhanji galloped in the moonlight, her breasts shook and were pressed against his arms holding the reins. She leaned on him as they travelled.

Though they knew that it was wrong, they could not control their bodies, nor did they wish to. Their desire which had been awakened induced them to long for the next stage. However, both were reluctant to make the first move, and so tried to remain calm. But, how long could they pretend to be stoic and remain in self-imposed abstinence?

They reached the river on Mahendra Parvatha. Did their love not originate in this place of a thousand lingas? Was this not where they learnt of their love for each other? On coming to the same place again, their emotions overflowed.

Dismounting from Vibhanji, they sat on a rock near the bank of the river. The first time they came, the river had been dry, and the Siva lingas could be seen above the water. But now, they were submerged. Was the river alone in spate? Their bodies too, were filled with fires of desire.

He was the first to begin. "Mandagini" he said, and held her by the waist with his right hand. She did not prevent him. "Mandagini, I do not wish to tarnish your purity. I do not see you as an object of lust. I respect everything about you: your intelligence, your wit, and your fighting skills. I love you. Though my head tells me that I am transgressing, I cannot desist from touching you."

Saying thus, he turned her face towards him with his left hand and kissed her.

She did not resist. She had been longing for this all day. It was this embrace and kisses that first made her aware of her feminity. Why should she prevent that now? Her latent feminine feelings woke up again with new vigour. Though she had been a dutiful wife to Mahendra, it was Adithya who drew her to him like a magnet. The quality of the music produced by a veena depends on the player. Thus, the only man with whom she could connect at all levels - physical, mental and spiritual - was Adithya.

With their clothes taking leave of them, the drama of physical union was enacted in earnest, the hard ground serving as a mattress and the moonlight as a blanket. This was no mere physical union. It was a total union at all levels. That of two souls longing to come together. It was not just sexual release. It was total bliss! At its peak both died and were reborn. The last days of the Angkor Kingdom; the certain death that Adithya was to face in the near future; everything lost its meaning. Nothing mattered anymore. They lived **in** that moment alone; **for** that moment. Had it been their last breath, they would have accepted it very happily.

Exhausted and totally spent by their activity, they slept off on the banks of the River, in an embrace. Vibhanji stood near them, a witness and a guard.

At midnight, Adithya woke up to answer the call of nature. That finished, he lay down beside her again. Seeing the goddess of beauty sleeping soundly near him without a care in the world, he felt very guilty. He chastised himself for having tarnished the immaculate image of this angel, for having stained a spotlessly pure maiden.

Moving a little in her sleep, Mandagini apparently felt his gaze on her. She opened her eyes slowly and smiled.

"Mandagini, forgive me" said Adithya.

Ezhuth Aani

"For what?" she asked.

"I have done wrong" he said.

"When both have been equal partners in the deed, why should only one be guilty?" asked Mandagini.

"Mandagini, I am elder to you. I know the shastras. Knowing that it was wrong, I induced you to do it. And I was the one who started it," said Adithya.

"Stop, Adithavarma. What is wrong in this? Have we deceived anyone? Codes of conduct and virtues have all been determined by man. We are beyond that. You are the only true lover in my life. Different events may have taken place due to circumstances beyond our control. But I have never betrayed my conscience. When I slapped you, I was under compulsion to adhere to a certain social discipline. Moreover, I thought you should dislike me. I wanted you to hate me. Only then will you have the resolve to bear our separation, I thought."

She continued: "I am the only one who knows the anguish I felt when I slapped you." So saying, she caressed his cheek. The feather-like touch of her hand was very soothing. "Mandagini, will your slap ever pain me?" said he, and taking her hand he placed it on his cheek.

"Adithavarma! Our love is divine. Social norms, codes of conduct and laws laid down by man will not bind us. We are beyond them. If our minds are pure there will be nothing wrong in our deeds."

Saying this, she drew him closer, kissed him and asked "Is this wrong?"

She then went to the river, performed her ablutions, and returned to him.

As she walked towards him, nude and her tresses wet, her form shone in the moonlight. More than that, there was a different light in her eyes. It was not affection or love that he saw in her look. It was a look of one possessed. He did not know whether it was lust or something else. It was beyond his comprehension.

"Adithavarma!" she called in a haughty voice; "Look here! See these thousand lingas. What do they denote? Do they not symbolize the union of the yin and the yang? Do they not denote the cosmic dance of Siva and Shakthi mating? You are Siva! I am your Shakthi! Plant your seed in me! I shall bear your child. Even if you die, I shall save and nurture your progeny. Our love shall live forever! Enter me, my love!" she said, as she sat on him.

For the next several hours, the Dance of Bliss of Siva and Shakthi was enacted and reenacted. Both participated as equals, competing with each other in this mating ritual. Who was male, and who female? It was Nature's law, was it not? Death is as certain as birth. In this cycle of Nature, if there is no dance called mating, there will be no birth. And if there is no birth, there'll be no death.

Death was fast approaching them. Adithya was almost certain to die. At this moment, birth too was quite close. Yes. For Adithya's lineage to flourish, their union was necessary.

What happened before midnight was a physical union; the union of two souls. But, what happened after midnight was a cosmic dance. In truth she was Shakthi and he Siva. After several such unions lasting many hours, they slept. When Adithya woke up the next day, Mandagini had already bathed, dressed and was ready.

Now, there was no sadness in her face. No confusion. Her eyes were serene in the contentment that everything was over. There was a resolve in her demeanour. She was not yesterday's Mandagini. She had changed back into a dominant princess.

When he saw the transformation in Mandagini's attitude, Adithya felt assured. Was this the calm after her sensual storm, or was it a prelude to the cyclone of war in the near future?

Whatever it was, the thought that the beloved whom he loved wholeheartedly in his life, continued to love him still, was enough for him to die happily not only in this life but in the next seven lives also. It was sufficient that even if he were not alive, his offspring would continue to live.

The next day; at sunset. This was the last ship removing the civilians. Angkor Wat and Angkor Thom had become mere skeletons.

Mandagini was standing at the rear of the ship. As the princess, she was supervising the last minute arrangements from the last ship.

A major part of the army had moved towards Pnom Penh by land. A few handpicked soldiers under Adithya's leadership stood guarding the Angkor region. The next morning they would join the forces stationed in the east on the banks River Mekong.

It would take about a month for the Ayutthaya armies to enter this region. Adithya's task was to keep the Champa forces at bay till then. They knew that most of them would die in this war. If any survived they would escape to Pnom Penh eventually.

In the fading light, the form of Adithya shrank slowly into a dot. Without revealing her sorrows, Mandagini stood issuing orders to her charges.

The dot called Adithya now vanished into the void. Was this the end? Can't he be seen ever again?

Ezhuth Aani

Towards the Sunset

Is this a bridge or a jetty?
Is that the shore or midsea?
Is the reddened water flowing across
The reflection of the setting sun
Or the blood of the dead?
Is the smell carried by the gentle winds
That of the sea mud
Or that of decaying corpses?
Is the red horizon seen afar
The sunset or another sunrise?
He walked and walked
Over the dead and the maimed
The shoulders slouching with the burden
The swords tired of fighting
Bullet ridden garb adorning
Are they symbols of his defeat?
Is this the end?
Was this all a dream?
In the lap of Fate
Is there no dawn?

*** THE END***

www.ingramcontent.com/pod-product-compliance
Lightning Source LLC
Chambersburg PA
CBHW051330250626
47155CB00007B/2538